NOW SHE'S DEAD

Ben Cheetham

Visit the author's website at www.bencheetham.com

Printed in the United Kingdom

First Printing: April 2018

ISBN-13 978-1-7201885-2-0

CHAPTER 1

2016. Somewhere near Hastings.

Jack Anderson had no words left to say to his wife. All he could think to do, as the long hours of night closed in, was hold Rebecca close. She felt distressingly limp in his arms. Her face, naturally pale, was as white as the bedsheets, making her long hair look even blacker. Her eyes – the bluest eyes he'd ever seen – stared into nowhere. Every so often he kissed her gently, feathering his thumb over the gold wedding band on her ring finger. She showed no sign of knowing he was there.

He didn't want to take his eyes off her, but during the early hours sleep ambushed him. He awoke with a jolt. Rebecca's side of the bed was empty! He sprang from beneath the duvet to search the upstairs rooms. All were unoccupied, except for one with a little girl sleeping in it. The girl's hair was as glossily dark as her mother's. Her soft round cheeks were flushed with the warmth of bed.

Jack winced as the question Naomi had asked the previous day came back to him: "What's wrong with Mum?"

He'd looked into his daughter's eyes – the eyes of a seven-year-old coming to terms with the realisation that the world isn't all love and laughter – and it was as if a vice was squeezing his chest. "She's just tired, sweetie," he'd replied in a voice that sounded dishonest to his own ears. "She'll be fine once she's had a good night's sleep."

Wrenching his gaze away from the sleeping child, Jack hurried downstairs. There was a note on the bottom step: 'Gone for a walk'.

Normally there wouldn't have been anything unusual in that – Rebecca loved walking along the towering coastal cliffs a short drive from their home – but things had been far from normal lately.

He looked out of the front door. Rebecca's Toyota was gone. He snatched up the phone and dialled her mobile. His call went through to voicemail. He tried again with the same result. Uncertainty creased his forehead. He couldn't go out in search of her and leave Naomi alone in the house. He considered waking Naomi and taking her with him, but decided against it. She'd been through enough worry already.

Jack paced around, phoning Rebecca every few minutes to no avail. When he heard Naomi get out of bed, he forced his lips into the semblance of a smile and went upstairs. Naomi was sleepily clutching a stuffed doll that Rebecca had bought her. His heart hurt at the sight. "Morning, sweetheart. Did you sleep well?"

"I dreamt Mum was better. *Is* she better?"

"She's a lot better today." Jack hoped with everything in him that he wasn't compounding yesterday's lie.

Naomi's face brightened. "Can I see her?"

"She's gone for a walk."

There was no point telling Naomi her mum was asleep. She was like Jack – she had sharp eyes. She'd spot that Rebecca's car was gone the moment they left the house. Naomi's big blue eyes widened in surprise, but she said nothing. He noticed something shining on her wrist – a silver bracelet. His heart skipped. The bracelet had been a first anniversary present from him to Rebecca. She'd never taken it off from the day he'd put it on her until now.

Why now?

The question increased his anxiety tenfold. "When did your mum give you that?"

Naomi's porcelain-smooth forehead creased faintly. "I don't know. It wasn't there when I went to bed. Shall I take it off?"

Jack concealed his anxiety with another smile. "No, sweetheart."

He rushed Naomi through the morning routine – eat breakfast, wash face, brush teeth and hair, put on school uniform – then drove her to school and kissed her goodbye. For the first time in weeks, she ran into the playground with a smile on her face.

Jack sped off towards the coast. He found Rebecca's Toyota parked in the usual place. He sprinted along the windswept clifftop path as if he was in a race for his life. The sun was shining in a cloudless sky. People were out walking and admiring the sparkling views from the sandstone cliffs. The vice in his chest turned several twists tighter when he spotted a small crowd at the cliff's edge.

"What's going on?" he gasped with what little breath he had left.

"A woman fell," someone replied.

"She didn't fall," put in someone else. "She jumped."

Jumped. The word almost crushed Jack to his knees. He gaped over the cliff – thirty-odd metres straight down to broken rocks and churning waves. There was no sign of a body, but no one could have survived such a drop. He grew dizzy and swayed on his feet. Hands caught hold of him and pulled him to safety.

After that things became blurry. Jack remembered the police and coastguards arriving. He remembered the witnesses providing them with a description that fitted Rebecca. He remembered a helicopter circling above the sea in search of her. But all of it was filtered through a black-and-white haze of pain. The next thing he remembered with vivid colour was finding the text message from Rebecca on his phone.

CHAPTER 2

One year later. Manchester.

All the photos scattered across the bed were of the same willowy, almost ethereally beautiful woman. Jack Anderson lay amidst them, his bloodshot eyes fixated on a photo of Rebecca and himself. She was wearing a simple white satin wedding-dress and holding a bouquet of pink roses. He was standing beside her in a pin-striped grey suit with a blue carnation in the lapel. Both were beaming into the camera from the arched stone porch of the church where they'd just said, "I do." They looked like the perfect couple. There was no hint in their faces of the heartbreak to come.

Jack asked the question that had passed his lips a thousand times and more since his wife's death, "What happened, Rebecca?"

There was no answer and never would be, but that didn't stop the question from hammering at him.

His mind looped through the weeks that had led up to *that* day. Rebecca's depression had deepened relentlessly. Nothing – no pills, no therapists – had stopped her deterioration. It wasn't the first time she'd been depressed. After Naomi's birth, postnatal depression had laid her low for months. But this was different. It had hit her out of the blue, like a breezeblock dropped from an airplane.

"Where's this coming from?" Jack had asked her in bewildered desperation. "We love each other, we've got a beautiful daughter, a house of our own, good jobs. What is there to be depressed about?"

In reply, Rebecca had looked at him with her big sad eyes as if to say, *If you don't know, I can't tell you.*

At first there had been lots of tears. Rebecca would lock herself in the bathroom and Jack would listen to her sobbing through the door. Then came the silence, the staring off into a place only she could see. That was infinitely worse than the tears.

A sob rose from the pit of Jack's stomach as scenes from the day Rebecca died spooled out in front of him. He saw everything as if it was happening right that second – the crowd on the cliffs, the waves frothing against the rocks, the circling helicopter, the text message.

Jack reached for his mobile phone and found the message: 'I love you and Naomi more than I can bear. I'm so sorry.'

That 'sorry' haunted Jack. What did it mean? Was Rebecca sorry for killing herself? Was she sorry for something else she'd done, something that had pushed her over the edge? Or had she simply been sorry for being depressed? Maybe she hadn't killed herself. Maybe she'd been on her way home, determined to defeat her depression when she slipped and fell. He would never know. The coastguard hadn't recovered Rebecca's body. A verdict of accidental death had been recorded. Jack and Naomi had wept over an empty coffin at the funeral.

Jack's phone rang. It was Laura. He didn't answer the call. He couldn't speak to his sister right now. Not on this day, this first anniversary.

Like a merry-go-round of pain, the images came around and hit him again. The crowd, the cliffs, the sea, the helicopter... Oh Christ, it was too much to bear.

He needed to drink – not merely to get drunk, but to obliterate himself. That was the only way he knew to escape the memories for a few hours. He headed down to the kitchen, stepping over cardboard boxes. He'd been in the new house for nearly two months, but still hadn't got around to unpacking. He grabbed a bottle of vodka from the work-surface. Vodka had been Rebecca's favourite drink. Now it was his chosen route to oblivion. There were only a few centimetres of liquid left in the bottle. Not nearly enough for his purpose. He knocked it back and made for the front door. He hit the street at a jog. The constricting sensation in his chest was agony. He hadn't realised until Rebecca's death that heartbreak was a physical thing. Every sober second of every day since then it was as if his heart was literally being ground into dust.

He bought 70cl of vodka from the nearest off-licence and gulped it down. He retched a few times, drawing glances of indifference, disgust or sympathy from passers-by. He knew how he looked – unshaven, crumpled clothes – but he'd long since ceased to care what others thought of him, except that is for Naomi. He would be mortified if she saw him like this.

A spasm of guilt tugged at Jack's haggard features. *Naomi.* He wasn't the only one suffering. She was in pain too. *Oh Naomi. My beautiful little girl.* "You selfish prick," he muttered at himself. "You should be with her." It was too late for that though. He was too far gone to get himself straight tonight.

The guilt and pain subsided as the drink did its work. Head bowed, not noticing where he was going, Jack continued walking. The night-time streets were quiet. He paused in the pool of a streetlamp to take another swig from the bottle. A woman came around a corner and pulled up at the sight of him. She stared at him nervously for a heartbeat before crossing to the opposite pavement.

"What happened, Rebecca?" he mumbled as he continued on his path to nowhere.

After a while, he became aware that his legs were struggling to carry him. Lifting his head, he saw that he was walking alongside a park. He staggered through a gate and slumped to the grass beneath a tree. A sultry summer breeze brushed his face as he stared through the branches at glimpses of stars and space.

He finished the bottle. The alcohol weighed down his eyelids. His eyes fluttered open as a scream split the night. He struggled up onto an elbow, squinting blearily into the encircling darkness. There was no one to be seen. "Anyone there?" he slurred. Silence. He tried to stand up, but his limbs were reluctant to cooperate. "Fuck it." He fell back, closing his eyes again. He drifted in a fog of drunken self-pity for a while before merciful blankness took him.

CHAPTER 3

Pale morning light streamed through the branches, illuminating drops of dew on Jack's face. He awoke with a pounding headache and a mouth like sawdust. Sitting up, he dug out a packet of Marlboro and lit one with a scuffed old Zippo. His gaze landed on a group of people gathered around something towards the far side of the park. A frown touched his forehead as he hazily recalled the scream. On stiff legs, he headed over to the people. From beyond the park's perimeter came the wail of approaching sirens. A woman was sobbing into a man's shoulder. Other people were pressing their hands to their mouths as if they might vomit.

"Don't look," a pasty-faced man said to Jack. "Trust me, you don't want to see it."

Jack made his way to the front of the little crowd. The woman was lying on her back between bushes a few metres from the path. She was slim with long dark hair. She looked to be in her twenties or early thirties although her face was so bloody it was difficult to tell. There were what appeared to be knife wounds on her face, neck, chest and arms. The surrounding grass was black with blood. She was dressed as if for a night out: shoulderless black dress, matching high-heels. The dress was pulled up to under her small breasts. Her underwear had been removed and lay nearby along with an unopened handbag. Her legs were splayed as if she was waiting for someone to climb between them. Her buttocks and inner thighs were stained with faeces. Most horrifyingly of all, her stomach was horizontally slashed open just below her belly button. Glistening coils of vital organs bulged through the wound.

A shudder of disgust shook Jack – not simply at the sight of the dead woman, but at himself. It was surely her he'd heard screaming. She might still be alive if he hadn't been too drunk to get up and investigate. He turned his back on the sickening sight. Police cars had pulled up at the park's main gate. Constables were getting out of them. Jack moved off in the opposite direction. There was nothing for him to say to the police. He didn't have a clue what time he'd heard the scream.

He went into a cafe for a coffee. "What are those sirens about?" wondered the man who served him.

"A woman's been killed in the park," said Jack.

The man's eyebrows lifted. "Another one."

"What do you mean?"

"A girl was killed three nights ago. Not in Alexandra Park. Over in Didsbury. Don't you watch the news?"

Jack hadn't kept up with the news in a long time. Since Rebecca's death his world had shrunk to a tiny bubble of his own misery. There was no space in there for anyone else's. "How was she killed?"

"She was stabbed like twenty or thirty times. Whoever did that's got to be crazy, don't you think?"

Jack nodded. He drank his coffee as he walked. The caffeine cleared away the cobwebs of his hangover. He was no longer thinking about the dead woman in the park. His mind was back in the same old loop: *What happened, Rebecca? What were you sorry for?* He stopped at an off-licence to buy a bottle of vodka for when the need to escape himself overwhelmed his need for answers.

He heaved a sigh at the sight of the little suburban semi he'd bought for Naomi and himself to make a new start in. The house had an unoccupied look – the lawn was overgrown, there were curtains in some windows, others were blacked out with newspaper. As he stepped into the hallway, he was struck by how lifeless and alien it felt. A blanket and pillow were screwed up on the sofa in the bare-walled living-room. He'd rarely slept in a bed since Rebecca's death. He doubted if he would ever get used to sleeping alone in a double-bed.

He dropped into an armchair and closed his eyes, but not for long – too many images, too many questions. "She's gone and there's nothing you can do to change that," he told himself sharply. He knew his words were true, just as he knew they would have no effect. When Rebecca died, it was as if he'd died too and been plunged into hell.

An insistent knocking started at the front door. Jack knew it had to be Laura. No one else knocked on his door like that. He wearily rose to his feet. Ignoring her wasn't an option this time. Laura wasn't the type to give up easily. Besides, it occurred to him with a little tightening of his chest that she might have something to tell him about Naomi.

"About bloody time," Laura said as he opened the door. She was wearing her pale blue nurse's uniform and holding a full carrier bag in each hand. Her hair – mousey brown like Jack's – was tied back in a ponytail. She had the same hazel eyes as him too. But unlike his, her eyes were clear and keen. They examined him as if he was a patient – firmly but with care. "God, Jack, look at the state of you."

He opened his mouth to speak, but she continued, "Before you ask, Naomi's fine. I dropped her off at school on my way over here."

"Did she mention Rebecca at all last night?"

"Once or twice. She had a little cry, but I put a movie on and she settled down."

Jack gave his head a shake of self-recrimination. "I'm sorry, Laura, I should have come over."

"From the looks of you, you wouldn't have been much use if you had done."

Jack acknowledged the truth of Laura's words with a sigh and repeated, "I'm sorry."

"Listen, it was the first anniversary of Rebecca's death. I understand that you needed to be alone."

"But does Naomi understand?"

Jack waited for Laura to say, *Yes*. Instead, agonisingly, she avoided his gaze. She manoeuvred past him into the hallway, sniffing the air. "This place smells worse than the geriatrics ward," she joked grimly, putting the carrier-bags down in the kitchen. She pointed at Jack. "Upstairs now. Shower, shave, put some clean clothes on if you've got any. I'll make breakfast."

"There's no food in."

"Yeah, I know. That's why I brought some with me."

There was no point arguing with Laura when she was in this mood. Jack went upstairs. He stood under the shower, trying to feel the hot water and nothing else. Then he shaved at the sink. The face that emerged from under the heavy stubble was thinner than it had been a year ago, more lined. The eyes stared back at him from hollows of grief. He dug jeans and a t-shirt out of a suitcase. Mixed in amongst his clothes was one of Rebecca's blouses. He pressed it to his face and inhaled. He could still smell her on it, but the scent was fading.

"Breakfast's ready," Laura called to him.

The sizzle of frying bacon greeted Jack as he descended to the kitchen. The windows were wide open. Laura surveyed her brother approvingly. "There you go. You almost look like a member of the human race."

Laura had set the table. She served up two fried breakfasts, which they ate in silence. Laura leaned back in her chair, looking steadily at her brother. Now it was his turn to avoid her eyes.

"You know what I'm going to say, don't you?" she began. There was no firmness in her voice, only compassion. "I love having Naomi. She's welcome to stay with me for as long as necessary. But it's not me that she really needs. She needs her dad."

Jack lifted his guilt-wracked gaze to Laura's. "Don't you think I know that? She's the most important thing in my life. I want to be there for her more than anything. I just... I can't stand the thought of her seeing me like this."

"So sort yourself out."

"I wish I could, Laura, but I don't even know where to start."

"Start by doing something to bring you out of yourself. Go back to work."

"I'm not ready."

"Well you can't keep on like this, Jack. You seem hell-bent on slowly killing yourself, but you don't have that luxury." Laura reached to rest her hand on Jack's. "You have to be strong for Naomi."

He almost scoffed at the platitude, but caught himself. "Look at me. How am I supposed to be strong?"

"I don't know, but you won't find the answer in a bottle of vodka." Laura glanced at her watch. "I've got to go. I'm due on the ward in twenty minutes." She gave Jack's hand a squeeze and pushed her chair back.

"Leave them," he said as she cleared the table. "I'll do it."

At the front door, Jack kissed Laura on the cheek. "Thanks for breakfast, sis. Tell Naomi I love her."

"Phone and tell her yourself. Or better yet, come round and see her."

The crow's feet at the corners of Jack's eyes deepened. "I will."

"You'd better," Laura said in a mock-threatening tone.

Jack watched his sister get into her car and waved as she accelerated away. He returned to the kitchen and picked up the breakfast plates. He thought about Naomi's blue eyes, black hair and china skin. It was impossible to look at her without seeing Rebecca. He'd promised himself time and again that he would hold it together for his daughter, but every time he saw her he fell apart. He dropped the plates into the sink and moved through to the living-room. He drew the curtains and slumped into the armchair. *Rebecca.* He closed his eyes. *What happened, Rebecca? What happened?*

CHAPTER 4

Jack stood outside Laura's little terraced house for a long time, working up the nerve to knock on the front door. All he could see in his mind's eye were the cliffs and the sea. All he could hear was the whoosh of waves and the whump-whump of rotor-blades. His hand clenched into a fist, but instead of knocking he thudded it into his thigh. What was the matter with him? He hadn't lied to Laura. Nothing meant more to him than Naomi. So why was he standing out here instead of showing her how much he loved her? He already knew the answer. It wasn't simply that she reminded him of Rebecca. That was part of it, for sure, but there was something else. The way she looked at him with such need, hope and vulnerability. It terrified him because he knew he was going to fail her the same way he'd failed to save Rebecca.

He turned suddenly and walked away from the door. "You're a fucking coward," he told himself.

As he trudged along, Jack tossed vodka down his throat. His face glistened with the drizzle that had been falling for the past hour or so. The fine droplets were thickening into heavy rain. He glanced upwards as thunder rumbled across the starless night sky. On the other side of the road were tall wrought-iron gates set between stone posts. Beyond the gates a tree-lined avenue led through ranks of graves.

Jack had spent a lot of time in graveyards since Rebecca's death. He'd visited her memorial plaque at Hastings Crematorium a few times, but he felt no connection to her there. Rebecca wasn't in the urn behind the plaque. She was somewhere at the bottom of the Channel. Besides, the Crematorium was always busy. He preferred the solace of old cemeteries. He felt more comfortable with the dead than the living. They didn't judge or expect anything of you.

He staggered across the road and rattled the gates. Padlocked. He put the bottle through the bars and scaled the gates. His t-shirt caught on a fleur de lis spike. He pulled it free with a tearing sound and lowered himself to the path.

As Jack wandered deeper into the cemetery, the sounds of the city receded and silence stole over him. He looked almost jealously at the graves. For their occupants the suffering was over. No more memories. No more questions. No more pain.

Most of the graves were marked by standard headstones. Interspersed amongst them were clusters of elaborate memorials – tall pedestals with winged angels atop them, miniaturised classical temples, pointed obelisks.

The rain was weighing Jack down. He felt as if he could barely take another step. He veered off the path, dragging his feet along in search of somewhere to shelter. Neatly tended graves gave way to weed-choked plots occupied by cracked and fallen headstones. Light from a building that formed part of the cemetery wall faintly illuminated an altar tomb half-shrouded by ivy and enclosed by a low rusty fence. The altar tomb was carved into the likeness of a church ornamented with spires and arches. The church roof overhung the walls sufficiently to provide some shelter.

Jack stepped over the fence and squatted under the overhang. He put out a hand to balance himself. It passed straight through the ivy. He lifted the tangled veil aside, revealing a collapsed section of wall. He sparked his Zippo into life. The flame illuminated a patch of compacted earth long enough to lie out on. He crawled into the tomb's hollow interior. It smelled of old stone and damp earth. Rain drummed against the arched roof, dripping through unseen cracks. He swallowed more vodka and closed his eyes. He imagined he was the grave's occupant, buried six feet under, and that all he knew was darkness. He wished he could stay in that place where there was no past to torment him – not forever, but long enough for the pain to fade. He would gladly have given up a year or two of his life if only it allowed him to live again.

A drip hit his forehead. He wiped it away. A sliver of bright light at the rear of the tomb caught his eye. Had someone seen him climb the gates? Were they searching for him with a torch? He pressed his eyes to a flared horizontal crack. His breath stopped in his throat. The crack looked towards the nearby building – a big old house with tall windows. A light had come on in a first floor window. The curtains were open and the sash-window was drawn up as if to let in the sounds of the storm.

A woman was sitting in the window. A red blouse hung off one of her slender shoulders. She was brushing long black hair that framed a china-white, strikingly beautiful face. Jack watched the motion of the hairbrush as if mesmerised. His gaze glassily traced the lines of her neck, jaw, lips, nose, cheeks and eyes. She was about fifteen metres away. He couldn't tell the colour of her eyes from that distance, but in his mind they were startlingly blue. It was as if he was looking through a window into heaven.

"Rebecca," he murmured. "Rebecca."

His heart plummeted as the woman rose and moved away from the window. "No," he whispered. "Come back."

A light came on in a larger neighbouring window. Jack exhaled as the woman reappeared. She stood at the window, staring into the rain. Her blouse's plunging neckline revealed a swell of cleavage. It wasn't the kind of thing Rebecca would have worn, but that didn't matter. Everything else was as it should be – the hair, the skin, the facial features, the build. She even looked about the same age as Rebecca had been. Jack ached to reach out and touch the woman, pull her into his arms and crush her to him.

She glanced over her shoulder as if at a sound. A low moan rose in Jack's throat as she moved away from the window. Long minutes passed with no sight of her. The light went off in the larger window. Seconds later, she approached the other window and closed the curtains. The light went off behind them too.

Jack continued to stare through the crack until it became obvious that he wasn't going to catch another glimpse of her. He collapsed face first to the earth, trembling all over. Behind his eyelids he saw Rebecca, only now she was wearing a red blouse. Tears filled his eyes as he asked her, "What happened?"

If you don't know, I can't tell you, she replied in her soft Sussex accent.

CHAPTER 5

When Jack came to, the first thing he did was put his eyes to the crack. He blinked at the sun peeping over the house's slate roof. It was the sort of oversized Victorian mansion that developers loved to convert into flats. It was positioned side-on to the cemetery, facing a quiet, leafy street. The curtains were open in both first floor windows. The window where the woman had sat brushing her hair was now closed. She was nowhere to be seen. Had she gone to work? From the position of the sun, Jack guessed it was around eight o'clock. He'd been passed out for a good seven or eight hours. He felt a twinge of disappointment. He'd hoped to see the woman in daylight, partly to get a better look at her, partly to confirm she hadn't been a phantom of his inebriated mind.

He watched the windows for a while before skulking out of the tomb. If the woman was in, he didn't want her to see him. The cemetery gates were open. He made his way back to Chorlton, feeling set apart from the bustle of the rush-hour streets. Noises and faces seemed distant, vaguely unreal. He went into a shop for vodka. A schoolgirl was standing in the queue. She looked curiously at him. He thought about Naomi. She would be just about to leave for school. He found Laura's number on his phone. His finger hovered over the dial button.

Coward! Failure! The familiar words rang in Jack's mind like accusations in a courtroom. More followed them. *You couldn't be the husband Rebecca needed and now you can't be the father Naomi needs. All you're good for is wallowing in self-pity and booze.* As if to confirm the words, he returned the phone to his pocket and took out his wallet.

Upon arriving at his house, Jack pored over the photos of Rebecca. He conjured up a mental image of the woman in the window. The photos reinforced her striking similarity to Rebecca. They could have been related. Sisters even. The thought of the woman's black hair, pale skin and long slim body made his heart pump with, if not renewed life, then at least something that resembled it. Who was she? What was her name? He *had* to know.

He rooted through boxes until he found what he was looking for – a pair of binoculars he'd used for birdwatching on the Sussex coast. He'd often taken Naomi with him. She'd enjoyed listing the birds they spotted. Sometimes she would grow bored and noisy in the way all children do, but Jack hadn't cared. He'd simply been happy that she wanted to be there with him. That seemed like a different life now.

Jack showered, shaved and dressed. He ate what remained of the bacon and eggs Laura had brought. A free local newspaper landed on the doormat. 'Were They Killed By The Same Assailant?' ran the cover headline. Underneath were two photos of attractive young women. Both were dark-haired and slightly built. 'On July 16th the body of Abigail Hart, 26, was found near a lonely road in Didsbury.' began the article. 'She had been brutally stabbed and mutilated whilst making her way home from a night out in the city centre. Her body had been posed in what police describe as a sexually provocative position. Two days later, Zoe Saunders, 29, was also making her way home after a night out. Her body was found the following morning in Alexandra Park, Moss Side–'

He tossed the newspaper aside. He wasn't interested in the murders. Right that moment, he wasn't even interested in finding a way to break through his fears and doubts about his ability to be a dad. All he was interested in was the woman in the window.

With the vodka bottle stuffed into one jacket pocket and the binoculars in the other, he headed back out. It was a warm day. Vodka-scented sweat beaded his forehead by the time he got to the mansion. It was at the head of an affluent-looking street of similar properties, many of which had been broken up into flats and offices. Jack approached the mansion's front door. An intercom indicated that it comprised of four storeys of flats, including a basement level. Each floor had three flats on it, which meant the flats on the first floor were numbered 7-9.

He continued around the back of the building, holding himself as if he had a right to be there. A slatted wooden fence screened communal bins. There were large bins for general waste and smaller ones for recyclable materials. He upended a paper bin. Amongst the newspapers, magazines, cardboard and junk mail, there were personally addressed envelopes and letters. Some letters had been torn to pieces. Others had been screwed up. He found a fragment of one addressed to a Mr Zhang in flat 8. The name was Oriental, unlike the woman. So, unless she and Mr Zhang were an item, she most likely lived in flat 7 or 9. More searching revealed an empty brown envelope addressed to a Miss Camilla Winter, flat 7. He sifted through the rest of the rubbish, but didn't find anything for flat 9. He headed for the street.

A sporty little car was pulling into the carpark. 'DALE 1' boasted its personalised number plate. Jack wondered what sort of arsehole would drive around with a reg like that. A man got out of the car. Dale – assuming that was his name – looked to be in his early thirties and was dressed in a polo shirt, jeans and sockless loafers. He was a little taller than Jack, broad-shouldered, blonde and handsome in a catalogue model sort of way. He cast an uninterested glance in Jack's direction, walking with a swagger that made it seem as if he owned the entire building.

Jack avoided eye contact. He found a shady bench in the cemetery and Googled Camilla Winter on his phone. A list of hits came up. Top of the bill was a link to the Manchester Evening News: 'Rising Opera Star To Headline Hometown Charity Concert'. He followed it and found himself staring at a photo that made his hands shake ever so slightly. Camilla was wearing a low-cut black dress. Sleek black hair cascaded down her back. She was casting a seductive look towards the camera over her shoulder. Her full lips glistened with crimson lipstick. A hint of blusher highlighted her high cheekbones. Mascara outlined her eyes – eyes that were as blue as Rebecca's.

He tenderly traced her outline. The shadows had shifted a couple of centimetres by the time his gaze moved on to the text. 'Camilla Winter has deservedly won plaudits for her performances with La Bella Vita Opera Company. Now the talented young soprano is bringing her silky voice to Manchester Opera House. On Saturday 22nd July she will be singing the role of Violetta in Verdi's La Traviata. All proceeds from the concert will go to Royal Manchester Children's Hospital. Miss Winter, who grew up in Didsbury, commented, "It's wonderful, if a little nerve-racking, to be performing in my hometown for the first time. I've been lucky enough to perform all over Europe, but it's been a lifelong ambition of mine to take to the stage at Manchester Opera House."

At the end of the article there was a ticket line number. Jack rang it. There were single seats still available. He booked the one with the best view. Then he weaved his way through the headstones to the altar tomb. He glanced around to make sure no one was about. A small, empty silver car was parked outside the cemetery railings near the entrance to the flats' carpark. He took out his binoculars for a close-up view of the interior of Camilla's flat.

The smaller window looked into a bedroom. The walls were hung with paintings of naked lovers embracing. There was a mirrored wardrobe and a dressing-table. From that angle, he couldn't see the bed. The other window looked into a living-room. There wasn't much to see – a few more paintings, a mantelpiece with two candles on it and a flat-screen television attached to the chimney-breast above it, shelves of books and ornaments, a closed door.

Jack ducked behind the altar tomb as the door opened and a figure stepped into view. It was the man from the carpark – Dale. Jack's eyebrows knitted together. Who was he? A friend or relative of Camilla's? Her boyfriend?

Dale dropped from view and the television came on. Jack crawled inside the tomb and kept watching. The morning tipped over into afternoon. It was pleasantly cool in the stone cavity. Jack's eyes began to drift shut. They sprang wide when Camilla appeared in the living-room doorway. The binoculars made her seem close enough to touch. She was wearing a white summer dress that clung to her tiny waist. Her hair was up in a tight bun. There was little makeup on her face other than eyeliner and pink lipstick. Her lips were drawn into a smile that reached up higher on one side than the other. Jack's heart thumped against his ribs. Rebecca had used to smile like that before depression sank its claws into her. Dale rose back into view. He approached Camilla, and they kissed passionately.

Jack's knuckles paled on the binoculars. It was almost as if he was spying on Rebecca and a lover. Camilla led Dale by the hand into the bedroom. They made a beautiful couple. Dale was almost a head taller than her. His blonde hair and tanned skin contrasted with her dark hair and pale features. They were equally good looking, unlike Jack and Rebecca had been. Next to Rebecca, Jack had always felt like a carthorse paired with a thoroughbred. She could have had any man she wanted. He'd often wondered why she was with him. He'd asked her that question more than once over the years, to which her reply was always the same, "I don't want *any* man. I want you."

Dale pulled Camilla to his chest. They kissed again for what seemed like a long time. Camilla moved to close the curtains. Jack let out a breath of relief as if he'd been freed from a sight that was as hypnotic as it was painful.

He put the vodka bottle to his lips. As the liquid seared his throat, images of Rebecca and himself making love swirled in his mind. Most of the time she'd been happy for him to dictate their lovemaking, but occasionally she would take control. "I'll do anything for you," he'd used to tell her at such times. "Just ask and I'll do it."

He'd been true to those words, except for one occasion. He'd pored over that incident countless times since her death, wondering if it had any significance. A year or so after Naomi's birth, their dormant sex life had awoken with a ravenous appetite. They'd got drunk and were going at it on the living-room floor. The booze had ignited a wild light in Rebecca's eyes. She'd kept gasping, "Fuck me harder, Jack. Harder. Harder!" Suddenly she'd grabbed one of his hands and pulled it to her throat. "Strangle me, Jack!"

"No. I don't want to," he'd replied in a shocked tone.

His refusal had extinguished the light in Rebecca's eyes. She'd squirmed out from under him and lain with her back to him. He hadn't known what to say, other than, "Sorry."

"You've got nothing to be sorry for," she'd said in a flat voice. "Please let's just not talk about it."

And they hadn't talked about it. Jack had all but forgotten it even happened until after Rebecca died. Then it had come back to him and he'd wondered, *Did she need something I couldn't give her? Had she looked for it elsewhere?* He'd scoured her belongings and emails, talked to her friends and colleagues, but found nothing to suggest his suspicion was justified.

It was late afternoon and Jack was halfway through the vodka when Camilla opened the curtains. A silky red dressing-gown loosely tied at the waist exposed the valley between her breasts. Her thick hair hung around her shoulders. She seated herself at the dressing-table and brushed it.

Dale appeared fully dressed behind Camilla and nuzzled her neck. She lifted a hand to cup his cheek, then he turned to head for the door. A minute later a powerful engine revved on the other side of the wall that divided the cemetery from the carpark. The sound faded as the car – surely Dale's sports car – accelerated into the distance. Jack hoped Dale didn't return that day. He ached to spend the evening alone with Camilla.

She rose and moved into the living-room, picking up a sheath of papers somewhere along the way. Pacing back and forth, she leafed through them.

She stopped to open the sash-window and lift her face to the afternoon breeze. Taking a step back, she broke into song, her voice rising as clear and high as the sky. The language was foreign. It sounded like Italian. Little shudders ran through Jack. He'd never heard anything so lovely, except perhaps Rebecca's laugh.

Camilla broke off, frowning as if she'd heard something she didn't like. She sang the same few words nine or ten times before slapping the papers down on the windowsill. She grabbed a packet of cigarettes, lit one, took a drag, then hurled it out of the window as if disgusted by it. A faint spiral of smoke rose from where it landed in the cemetery's long grass. She put a cordless phone to her ear. Jack caught a few snatches of half-shouted words. "I can't... I've tried... I can't hit it!" Her voice quivered as if she was ready to burst into tears.

She hung up, returned to the bedroom and untied her dressing-gown. Jack looked away as the robe fell off her shoulders, but his gaze slid back to her. Her body was as flawless as her face. Beneath the soft curvature of her breasts, a flat belly led down to a triangle of dark hair between milky thighs. She put underwear and a summer dress on, slung a handbag over her shoulder and left the room.

Jack gave it a moment to make sure she didn't return before creeping out of the tomb and over to where the cigarette had fallen. A brief search exposed the nub-end. A hint of lipstick stained its filter. He placed it between his lips. It had a sweetish taste. He put it in his jeans pocket and headed for the cemetery's entrance. His stomach was full of vodka and not much else. If he was going to stave off unconsciousness long enough to see Camilla return, he needed something to eat.

CHAPTER 6

Jack was eating a sandwich in a fast-food restaurant when his phone rang. It was Laura. He guiltily remembered saying he would call or visit Naomi. Laura wasn't about to allow that one to slip by. She'd become fiercely protective of Naomi since taking her in. Doubtless, she was ringing to give him an earful. It was no less than he deserved. Steeling himself, he put the phone to his ear.

"Sorry, sis," he began, "I've got no excuses. I just–"

"It's not Aunt Laura," a small nervous voice broke in, "it's me."

Jack was startled into silence.

"Daddy, are you there?" asked Naomi.

Jack sucked in a head-clearing breath and tried to inject a little lightness into his voice. "Hello, sweetheart. I wasn't expecting it to be you."

"Aunt Laura said you wanted to speak to me. You do, don't you?"

His heart squeezed at the doubt in Naomi's voice. "Of course I do..." He scrambled for something else to say. "How's school?"

"It's OK." The response was a verbal shrug. "Are you OK, Dad?"

"I'm a lot better."

"That's what you said about Mum."

"I know, but I really am a lot better." Jack hated himself for lying, but what else was he supposed to say? *I'm a drunken mess who'd rather spend his time peeping on a stranger than face the reality of bringing up a child alone.*

"Does that mean I can come to live with you?"

He winced. Naomi's hope was even more painful than her doubt. "Not quite yet."

She made a disappointed little sound. "When then?"

"I don't know, sweetie. I thought you enjoyed living with Aunt Laura."

"I do, but I want to be with you. Why can't I be with you, Dad?" There was a tremor of tears being held back.

Jack closed his eyes to dam his own tears. "You can, just not right now. I'm working through a few things. Tell you what, I'll decorate your bedroom. What colour would you like it to be?"

"Blue like the sky is blue."

Jack was silent. Naomi's old bedroom had been summer sky blue. Rebecca had chosen the colour because it matched her and Naomi's eyes.

"Is that OK, Dad?"

It wasn't OK – Jack knew the colour would hurt him every time he saw it – but how could he say no. "Of course, sweetheart. Listen, I love you very much. I only want what's best for you. And right now what's best for you is staying with Aunt Laura. But it won't be forever." *Nothing is,* he thought. Life had a way of tricking you into thinking things would just go on and on as they always had when the reality was the exact opposite. The only certainty – apart from death – was that nothing was certain. Rebecca had taught him that.

"Do you promise?"

"I promise."

"Cross your heart and hope to die."

"Cross my heart and hope to die. You'll be moving into your new bedroom before you know it, sweetie. I love you," Jack said again. "You know that don't you?"

"Yes, Dad."

He let out a little sigh of relief. He'd needed to hear Naomi say that. "Is your aunt there?"

"Uh-huh."

"Put her on."

Laura came on the phone. "Hi there."

"You could have warned me before putting Naomi on the phone," said Jack.

"Why would you need warning?" Laura asked curtly. "Have you been hitting the bottle again?"

Jack didn't try to deny it – he could hear the slur in his voice. All he could offer was another lame, "I'm sorry."

"It's not me you should be apologising to."

He took a deep breath of resolve. "I'll make this up to her. I don't know how, but I will."

"Well decorating her bedroom will be a good start," Laura said more softly. "And when you're finished, maybe you'll give serious consideration to what I suggested last time we spoke."

"You mean going back to work?"

"I mean putting that brain of yours to proper use. Have you seen the news today? Another body's been found. The third in four days."

"Where?"

"Chorlton."

Jack frowned. His house – he couldn't bring himself to think of it as a home – was in Chorlton. He'd chosen the area because it was a quiet suburb with good schools, plenty of green space and a low crime rate for Manchester. "Was it a dark-haired young woman?"

"Got it in one. Some psycho stabbed the poor cow to death in her flat. They're saying there might be a serial killer out there."

"But the police are saying there's no evidence the murders are linked."

"How did you guess?"

"Denial is their default position. Had the woman's stomach been cut open?"

"It didn't say so on the news." A hopeful rise came into Laura's voice. "Have you been making some sneaky inquiries?"

"No."

"So how do you know about that stuff?"

Jack thought about the woman in the park – her bloodied and battered face, her spread-eagled legs and the grotesquely smiling stomach wound. He changed the subject. "Please don't pull this trick again, Laura. I understand why you did it, but what you've got to understand is I'm trying to protect Naomi."

"Hmm, I'm not sure that's completely true. I think this is more about you than her. But I don't suppose I've got much choice other than to go along with you. I'm telling you, though, Jack, next time I come round to your place you'd better have at least slapped some paint on Naomi's room."

"I'll..." Jack fell silent. He'd intended to say *I'll phone Naomi when it's done,* but he realised how hollow the words would sound.

After hanging up, he rose and left the restaurant. The conversation had killed whatever appetite he'd had. His gaze slid longingly towards the cemetery. "What do you think you're playing at?" he muttered. With a disgusted shake of his head, he turned in the opposite direction.

CHAPTER 7

Jack browsed the DIY store's paint aisles. He gingerly ran his fingers over a sky blue label, before putting the tin it was stuck to in a trolley along with gloss, turps, brushes, rollers and dustsheets. He lugged his purchases back to Chorlton. A street of large houses tucked away behind hedges and trees was cordoned off by blue-and-white plastic tape. Halfway along the street, police vehicles were clustered outside a 70s-style, flat-roofed block of flats. A team of forensic officers in full white scene suits were trooping into the flats.

Jack didn't stop to watch. His house was only four streets away. Although it was hot outside, the hallway felt cold. He headed upstairs to the room that Naomi had chosen to be hers. Boxes of her belongings were piled on the carpet, along with a plastic-wrapped mattress and sections of a bed waiting to be assembled. The plan had been that Naomi would stay with her aunt for a fortnight while Jack sorted out the house. She'd been there for the better part of two months now.

An almost unbearable heaviness weighed down on Jack as he contemplated the room. With laboured movements, he shifted the boxes onto the landing. He spread out the dustsheets and poured paint into a roller tray. The paint went onto the walls dark, but dried to a pale but bright blue. It was a colour in which you could lose yourself and never find your way back.

What happened, Rebecca? Did you fall? Did you jump? Oh god, please somehow find a way to tell me...

Jack realised that he'd stopped painting. The roller hung like a dumbbell at the end of his arm. All around him all he saw was blue, blue... The blue suddenly changed to red. He jerked up his arm and hit the wall with the roller, denting the plaster. Next, he snatched up the paint tin and hurled its remaining contents over the room like an unhinged artist. He flung the tin aside and stalked down to the living-room. He dropped into the armchair and set to work on the rest of the vodka, not caring that his hands and clothes were smeared with wet paint.

"Who are you kidding?" he scowled. "You'll never sort this house or yourself out."

The vodka worked its black magic. Jack felt as if he was shrinking into himself. The room receded from him like a light at the beginning of a tunnel...

When he next opened his eyes, the room was bathed in purple twilight. The first thing he thought about was Camilla. A desperate desire to see her throbbed through his veins. This time, he didn't fight the urge. He drunkenly fought his way into clean clothes and left the house.

As he swayed along the pavement, a police car cruised towards him. It slowed down and its driver gave him a long look. Then it stopped and two constables got out. "Excuse me, can we talk to you a–"

"I can't help you," interrupted Jack. "I wasn't in the area last night."

"Do you live around here?"

Jack nodded, thumbing over his shoulder towards his house.

"Can we see some ID?"

Jack took out a wallet and flipped it open. The constables looked at his ID. They exchanged a glance. "Sorry for bothering you, sir," said one. "We'll let you get on your way. Have a good evening."

"Yeah right," Jack said with a scoff of laughter as they returned to their car.

The streets were eerily quiet. Apart from a few foolhardy teenagers and the odd man with the purposeful stride of someone on their way to the pub, Jack saw no one. Word was out. There was a killer on the prowl. A maniac. Lock your doors and don't open them to strangers.

He detoured to buy more vodka. It was dark by the time he reached the cemetery. He dragged his alcohol-sodden body over the locked gates and found his way to the altar tomb. The lights were off in Camilla's apartment. He settled down to await her return, taking occasional sips from his new bottle – just enough to stave off the pain without knocking him out.

It was almost eleven o'clock when Camilla returned home. Jack's heart soared at the sight of her, but nosedived as Dale stepped into view. Dale was sharply dressed in a grey suit. His face was flushed, his movements jerky – symptoms Jack recognised only too well from his own heavy drinking. Dale dropped out of sight in the middle of the living-room. Camilla left the room and returned a moment later with two tumblers of what looked like whisky. Strands of hair had come loose from the bun on her head. Jack could see tension in her expression.

Dale's hand rose into view to take a glass. Camilla approached the window and opened it wide to the muggy night before picking up the sheath of papers. Glaring at them as if they were an old enemy, she broke into a snatch of song. Jack closed his eyes and, for a shuddering few seconds, he could feel her voice touching him like silk.

Camilla broke off momentarily. Then her voice rose again, this time in anger. "Give it a rest? How dare you tell me to give it a rest!"

Jack's eyes snapped open. Camilla's back was to the window. Dale stood up, pointing at his forehead and saying something that Jack couldn't make out.

"I don't care if you've got a headache," Camilla yelled, theatrically flinging her arms apart. "In two days I have to perform in front of thousands of people. The national press will be there. If I'm not note perfect, they'll tear me to shreds."

Dale's voice rose in response. "Oh stop being so bloody melodramatic. This is Manchester not Vienna, *darling*." He emphasised the final word sarcastically. "No one gives a shit if you don't hit every note."

"I give a shit. Don't you understand?"

"Yeah, I understand." Dale's lips curled into an ugly sneer. "You want them to love you for your voice. I hate to be the one to break this to you, babe, but you didn't get the part just because of your voice."

"Oh my god, you're so fucking ignorant."

Dale approached Camilla and said something else, his voice dropping too low for Jack to hear. He reached for her breasts, but she slapped his hands away and spat a retort at him. "You disgust me."

Dale's voice grew loud again. "Don't play the offended innocent with me, Camilla. I know how your filthy little mind works. You'll make a perfect Violetta because the thought of being a prostitute secretly gets you wet."

Camilla's hand flashed up. The contents of her tumbler flew into Dale's face. He grimaced at the stinging alcohol. His hand shot out to encircle her throat.

"No." Jack dropped his binoculars and scrambled out of the tomb. Dale's hand was still on Camilla's throat. She didn't try to prise it away. Instead, she threw her head back defiantly as if challenging him to tighten his grip.

Jack started running, his eyes scouring the wall for somewhere to scramble over. "Don't you hurt her," he said to himself. "Don't you hurt my Rebecca." He saw himself kicking in the flat's front door, wrenching Dale away from Rebecca and twisting the bastard's arm so hard that the bones snapped.

His foot hit a fallen gravestone. He tripped and fell flat on his face. Winded, he stared up at the window. Dale let go of Camilla and flung his glass at the wall. She spun away from him as shards of glass went flying. Jack glimpsed her face. He saw no fear. She appeared to be relishing the confrontation. She whirled back around to Dale. "Get out of my flat!"

My flat. Those words gave Jack a lift. They meant that Camilla and Dale didn't live together.

Dale glared at Camilla for an instant longer before storming out of the room. She stalked after him. Jack struggled to his feet, staggered back to the tomb and resumed his vigil. After a minute or two, Camilla returned to the living-room. As if re-energised, she snatched up the sheath of papers and belted out a spine-tingling burst of song, her voice soaring higher than before. She threw the papers down, this time not in frustration or anger, but in triumph. She switched off the light and left the room. Minutes later, she reappeared in her bedroom, having let down her hair, removed her makeup and changed into her dressing-gown. With her face unadorned and her hair flowing free, she looked even more beautiful to Jack – just like Rebecca used to do.

Rebecca...

Jack recalled with a jolt what he'd said as he ran towards the cemetery wall: *Don't you hurt my Rebecca.* "You're going to lose your mind, Jack," he told himself. "You need to leave here and never come back. Get up, Jack. Get up and leave right now."

But he remained where he was, watching Camilla perform her nightly ritual of brushing her hair at the dressing-table. Even when she closed the curtains and the light went out he continued watching, hoping to see her again, if only for a fleeting instant, before the night was through.

CHAPTER 8

When Jack awoke from a sleep he hadn't intended to fall into, soft morning light was seeping into the tomb. Shivering and rubbing life into his hands, he put his eyes to the crack. The bedroom curtains were still closed. He squinted at the vodka bottle. There were two finger-widths left in it – enough to take the edge off his pounding headache. He drank it down, suppressing a cough as it hit his raw throat. He lit a cigarette chaser and settled back into watching the flat.

He didn't have to wait long before Camilla emerged from her bedroom, looking as fresh as the morning. She perched on the windowsill in her dressing-gown, sipping from a teacup and perusing the sheath of papers. When she next left the room, Jack squirmed out of the grave and headed for the cemetery's entrance. He made his way past the block of flats to a tree from behind which he could inconspicuously watch the front entrance.

Three-quarters-of-an-hour later, Camilla stepped outside. As usual, her hair was pinned up and her face was flawlessly made-up. She was wearing a close-fitting pastel-blue summer dress and matching heels. A little black handbag dangled from her shoulder. She walked with the easy grace of a catwalk model, looking more like someone you would see in Cannes than Manchester.

Desire surged through Jack. "Rebecca," he murmured.

To his delight, Camilla set off on foot. He waited until she'd gone a hundred or so metres before following her. He was careful not to close the distance as he tailed her along leafy suburban streets. Puffs of cloud scudded across the sky, but wherever Camilla went the shadows seemed to draw back. She made everything around her seem grey and drab by comparison.

This is so wrong. You have to stop this.

The thought entered and left Jack's mind as fleetingly as the clouds veiled the sun. "She's in an abusive relationship," he told himself. "She needs protecting." But he knew his words were an empty excuse. He didn't simply want to protect Camilla, he wanted to hold her, look into her eyes and call her by a name that wasn't hers.

Camilla stepped into a newsagent. She paused on her way out to open a packet of cigarettes. She took a couple of drags on one before stubbing it out and hailing a passing black cab. The taxi accelerated away in the direction of the city centre with her in it. Jack had a good idea where it was going. He phoned for a minicab. When it arrived, he directed the driver to Manchester Opera House.

The minicab crawled along a busy dual-carriageway lined by post-war semis, fast-food outlets and retail parks. Suburbia gave way to bland blocks of flats and glittering steel-and-glass towers. Construction cranes punctuated the skyline, signalling a city on the up. Closer in to the centre, the stark modern buildings were offset by streets of Edwardian redbrick and pale stone edifices. The cab pulled over outside the opera house – a wide building of stuccoed brick with a roof like a Greek temple supported by six fluted columns. Above the two central columns a stone lintel was engraved with: 'The Play Mirrors Life'. Half-a-dozen posters along the building advertised 'La Traviata'. Camilla – or rather, Violetta – stared wantonly out of them, draped in an off-the-shoulder crimson dress.

Jack stood motionless for a moment, spellbound by the paleness of Camilla's skin, the blackness of her hair and, above all, the blueness of her eyes. He peered through a glass door into a deserted foyer. He tried the door. Locked. He caught sight of a black cab reflected in the glass. Camilla got out, along with two other women. Jack put his head down and moved away from the doors. Camilla didn't look in his direction. She and her companions approached a windowless side-door. It was opened by someone he couldn't see and they went inside.

He took up a position on a street corner opposite the opera house. With only a day to go until Camilla's performance, he guessed she was in for a long rehearsal. He was right. The day had worn away into a pink-skied evening by the time she eventually emerged from the windowless door. Office workers on their way out of the city centre had been replaced by a steady stream of revellers heading into it. Camilla was at the middle of a chattering, laughing little crowd. She was smiling as if she was happy with the way things had gone. Exchanging kisses and waves, several of the group broke away and flagged down a taxi. The rest, Camilla included, joined the revellers. Jack shadowed them, his eyes fixed on her every move.

A few hundred metres along the road, the group entered a busy, glass-fronted bar. Jack watched them mingle into the crowd. His heart tugged as he lost sight of Camilla. The tugging pulled him into the bar. Towards the front, people were perched on tall stools at small round tables. Further back, they were gathered at rectangular tables and a spot-lit bar counter. Blackboards advertised 'Tapas' and 'The Cuban's legendary Cuba Libre Granitas'. Lilting Latin music played over the hum of conversation. Jack spotted several of Camilla's group at the bar counter. She wasn't amongst them. His gaze swept the room, stopping with an electric jolt on a booth against the left-hand wall. Camilla was sitting side on to him. A spotlight highlighted her every feature. In profile she looked so much like Rebecca that it dazzled Jack. He became aware that people at a nearby table were casting curious glances at him. In a daze, he approached the bar counter.

"What can I get you?" asked a barman.

"Vodka."

"Do you want tonic and–"

"Vodka. Straight."

Jack knocked back his drink and motioned for a refill. Camilla's companions clustered around her, partially blocking his view. He adjusted his position, drawing nearer. He wasn't worried about being conspicuous anymore. All he cared about was drinking in her face as thirstily as he downed shots of vodka. With bitter-sweet pleasure, he imagined himself touching her, kissing her, whispering in her ear how much he loved her. He could almost hear her murmuring back, *I love you too, Jack.*

A tall, suited figure stepped between him and Camilla. He found himself looking into a face that was tanned and moisturised to within an inch of its life. Dale stared back for a second, his eyebrows pinching together as if he was trying to place Jack's face, before turning to order drinks. Jack dropped his gaze, but he was aware of Dale shooting further glances at him. Dale took a tray of rum shots to Camilla's table and doled them out amongst the group.

"Just finish your drink and go," Jack told himself, but he might as well have been talking to a wall. As if he was being manipulated by an irresistible force, his eyes returned to Camilla. His breath caught in his throat. She was staring back at him! There was no uneasiness in her eyes, only a faint curiosity. He gripped the bar counter as if to keep from losing his balance.

Dale was staring at Jack, too, with far from friendly eyes. As Dale rose to his feet, Camilla caught hold of his arm. He shrugged her off and strode towards Jack. The sight broke the spell holding Jack in place. He turned and made for the front entrance. Dale moved to intercept him and placed a hand firmly on his chest. Dale's too-white-teeth flashed as he said, "I knew I recognised you from somewhere. I saw you outside the flats the other day, didn't I?"

"I think you've mistaken me for someone else."

"I don't think so. I've got a good memory for faces." Dale's lips curved into a smile that seemed to suggest he could wipe the floor with Jack if he so wished.

"Take your hand off me."

37

Jack's voice was steady, unintimidated. Dale's smile faltered, but he didn't back down. "What's your deal? Are you a pap or some kind of saddo stalker?"

Stalker. The word echoed in Jack's mind. *Is that what I am? Is that what I've become?*

"Whoever you are, I'm warning you," continued Dale, "stay away from my woman. Do you hear me?"

Jack made no reply.

Dale's voice dropped to an angry hiss. "I said do you fucking hear me?"

Knock this prick's teeth down the back of his throat, Jack's instincts shouted at him. Resisting the urge, he nodded. Dale stepped back, grinning again, pleased with himself. "Now fuck off and don't come back."

Jack headed outside. "I won't," he promised himself. As if to reinforce the words, he repeated them over and over, "I won't. I won't..."

CHAPTER 9

Jack suddenly felt an overwhelming urge to see Naomi. He broke into a run. Two groups of lads were drunkenly squaring up to each other on Deansgate. Cutting across the road to avoid them, he turned onto Bridgewater Street. Sweat poured out of him as he passed into the exhaust-fume scented darkness beneath the Metrolink Bridge. His lungs struggled to keep up with his legs. He came to a stop with a searing stitch in his side. A year ago he could run ten kilometres without getting out of breath. There was a whole sea of vodka between then and now.

"No more," he told himself. "This stops right now."

He flagged a passing taxi and told the driver where to go. The driver eyed Jack's sweaty, unshaven face. "Hard day?"

Resting his head back against the seat, Jack sighed heavily. "Hard year."

Twenty-odd minutes later the taxi pulled over outside Laura's terraced house. A light glowed behind the downstairs curtains. Upstairs was dark. A low gate led to a postage stamp front yard. Jack knocked softly on the front door as if afraid of making too much noise. Laura's face appeared between the curtains. Her eyebrows twitched with surprise at the sight of Jack. The curtains fell back into place. A moment later the door opened. Laura was wearing a dressing-gown and slippers. Vertical lines clustered between her eyebrows as she took in her brother's tired and drawn features.

Jack pre-empted her. "Yeah, I know. I look like shit."

"And then some." Laura motioned him inside, adding in a hushed voice, "Naomi's in bed."

They went into a living-room furnished with a comfortable-looking sofa and armchair. There was a thick rug in front of a cast-iron fireplace. A television was muted in a corner. Everything was clean and fresh – the opposite of Jack's living-room. Laura picked up a glass of white wine and took a sip. "I would ask if you want a glass, but..." she tailed off meaningfully.

"I'd say no if you did. I'm off the drink."

Laura arched a doubtful eyebrow. "You smell more like you've been on it all day."

"I have. But that was the last time. From now on I'm teetotal."

"What brought on this decision?" There was a cautious note in Laura's voice, as if she'd heard this speech before.

With a stab of shame, Jack thought about the past few days of lurking like a ghoul in the cemetery. Every time he'd gone there, he'd felt as if he was moving a little further away from the world of the living. It was on the tip of his tongue to confess all, but he couldn't bring himself to do so. "I've been thinking about what you said. You're right, Laura, if I keep on like this I'll end up dead. Naomi's already been through more than any kid should ever have to without me doing that to her. I want to be there for her whenever she needs me, be it tomorrow or thirty years from now."

A smile in which happiness and sadness were intertwined broke through Laura's caution. "I can't tell you how glad I am to hear you say that, Jack."

"I'm sorry, Laura. I've been so selfish." He rested his forehead on her shoulder. "Why has this happened to me, sis? What did I do to deserve this?"

"You did nothing to deserve it. Sometimes bad things happen to good people."

Jack didn't argue. He'd seen the truth of those words demonstrated hundreds of times. Somehow, though, it hadn't crossed his mind that one day he would be on the receiving end of that pitiless reality. He'd thought that if he did the right thing, followed the rules, played nice, he would be insulated from that pain. For months after Rebecca's death he'd despised himself for being so blinkered. Even now, all he could say in reply was, "I just don't understand."

"Perhaps that's because there's nothing *to* understand," suggested Laura.

"There has to be. Otherwise how am I ever supposed to get past this?"

"You have to stop asking yourself these questions, Jack. All you're doing is beating yourself up over and over." Laura stepped away from him. "Sit yourself down. I'll make you a cup of tea and a bite to eat."

As she left the room, Jack dropped onto the sofa. He only remained seated a few seconds before standing and moving into the hallway. He padded upstairs to an open door. Naomi hadn't been able to sleep with her bedroom door closed since her mum's death. For weeks, she'd kept seeing Rebecca's face in the darkness. "You were just having a bad dream," Jack had tried to explain, but she always insisted that she hadn't been asleep. She'd been so certain that one night Jack crept into her room and sat watching her. Deep into the early hours, she'd woken with a sob and called for him. "I saw mum again," she'd said when he moved to comfort her. A strange sense of disappointment had filled him. He'd seen nothing.

Jack peeked into the bedroom. Naomi was lying on her side, knees drawn towards her chest. Her fawn-like limbs poked out of too-small pyjamas. The anniversary bracelet gleamed on her wrist. The bracelet haunted him almost as much as Rebecca's final text message. Why had she given it to Naomi? Was it because she'd known she wouldn't be returning home? Or had it simply been an impulsive present? Something to assuage her guilt about the pain she'd caused?

More questions with no answers.

Naomi's sleeping face looked peaceful. Jack saw nothing of himself in her. He only saw Rebecca. The familiar urge to turn away swept over him. He forced himself to keep looking. His mind returned to Camilla, only now he seemed to see her face clearly for the first time. It was broader and more angular than Rebecca's. Her eyes held a confidence bordering on arrogance that Rebecca had never possessed.

Rebecca, what happened? Make me understand...

He turned at a touch on his shoulder. "Beautiful, isn't she?" whispered Laura.

"She's the most beautiful thing I've ever seen."

Tiptoeing forwards, Jack ever-so-gently covered Naomi with the duvet. She stirred, but didn't open her eyes. "Sleep tight, sweetheart," he mouthed. "Don't dream."

They returned to the living-room. Laura had made Jack a mug of tea and a sandwich. "Thanks," he said, "but I'm going to head off."

"Stay a while."

He shook his head. "There's a lot to do to get the house ready for Naomi."

"Yeah but surely you're not going to do anything tonight?"

"I've wasted enough time, Laura." Jack headed for the front door and turned to kiss his sister.

She grimaced at his stubble. "Do me a favour and have a shave. It's like being kissed by sandpaper."

Jack attempted a smile. It almost looked like the real thing. "I'll see you soon."

He walked away fast, trying to think about Naomi and nothing else.

CHAPTER 10

Jack washed the pots and disinfected the kitchen. He flung out a bulging black sack of empty vodka bottles. He filled the washing machine, emptied boxes, set up the television, hoovered, dusted and scrubbed. He opened every window. It was getting light by the time he started on Naomi's bedroom. After pulling up the paint-encrusted carpet and throwing it in the back garden, he built Naomi's bed. He worked at it with borderline-manic urgency, afraid that if he slowed down the questions would come flooding back and with them the compulsion to find his way to an off-licence and then the cemetery.

Finally, he accepted that if he didn't take a break he would collapse. After showering, shaving and putting on clean clothes, he drove to a nearby retail park. At a red traffic-light, his gaze was drawn to a billboard with Camilla staring out of it. He gaped up at her, sinking into the blue of her eyes. The beeping of a car behind brought him back to the now green light. He accelerated away.

He ordered a carpet for Naomi's bedroom, bought another tin of paint and filled a supermarket trolley with all Naomi's favourite food. Back at the house, he painstakingly emulsioned the bedroom. He surveyed his handiwork with satisfaction, thinking about what he needed to do when the paint was dry – set out Naomi's stuffed toys and dolls, her books, her collection of miniature ceramic cats. Everything would be just so for her first night in her new home.

"Home," Jack said with a certain reluctance. Was that what this place was now?

He went around the house, looking for jobs to do. In his bedroom, he caught sight of a photo of Rebecca. For an instant he was caught between the yearning to drop to his knees like a worshipper at an altar or to turn and run and not stop until he had a bottle to his lips. He did neither. Instead he snatched up the photo and put it in a drawer. Downstairs, he set about cooking Naomi's favourite meal – spaghetti Bolognese. The bedroom wouldn't be ready today, but he could invite her and Laura over for a meal. He figured that would ease Naomi into the idea of moving in.

Jack left the sauce simmering and moved into the living-room. It felt like a different room –welcoming instead of oppressive. Even the sunlight shining through the window somehow seemed brighter and friendlier. To occupy his mind, he turned on the news. A swarthy, middle-aged man was addressing a scrum of journalists. The man had short salt-and-pepper hair and was handsome, if stern-featured. He wore a grey suit and a suitably sombre expression. A caption at the bottom of the screen identified him as 'Detective Chief Inspector Paul Gunn'.

"...newspapers seem convinced that these murders are the work of one individual," the chief inspector was saying in a reedy southern accent. "I would like to stress once again that we have no evidence at this time to support that theory..."

Still wheeling out the same old company line even though he must know it's bullshit, thought Jack. *No wonder he looks so stressed.*

"...However, I would also urge caution – especially for women in the Greater Manchester area. If you're planning on a night out, don't travel alone to and from your destination. If you're staying in, make sure your doors and windows are secure. And If someone comes knocking after dark, don't open the door unless you know and trust the person on the other side of it."

Jack snorted a humourless laugh. DCI Gunn might as well have said, *We haven't got a fucking clue who's doing this or why, so don't blame us if your stupidity gets you killed.* The chief inspector said something else, but Jack tuned out of his voice. He'd heard enough to know there was nothing worth hearing. Christ, he was so tired. He felt like he could sleep for a month. He allowed himself to close his eyes. As always, Rebecca was there in the darkness. He inhaled slowly through his nose and out through his mouth. "Accept the pain, accept that this is your life," he murmured. "Just let it come and let it go. Let it come and let it go..."

It was a mantra he'd repeated hundreds of times over the past year. A therapist had explained the importance of accepting reality for what it was, rather than what you wanted it to be. "Don't run away from painful thoughts, but don't indulge them either," the therapist had told him. "Take a step back and let them be. That way they'll gradually lose their power over you." At least that was the idea. It hadn't worked for Jack so far, but that hadn't stopped him from trying. For Naomi's sake he would have attempted anything to release Rebecca from his mind, even if it was the last thing his heart wanted.

Jack's eyes popped open and refocused on the screen. DCI Gunn was gone. In his place was an incongruously bubbly female 'Entertainment Correspondent'. She was outside Manchester Opera House. "I'm delighted to have with me the star of tonight's show," she said. "Camilla Winter is a home-grown talent who, after a series of critically acclaimed performances, has the world of opera at her feet."

"I wouldn't go so far as to say that," Camilla put in modestly.

Jack leant forwards, his eyes shining. A lacy white dress pushed up Camilla's breasts and flared outwards below her impossibly narrow waist. A silver necklace set with blood-drop gems adorned her long neck. Earrings dangled like chips of ice from her earlobes. Corkscrews of hair spilled from beneath a crown of white flowers. Makeup made her lips as plump as ripe cherries and her eyes as big as the sky.

"Tell us how it feels to perform the lead role in one of the world's most famous operas in your hometown," said the correspondent.

"Ever since my mother first brought me to this place as a young girl, I've dreamed about singing here."

"So it's a dream come true."

"It really is, yes."

Camilla's voice was soft and assured, but Jack detected a tiny wobble of nerves. A hint of vulnerability that did more to enhance her beauty than any amount of makeup. Tingles rose from the nape of his neck to the crown of his head.

"And the entire proceeds from tonight are going to Royal Manchester Children's Hospital," said the correspondent.

Camilla's glistening lips parted to reply. With an immense effort of will, Jack reached for the remote and switched off the television. He closed his eyes again. Rebecca and Camilla's faces flashed at him like superimposed images.

He repeated Laura's words. "You have to be strong." Platitude though it was, he needed it right then.

He returned to the kitchen, tasted the Bolognese sauce, then looked around himself with a glint of desperation in his eyes. His gaze fixed on the overgrown garden. He dragged the lawnmower out of the shed, pushed it back and forth across the lawns, then set to work on weeding the flowerbeds. Sweat lathered his face beneath the afternoon sun. He continually ran his tongue over his lips. He had an itch, but not one he could scratch with his hands. It seemed to start at the centre of his brain and spread through his body like a virus. God, he needed a drink so badly. Even more than that, he needed to see Camilla.

"Be strong," he said again, but there was less conviction in his voice.

He uprooted weeds like his future depended on it. The itch became tongue-chewingly intense. He wondered if this was how the killer felt. Maybe they'd fought the urge to kill for as long as possible before caving in.

"Why should I even try to fight this?" he muttered bitterly. "Tell me Rebecca. Why should I?"

A single word echoed in his mind: *Naomi.*

He shook his head as if he didn't want to hear it. "All I ever wanted was to be a husband and a dad. Now I don't know how to be either. What happened, Rebecca?" His voice rose in grief and anger. "What fucking happened?"

He strode into the house, turned off the hob and went upstairs. After showering, he put on a white shirt and a navy blue suit. He didn't inspect his appearance in the mirror. He couldn't bear to look himself in the eyes. He phoned for a taxi to take him to the city centre. The opera didn't start for several hours. That suited Jack just fine. He had some catching up to do before then.

CHAPTER 11

Jack drained his glass and glanced at a clock. Quarter-to-eight. Not long till the show started, but long enough to toss back a couple more drinks. His gaze roamed the barroom. It was quiet for a Saturday night. The few customers who came through the doors were all in groups of two or more. Manchester's citizens, it seemed, were paying attention to Chief Inspector Gunn. Jack clocked several of them shooting him – the only solitary drinker in the place – wary looks.

He wondered if everyone who'd bought tickets would turn up for Camilla's show. He drifted into a fantasy where he was the only spectator in the auditorium. Camilla sang to him and beckoned him onto the stage. They embraced and when they drew apart he found himself looking into Rebecca's face. *I love you more than I can bear,* she told him with tears in her eyes.

"Why is it more than you can bear?" he asked.

She closed her eyes as if afraid he might see the answer in them.

"I miss you so much, Rebecca. I miss you so–"

Jack flinched at a tap on his shoulder.

"Listen, mate, I don't want any trouble," said the barman, "but you have to leave. You're making my other customers nervous talking to yourself like that. And everyone's nervous enough already."

Jack left without protest. It was a perfect summer's evening – turquoise sky, air like a caress. On evenings like this Rebecca and he had used to sit on the patio, sipping wine and watching swifts draw circles in the sky. Sometimes they would let Naomi stay up and she would lie snuggled in the crook of his arm, chattering on, asking endless questions. *Do birds talk to each other? Where does the sun go at night? Why is the moon white when the sky is black?* Jack would try his best to answer her. But sometimes he would have to admit, *I don't know, sweetheart.*

People were queuing out of the opera house's doors. Many were older couples not put off by the threat of a killer stalking young women. The queue led into a red-carpeted lobby where stalls sold 'Confectionary' and 'Merchandise'. Jack purchased a glossy programme with Camilla on its cover. He handed his ticket to an usher and followed a sign for 'The Gallery & Bars'. A tannoy called people to their seats. Jack continued against the general flow into a bar area. He knocked back a quick vodka and ordered another to take to his seat.

The auditorium was an echoing space with an arched ceiling of illuminated square panels. Banks of green velvet flip-seats shelved steeply towards balcony rails. Fluted pillars flanked private boxes. A green velvet curtain fringed with gold tassels screened off the stage.

The orchestra were fine-tuning their instruments in the pit. People were milling about in search of their seats. Jack found his near the back of the second floor gallery. Apart from the odd empty seat, the auditorium was at capacity. Despite his fantasy, Jack felt comforted by the anonymity of numbers. The last thing he really wanted was for Camilla to see him. After his confrontation with Dale, she was sure to be thrown by the sight of him. He would have hated to ruin her big night. Even worse was the thought that she might try to put a stop to his stalking.

Stalking. His forehead creased at the word, but there was no dressing it up as anything else. He'd become the very type of person he despised – a prowler, a deviant – and the worst part of it was that right then he didn't care. He had no thoughts of Naomi, no thoughts of his career or future. The only thoughts he had were of Camilla and of drinking until the final shreds of his personality were stripped away.

The lights dimmed. The audience broke into applause as the conductor appeared from the wings and took up his position in front of the orchestra. The conductor bowed to the audience, then turned to the musicians and raised his baton, bringing the string section to life. The horn section joined in and the pace gradually built. There was a lull in the music. Applause filled the auditorium again. The conductor resumed at a furious pace. As the orchestra responded in kind, the curtain rose to a peal of laughter from the stage.

The scene was a lavishly furnished candlelit room. Gilt-framed oil paintings of voluptuous naked women and arrow-wielding cherubs adorned the walls. Men in evening suits were drinking Champagne and smoking cigars at a long table decorated with bouquets of red roses. A line of women in ruffled silky dresses danced into the room. At their head was Camilla – or rather, Violetta. They milled around, fluttering fans in front of their pale powdered faces as the men broke into song. White-wigged servants carried in trays piled comically high with cream cakes.

Opera glasses were attached to the back of the theatre seats. Jack hired a pair and focused in on Violetta as she took centre stage, surrounded by men who eyed her like a prime cut in a butcher's shop window. She accepted the hand of one and led him to the table, singing words that made Jack shudder though he didn't understand them. Her voice soared over the orchestra, the other sopranos, the altos, the tenors, the baritones and the basses, leaving them so far behind that he lost sight of them. He watched Violetta like someone lost in a memory. When she sank onto a divan sofa theatrically coughing and clutching her chest, he made as if to rush to her aid. He was halfway to his feet before he came to his senses and sat back down. Minutes or hours might have passed when the curtain fell in front of Violetta, leaving the auditorium in darkness.

Jack blinked as the lights rose. Camilla appeared from the between the curtains to rapturous applause. She bowed, blew kisses and mouthed thanks to the audience. Other cast members emerged to share in the applause before all retreated from view. The tannoy announced that there would be a short interval before act two. Jack headed for the bar. Two drinks later he was back in his seat.

Act two began in a wood-panelled sitting room. The paintings of voluptuous women had been replaced by sombre portraits; the Champagne flutes had been swapped for china teacups. There followed what seemed to Jack an interminable scene involving a country gent and a maid. Jack's eyelids drooped. He had no interest in these characters. Finally, they left the stage and Violetta reappeared. His eyes popped wide open, following her every movement. His ears hung on her voice. Other characters came and went without him noticing. When Violetta broke down in tears, he felt a sting in his own eyes. All too quickly, she departed the stage again. The country gent returned. So too did Jack's drowsiness. It settled over him so heavily that before he realised it his chin was resting against his chest.

He awoke with Rebecca's voice seeming to echo in his ears: *I love you more than I can bear... More than I can bear...* A brightly illuminated bed with Rebecca lying on it filled his vision. Her hair was lank. Her pallor was sickly. Fear and something else that he read as a desperate appeal for understanding lined her face. She clutched a pillow to herself as if struggling against pain. Jack stood up, stretching out a hand to comfort her.

"Could you please sit down?"

The annoyed voice came from behind him. He blinked as if jolted out of a trance. The woman on the bed was no longer Rebecca, it was Camilla or Violetta. "Sorry," he fumbled out. He suddenly felt suffocated. He had to get outside into the fresh air.

He squirmed his way to the end of the row and half-ran out of the auditorium. Upon reaching the street, he leant against a wall heaving in lungfuls of air. Light-headed, he swayed across the road, forcing a carful of young lads to brake sharply. "Wanker! Freak!" they shouted.

Jack knew they were right on both counts – he was a wanker for letting down Naomi and a freak for stalking Camilla. And yet he also knew he wasn't going to sober up and make another desperate attempt to pull himself together. He was going to buy a bottle and take it to the cemetery.

CHAPTER 12

Jack made his way to the cemetery on foot. He just barely had the energy to haul himself over the gates and worm his way into the tomb. Camilla's windows were dark. He wasn't surprised. She would be at an after-show party, celebrating her success, soaking up the congratulations. No doubt Dale would be with her, basking in her reflected glory. He wrinkled his nose as if he'd caught a whiff of something nasty. Now there was an arsehole who deserved to be put in his place.

He shone his phone light at the opera programme, running his eyes and fingers over Camilla's face.

Muffled laughter attracted his attention. The living-room light was on. Camilla and Dale were holding each other. Dale was wearing a black suit and bow tie. Camilla had changed into a red dress. They danced round the room, laughing, kissing and swigging from Champagne flutes. They looked luminously alive. They made Jack feel like something dead and decaying.

Dale upended a Champagne bottle, but nothing came out. Pulling a mock-sad face, he retreated from Camilla and out of the door. She pirouetted towards the window, snatched up the sheath of papers and triumphantly flung them into the air. As they fluttered down around her like oversized confetti, she danced through to the bedroom.

Jack felt a crawl of pleasure as Camilla examined her reflection at the dressing-table, running her tongue over her lips and applying fresh lipstick. She let her hair down and brushed it slowly, sensuously. From the length of time Dale had been absent, Jack guessed he'd gone out to buy more Champagne. He hoped some accident befell Dale on the way to the shop.

Nothing too serious. A sprained ankle would do. *Ten more minutes, that's all I want with her,* he told himself. But he knew it wasn't true. Ten minutes, an hour, a day... It would never be enough.

A flicker of movement drew Jack's gaze back to the living-room. He squinted as if unsure of what he was seeing. It wasn't Dale – unless Dale was playing a trick on Camilla. *No, definitely not Dale,* decided Jack. Whoever it was, they were a good few inches shorter than Dale. The figure was wearing a bulky black raincoat that made it impossible to tell if they were a man or woman. Thin black hair curtained a face like something out of a horror movie. The skin was as yellowish-green and wrinkly as a week old corpse. The nose was witchily long and hooked. The eyes were lost in black-ringed sockets. *It's got to be a mask. Hasn't it? But if it's not Dale underneath, who is it?*

The figure pressed their back to the wall next to the living-room door and raised an arm. The light caught on something in their gloved-hand. A knife! The sight pierced the alcoholic-miasma of Jack's mind. He sprang up so suddenly that his head crunched against the roof of the tomb. He fell back to his hands and knees, dazed. His gaze swam towards the living-room window. He saw what had put the figure on alert. Dale appeared in the doorway, a bottle of Champagne in one hand, a bouquet of red roses in the other. He stepped into the room with a big, dumb smile on his face.

"No, you idiot! Look behind you," Jack slurred like a drunk at a panto.

The knife flashed downwards, plunging into Dale's back. An almost comical look of bewilderment replaced his smile. His expression turned to horror as the knife rose and descended again. He took a few faltering steps before turning towards his attacker. A groan whistled past Jack's teeth. The knife blade was buried to the hilt in the back of Dale's head. The Champagne and flowers dropped to the floor. Dale swayed on his feet for a second before following them. His killer stooped to retrieve the knife and turned towards the hallway.

Jack's gaze darted to the bedroom. Camilla was staring towards the door as if she'd heard something. Dale didn't appear to have cried out, but his body must have made a thud when it hit the floor. She rose to her feet. Jack moved too, flinging himself towards the hole in the tomb's wall. As he scrambled outside, the ivy seemed to clutch at him like restraining hands. He threw a glance at the living-room window. The knife-wielding figure was gone. He hesitated as a possibility tumbled through his mind: maybe they hadn't been there in the first place. Maybe the figure and Dale had been a hallucination conjured by grief, alcohol and lack of sleep. He hoped he was right. Better that he was losing his grip on his sanity than any harm came to Camilla.

"It's not real, it's not real," he chanted, willing his words to be true.

He looked at the bedroom again. Camilla was gone too. A heartbeat later, she reeled back into view. She wasn't alone. The killer sprang after her, stabbing downwards. Camilla twisted so that the blade skimmed past her. She grabbed her attacker and they staggered around as if in a clumsy parody of her dance with Dale.

It's real! Jack's mind screamed. *It's real!*

He started running. Although he pumped his legs as hard as possible, it felt as if he was moving in dreamlike slow-motion. Then he was at the cemetery wall. He half-climbed, half-threw himself over it, landed off-balance, pitched forwards and hit the tarmac. A little winded, he scrambled upright and ran to the front door. It had been wedged open with a stick. A light automatically clicked on in the high-ceilinged hallway. To the right and left were doors to ground floor flats. He raced up a broad staircase and came to an abrupt halt on the first floor landing outside flat '7'. There was no sign of forced entry. He reached for the handle, but hesitated.

Easy now, Jack, he cautioned himself. *That fucker's got a knife.* He glanced around for something he could use as a weapon or at least to defend himself with. There was nothing. He snatched out the opera programme and rolled it up. It wasn't much, but it could deflect a knife thrust.

He tried the handle. The door clicked open. Had Dale left it unlocked? Was that how the intruder had got in? The door led to a hallway with a parquet floor. Numerous pairs of high-heels were balanced haphazardly on a shoe-rack. A jumble of coats, jackets and gossamer-thin scarves hung from pegs. Photos of opera singers cluttered the walls. A rich, dark scent rushed up Jack's nostrils – surely the smell of Camilla's perfume. Rebecca had rarely worn perfume. When she did, it was always something subtle, a scent that was all the more lovely because it was only caught in passing.

There were two doors to the right, two to the left and one straight ahead. The door straight ahead was open. A brown leather sofa, a tall uplighter lamp and the sash window were visible through it. Dale was lying face down on the floor. The roses protruded from under his chest, their petals almost as dark red as the blood pooling around him. Jack knew Dale was dead. Dale had been stabbed at the base of his head. Even a seemingly innocuous injury to that area could fatally damage the brainstem.

Jack's gaze moved to the second door on the right. It had to lead to Camilla's bedroom. The door was a few centimetres ajar. There was no sound from beyond it. The silence was as threatening as a snake coiled to strike.

Heart going like a piston, Jack crept to the door and prodded it open with the magazine. Next to the door was an unmade double-bed with clothes strewn over it. At the far side of the bed stood an antique-looking wardrobe with a mirrored door. Jack caught sight of his reflection – wide eyes, sweat-sheened forehead, dishevelled hair. A stool lay overturned in front of the dressing-table. The dressing-table mirror had been smashed. Jagged fragments of glass gleamed amongst a wreckage of perfume bottles and other beauty products. The bedroom appeared to be deserted.

Then Jack heard it – a sound like water bubbling from a leaky radiator. He glanced behind the door. Nothing. He edged towards the foot of the bed. The first thing he saw was a pair of bare feet, red-varnished toenails facing upwards. The feet were attached to slender, smooth legs. The wet sound came again, louder. Jack took a quick step forward. His breathing accelerated in turn.

Camilla was lying on her back, her eyes bulging at the ceiling. Bright red blood was frothing out of her mouth. Her right hand was flung out to the side. Her left hand rested close to a large shard of mirrored glass protruding from her neck. Blood streamed along the shard, pooling like spilt ink on the floor.

Forgetting his caution, Jack grabbed a dress from the bed. He bundled it up and pressed it against the wound, taking care not to dislodge the shard. Blood soaked through the material. Camilla's eyes slid towards him, radiating pain and fear. He pressed another item of clothing over the sodden dress. Pressure, that was the key to stopping the bleeding. The second layer of material seemed to do the trick.

He reached for his phone. Explaining how he saw the attack on Camilla would destroy his career. That was bad enough, but infinitely worse was that Naomi would find out what he'd been up to. Dale's voice echoed back to him, *Are you some kind of saddo stalker?* It made Jack shrivel with shame to think of Naomi knowing that that was exactly what he was. But if it meant Camilla survived, it was a price he was willing to pay. Wasn't it? Of course it was! *Christ, how can you even ask yourself such a thing?* he rebuked himself.

As Jack dialled, Camilla's left hand twitched downwards. "Try to stay still," he cautioned. "If the shard comes loose, I won't be able to stop–" He broke off in dismay as Camilla's eyes rolled white. "No, no! Keep looking at me, Camilla." Her dilated pupils flickered back into view. "That's it. Good girl. Just hold on, Camilla. You're going to be OK. An ambulance will be here soon."

Her hand moved again, pointing. Jack followed the line of her finger. Her red dress clung wetly to her stomach. The hem of it was ruckled up to just below her groin. He lifted it with the magazine. She was wearing a thong whose string had been cut. He lifted the dress higher. What he saw made him want to squeeze his eyes shut. Camilla wasn't going to be OK. Even a trauma team couldn't have saved her. She'd been slashed halfway open from her left side to her navel. A bloody, veiny tangle of lacerated organs bulged through the wound. It was as if a crazed surgeon had gone to work on her.

He looked into Camilla's eyes. She didn't have long. The gurgle of her breath was subsiding. Such beautiful eyes. Suddenly it was as if a light had been snuffed out in them. Then there was silence.

CHAPTER 13

Jack ground his teeth so hard it felt like they might shatter. Why did ugliness always seem to triumph over beauty? His face was ashen. He felt empty, drained to the point where his own heart might give up the ghost. He closed his eyes and bowed his head. A shuddering breath later, he looked at his phone again. The killer couldn't be far away. If he gave the police the heads-up, they might get lucky and catch the bastard. He would still have a hell of a job explaining his presence, but there was one crucial difference – without Camilla alive to ID him as a suspected stalker, he didn't have to tell the whole truth. He could spin a tale that he'd seen someone acting suspiciously outside the flats and decided to investigate. Lying to the police was a huge risk. One that could land him in prison for a long time. Was it a risk worth taking? Not for the sake of his job it wasn't. But what about for Naomi? He thought about the way she used to look at him, her eyes so full of a pure and loving trust. That trust had already been dented. It would be shattered if the truth came out.

His phone pinged, once, twice. Two messages. No caller ID. He opened the first message. It was a video file. His eyebrows pulled into a knot. The camera lens was directed through the window of a busy bar. People were chatting, smiling, laughing and enjoying cocktails to the sound of Latino music. Towards the back of the barroom, customers were lined up at a counter. Amongst them was one man who stood apart from the crowd. Not because he wasn't smiling. Or because his cheeks were sunken and shadowed with stubble. But because of the look in his eyes. Jack had seen plenty of people like him in the streets – rough-sleepers, addicts, prostitutes, beggars. People existing on the fringes whose wild, lost eyes inspired sympathy and unease in equal measure. He realised with a shudder that he was looking at himself.

The camera panned across to the object of his attention – Camilla. She was staring back at him. She stood apart from the crowd too, but for different reasons. Like a diamond amongst lumps of coal. Dale's angry face came into the picture. The lens followed him as he moved to intercept Jack.

The two men squared up to each other. Watching himself eyeball Dale, Jack thought, *He's not the arsehole, you are. He was right to warn you off. You would have done the same if some guy had been looking at Rebecca like that.*

The video finished abruptly as Jack hurried from the bar. He thought back to that night. He'd turned right out of the door, meaning he'd passed the killer – who else but the killer could have shot the footage? – but his head had been down. He'd seen no one.

Jack opened the second message. It was a photo of him in the cemetery, peering into Camilla's window through binoculars. This was the money-shot. The scene in the bar was damning, but didn't explicitly identify him as a stalker. There was nothing ambiguous about the photo. The man in it was a voyeur, a peeping-tom. The photo had been taken earlier in the day of his altercation with Dale. There had been no one around. The only thing that had caught his eye was a silver car parked outside the cemetery railings. Did the car belong to the killer? Was that the moment they'd realised they weren't the only one stalking Camilla?

He flinched as his phone rang. No caller ID. *Don't answer it,* warned part of him. *Call the police. You need to get to them first, tell them the whole truth and nothing but. If someone else beats you to them, you could be implicated in the serial murders.* There was no doubt in his mind that Camilla and the other three women had been killed by the same assailant. The slashed stomachs, the blue eyes and black hair – it couldn't be a coincidence.

But another part of him cried out, *Answer it! You might pick up some scrap of information that leads to the killer. If the killer's caught, the police may well be willing to overlook the role you played. Naomi would never have to know about this. It's worth the risk.*

"It's worth the risk," Jack repeated out loud.

He put the phone to his ear and waited for the caller to speak. Tentacles of silence seemed to reach out of the earpiece and squeeze the breath from him. Finally, a voice – softly spoken, not identifiable as male or female – came over the line. "Who's been a naughty boy then, hmm Jack?"

Jack fought for calm in the wake of those chilling words. "How did you get this number?" he asked, noting that his voice echoed back at him.

He could guess the answer. After watching him watch Camilla, the killer had followed him home. From there it would be simple enough to find out his name. A quick rifle through his bin would do the trick. It was full of mail he hadn't bothered to open. It wouldn't be difficult for someone armed with that information to find out his mobile number. After Rebecca's death he'd put out online appeals for witnesses to contact him. The only response of any real note had come from a woman who'd been walking her dogs on the clifftops. She'd seen Rebecca looking out to sea. She remembered thinking Rebecca was dangerously close to the edge. That was about a quarter of a mile from where Rebecca plunged to her death. At that spot the cliffs weren't sheer. A falling body would bounce off rocky outcrops on the way down. Had Rebecca been looking for a suitable place to jump? Or had she been taking in the view? More questions to torment him. There had to be some logic, no matter how twisted, to their answers. There just had to be. Didn't there?

Right that moment other questions were tying Jack's mind into knots. Why had the killer contacted him? Just for the hell of it? Or did they want something from him? That was why he'd asked a question to which he knew the answer. It was psychology 101: questions create communication,

communication creates a connection, the more you communicate the deeper that connection becomes, and the deeper the connection the more likely you are to find out what you really want to know.

"What do you think of my little film?" asked the voice.

Clever bastard, thought Jack. Answering a question with a question was an old trick favoured by psychiatrists, policemen, politicians and paranoid killers since time immemorial. The killer wasn't going to play his game. But that didn't mean he had to play the killer's game. "I thought it was..." he sought a word that disclosed as little as possible of what he was thinking, "interesting."

There was the sound of low laughter. "You're a cagey one, aren't you? I can tell we'll have fun together."

Fun. The word made Jack shudder. He said nothing. What were you supposed to say to something like that?

"Don't go quiet on me, Jack. I hate it when people do that."

He ran his tongue dryly over his lips. The conversation was slipping out of his control. Time to cut to the chase. "What do you want?"

"Patience, Jack. We'll get to that soon enough. For now I just want to talk. Rebecca was a beautiful woman. Even more beautiful than Camilla. You must have loved her with all your heart."

A scowl twisted Jack's face. *Rebecca.* It sounded like blasphemy coming from this fucker. "Don't say my wife's name," he growled and instantly wanted to kick himself for letting emotion get the better of him.

The killer chuckled again. "That's more like it, Jack. Now we're getting to know each other. You know I don't like being given the silent treatment and I know you don't like talking about your dead wife. You know I like spying on beautiful young women. And I know you like to do the same."

"No–" Jack began to blurt out a denial, but broke off.

"What were you about to say? I hope you weren't about to deny it because we both know that would be a lie. Don't we?"

Jack was silent.

With a little rise of irritation, the killer repeated, "Don't we?"

"Yes," Jack replied in a voice weighed down by shame. Christ, what the hell was he thinking answering the phone? Perhaps there'd been a time when he could have outwitted this psycho. But that time was long past. All he was achieving was to allow the killer to put more distance between his or herself and the crime scene – the echo on the line was a sure sign that the killer was on hands-free whilst driving. He couldn't hang up though. If the killer had issues with people going silent on them, god knows how they'd react to him hanging up. It could send them into a homicidal rage. Someone else might die because of his stupidity. And the burden of that on his conscience, along with everything else, might well be enough to drag him under for good.

"I'm glad to hear you say that, Jack, because it's important that we're honest with each other. There has to be trust. If there's no trust then... Well, then I think you know what happens."

Jack called the killer's bluff. "So do it. Send the video and photo and anything else you've got on me to the police. What'll happen? I'll lose my job and get a slap on the wrist. Big deal."

"Who said I would send them to the police?"

Jack's stomach was suddenly like ice. The insinuation was clear. The bastard would send them to Naomi. He held his tongue in the slim hope he was wrong. After all, the killer couldn't have seen Naomi at the Chorlton semi and her name had been kept out of the newspapers after Rebecca's death.

"Social media's a big problem for parents these days, don't you think?" continued the killer, seemingly unbothered by Jack's silence this time. "It's so difficult to keep track of what kids are doing online. Especially if you're a single parent who doesn't have much time to talk to their kids. For instance, Jack, did you know your daughter has a Facebook account? You're supposed to be thirteen before you can open an account, but it's so easy to lie about being older than you are. The reverse is also true. An adult can pretend to be a child. They can follow the timelines of children. Find common ground. Make friends with them. Groom them. That's become a nasty word, hasn't it? Groom. It used to make me think of horses and weddings. Nowadays it makes me think of kiddy fiddlers. That's not what I am, Jack. I hate those sick fucks. If it was up to me, I'd round up every last one of them and put their heads on spikes. But anyway, back to the point... Common ground. I love cats. So does Naomi. She's been feeding a stray on your sister's street. Every evening after school she goes out with a bowl of–"

Words were surging up Jack's throat like lava. He couldn't contain them any longer. "Stay away from my daughter or I'll rip your fucking heart out!"

"Whoa," the killer said delightedly. "I don't doubt for a second that you would. You're like me."

Jack just about reigned in his anger. "I'm nothing like you."

"Don't fool yourself, Jack. Under the right circumstances, you could end up just like me. You're already halfway there. All it would take is a little push in the wrong direction."

"Who pushed you? Didn't Mummy and Daddy give you the attention you needed?"

Jack drew a cruel pleasure from the question. It only lasted a second, then he shook his head in self-disgust. *Are you trying to get someone else killed? Don't provoke the bastard.*

"Wouldn't you like to know," the killer replied in a voice that gave nothing away. "Which brings me to my next point. Do you know what the maximum sentence for voyeurism is? Two years. You wouldn't get anything close to that. Not considering your background. You'd end up doing a few weeks. Three or four months at most. Like you said, a slap on the wrist. Just enough to ruin what's left of your life. Imagine getting out of prison with no job. You wouldn't be able to find another job because no one employs ex-cons. Especially not ones on the Sex Offenders Register."

"I'm not a sex offender."

"You're a stalker, Jack. You spied on Camilla in her own home. I'll bet you felt a little stirring down there when you watched her getting undressed, didn't you? Did you wank yourself off?"

"No," Jack retorted. "It wasn't like that. She–" He broke off. He wasn't about to talk to this sicko about the feelings Camilla had reawakened.

"She reminded you of Rebecca. Watching her must have been sweet torture. I'll bet it felt like your guts were being torn out when you saw Camilla and Dale getting it on."

Jack bit his tongue so hard that he tasted blood. He knew that if he allowed one more word out others would erupt from him. He would lose the plot; threaten every type of violence. He also knew that doing so would only play into the killer's hands. Power. That's what it was all about. Power was everything to psychos like this. But to get power, you first needed control. And the easiest way to control people was through their emotions. That was another thing Rebecca had inadvertently taught him. She'd put him through so many emotions – love, elation, sympathy, confusion, fear – that it had got to where he would have done whatever she asked to try to keep her happy.

A sharp sigh filled the line. "Are you really going to play the silent card again, Jack? Do you want me to contact Naomi?"

Keeping his teeth clamped together, Jack made a negative noise.

"Of course you don't," said the killer. "Because you know what things like this do to people. They stay with you for life. Like a stain nothing can wash out. Whenever Naomi looks at you, she won't just see her dad. She'll see a pervert. Perhaps she'll even see a killer. Because if the police can't catch me, they'll look for someone else to pin this on. And you're the prime candidate."

"Not if I hand myself in I won't be. Killers like you don't hand themselves in. They carry on doing whatever floats their boat until they're caught or killed." Jack's voice was steady. He felt on surer ground, talking about a subject he was well versed in. "Even if they try to pin it on me, it won't stick because when you kill again – which you will do – I'll either be in prison or far away from here."

He noted with satisfaction that the killer was silent for a moment. "You've no idea how patient I can be, Jack," came the insidious voice. "If I have to wait years to get what I want, then I'll wait years. And Naomi will spend that entire time wondering, *What if, what if...* That kind of doubt can send a person off the rails."

"Not Naomi. She's too level headed." The tremor was back in Jack's voice.

"You mean like her mum was?"

Jack winced. *Naomi's nothing like her mum was,* he tried to reassure himself. *She's more like... Like who? Like you? Look at yourself. Laura told you to be strong, but you're a weak, self-pitying drunk. Is that what Naomi's got to look forward to? Depression, alcoholism, maybe even suicide? Will that be your and Rebecca's legacy to her?* He gave a hard shake of his head. No. He'd do anything to make sure Naomi didn't end up like Rebecca or him. Anything!

"Why are you doing this to me?" he asked.

The killer's voice rose again, not in irritation, but in throat-constricting anger. "Imagine the biggest rush you ever had. The highest high. You stole that from me, Jack."

He glanced at the sickening wound to Camilla's stomach. It was only half as long as the injury inflicted to the Alexandra Park victim. He'd disturbed the killer before they could reach the climax of their ritual. "And how do you expect me to pay you back?"

"There's no need to sound so down, Jack. It's not as bad as you think. It's not like I want you to cover up my crimes."

Then tell me what the fuck you do want! Jack felt like screaming.

"So here's the thing, Jack. Believe it or not, I..." The killer paused theatrically. "I want you to catch me."

Jack's frustration turned to scepticism. "Why?"

"Why do you think? I'm a psycho killer. I have to be stopped before more people die."

Was the bastard serious? Jack couldn't tell. The voice was deadpan. "Tell me where you are. I'll come and take you in right now."

There was that chuckle again. "Where would be the fun in that? Oh and I'm using prepaid GSM phones in locations that won't lead you to me. So don't waste your time trying to catch me that way."

"And what happens if I catch you?"

"I go to prison and you're off the hook. You have my word on that."

Jack almost let slip a derisive laugh. Psycho killers weren't exactly known for keeping their word. "How can I be certain you won't try to take me down with you?"

"I gave my word, didn't I? Like I said, this won't work unless we trust each other. Do you think you can do that, Jack, after everything you've been through?"

That was a good question. Since Rebecca's death, Jack had struggled to trust anyone, least of all himself. Just about the only person he had any faith in was Laura. So he wasn't about to trust this scumbag. "I'm not sure," he said for fear that an outright 'no' might anger the killer even more than silence.

"I hope for Naomi's sake you can, Jack, because the alternative doesn't bear thinking about. She's such a beautiful girl. Try to imagine where she might be in five or ten years if she goes off the rails. She could fall in with the wrong crowd, get hooked on drugs, get in trouble with the police. She might even end up selling herself on the streets. Can you picture that, Jack? Can you picture Naomi sucking some old man's cock for twenty quid? Answer me, Jack. Can you picture it?"

Jack would have rather put a bullet in his brain than picture those words, but he forced a, "Yes," through his teeth.

"That's good, Jack. Hold on to that image. It'll help you do what you need to do."

"Which is?"

"Right now you need to get some sleep. But first you're going to phone Paul Gunn and tell him you want to return to work. And don't try to pretend you don't know who Paul Gunn is. You two used to work together in Sussex. He got you a job at GMP after Rebecca died."

Jesus, this bastard's really done their homework, thought Jack.

The killer's words transported him back to Rebecca's funeral. After the agony of watching the empty coffin slide through the velvet curtains, the mourners had traipsed to a wake at a nearby hotel. Paul and his wife Natasha had driven down from Manchester. A traffic-jam on the M25 caused them to miss the memorial service. After apologising, Paul had told Jack, "I realise now's not the time, but a position will soon be opening in SCD." A year or so before Rebecca's death, Paul had snagged a plum job with the Serious Crime Division of Greater Manchester Police. Laura – Jack's only family besides Naomi – was a ward sister at Manchester Royal Infirmary. The move made sense, but Paul had been right – Jack couldn't bear to even think about selling the house Rebecca and he had once been so happy in. Several months of living with its strange new emptiness and listening to Naomi crying in her sleep had changed his feelings.

He'd been a nervous wreck at the interview. He wouldn't have had a cat-in-hell's chance of getting the job if it hadn't been for Paul. He'd hoped the change of scenery would help Naomi and him overcome their grief. His hope proved to be party justified – Naomi's nightmares had eased off, but for him there was no outrunning the memories. On what was supposed to be his first day in his new job, he'd sat paralysed in the carpark of GMP headquarters. Nothing – not his sense of duty, not guilt at letting Paul down – could have incited him to enter the building. After an hour, he'd driven to the nearest off-licence and bought a bottle of vodka. The following day he'd gone to his GP and asked to be signed off sick. Paul hadn't been angry. He'd told Jack to take as much time as he needed to get himself together. The job would be waiting for him when he was ready.

"It's not as simple as just making a phone call," said Jack. "I'm on long-term sick leave. First, I have to provide a Fit Note. Then I have to attend a Return to Work Discussion. And even if I can convince them I'm ready, they won't throw me straight into a high-profile investigation. After the way I've messed them around, I'll be lucky if they let me chase up parking fines."

The killer tutted. "Don't undersell yourself, Jack. I've read all about you. You're a highly decorated officer. I'm sure they'll make an exception for you."

"No exceptions."

"Well then I'm sorry to say that you-know-who's in for another nasty little reality check."

Jack's fingers contracted on the phone. "I'll try."

"I know you will, Jack. I think I've said all that needs saying for now. And you've got a lot to be getting on with, so I'll leave you to it. Just remember to keep *that* picture in your mind before you make any decisions. We'll speak again soon."

The killer hung up.

CHAPTER 14

Jack pressed his hands to his face. His head was spinning. Blood was pounding in his ears. Everything seemed surreal. Like a bad dream. *Is this even happening*? he asked himself once again, peering through his fingers at Camilla. The pool of blood had spread from her stomach and throat almost to his feet. A strong smell of faeces and urine assaulted his nostrils. The muscles controlling her sphincters had relaxed, evacuating the contents of her bladder and bowels. Her facial muscles had slackened too, giving her a blank expression. She was no longer beautiful. Yes, this was happening. Camilla and Dale were dead. Naomi, his career, his freedom, they were all slipping away.

Shit, shit, what are you going to do?

"Calm down," Jack told himself. He took a few slow breaths. *Focus. Think! You answered the phone because you wanted to learn something about the killer. Well, what have you learnt?*

He'd learnt one thing for sure: the killer was a good actor, adept at donning disguises, whether of clothes, speech or personality. Obviously homicidal tendencies were not considered to be a positive character trait. For people who carried that craving with them, concealing their true self became second nature. That often meant surrounding themselves with the trappings of normality – friends, lovers, family. They went to work, came home, kissed their wives, played with their kids, ate, drank, laughed, argued and screwed. Even those closest to them didn't know the truth about who they really were. So what chance did the police have of identifying them based on speculative psychological profiling? Almost zero. Better to start with the facts – or, at least, near facts – and build from there.

Fact – the killer had a phone. Near fact – they almost certainly had a car, possibly a small silver one. That meant they had money, and most likely, a job and a place to live. They weren't some down-and-outer on a suicide mission. Fact – the killer had stalked Camilla. They'd watched and waited for their opportunity. They hadn't panicked even when things went awry. That meant they were organised and cool headed. In other words, they were a copper's worst nightmare. Near fact – unless it was a part of the act, the killer didn't like being given the silent treatment. Who did? But then again, he hadn't actually ignored the killer. He'd been at a loss for words. The killer's reaction was symptomatic of a fragile ego. Perhaps it went back to the way their parents had treated them. Or perhaps they'd been spurned by a love interest. Logically it followed that the love interest was a dark haired, blue-eyed woman. Which in turn suggested – although by no means proved – that the killer was a man of a similar age to the victims.

I'll bet it felt like your guts were being torn out when you saw Camilla and Dale getting it on, the killer had said.

Those words were an interesting choice, especially when you considered how the victims were mutilated. Had the killer seen his or her partner, wife or whatever 'getting it on' with a lover? Is that what had pushed them to act out their homicidal urges?

Jack cautioned himself not to go too far into the realm of guesswork. Back to the facts. Fact – the killer had been following and possibly even contacted Naomi through Facebook. They would be using a fake profile, but it was worth finding out if that led anywhere. Fact – the killer claimed to love cats. Maybe they had a pet cat or simply admired the way cats stalked and played with their prey. Fact – the killer had watched Naomi feeding a stray cat over the course of more than one day. Someone on Laura's street might have seen them doing so. Fact – the killer claimed they wanted to be caught. No amount of grief or alcohol could have made Jack blind enough to take that statement at face value. The killer hadn't exactly sounded chewed up by guilt. Maybe they did want to be caught or even killed, but not before they'd played out their game.

The muffled wail of a siren drew Jack's gaze towards the window. The pitch identified it as an ambulance siren. The noise faded into the distance. Another crucial fact. He'd been in Camilla's flat too long. He needed to decide. Dial the emergency services operator or Paul? Play it straight or play the killer's game? *The killer's game,* he repeated to himself. *They make the rules. They control the outcome. If you join in, the bastard will own you.*

With a sudden movement, Jack dialled 999. An image rose from some dark place in his mind: Naomi and an old man... Oh Christ, it was almost enough to make him retch. He cut the call off before it connected and shook himself as if trying to dislodge the sickening image. The way the killer had described what could happen if things went bad for Naomi hinted at personal experience. Yes, the killer was a master of manipulation. But Jack was sure he'd heard a flash of something real in their outburst about putting kiddy fiddlers' heads on spikes. Had childhood sexual abuse set them on a path to drug addiction and prostitution? If so, it was likely they'd come into contact with the police. That would hardly narrow down the list of possible suspects. The world was a conveyor belt of such tragic cases.

But not Naomi, Jack swore to himself. *Not my little girl. I'll make sure of that, no matter what.*

You mean like you were able to save Rebecca? scoffed another voice in his mind. *Nothing you did made any difference to her. And it won't make any difference with Naomi either. The killer's right. There's only one way out of this. You've got to play the game and you've got to win. You can do it. You can catch this bastard.*

To his surprise, Jack realised there was a degree of conviction in the thought. The investigative part of his brain had been in hibernation for so long. Now he could feel it stirring back into life, sharpening his senses, calming his nerves. Yes, he *could* catch the bastard. But what then? Could the killer be trusted to keep their word? Of course not. But if he could get his hands on whatever incriminating material they had and destroy it, then it would be the killer's word against his. And no one would believe a scumbag murderer over a policeman.

He scrolled through his phone's list of contacts to 'Paul Gunn'. His finger hovered over the dial button. His mind was a mess of conflicting voices. *What if I've lost the ability to be a copper, like I've lost the ability to be a dad? Then you fight to get it back. What if I get someone killed? What if you save someone's life? Where did it all go so wrong? Was it your fault? Was it something you did or didn't do? What happened Rebecca? What—"*

He cut his thoughts off. This wasn't the time for losing himself in *that* question. "You know what you've got to do, so just fucking do it."

He pressed dial, and this time he didn't hang up. A voice came over the line – the voice of someone happy to hear from an old friend, but also concerned. "Hello Jack."

"Sorry for calling so late, Paul. Hope I didn't wake you."

Paul blew into the receiver. "Have you been following the news?"

"On and off."

"Then you'll know I've slept about three hours in the past three days. How are you holding up? Still not sleeping?"

"Actually I'm a hell of a lot better than I was last time we spoke."

"Glad to hear it. And how about Naomi? Is she settling in to school and making new friends?"

Making new friends. Those words sent a shiver down Jack's back. "Yes."

"It always amazes me how adaptable kids are," remarked Paul. "Whatever life throws at them, they–"

"Listen, Paul," interrupted Jack, "the reason I'm calling is I want to return to work."

"Are you sure? Your job's safe. Don't feel you have to come back before you're ready."

"I'm one hundred percent ready."

"OK, well you know the procedure. You sort out the Fit Note and I'll arrange the rest of it. I'll be in contact in a few days."

A note of urgency quickened Jack's voice. "No, not in a few days. Monday."

There was a pause, followed by, "What's the rush?"

A warning prickle passed through Jack at Paul's inquisitive tone. Back in Sussex, Paul had been dubbed the 'Duracell Bunny' for working cases tirelessly and meticulously. If he suspected something was off, he would chip away until he found out what it was. Jack forced a note of levity into his reply. "I'll tell you what the rush is, Paul, I'm bored shitless sitting here watching crap on the TV all day. If I don't get some action soon, my brain will turn to mush."

Paul made an approving noise. "Well I can understand that. Personally I find holidays more stressful than work. I'll tell you, though, Jack, this case is pushing me to the limit."

"Sounds like you don't have much to go on."

"Sod all. But sooner or later these psychos always make a mistake. And I'll be there when this one does."

Not if I'm there first, Jack said to himself. "So you think it's the work of one individual."

"It looks that way, but then again..." Paul trailed off.

Jack understood where his reticence came from – it was dangerous to assume that the same MO signified one killer, there could be copycats out there seeking to exploit the situation.

"As far as the public's concerned, the official line is that we can't say whether the murders are the work of a serial killer," said Paul. "You know what happens when we start using *those* two little words."

Jack knew. He'd been involved in cases where speculation about whether a serial killer was at large had played havoc with the investigation. First, the media went into a feeding frenzy, pumping out all sorts of panic-inducing crap. Then the cranks came out to play – false confessors, psychics, people with grudges to settle, serial killer groupies. Even level-headed coppers could get caught up in the hysteria. They started thinking, *I can make a name for myself if I catch this bastard.* The next thing you knew they were hounding some innocent who just happened to be in the wrong place at the wrong time.

"Look, I'd love to talk longer, but I've got to crack on," continued Paul.

"No problem, mate. See you soon. I'm looking forward to getting my teeth back into the job."

"That's the best news I've had in ages, Jack. We need you."

Jack got off the phone and drew in a steady breath. *A hell of a lot better than I was last time we spoke.* He realised those words weren't an outright lie. Considering his predicament, his stomach should have been churning with anxiety. Instead, for the first time since Rebecca's death, he felt a clear sense of purpose. The SCD might not have any leads, but he did.

CHAPTER 15

Jack peered into the hallway. The front door was shut. That was good. A door left open at this time of night would have aroused the curiosity of any residents who happened by. He approached it, pulled his sleeve down over his hand and flicked the Yale lock closed. He knew what he had to do – he had to remove any trace of himself from the flat. At the same time, he had to try not to disturb any forensic traces the killer might have left behind.

Taking care not to touch anything with his bare skin, he found a carrier bag, duster and polish in the kitchen. He listened at the front door for sounds of movement before easing it open and polishing the exterior handle. The killer had worn gloves, so the only fingerprints of any relevance he would be removing were his own.

He returned the duster and polish to the kitchen, then put the blood-soaked clothes he'd used to staunch Camilla's neck-wound into the carrier bag. Their absence might be noticed, but he couldn't risk leaving them behind. Not only would they muddy the crime scene reconstruction, but advances in vacuum metal deposition – the coating of evidence with fine layers of metals at low pressures – allowed fingerprints and palm impressions to be recovered from fabrics.

A search revealed a hoover in a store cupboard. A conflicted expression pulled at Jack's features as he considered whether to use it. There was a good chance he might have left behind clothing fibres and hair fragments. Of course, the same went for the killer. The hair root was needed to extract a DNA profile. The vast majority of naturally shed hairs didn't have the root attached. So the chances of either him or the killer being identified by a hair were slim. But hair provided evidence aside from DNA. In particular, ethnic characteristics and colour. Clothing fibres too could provide many investigative leads. They might retain particles from where the killer lived or worked. They might even identify the make and manufacturer of the killer's clothes. And if those clothes were individually tailored, they could lead right to the killer. Jack thought about the killer's wizened yellow-green face, witchy nose, hollowed-out eyes and long black hair. If it was a mask, then perhaps a strand of that hair had come loose during the killer's struggle with Camilla. And just maybe that strand would prove to be a vital clue.

He shook his head. No, he couldn't bring himself to use the hoover. His suit was an off-the-rack thing. Impossible to trace to him. His hair was medium brown. The same medium brown as thousands of others in the surrounding area. Apart from the risk of disturbing Camilla's neighbours, he would be compromising the integrity of the crime scene for little or no reason.

He glanced at a clock on the wall: 12:42. How long had it been since he first saw the killer? Forty minutes? Fifty? He wasn't sure. It seemed like hours. He took a last quick look around. He'd done everything he could to mask his presence. He knew that. Yet he couldn't help but feel he'd forgotten something. Rebecca had used to get the same feeling when they went on holiday. One time, she'd got so stressed about it that she broke down in tears. After that, they'd always made a list of items – clothes, sunscreen, toiletries etc. – to tick off as they packed their suitcases. He sighed. Rebecca had been high-maintenance for sure. A fact of which she'd been acutely aware. He'd lost count of the times she'd apologised for making his life a misery. His reply had always been the same: "I'd rather be miserable with you than without you."

His gaze moved between Dale and Camilla. Dead lovers. Separated by only a few metres, but forever beyond each other's reach. Grief swept over him like a tidal wave. He closed his eyes and pictured Naomi, using the image to restrain the sobs that threatened to burst from him.

He poked his head out of the front door again. The landing was deserted. He considered leaving the door open, but reluctantly decided against it. He couldn't risk an inquisitive neighbour discovering Camilla and Dale's bodies before he disposed of evidence linking him to the scene.

He padded downstairs, keeping an eye out for CCTV cameras. There weren't any. The lobby door was shut. Had Dale dislodged the stick wedging it open on his way in? Or had the killer done so on their way out? It didn't matter. What mattered was getting off the premises without being seen or heard.

Watching for people returning from a night out, he headed for the street. There was a light on behind curtains in a top floor flat. The carpark was full. Dale's Porsche was amongst the cars.

Jack slunk through moon-splashed streets, walking fast but not so fast as to draw unwanted attention, dropping his head whenever an occasional vehicle – usually a taxi – passed by. He resisted the urge to head to Laura's house, wake up Naomi and give her the fifth degree about Facebook. That would have to wait until morning. There was plenty to keep him occupied until then.

Upon arriving at his house, Jack changed his clothes, bagged up everything he'd been wearing along with the opera programme and scrubbed the blood off his hands. He packed a baseball cap, torch, gloves and lighter-fluid into a rucksack. His car was in the garage at the side of the house. He mixed a handful of earth with water in a bowl and pasted mud over the number plates and maker's badges. He smeared more mud over the bumpers and hubcaps to make the camouflage seem natural.

He drove towards the eastern outskirts of the city, taking care to observe the rules of the road. If he was stopped by the police, it was all over. His blood-alcohol level must have been ten times the legal limit.

Suburban housing estates gave way to a semi-rural landscape of sooty buildings, boarded up old industrial mills and modern light-industrial estates. He spotted what he was looking for at the far side of a railway bridge – a narrow lane that branched off towards a patch of woodland enclosed by a spiked fence. After following it for sixtyish metres, he saw a mound of fly-tipped junk – mouldering mattresses, torn plastic bags, broken furniture, rusty kitchen appliances, builders' waste – that had clearly built up over time. That was good. It meant few people passed by here.

He pulled over, put on the gloves and baseball cap and got out. He extracted a washing machine from the mound and pushed it against the fence. Next, he dragged a sagging mattress to the same spot. He clambered on top of the washing machine and draped the mattress over the spikes. Then he took the carrier bags that contained his and Camilla's clothes out of the boot.

He dropped the bags over the fence and boosted himself after them. Following the beam of his torch, he made his way into the thickest part of the woods. The whoosh of a passing train came from nearby as he piled up twigs and leaves. He put the carrier bags on the pile and squirted lighter-fluid over them. He sparked his Zippo and held it against the leaves. Flames crackled into life.

When the pile was reduced to blackened globs of melted plastic, he climbed over the fence and returned the mattress and washing machine to where he'd found them. He turned the car around and set off back the way he'd come, not switching on the headlights until he hit the main-road.

CHAPTER 16

During the journey back to Chorlton, Jack ran through the night's events. Was there anything he'd missed? Anything else he could do to cover his tracks? No, he'd done everything possible. He just had to hope it was enough.

There were factors he couldn't control. Someone besides the killer might have seen him at the block of flats. He might have been caught on CCTV near the crime scene. And then there was the killer to consider. Perhaps the bastard was already homing in on their next victim. Jack had done his best to preserve the crime scene, but that wouldn't help much if no one alerted the police. Tomorrow was Sunday. There was a good chance Camilla and Dale's absence wouldn't be noticed until at least 9 a.m. Monday – 33 hours after the killings took place. The first 48-72 hours were critical in any murder investigation. With every hour that ticked by, evidence became degraded, witnesses scattered, potential leads went cold and the chances of success dropped dramatically.

It made Jack's jaw clench to know more women might die because of his actions. Beautiful young women whose lives would be prematurely snuffed out in the worst way imaginable.

"You had no other choice," he told himself. But it was a lie. There was always a choice.

And there was no point agonising over that choice now. What was done was done. The only way to atone was to catch the killer. *But what if you can't? What if you're not up to it? What if–*

Jack cut off his thoughts. Those kinds of doubts would paralyse him. Perhaps he'd never been much good at being a husband or a dad. But there was one thing he'd always been good at – catching criminals.

"You will catch this fucker before they can hurt anyone else," he told himself as if he was stating a fact.

Jack pulled into his garage, rested his head against the steering wheel and heaved a breath. His body buzzed with physical and nervous exhaustion. His feet dragging as if he was wearing concrete boots, he went into the house. His mouth tasted of vodka and anxiety. He put it to the kitchen tap and swallowed water until his stomach was full. He took the hoover to the garage and meticulously hoovered the car's interior. Then he cleaned it inside and out with hot soapy water and disinfectant and rinsed the exterior down with a hosepipe.

Back inside the house, Jack cut his fingernails, taking care to collect all the clippings and flush them down the toilet. After that he scrubbed himself from head to toe in the shower until his skin shone like sunburn.

Downstairs, in his dressing-gown, he slumped into an armchair. Christ, he was so tired. But sleep wasn't an option.

What now? Where to start?

Jack frowned thoughtfully before booting up his laptop and Googling 'Halloween Masks'. He scrolled through pumpkin, skeleton and witch masks. Nothing resembled the face he'd seen in Camilla's living-room window. He tried 'Scary face masks' – more ghouls, devils, zombies, werewolves and killer clowns, interspersed with images of real faces grotesquely transformed by makeup or digital effects. He typed in variations of the search term – scary woman masks, scary man masks, horror masks, ugly face masks. A witchy face with hollowed-out eye sockets and long black hair caught his eye. He followed a link to a site selling 'Popular, cheap Halloween masks'. *Too unrealistic,* he decided. The next image his gaze paused on was labelled 'Ugly Mask' – yellowish skin, hooked nose, black lips, thin black hair.

"That's close," he murmured.

The adjoining link took him to a gallery of intricately detailed masks in various stages of completion. The mask he was interested in was described as an 'Ugly hag straight out of a fairy tale'. The downturned lips and deeply lined skin seemed designed more to express disgust than incite fear. Its creator was a 'lucreziamoretti'. He clicked the name and brought up a profile of the artist. There was a photo of a waifish, dark-eyed woman with crimson hair and Goth clothes. She was in a studio surrounded by her creations – witches, vampires, werewolves and other supernatural creatures. Her profile read: 'Lucrezia Moretti. Character Artist. United States. Ciao a tutti. I am an artist from Italy, now living in San Diego and working at Monstrous Creations. For more information visit my website www.lucreziamoretti.com.'

Jack did as suggested. There was a 'Shop' page, where the mask was on sale for $699. Not exactly a mass-market product. There couldn't be many of those things out there, especially in the UK. He headed to the 'Contact Me' page and typed a message into the contact form: 'Dear Miss Moretti. My name is Jack Anderson. I am a Detective Inspector with the Serious Crime Division of Greater Manchester Police in the UK. I have reason to believe that your 'Ugly hag' mask may have been used in a crime in the Greater Manchester area. There is no reason to be alarmed. You are not under any suspicion. However, could you please contact me? This is a matter of the utmost urgency. I would also ask that you do not contact anyone who has purchased this mask. I cannot stress this last point enough, with regards for both your personal safety and that of persons here in the UK.'

After pressing 'Submit', Jack looked at the 'Ugly Mask' again. 'Moulded from high-grade silicone and hand-painted, this hideously wrinkled and warty old hag has a terrifyingly realistic appearance.' boasted the product description. 'Her greenish skin, crooked nose and pointed ears are the stuff of nightmares.' That description certainly fitted the face he'd seen in Camilla's window. Was this the same mask? If the killer was careless enough to wear something so traceable, perhaps they were also careless enough to buy it using their real name. In which case, a list of customers would be all he needed to nail the killer.

Surely it couldn't be that it easy, could it? Paul's words came back to him: *Sooner or later these psychos always make a mistake.* That wasn't strictly true. Some serial killers were never caught. But there was also a lot of truth in the words. The more victims serial killers claimed, the more it fed their sense of invincibility. And that was often their undoing. They let their guard down and took unnecessary risks. Sometimes they even taunted the police.

Jack wondered whether the killer had known he was watching Camilla's flat tonight. Maybe they'd wanted him to see her die in order to draw him into their game. *Imagine the biggest rush you ever had. The highest high. You stole that from me, Jack.* Those words of the killer suggested otherwise. More likely, they'd watched him working on his house and garden and thought he was turning over a new leaf.

Jack checked his inbox. Empty. What was the time difference between California and England? Eight hours. It would be almost midday over there. Lucrezia would be awake. An email alert might have pinged up on her phone. Another minute or two crept by. He hit refresh. Still empty.

Waiting for an email that might never arrive would get him nowhere. But what else was there to do? The silver car was an interesting lead. It would be worth finding out if any of Camilla's neighbours had noticed the car hanging around. Obviously he couldn't go asking those sorts of questions before the crime was discovered though. It would also be worth finding out if the car had been picked up on CCTV. It wasn't likely that he would be able to single out the car from footage captured near Camilla's flat. The vast majority of security cameras in that area would be privately owned by shops, pubs, offices, warehouses and the like. They tended to be angled to catch anyone breaking into the premises. The council CCTV cameras that were thinly spread throughout the suburbs would, of course, have picked up plenty of silver cars. But how to identify the one he was looking for? Crooks loved silver cars because they were by far the most popular coloured car. Police hated them for the same reason. The city centre was a different matter. It was watched over by a network of cameras. The killer had been outside The Cuban cocktail bar at around 10 p.m. on Friday. There was every chance they'd been caught on CCTV.

The footage was held on file at the council's CCTV Control Room. If this had been Hastings, Jack would have known who to contact to get a sly look at it. But this was Manchester. He was a stranger here. If, by some miracle, he convinced his superiors to assign him to the murder investigation, he would have access to the footage. But even then he would have to put in an official request, which might raise awkward questions.

With a gnawing sense of frustration, Jack mentally shelved the silver car for now. The next thing was to look at the victims, search for connections between them. Paul and his team would be all over that, but they didn't know about Camilla. Jack found his way to a local news segment about the murders. To dramatic music, photos of the three known victims scrolled across the screen. He recognised the first woman from the newspaper. The second he recognised from the park. The final photo was of a pretty woman with shoulder length dark hair and a friendly smile. "Abigail Hart, Zoe Saunders, Erica Cook," a voice announced sombrely. Jack committed the names to memory.

A camera panned in on a reporter in the city centre. A police van was conspicuously visible in the background. "Good evening," said the reporter. "Welcome to Manchester, a city living in fear after what has been one of the most shocking weeks in its recent history. Three young women are dead, three lives brutally cut short. Their killer is on the loose and the police desperately need a breakthrough. Earlier today I spoke to Detective Chief Inspector Paul Gunn of Greater Manchester Police. This is what he had to say."

Paul's battle-worn face appeared on the screen. He spoke to the camera. "We are investigating the possibility – and I stress it's only a possibility – that the three incidents are connected," he admitted, before appealing for anyone who might have seen anything suspicious in the Chorlton area on Wednesday night – the night of Erica Cook's murder – to get in contact. "It doesn't even have to be something suspicious," he emphasised. "Someone out there might have seen something critical to our investigation without even realising it."

The video ended with the reporter giving out the hotline number. Jack scanned the sidebar for links to related stories. His gaze pulled up on the headline 'La Traviata wows audience and critics alike at Manchester Opera House'. He stared at it for a long moment before clicking it.

It took him to a video-still of a stage with a painfully familiar figure at its centre. He pressed play and a bubbly entertainment reporter declared that, "The performance was a sparkling success." and Camilla was being touted as, "The next big thing in the opera world." A camera swept in on the stage. Camilla was bathed in a spotlight, pale with makeup but radiant with life. Her eyes seemed to reach out of the screen. Jack's gaze fell away from them.

But he couldn't look away from the jumble of images in his mind – Camilla's dead eyes, Rebecca's desolate ones, the crowd on the cliffs, the crowd in the park, Zoe Saunders's mutilated body

Jack pinched the bridge of his nose with a trembling hand. "Focus," he said through gritted teeth.

... The waves frothing against the rocks, the blood pouring from Camila's throat, the helicopter circling, the text message... *Rebecca. What happened?* He shook his head. *Don't think about that. Think about what you need to do.*

As if a heavy hand was pressing down on him, he raised his eyes to the screen. He navigated to an article about the first victim – Abigail Hart – and read 'A murder investigation has been launched after a woman's body was found in Fletcher Moss Park, Didsbury.'

Fletcher Moss Park. So assuming the known victims are the only victims, victims one and two were killed in public parks. But victims three and four were killed in their flats. What made the killer change their MO? What... What happened? Speak to me, Rebecca... Don't go quiet on me. I hate it when people do that...

"Stop," Jack hissed at himself. "Just stop."

He refocused on the article. 'The body was found after police were called at around 7:00 a.m. on Thursday. Detectives are...' *...not treating the incident as suspicious. Rebecca Anderson is believed to have been out walking alone when she fell from the cliffs near Fairlight Coastguard Station...*

Jack couldn't see the words anymore. His eyes were wet with tears, but his mouth was a desert begging to be watered with alcohol. Before he even knew what he was doing, he was hurrying into the kitchen and rooting through the cupboards. Nothing. He stuck his head into the outdoor bin. Empty bottles. Their scent made him groan with yearning. He continued his desperate search, flinging cushions off the sofa, overturning the armchairs. He upended the bathroom bin, pulled towels out of the airing-cupboard. There had to be a bottle somewhere. Just one bottle with one mouthful left in it. He peered under the bed and there it was! He clasped the bottle to himself as if it was the Holy Grail. Several centimetres of liquid sloshed around in it.

He unscrewed the top. His hand was shaking so much he could barely put the bottle to his lips. He grimaced as if a hand was twisting at his guts. *Be strong for Naomi.* Tears rolled down his cheeks. *I'm sorry, Laura. I can't do it.*

His phone rang. He flinched so hard he dropped the bottle, spilling its contents. He snatched his phone out. 'No Caller ID'. Rage surged up his throat. No Caller fucking ID! He wanted to hurl his phone at the wall. Smash it to pieces. But he knew he had to find out what the killer wanted. He put the receiver to his ear and waited for them to speak.

"Hello again, Jack," began the softly spoken voice. "It didn't take you long to answer the phone. Were you already awake? Have you begun your investigation? I'm impressed, but don't tire yourself out too much otherwise you'll be of no use to anyone."

"What do you want?" Jack muttered.

"You could at least pretend to be happy to hear from me, especially as I'm calling to congratulate you on making the right choice."

The right choice. How does this bastard know what choice I made? Two possibilities occurred to Jack: the killer had watched him sneak away from Camilla's flat or was listening in on a police scanner. If the first possibility was the case, perhaps they were still watching him. "Was it the right choice?" Jack asked, more so as not to irritate the killer than because he was interested in their answer.

Daylight light was creeping through the newspaper taped over the bedroom window. He peeled it aside. The street was deserted. It was a little after 6 a.m. Most people were still in bed and, considering it was Sunday, would remain there for several more hours. The car he'd seen at the cemetery wasn't amongst the vehicles parked in the street.

"How can you even ask that? What matters more than Naomi?"

"Nothing."

"Life is full of difficult choices, Jack. Good or evil? Failure or suicide?"

Jack's forehead creased into deep furrows. "Failure or suicide, what's that supposed to mean?"

"You know what it means. Bye for now, Jack."

The line clicked off. *Failure or suicide?* The words reverberated in his mind. They bothered him as much as anything else the killer had said. More! Did they refer to Rebecca? Did the killer know something about her death? He shook his head. It wasn't possible. The bastard was playing mind games.

That's what sickos like that did. They found a chink in your armour and jabbed at it until you would do anything to make them stop.

He looked at the now empty bottle, reflecting bleakly that he should have thanked the killer. They'd stopped him from making yet another mistake. The killer had been right about one thing – if he didn't get some sleep he would be of no use to anyone. He lay down and closed his eyes. He felt strangely still as if nothing – not even his heart – was moving inside of him. The calm after the storm. It wouldn't last. It never did.

The killer followed him down the rabbit hole of sleep, stalking him through lucid dreams, stabbing him, slicing open his stomach. Except that whenever he looked down, to his horror and bewilderment, the hands holding the knife were his own.

CHAPTER 17

A noise pried its way into Jack's sleeping mind. *Ping!* He awoke with a jolt and groped for his phone. Had the killer sent another incriminating text? He was only a little relieved to find two messages from Laura. The first had been sent at ten o'clock that morning: 'How's it going? I told Naomi you're getting the house ready for her. She's super excited.' An hour later, she'd sent another text: 'I hope you're keeping busy, Jack. Don't lie around dwelling on things.'

Eleven o'clock. "Shit," he muttered. He hadn't meant to sleep for that long. As he got up, a headache tried to pummel him back onto the pillows.

He phoned Laura. "Where are you?" he asked when she picked up.

"I'm at my house."

"Stay there. I'm coming over."

Before Laura could reply, Jack hung-up. He swallowed painkillers, showered, shaved and dressed. His pallor was off-white, but apart from that he looked surprisingly well considering what he'd been through. He couldn't remember the last time he'd slept five hours straight in a bed. He descended to the kitchen. His stomach grumbled at the aroma of Bolognese sauce. Realising he was ravenous, he spooned the cold sauce into his mouth. God, it was good. Since Rebecca's death everything he ate had been as flavourless as stale bread, but now his taste-buds had flowered back into life. He ate from the pan in front of the television. There was nothing on the news about Camilla and Dale.

"Shit," he said again. Twelve hours had already ticked by since their deaths. Twelve hours of lost possibilities for Paul and his team.

He checked his emails. Nothing. Triple shit.

After dumping the pan into the sink, Jack hurried to his car. On the way to Laura's, his eyes flitted between the road ahead and the rearview mirror. There were plenty of small silver cars around, but none of them appeared to be tailing him. Laura was waiting for him at the front door, wearing a concerned expression. "You sounded worried on the phone? What's going on?"

"I need to speak to Naomi."

"She's in her bedroom."

Jack moved past Laura and climbed the stairs. "You're not going to do anything to upset her, are you Jack?" asked Laura, following him.

He didn't reply. One day, if she met the right person, Laura would make a great mum, but until then she wouldn't understand that sometimes as a parent you had to do things that upset your children.

Naomi was messing around on her iPad as Jack entered her bedroom. She jumped up, smiling. "Dad, yay!"

It hurt to think about putting a dent in her smile, but not enough to stop him from doing what needed to be done. "I'm going to ask you something, Naomi, and it's important that you give me an honest answer."

She frowned at her dad's serious tone. He motioned for her to sit down and dropped to his haunches in front of her. "Do you have a Facebook account?"

Her big blue eyes got even bigger. "Who told you that?" She shot a suspicious glance at Laura.

"Don't look at your aunt like that. It wasn't her. Besides, it doesn't matter how I found out. What matters is that you tell the truth?"

Naomi's gaze dropped to her lap. Her fingers fidgeted with each other.

"I'm not angry with you, sweetheart. But I will be if you lie," Jack gently pressed.

Naomi looked at him sheepishly from under her dark eyelashes. "I'm sorry, Dad."

"So you do have an account."

She nodded.

"I didn't know about this," said Laura. "I'd have told you straight away if I had done."

"I know," said Jack. "If anyone's to blame for this, it's me not you." He returned his attention to Naomi. "How long have you had an account?"

"Not long. Loads of the girls at school have them. They showed me how to open one. I only speak to my friends on it. That's all."

"Show me."

Naomi navigated to Facebook on her iPad. Jack noted down her password, took the iPad from her and opened her timeline. He didn't have a Facebook account, but he'd used it plenty of times to help with investigations. It never ceased to amaze him how many criminals were stupid enough to boast about their offences on social media. At the top of the timeline were selfies of Naomi and several other girls her age. The photos were innocent enough, but Jack was only too well aware how these things could attract the attention of undesirables. He resisted the urge to launch into a lecture. There were more immediate concerns. He pointed to the other girls. "Are these school friends?"

Naomi nodded. "That's Joanna and that's Lucy and that's Ellie and Phoebe." Her voice rose apprehensively. "You're not going to tell their parents, are you? They'll all hate me and they're my only friends."

"We'll talk about that later." Jack scrolled down the timeline. The bulk of it was taken up by the five friends chatting about classmates, films, pop songs, pets, birthday parties, YouTubers etc. Other people had joined in the conversations. He scanned through them one by one. "Who's this girl?"

"She's a friend of Joanna's from year six."

"Who's that?"

"That's Henry, a boy from my class. And that's his sister Nicki."

Jack came to a post from 7:34 p.m. on Thursday 20th July– a few hours after he'd first seen the silver car. "And what about him?" He pointed to a photo of a good looking boy with coiffured brown hair. "He looks far too old to be at your school."

"That's Harry Styles."

"Why is that name familiar?"

"He used to be in my favourite pop group."

"Ah yes, I remember. What are you doing talking to him?"

Naomi rolled her eyes. "It's not really him, Dad. It's just someone who calls themselves Harry Styles."

"So if it's not him, who is it?"

"I think he's friends with someone Ellie knows. Ellie and me were talking about songs we like and stuff and Harry joined in."

Jack read through the conversation. Once again, it all appeared to be innocent enough. As Naomi had said, Ellie and she were discussing which was their favourite One Direction song. Then Harry had joined in with 'Hi, people say I look just like Harry. What do you think Naomi?'

Jack frowned. The way Harry singled out Naomi rang alarm bells.

'Lol you are funny,' she replied followed by a series of emoji.

'You look like Katy Perry.'

'I love Katy Perry!' butted in Ellie.

'Do you want to be a pop star Naomi?'

Jack's frowned tipped towards a scowl. This 'Harry', whoever the fuck they really were, was interested in one thing – Naomi. He navigated to their profile. The only conversation on the timeline was the one he'd just been reading. The only uploaded photo was of Harry Styles. Their only friend was Naomi. He clicked on 'About'. Their work was listed as 'Professional lookalike'. 'Gender: Male'. 'Places he's lived: Manchester, Greater Manchester'. Everything else was blank.

It had to be the killer. Didn't it?

He read the rest of the conversation. 'I want to be a singer,' said Ellie. Again, Harry didn't reply to her. That was at 7:41. The next post was at 7:45: 'Naomi are you still there or what?' Jack's stomach knotted. It was the killer alright. He could almost hear the irritation in the question.

'Yes,' replied Naomi. 'But I am going to bed soon.'

'You didn't tell me what you want to be when you grow up.'

'That's cos I do not know. I guess I just want to be happy.'

Jack felt a sudden sting of tears at the back of his eyes. *I just want to be happy.* The insinuation was clear: Naomi was unhappy. It hardly came as a surprise. But it still hurt like hell to see it written there.

'I hope you get what you want,' replied Harry. 'Sleep tight Naomi xx.'

'Thanks xx.'

Those digital kisses made Jack want to reach into the iPad and break Harry's fingers so that he could never elicit affection from Naomi again. *He.* Was the killer a he? Who the hell knew? Maybe even the killer wasn't sure what gender they themselves were. One thing had the ring of truth though. The killer very possibly lived, or had once lived, in Manchester. More specifically: the south side of Manchester. The victims had all been killed within a few miles of each other, suggesting the killer was confident with the area's geography.

Jack let his anger simmer down, before asking Naomi, "Are you on any other social media sites? Twitter? Instagram?"

"No."

"So you've not had any other online contact with Harry or other strangers?"

"No, Dad. Honestly."

Jack had no reason to doubt her. She'd never lied to him. But the killer must have known he'd stop her from using Facebook. Did that mean they had another way to contact her? He held up the iPad. "I'm confiscating this."

Naomi looked at him as if he'd told her he was amputating one of her limbs. "For how long?"

"As long as necessary."

Naomi opened her mouth as if to protest further, but thought better of it. She pouted at the floor. Jack gave her an uncertain look. His mind had moved on from Facebook to another uncomfortable topic: was she better off staying here or moving in with him? His first instinct was to keep her as close as possible. But if he got on the investigation, he would be working long, odd hours. There was no way he'd be able to keep a close eye on her even if she was living with him. He told himself that the killer wouldn't harm her so long as she was being used to leverage control over him. But still, he couldn't bear the thought of leaving her or, for that matter, Laura unprotected. This very moment, the killer could be watching them. A solution occurred to him. "I need to talk to your aunt for a moment."

Jack and Laura headed down to the living-room. "You don't think this Harry is some kind of predator, do you?" Laura asked.

"Whoever they are, I'm not comfortable with it. I think I should stay here for a few days."

"Why? Do you think Naomi's in danger?"

"I'm probably just overreacting, but it's best to be on the safe side."

Laura looked at him closely. "Is there something that you're not telling me, Jack?"

"I've decided to return to work."

Laura's voice lifted in pleasant surprise. "That's great news. When do you start?"

"Hopefully this week."

"Isn't that a bit soon? Don't get me wrong, I'm over the moon you're returning to work, but it would be good if you and Naomi could spend time together first. Go on holiday. Get out of the country. A week or two on a beach would do you both the world of good."

"I'm sure you're right, Laura, but it's just not possible at the moment." Jack didn't elaborate. Laura knew him better than anyone alive. He couldn't tell her the truth and she would spot an outright lie a mile off. Better to say as little as possible. "I'm heading back to Chorlton to pack some things. I won't be long. In the meantime, do me a favour, keep Naomi in the house."

He darted a glance out of the window at a passing vehicle – a red car. The midday sun was shining from a cloudless sky. The window was wide open. He closed it. He moved through to the kitchen, closed the window in there too and checked the backdoor was locked. Laura watched him with troubled eyes. "You're starting to really worry me, Jack. This isn't just about Facebook, is it?"

He made no reply.

"Don't do your silent thing. Talk to me," persisted Laura.

Jack's stomach tightened again at this distorted echo of the killer's words. "Like I said, I'm probably just being overprotective. But the thing is, well..." he threw Laura a pained glance, "Naomi's all I've got left."

Laura's frown faded. She smiled sympathetically. "She's not *all* you've got left," she said, following Jack to the front door.

He returned her smile. "I won't be long."

Laura closed the door. Jack waited to hear the key turn in the lock before heading to his car.

CHAPTER 18

Jack packed a bag with enough clothes for a few nights, an extendable steel baton and a set of handcuffs. It was unlikely that, even if he flat out refused to cooperate with their demands, the killer would try anything with him around. The four victims were slightly built women, doubtless targeted for their vulnerability. Like any hunter, the killer wanted to maximise the chances of a successful kill. That meant not attacking anything that might fight back and win. But then again, hunters of human game were unlike other hunters. They weren't driven by hunger or pleasure – well, at least not in the conventional sense. They were driven by hate. Pure, unadulterated, insane hate. And that made them dangerously unpredictable.

He put his bag and laptop into the boot and headed out again. He detoured to a retail park and bought a smartphone with parental controls and location tracking. It was mid-afternoon when he arrived back at Laura's. His heart gave a little lurch when he saw Naomi in the front yard stroking a skinny black cat. Laura was watching over her from the doorway. Jack's gaze scoured the street – a woman walking a dog, a group of teenagers, nothing suspicious.

He parked up and retrieved his things from the boot. "Who's this?" he asked as he entered the yard, taking care not to show his concern to Naomi.

"It's Elsa," said Naomi. As Jack stooped to stroke the cat, she added, "Aunt Laura says you're coming to stay with us.

"Just for a few days."

"Because of what I've done?"

"No, sweetheart. Because I've been away from you too long. I'll stay here until the house is ready, then we'll move there together." Jack ran his hand over Naomi's hair that was as smooth and black as the cat's. "I won't be apart from you like that again."

They stroked Elsa for a while before going inside. The smell of roasting meat filled the air. "I'm cooking Sunday lunch," said Laura, heading into the kitchen

Jack followed her, leaving Naomi in front of the television. "Sorry," she said, "The cat was whining to be fed. I didn't see any harm in it."

He waved away her apology. "I meant what I said about not being apart from Naomi again."

"I know." Laura reached for a glass of white wine, but hesitated glancing concernedly at Jack. "How are you feeling?"

He lifted his hand, displaying a slight tremor. "I've got a touch of the DTs, but I'll be alright. Drink your wine."

Jack returned to Naomi. "I've got something for you." He took out the phone. "Don't get too excited," he added as her eyes widened. "It's programmed to only ring two numbers – mine and your aunt's. If you can't get through to either of us in an emergency, you can also ring 999. I want you to keep this on you at all times when you're out of the house. Understood?"

"Yes, Dad."

"Good girl."

Naomi pressed her head into Jack's shoulder – a sure sign that she wanted a cuddle. He put his arm around her. She snuggled in and resumed watching TV. Jack knew he should be doing whatever he could to dig up leads on the killer, but he couldn't bring himself to move. It came to him with a jolt that he hadn't thought about Rebecca all day. He was content just to sit and be with Naomi.

They stayed like that until lunch. Afterwards, Laura helped Naomi with her homework while Jack went out on the pretence of buying toiletries.

Instead, he knocked on every door along the street, showed his police ID and asked a few questions that were specific enough to get what he wanted without revealing details that might come back to bite him. *Have you seen any strangers hanging around or acting suspiciously? What about vehicles you don't recognise?*

No one had seen anything of interest.

Jack returned to Laura's and got on his laptop. Still no reply from Lucrezia Moretti. Still nothing on his news feeds about last night's murders.

He turned his attention to the victims the police knew about. The first to die had been Abigail Hart. An hour later, he'd dug up most of what the internet had to offer on her. She had profiles on Facebook, Instagram and LinkedIn. For anyone who wanted to stalk her or steal her identity, all the information they needed was easily accessible. Abigail had been a junior estate agent at the Booth Street branch of Barlow & Coe Estate Agency – the agency he'd bought his house through. Before that she'd studied for a degree in real estate development at The University of Manchester. She was twenty-six-years-old and originally from Coventry, where her parents Russell and Suzanne Hart still lived. Russell was a fifty-one-year-old chemistry teacher at a Coventry high school. Suzanne was a fifty-year-old PE teacher at the same school. Abigail was their only child. There were photos of her out drinking with friends, at concerts, hiking in the Pennines. All perfectly normal. Nothing that marked her out as the potential victim of a serial killer.

Zoe Saunders came next, but she would have to wait. Naomi was at school in the morning. It was time to get her ready for bed. Jack bathed her and helped her into her pyjamas. He read her a story and tucked the duvet around her. Her eyes glimmered with heart-breaking uncertainty.

"Are you all better now, Dad?"

As Jack opened his mouth to say yes, some other words of Naomi's came back to him: *I dreamt Mum was better. Is she better?*

She's a lot better today, he'd replied. A short time later Rebecca had plummeted to her death.

There had been more than enough lies already. "All you need to know is, I'm not going anywhere. I'm staying right here with you. OK?"

"OK."

Naomi closed her eyes. Jack held her hand until her soft, rhythmic breathing told him she was asleep. He padded down to the living-room. Laura was stretched out on the sofa. "Is she asleep?"

Jack nodded, settling into an armchair with his laptop. "I've made such a mess of things," he sighed. "I just hope I haven't done her any permanent damage."

"If anyone's done her permanent damage, it's Rebecca." There was a sharp edge to Laura's voice that Jack had heard before when she mentioned Rebecca. "But I don't suppose she was thinking about that when she—" She broke off as if she'd thought better of speaking her mind.

"When she what?" said Jack. "Go on, say it: when she threw herself off the cliffs."

"Sorry, Jack. Just ignore me. I've had too much wine."

They sat in silence with the television murmuring in the background. Laura had never said outright that she thought Rebecca killed herself, but she'd made enough sideways comments for Jack to know that was what she believed. He thought about the killer's parting words: *Failure or suicide?* Which one was it?

He wrenched his attention back to Zoe Saunders. He worked intensely, using the details of her short life to blot out everything else. Through newspapers and social media, he learnt that Zoe had been a pharmacist at Moss Lane Pharmacy, three-quarters of a mile from where she lived on Stanley Road. She'd studied pharmacy at the University of Central Lancashire in Preston. She was twenty-nine-years-old and originally from Blackburn. Her parents were Greg and Ellen Saunders. Greg was a fifty-five-year-old occupational therapist at HMP Preston. Ellen was a fifty-six-year-old housewife. They had two other children – Joshua and Adam.

Laura left the room and returned with a bundle of sheets and a pillow. "I'm off to bed. Are you taking Naomi to school tomorrow?"

"Yes. Goodnight."

Laura looked at Jack as if contemplating saying something else. To his relief, she turned and left without doing so. He didn't want to get into any difficult conversations about Rebecca or anything else relating to him and Naomi. He needed all his energy for the task ahead.

After checking the doors and windows were locked, he made himself a strong coffee and got back down to it. He moved on to the third victim. Erica Cook had been a bank teller at the Chorlton branch of RBS. She'd worked there since finishing her A-levels at The Manchester College in 2004. She was thirty-three and from Wythenshawe. Her parents, Roger and Stacy, still lived there on Greenbrow Road. Roger was a fifty-eight-year-old bus driver for Stagecoach. Stacy was a fifty-six-year-old cashier at Asda Wythenshawe. They had three other children – Heather, Mark and Evan.

Jack sighed. So many names. So many lives reduced to rubble. There would be others to add to the list – grandparents, aunts, uncles, cousins, nieces, nephews... The shock waves travelled outwards and outwards.

Nothing about the three women jumped out at him, but a few details piqued his interest. First, all had worked in customer-facing jobs. It was possible that the killer had used their services – Camilla's face had been in the public eye too, albeit in a different way. Second, Greg Saunders worked in a prison. Jack looked up HMP Preston. It was a category B prison for adult males. That meant there were all kinds in there, except the highest-risk violent offenders such as murderers and terrorists. Could the killer have passed through HMP Preston, perhaps even come into contact with Greg? No doubt Paul was all over that possibility.

Jack's thoughts returned to the female victim the police didn't know about. Camilla Winter. What did he know about her? She'd toured with La Bella Vita Opera Company. She'd been in a stormy relationship. Apart from Rebecca, she'd had the most beautiful eyes he'd ever seen. Oh god, those eyes. So blue... He took a deep breath.

Google led him to Camilla's website. The homepage was dominated by a photo of her that threatened to destroy his focus. He navigated to her bio. 'Camilla Winter was born 19th March 1986 to Gabriel and Lilith Winter.' Jack did a quick calculation. Thirty-one-years-old. Two years younger than the oldest victim. 'She grew up in Didsbury, Manchester and attended Manchester High School for Girls.' He opened another tab and looked at the school's website. It was a private school with fees running into thousands of pounds a term. Camilla came from an affluent background. No surprise there. Everything about her had reeked of a privileged upbringing. 'She showed a talent for singing from an early age that was nurtured by her mother. After high school, she was accepted into the Royal Northern College of Music, where she received operatic training at The School of Vocal Studies and Opera.'

The bio described how Camilla was mentored by a renowned Russian conductor, under whose guidance she sang many prominent roles. After joining La Bella Vita Opera Company, she performed to growing acclaim throughout Europe. However, she returned to Manchester after her mother fell seriously ill.

Jack had a scout around for information about Lilith and Gabriel. There was nothing to be found – no social media profiles, no phone book listing, nothing on the electoral roll's open register. Probably to spare them from being pestered by Camilla's fans, journalists and, well, stalkers like him.

He sat back thoughtfully. He'd found nothing to suggest a connection between Camilla and the other victims. If anything, what he'd learnt pointed in the opposite direction. Abigail, Zoe and Erica came from different strata of society to Camilla. They might have crossed paths with her with on a professional level, but not on a social one. Estate agents, pharmacists and bank tellers rarely tended to mingle with opera singers.

Yawning, he glanced at the time. 2:31 a.m. Barring delving into genealogical records, he'd gone as far as he could without access to police resources. He had to be up in a few hours to take Naomi to school. And after that there was the Fit Note to sort out. He would need to look at least half-alive if he was to convince his GP to hand over the required note.

He made up his bed on the sofa and got into it. He lay awake for a long time alert to every nocturnal sound, his fingers twitching against the steel baton, before sleep finally took him.

CHAPTER 19

Jack watched Naomi all the way into school. She gave him a final wave before disappearing from sight. He lingered near the gates, scanning for anything suspicious. There was nothing. It was 8:55 a.m. He'd made a doctor's appointment for half-past nine. With a last look around, he returned to his car.

He examined his reflection in the sunshade mirror. Not bad, apart from the bags under his eyes. Those things were big enough to fit a body inside.

On the way to the surgery, Jack rehearsed what he needed to say – *I've stopped drinking, I'm sleeping well, I'm getting the house ready for my daughter to move in. I think I'm really getting my life back under control.* In the waiting room, he looked at his hands. There was a slight DT's tremor. Nothing that couldn't be concealed. He exchanged a few pleasantries with the doctor before getting down to business. He was careful to keep his performance believable and balanced. The most important thing was to appear on an even keel – neither too low nor too high.

Twenty minutes later, Jack was back in his car with the Fit Note. His phone rang. It was Paul.

Jack answered it and said, "I was just about to phone you."

"I hope it was to tell me you've got the Fit Note, because I've wrangled you an appointment with your Line Manager for eleven o'clock this morning."

"I've got it right here."

"Great Pop in to see me afterwards."

"Thanks, Paul. I owe you big time."

Jack got off the phone. He scanned his surroundings. No silver Punto. He checked the location of Naomi's phone. It was right where it should be. *Stop fretting,* he told himself. *The killer needs you. They're not going to harm her.*

He looked at his inbox. Empty. He skimmed through the local news. No mention of Camilla or Dale. That would change soon. Camilla hadn't worked regular hours, but Dale needed an income to pay for his flash car. He thought about Dale's grey suit – the sort of thing you'd wear in a swanky office. If Dale had a regular 9-5 office job, it wouldn't be long before his colleagues started to wonder where he was.

Jack's mind turned to his own clothes. He needed to put a suit on before seeing his Line Manager. But his suits were crumpled in a heap at the bottom of the wardrobe. He hadn't expected Paul to come through so quickly. Greater Manchester Police Headquarters was situated to the north east of the city centre. He would have to stop and buy a suit on the way there.

He checked his phone for the nearest men's suit shop, put its postcode into the Satnav and set off. A few minutes later, he was pulling over outside the shop. He ran in, grabbed what he needed, changed into it and paid. Catching sight of himself in a mirror as he strode out of the shop, he pulled up. He found himself looking at a man he hadn't seen in a long time – DI Jack Anderson, all business, ready for anything.

The roads were busy with mid-morning traffic. He chain-smoked his way to headquarters. It wasn't far off eleven o'clock when he arrived, but he didn't immediately leave the car. He sat staring at an imposing six-storey glass and concrete box adorned with a huge seven-pointed silver star. Dozens of tall, tinted windows seemed to stare back at him, blank yet watchful. The shiny new HQ was on a business park of soulless buildings, antiseptic lawns and high-security carparks. There were plenty of cars around but no people, giving the place a deserted air. He knew all too well, though, that the windows concealed a hive of unremitting activity. He could feel sweat forming under his armpits. He'd been here before in more ways than one.

He drew in a breath like someone about to dive into deep water. "You can do this," he told himself. "You *have* to do this."

He got out, approached the staff entrance, pressed an intercom and informed the voice on its other end of who he was and why he was there. The door buzzed open and he made his way along a corridor lined with glass cabinets of police memorabilia – helmets, truncheons, handcuffs and the like. One wall comprised of an illuminated blueprint depicting police officers in uniforms dating from the eighteenth century to the present day. The place had a clean, airy feel. Unlike many of the antiquated police stations he'd visited around the country, where the prevailing smells were coffee, sweat, cheap aftershave, rising damp and, if you ventured down to the holding cells, cleaning fluids with an aftertaste of faeces, urine, puke and something else indescribable.

Jack took a lift to a corridor whose inner-facing windows overlooked a glass-roofed atrium furnished with potted magnolias, round tables, barstools and benches. It looked more like a swanky hotel lobby than a police HQ. But to Jack's eyes there was something calculated about this display of modernity. It shouted a warning loud and clear – we're the best-trained, best-equipped force out there, fuck with us and we'll use every up-to-minute investigative technique available to bring you to justice.

He knocked on a door. A voice responded, "Come in."

Jack's Line Manager was a middle-aged woman with sympathetic eyes. She'd left half-a-dozen messages on his phone throughout his absence, inquiring after his welfare. He hadn't returned her calls. She smiled, gesturing him to a seat. The next hour tested Jack's nerves more than many major incidents he'd attended. Fighting to keep his voice steady, he answered a lengthy list of questions about the reasons for his absence and the general state of his health. His efforts were almost scuppered by the question, "How likely do you think it is that there'll be a recurrence of your issues?" *Recurrence. Issues.* Those words made Jack want to retort, *This isn't some passing phase. I'm not depressed about my love life. My wife's dead. I'll never get over it!*

Somehow he clung onto his composure. "It won't happen again. I'm ready for full operational duty."

The Line Manager wasn't so sure. She prattled on about action plans and recuperative duties. Jack didn't argue. He'd learnt long ago that in The Force – as in every area of life – if you wanted something, you spoke to the organ grinder not the monkey. When the interview was over, he wiped his palm on his trousers, shook hands and thanked the Line Manager for seeing him on such short notice.

He took the stairs to Paul's office, giving his nerves a chance to settle. DCI Gunn was almost lost behind a desk overloaded with a keyboard, a monitor, two telephones, framed photos of his wife and two kids, stacks of papers and plastic folders and a bucket-sized mug of coffee. His small office was wallpapered with a pin-dotted map of Greater Manchester, a heavily scrawled calendar, stick-it-notes, memos, newspaper clippings, headache-inducing charts, graphs and lists of names. The scene looked chaotic, but Jack knew there was an order to it. Paul was like a spider at the centre of a web, alert to the softest touch on any strand.

Paul was on the phone. He motioned Jack to a chair in front of the desk.

Jack's gaze lingered on photos of the three known victims. Not the smiling photos that had appeared in the newspapers. These were crime scene photos of the women's corpses. Their names were written in luminous marker. One in particular caught his eye: 'Zoe Saunders', the woman from the park. She was as he'd seen her – beaten, stabbed, slashed, legs akimbo.

Next to Zoe's photo was 'Abigail Hart'. She was nestled amidst overgrown grass, posed similarly to Zoe. One arm was flung up over her head, the other rested on her chest. Her blouse – it was difficult to tell if it

NOW SHE'S DEAD

was white or light pink – was torn open. She was naked from her bra on down. Her torso was one big smear of blood, but her face was untouched and looked strangely serene. Intestines protruded like a long sausage through a jagged horizontal incision in her abdomen. One of her legs was positioned at a right angle to her body.

The third victim 'Erica Cook' was on a blood-drenched beige carpet beside a sofa. The blood furthest away from her body was bright red arterial blood, that nearest to it was black gut blood. She was naked except for a wide-open dressing-gown. Her hands rested on her slashed stomach as if trying to hold in her internal organs. She was peppered with so many stab wounds it was difficult to count them. Her legs had been forced open to an almost impossible angle. There was a chunk of flesh missing from her inner left thigh as if a wild animal had taken a bite out of her.

Each photo represented a progression in the killer's evolution, an intensifying blood lust, a need to push the bounds of their depravity. For the officers working the case, each photo was a reason to start work early and go home late. Jack read those extra hours in the lines around Paul's eyes and the grey flecks in his hair. It was only midday, but Paul already looked as if he'd done a full day's work.

Paul put the phone down, smiling and extending his hand. "Good to see you, mate. You're looking better."

Jack shook Paul's hand. "You look as if you're working too hard."

"Yeah well, that's the job, isn't it?" Paul rested back in his chair, eyeing Jack. "So what have you been up to this past couple of months?"

"Not a lot. I've decorated the house, done a lot of thinking."

"And what about the drinking?"

"The vodka and I are getting a divorce. I'm filing for custody of my liver."

Jack's attempt to make light of the issue met with a frown. "I'm glad you've rediscovered your sense of humour, Jack, but this is no joking matter. The Super won't tolerate an alcoholic on his staff, and neither will I."

"I don't expect you to, Paul. All I want is a chance to do what I'm good at." Jack's gaze drifted back to the photos.

"Gruesome, aren't they? Someone did a real job on them."

"Any developments?" Jack was thinking about Camilla and Dale. Just because it hadn't been on the news didn't mean they hadn't been found.

"Nothing worth mentioning."

"No suspects at all?"

"We're working through a list of the usual lowlifes – violent offenders, perverts. We're also looking at family, friends, acquaintances and work colleagues of the victims, people who live near them, people who take part in hobbies and leisure activities with them. We're talking to local therapists to find out if some headcase with a grudge against women has sought help recently. What we really need to find is something that links the victims. A person more than one of them may have known or had dealings with. A place they may all have shopped, drank or eaten out at."

"How's the tip-line doing? Getting many calls?"

"Not as many as we'd like. We're releasing CCTV footage of Abigail and Zoe making their way home and timelines of all three women's final hours. Hopefully that should generate activity."

"Sounds like a good idea. What else are you doing?"

"We've got an army of plain-clothes on the streets and in bars and nightclubs, keeping an eye on women who look like potential victims. Wherever this arsehole pops up next, we'll be there."

"So basically you're waiting for the next incident and hoping the killer makes a mistake."

"That's not the way I'd phrase it, but I suppose that's what it amounts to," Paul agreed. "I'll be honest, Jack, we could be in trouble on this one. If we are dealing with a single perp, they're careful and well organised. I mean, you don't stab someone fifty times without getting a lot of blood on yourself. But no one's seen anyone with blood on them. In fact, no one's seen anything at all."

You're wrong about that, thought Jack. "What about Forensics?"

"There's next to no forensic evidence. We have found one thing – a fifteen centimetre long synthetic black hair at the Erica Cook scene."

The killer's long black hair came to Jack's mind. Surely this confirmed they'd been wearing a mask. "So her killer might wear a wig."

"We're working on one theory that we're dealing with a transvestite. Someone who's been sexually humiliated because of their proclivities. We're talking to local trannies and prostitutes. So far nothing." Paul sighed. "Three women are dead and I feel like I'm banging my head against a brick wall. What do you think? What's this sicko's deal?"

Jack was silent for a moment. Not so much because he need to think about what to say, but because he needed to think about what not to say. He had to give Paul enough to convince him he was ready to work such a big case, whilst being careful not to mention anything that suggested he knew more than he should. "For starters, there can't be much doubt that we're looking at the handiwork of one individual. The MO seems clear. The killer chooses dark-haired, blue-eyed women. All of whom are between approximately twenty-five and thirty-five-years-old, and all of whom are slim and attractive. Was anything taken from the victims?"

"Not as far as we know."

"So robbery isn't a motive. What about evidence of sexual assault?"

"No sexual discharge has been found on the victims or at the scenes. No signs of vaginal penetration. Erica even had a tampon left in."

"So we're not looking for a rapist. As for where the crimes took place: victims one and two were killed outside, victim three was killed in her flat.

That muddies the waters. You said you're releasing timelines for the nights of the murders. Can I look at them?"

Paul handed Jack a printout:

Abigail Hart. 16/07/2017 – 17/07/2017.

20:30 – Abigail and five friends (three females, two males) had drinks in Apotheca cocktail bar.

22:00 – The group went to Noho cocktail bar.

22:30 – Abigail felt unwell. A male friend accompanied her to Piccadilly Gardens. They walked via Lever Street,

22:40 – Abigail boarded the No.42 bus alone.

23:16 – Abigail disembarked at Didsbury, Wilmslow Road, Fletcher Moss Gardens.

23:17 – Abigail proceeded along Millgate Lane towards the flat she lived in on St. Michael Court.

06:56 – Abigail's body was found by a dog walker approx.100 metres to the west of Millgate Lane in an overgrown area of Fletcher Moss Park.

The next timeline followed a similar pattern:

Zoe Saunders. 18/07/2017 – 19/07/2017.

20:00 – Zoe met three female friends in The Fitzgerald cocktail bar.

21:30 – All four made their way along Portland Street and New York Street to The Alchemist cocktail bar.

23:20 – Zoe's friends left. She stayed in The Alchemist talking to a man who remains unidentified.

23:40 – Zoe left The Alchemist and made her way alone along Portland Street to Piccadilly Gardens.

23:50 – Zoe caught the No.101 bus.

00:06 – Zoe disembarked at Moss Side, Alexandra Park, Princess Road.

00:07 – Zoe proceeded into Alexandra Park towards her house on Stanley Road.

Where I was passed out under a tree, Jack added to himself. He knew what happened next: *Someone attacked Zoe. She screamed and I...* Suppressing a grimace at what he'd done – or rather, hadn't done – he moved on to the final timeline:

Erica Cook. 19/07/2017-20/07/2017

17:00 – Erica left work at the Chorlton branch of RBS, 464 Wilbraham Road. She proceeded homewards on foot.

17:05 – Erica called in at the Wilbraham Road Co-Op for bread and milk.

17:20 – Erica arrived at her flat on Whitelow Road.

18:50 – Erica's boyfriend phoned to invite her over to his house. Erica declined, saying she was suffering from 'period pain'.

08:00 – A neighbour leaving for work noticed the door to Erica's flat was ajar. She entered the property and discovered Erica's body. There was no sign of forced entry.

Jack handed back the printouts, running through a fourth timeline in his mind:

Camilla Winter. 22/07/2017.

20:00 – Camilla sings in front of a full house at Manchester Opera House.

23:40 (give or take ten minutes) – Camilla and Dale arrive at her Chorlton flat.

23:42 – Dale leaves to buy Champagne.

23:55 – A masked figure enters the flat.

23:56 – Dale returns. The masked figure murders him and Camilla.

23:59 – I enter the flat and–

Jack cut off the thought. He couldn't allow himself to relive what happened next. Not here.

"What are you thinking?" asked Paul.

Jack almost flinched. "I'm thinking Abigail and Zoe appear to have been opportunistic kills and Erica's murder looks like more of a pre-planned thing. The killer might have known of Erica's existence from before Abigail and Zoe were murdered. The lack of any sign of forced entry could mean Erica knew the killer well enough to let them in. Or it could mean the killer knows how to pick a lock. In which case, we may be looking for someone with a history of burglaries and other petty crime. What did Erica do at RBS?" He knew the answer, but he couldn't remember if it had been in the newspapers.

"She was a bank teller."

"We should speak to her colleagues and check through RBS's security footage, find out if any customers acted oddly around her or made a particular point of using her."

"We're already on it. Nothing so far, but we've still got a ton of footage to go through."

Jack's gaze moved to the map of Greater Manchester. Coloured pins showed where the victims had been found. They formed an uneven triangle with a mile-and-a-half between Abigail and the other two victims, and maybe three-quarters of a mile between Zoe and Erica. Camilla's flat was at the centre of the triangle. "There's not much distance between where the bodies were found. Could indicate the killer lives locally. At the very least, it suggests the killer knows the area well."

"That's good, but it's not what I need. What I need is to get into the head of this character. Find out what they're thinking."

"I can give you the same profile I'm sure you've already constructed." Jack ticked off points on his fingers. "We're most likely looking for a white male over thirty-years-old. There's a good chance he's single, separated or divorced. Conversely, he may hide behind the normality of family life. He may have a history of mental illness. He may also have a police record as a violent offender. He may have been betrayed or perceive himself as having been betrayed by a dark-haired, blue-eyed woman. His prime motivation is a need for power, control and revenge, not sexual gratification. The absence of sexual discharge may indicate that he's impotent. In which case he may have sought treatment for his problem."

At this last possibility, Paul picked up a pen and made a quick note.

"I could go on," said Jack. "But you know as well as I do that this type of guess work should be taken with a big pinch of salt. If you want something more substantial, I need to read the case files. More importantly, I need to get out there and speak to people."

Paul pressed his fingertips together. "I'd love to have you on my team, Jack. God knows we could use the extra manpower. The Super's been on my back day and night about the amount of attention this case is generating. But I'm not sure you're ready to be thrown in at the deep end. It makes more sense to ease you back in. You could do half-shifts for a few weeks. See how things go. There's a series of muggings we think are connected–"

"I didn't move up here to investigate muggings," interrupted Jack. His voice took on a faintly pleading tone as he thought about the consequences of not getting on the murder inquiry. "I need this, Paul. I swear I won't fall off the wagon if that's what you're worried about."

"It's not just about that, Jack." Paul grew hesitant, almost sheepish. "After we spoke the other night, I was looking at the victims and something occurred to me: they all bear a distinct resemblance to Rebecca."

Jack gripped his thighs to conceal the sharp tremors the observation sent through him. "What are you getting at? Am I a suspect?"

"What gave you that idea?" exclaimed Paul, visibly taken aback.

"Well let's see. I live locally. I'm white, over thirty. You could say I'm separated from my wife. You could also say I have a history of mental illness. Maybe you think I suspect Rebecca betrayed me in some way." The tremors found their way into Jack's voice. "And to be honest, I've often wondered if she did. Who knows? Perhaps she was having an affair and it drove her to suicide."

"Rebecca would never have done that to you."

"Wouldn't she? When someone you love dies like that it makes you question everything you thought you knew. Who was Rebecca really? Did she have some whole other secret life?"

Paul shook his head. "Sorry, Jack, but I won't listen to this. That woman loved you and her death was an accident. That's all there is to it."

"How can you be so sure?"

"Because if there's one thing I know it's people. And Rebecca wasn't the type to just give up on life."

"You didn't see her in those last few weeks, Paul. When I looked in her eyes, I saw nothing. It was like she was already dead."

Paul sat in furrowed silence for a moment. He gave another shake of his head. "No. I can't bring myself to believe it. And as for you being a suspect, I've never heard anything so ridiculous. I'm just worried that the only reason you want on this case is because you've somehow got Rebecca and those women," he pointed to the photos, "mixed up in your head."

Jack thought about the way Rebecca and Camilla's faces had seemed to blend into one another like shadows. Paul hadn't hit the bullseye, but he was disconcertingly close to it. Jack knew better than to feed his friend an outright lie. "Perhaps there's some truth in that, but I'm not on a personal mission here. Someone out there is getting their kicks from killing young women. Look at those photos. Look at the all-consuming rage. This killer's only just getting started. Like I said, all I'm asking for is a chance to–"

Paul held up a silencing hand. "Alright, you've convinced me. I'll speak to the Super. I'm not guaranteeing anything, but the way things are going I doubt he'll say no to an extra pair of hands."

Jack felt an almost tearful rush of relief. He was over the first hurdle. Now he had breathing room to work out how he would salvage the wreckage of his and Naomi's life. "You're a good friend, Paul."

Paul smiled. "I'm not doing this out of friendship." He glanced at the photos. "I'm doing it for them." He pushed back his chair. "Come on, I'll introduce you to the team." He paused at the door. "One thing. It's fine to talk like old mates when it's just you and me, but when we're around the others I'd appreciate it if you observe rank. You understand, I can't be seen to be playing favourites."

"Of course, sir."

Paul nodded as if he liked the sound of that. "You know, I always assumed I'd be the one who ended up calling you sir. Back in Sussex the brass were always singing your praises. It's funny how life turns out sometimes."

Yeah sometimes, thought Jack. *But not always.*

CHAPTER 20

'Incident Room. No Unauthorised Access.' warned a laminated sign. Paul tapped a security code into metal keypad and opened the door the sign was pinned to. The office was as functionally modern as the building it inhabited. Detectives – male and female, but mostly male – occupied a central bank of desks, their eyes glued to monitors, their ears to phones, their pens to paperwork. They worked surrounded by blown-up aerial photos of the areas where the victims were found; whiteboards with names, dates and locations scrawled on them in a variety of colours; crime scene photos; CCTV stills; shelves that – the longer the case went on – would become ever more overstuffed with documents and files. Red lines radiated from photos of the victims, traversing maps and stick-it-notes, probing for the elusive connection that would break the case.

Paul introduced his team. "This is DS Gary Crawley, and this is DC Olivia Clarke, and this guy with the impressive moustache is DI Steve Platts..."

More names came at Jack. The faces that went with them were instantly familiar. He'd worked with people like them half his life. They were the best people he'd ever known – serious, friendly, sharp-witted, generous, enthusiastic, overworked – and he was betraying them with every moment that he kept quiet about what he'd witnessed. Their smiles made the knowledge all the harder to bear. It was all he could do not to turn and walk out of the room. He conjured up an image of Naomi and held it tight.

Paul finished his introductions at a thirtyish, slim woman with no-nonsense short blonde hair and an angular, make-up free face. "This is DI

Emma Steele. Emma will you bring you up to date on the investigation. Right, Jack, I'll have to leave you to it. I've got calls to make. Give me a knock before you leave."

Paul headed back to his office. Emma spread her hands and said, "Welcome to hell."

The deadpan remark went a long way to easing Jack's nerves. "That bad is it?"

"I've trawled through god knows how many hours of CCTV footage in the past few days. Only another few thousand to go. So what do you want to know?"

"Everything you've got."

"We've got a lot, but not much, if you know what I mean. Tell you what, let's start at the beginning." Emma led Jack to an aerial photo of Fletcher Moss Park. She pointed to a wooded area at the eastern edge of the park. "This is where the first victim, Abigail, was found. There were traces of blood twenty metres to the east on Millgate Lane. The houses on the opposite side of the lane are screened by trees, so the killer could act without too much risk of being seen. Abigail was dragged through bushes into the park. She may have already been dead or unconscious since there was no evidence of defensive wounds. She was stabbed fourteen times in her back, chest and abdomen. The fatal blow entered her back and pierced her heart. Most of the other wounds were shallow. Further traces of blood were found forty metres to the south east at a dirt access road to the park. We believe the killer may have parked a vehicle there. It had rained that night and we were able to make casts of a pair of tyre prints and a partial footprint."

Emma rooted out photos of the casts and print. "As you can see, the tyre tread is worn down. They're of a size and type used on smaller cars. So that narrows it down to about twenty million cars."

Or one small silver car, thought Jack.

"We think the footprint was made by a trainer," said Emma. "Note the circular tread pattern and wide heel. We're still trying to id the brand. We estimate it's a size seven. There's a lot of wear on the inner heel. I used to do that to my shoes when I was a kid. My mum gave me hell for it. Said I'd end up flat-footed."

"And she was right," quipped DI Steve Platts, a crew cut forty-something who looked as if he'd found his way into the police from the army.

"Ignore Steve," said Emma. "He's just jealous because I've got bigger feet than him."

Jack started to smile, but stopped himself. He couldn't allow himself to be lulled into a false sense of security by the familiar banter. He needed to stay on his guard, keep his colleagues at arm's length.

"So you worked with the DCI in Sussex," said Steve.

"We joined up at the same time." Jack wondered what else his new colleagues knew about him. Had Paul told them about Rebecca? The possibility made him feel exposed and ashamed. As if they might wonder – as he so often did himself – whether he was somehow responsible for her death. He brought the conversation back to the matter at hand. "What about the second crime scene?"

"This guy's a bag of laughs," Jack caught Steve remarking as Emma moved on to an aerial photo of Alexandra Park. He was relieved to hear the sarcastic aside. It surely meant that DI Platts didn't know about Rebecca. Either that or he was an insensitive arsehole. Jack made a mental note to steer clear of Steve.

"There are similarities between where Abigail and Zoe were found," said Emma. "There are also differences. Zoe's body was approximately a hundred metres into the park. There was no sign of it having been moved."

"The killer was more experienced," observed Jack. "They chose a better spot."

"I don't know about that, but I'll tell you this: they were a lot more brutal. Zoe was stabbed thirty one times in the face, back, neck, chest etc. And the cut in her abdomen was twice as long." Emma scrunched her nose. "It was not a pleasant sight."

Imagine the biggest rush... The highest high. With those words echoing back to him, Jack said, "It only takes one hit to become a junkie. After that the junkie's always trying to recapture their first high."

"And the only way to do that is to up the dosage," put in Emma. "I think the words the behavioural analysist used were, 'An obsessional, almost erotic compulsion that grows stronger with every act.' Although I find that odd when you consider that no sexual discharge was found at the scenes."

"Plenty of people find power erotic and there's nothing more powerful than taking a life."

"I suppose that's true if you're a dickless psychopath." Emma traced a line on the map. "There was a blood trail in Alexandra Park too. This one led south towards Demesne Road."

"So on both occasions the killer went south. Seems to back up the theory that they live on the south side of Manchester."

"Or it could just be a coincidence. I've been screwed over by coincidence more times than I can count."

Jack replied with a wry smile that said, *You and me both.* He couldn't help but like Emma. She was a what-you-see-is-what-you-get sort of woman. Not the type he was attracted to, but the type whose company he enjoyed. "What about the guy Zoe spoke to in the cocktail bar? Any leads on him?"

Emma pointed out a CCTV-still of a burly, shaven-headed man with a face two-thirds hidden behind a thick blond beard. The man was wearing a black suit and shirt. He was at a bar-counter, talking to a dark-haired woman in a short skirt and high-heels. Jack recognised Zoe Saunders. "This guy's at the top of our hit-list," said Emma. "He spoke to Zoe for half-an-hour on the night of her murder. She left The Alchemist on her own at twenty to twelve.

At five to twelve, this same guy was caught on CCTV on Princess Street." She showed Jack a photo of the bearded man walking along a pavement with his head down as if trying to make himself inconspicuous.

Jack scrutinised the image. The man didn't look particularly tall – maybe 5'7" or 5'8", although it was difficult to get a proper perspective. His height was roughly in line with what Jack was looking for, but his shoulders looked far too broad. Even with a bulky raincoat on, the killer had been nowhere near that well-built. Had they? Thinking back on it, all Jack could see clearly was the witchy mask. Everything else was clouded by a haze of vodka. "He looks like a bouncer."

"That's what we thought. We're doing the rounds of the nightclubs and bars. No luck so far."

"I hate to prejudge, but he also looks like he might have a record. I take it you've run him through facial recognition?"

Emma nodded. "No match. Might be something to do with the crappy hipster beard."

"Where's Princess Street?"

Emma pointed out a long road about two hundred metres south west of The Alchemist.

"So Zoe went north to Piccadilly Gardens at twenty to twelve," said Jack. "Quarter-of-an-hour later this guy was heading in the opposite direction. That would seem to rule him out of the running for Manchester's most wanted."

"Unless he knew where Zoe was going."

"Doesn't seem likely that she would have told a stranger in a bar where she lived. They could have met before, but surely someone amongst Zoe's friends and family would know of him. I'm assuming that's not the case."

"Correct."

Jack pointed at the bearded man's black shoes. "Also, those look bigger than size seven."

"I agree, but it's a solid lead and we haven't got many of those right now."

Emma turned her attention to a third aerial photo. It showed an area of large houses, many of whose front gardens had been converted into carparks, marking them out as offices or flats. Her finger landed on a boxy building at the mid-point of Whitelow Road. "It's a much more built up area. Still it's not a bad spot for the killer. Erica's flat overlooks St. Jack's Church. There are bushes beside the church carpark from which the killer could have watched Erica. Her flat is part of quite a large block. A lot of young professional types live there. People coming and going at all hours. Wouldn't be too difficult for the killer to sneak in and out without attracting attention. None of the neighbours heard a disturbance, which is amazing considering the number the killer did on Erica. She was stabbed over seventy times and gutted like a fish."

"I noticed what looks like a bite mark on her left thigh."

"Yeah, I thought it was a bite mark too, but it turns out the flesh was cut away with a serrated knife. Erica had a tattoo of a red rose and cupid there. Before you ask, neither of the other victims had tattoos."

"Perhaps the killer took a trophy."

"Or perhaps they liked it so much they decided to get the same tattoo."

Emma's tone was jokey, but Jack's was serious as he replied, "You could be onto something. You should make an image of the tattoo. Take it around local tattooists. Find out if anyone's had the same tattoo done since Erica's murder."

"I'll speak to the DCI. See what he thinks. Anything else you want to know?"

"Can I have a look at the victims' background files?"

Emma retrieved the files and pointed Jack to an empty desk. She resumed poring over CCTV footage while he skimmed through the files. Erica Cook had been in a relationship with a man named Luke Fraser. Luke had rock solid alibis for Erica and Abigail's murders. Apart from that, the files told Jack almost nothing he didn't already know. There were, however, queries relating to them that he wanted answers to. "Greg Saunders."

Emma nodded as if she'd expected to hear that name. "Poor bloke's in a right old state. He's worked at HMP Preston for fifteen years. Says he's always very careful about not discussing his private life with the prisoners. A lot of cons have passed through that place in fifteen years. A fair few that Greg's treated are now living in Manchester. We've spoken to several of them. So far we've come up with sweet-f-all."

"Any suggestion that Greg has ever been involved in anything untoward? Inappropriate relationships with prisoners or anything like that?"

"No. Anything else?"

"Barlow & Coe Estate Agency and Moss Lane Pharmacy."

"We're going through lists of customers for both places. We've also got CCTV from the pharmacy. Nothing connects so far."

"Can I see the lists?"

Emma fetched them. They were hundreds, if not thousands of names long. Paul's team had found no connections, but they didn't know about Camilla. Jack was particularly interested in the Moss Lane Pharmacy customer list. Lilith Winter was seriously ill. Maybe she, her husband or someone else connected to the Winters had picked up prescriptions from there. He scanned through the names.

"You're wasting your time," said Steve.

"Not necessarily," countered Emma. "He's a fresh pair of eyes. He might pick up on something we missed."

Jack barely heard them. He was too intent on his task. The afternoon ticked away. Upon reaching the end of the pharmacy customer list, he glanced at his watch. It was almost half-past two. The Barlow & Coe Estate Agency list would have to wait. He'd told Laura he would pick Naomi up from school.

"Anything catch your eye?" asked Emma.

"No. Can I get copies of these?"

"Take those. Do you need anything else?"

Yes, a PNC password so I can dig deeper into the lives of Camilla and her family and also access to city centre CCTV footage, Jack thought. But he couldn't use official channels to investigate those lines of inquiry until after Camilla and Dale were found. "I think that covers everything for now. Thanks, Emma."

"My pleasure. I hope you get on the team. We could do with you."

Jack made a quick exit from the Incident Room. He didn't want to get caught up in conversation with any of the other detectives. He poked his head around Paul's door. Paul was on the phone again. He beckoned Jack into the office.

"Yes, sir. I understand completely. Thank you, sir." Paul hung up and turned his attention to Jack. "That was the Super. You're on the investigation, but there are conditions. First and foremost, if I get even the slightest whiff that you've fallen off the wagon, you're out. And I mean out for good. Second, if you feel you're struggling to cope you must tell me. I can't have you cracking up on me. It wouldn't be good for anyone, least of all you and Naomi. Do you hear me?"

"Loud and clear. Thanks again, Paul."

"Don't thank me, Jack, just do your job."

"I won't let you down." Jack despised himself for those words. He'd failed Naomi. Now he was failing Paul. Lines from his swearing-in oath rang in his mind: *'I will, to the best of my power, cause the peace to be kept and preserved and prevent all offences against people and property... I will, to the best of my skill and knowledge, discharge all the duties thereof faithfully according to the law.'* There was a time when he would rather have walked away from the job than break that oath. Now the words seemed to have no more substance than an echo in a cave. "When do I start?"

"Tomorrow. That's what you wanted, isn't it?"

"Absolutely."

"Then all that's left to say is, welcome to GMP, DI Anderson."

Jack gave a casual salute. He pointed to Paul's family photo. "Say hello from me to Natasha and the kids. I hope they're well."

"They are and I will."

CHAPTER 21

As Jack drove to Chorlton, his eyes strayed to an off-licence. The past few hours had left him feeling as frazzled as burnt bacon. What he wouldn't have given to lose himself in a bottle of vodka. But that wasn't an option. He needed to find the missing link and find it fast. The increasing violence of the murders suggested it wouldn't be long before the killer's rage overwhelmed them again. He mentally sifted through the evidence – the footprint, the tyre tracks, the blood trails, the synthetic hair, the tattoo cut from Erica's thigh, the bearded man who'd spoken to Zoe in The Alchemist. What did it all add up to? As Emma had said: *a lot but not much.*

The footprint might or might not belong to the killer. If it did, then that would seem to rule the bearded man out as a suspect. The guy was surely too big to have size seven feet. Moreover, as Paul had pointed out, the killer was careful and organised. Why would they risk talking to Zoe in a public place? The blood trails reinforced the theory that the killer had a connection to south Manchester. The tyre tracks were interesting, but too commonplace to be conclusive. The synthetic hair, on the other hand, removed any lingering doubts that the same killer was responsible for all five murders. The tattoo... What did the missing tattoo signify? Was it a trophy or was there more to it?

The dashboard clock caught Jack's eye: 3:13 p.m. Naomi finished school in twelve minutes. He put his foot down, weaving in and out of traffic. He didn't want her waiting around.

She was coming out of school when he rushed into the playground. "Daddy!" she called out, running to give him a hug. For a second, something clutched at his heart – those eyes, that hair, *Rebecca* – but only for a second.

He took her bag. "Hi sweetheart. How was your day?" he asked as they walked to the car, hand in hand.

During the drive to Laura's, they chatted about what Naomi wanted for tea and what presents she wanted for her upcoming birthday. Just a normal conversation, but it made Jack feel like crying. There'd been a time, not so long ago, when he'd wondered if they would ever talk like that again.

Naomi went upstairs to change out of her school uniform while Jack made them both a drink. He was pleased to note that he felt no temptation as his gaze passed over a bottle of wine. His phone rang and 'No Caller ID' flashed up. He scowled. Why did the bastard have to spoil this moment? He closed the kitchen door and put the phone to his ear.

"Hello, Jack," said the androgynous voice. "How's my favourite accomplice doing?"

Favourite accomplice. Were there others? "I'm not your accomplice."

"You mean like you weren't Camilla's stalker? Let's not get off on the wrong foot again, Jack. Now I'll ask you once more: how's my favourite accomplice doing?"

Jack pushed the required words through his teeth. "I'm doing OK."

"OK? Is that all you've got to say?"

"What else is there to say?"

"You could start by telling me how your meeting with Paul went."

So you are following me, thought Jack. "I start work tomorrow."

"That's good, Jack. Keep this up and the future will soon look bright for you and Naomi. So tell me how the SCD's investigation is going."

Jack's forehead wrinkled. "That wasn't part of the deal."

"The deal is, you help me and I help you."

"Why do you need to know how the investigation's going? I thought you wanted to be caught."

"I do. Eventually. So..." The killer trailed off meaningfully.

No fucking chance, Jack said to himself. *If you do this, this bastard will always be one step ahead of SCD.* But another part of him countered, *Calm down, you knew it would play out something like this. Give them a few scraps of information to chew on, nothing important.* "There's not much to tell. I haven't got access to the case files until tomorrow."

A soft sigh tickled his eardrum. "I thought we agreed to be honest with each other?"

"I am being honest. The police force is all about rules and regulations. I spend half my life wading through red-tape."

"Is that your final answer?"

Final answer? This isn't Who Wants To Be A Fucking Millionaire. Jack caught the retort on the tip of his tongue. "I can tell you what you already know: where the victims were found, the nature of their injuries. But as for the finer details..."

"OK, Jack. If that's how you want to play it. Bye for now."

The line went dead. Jack stared at the phone with troubled eyes. *If that's how you want to play it.* That had sounded like a warning. Was the killer going to show him the consequences of not fully co-operating? He clenched his fist. *Damn it, you should have just given them what they wanted. Better that than someone else gets hurt.* He thought about the crime scene photos. The blood. The entrails...

His gaze returned to the fridge. His hand trembled as he reached to open it. He ran his tongue over his lips at the sight of the wine.

He quickly closed the fridge as Naomi bounded into the kitchen. From somewhere, he found a smile for her. They took their drinks out to the backyard and sat in the late-afternoon sun. Laura arrived home. She joined them with a glass of wine. Jack couldn't watch her drink it.

He returned inside and checked his inbox yet again. Still no reply from Lucrezia Moretti. Doubts gnawed at him. *You're not going to be able catch the killer. You should have told the truth when you had the chance. More people will die because of you. Christ, no wonder Rebecca was depressed being married to an idiot like you.* He refreshed his inbox every few seconds. Empty, empty... The muscles of his jaw pulsed. The air seemed to whisper, *Rebecca, Rebecca... Vodka, vodka...*

Naomi and Laura came into the living-room. Naomi was in a good mood, dancing around and laughing. To Jack, every sound was like a nail scraping down a blackboard. He clasped his hands together to keep them from shaking. Laura gave him a concerned glance. When Naomi popped out of the room, she asked, "What is it? The DTs?"

Jack nodded, but it wasn't the DTs. She laid a hand on his wrist. "You're doing so well, Jack. I'm proud of you."

Proud. He held in a scornful laugh. The last thing anyone should be was proud of him.

"Why don't you have a lie down on my bed?" suggested Laura.

"Thanks, I think I will."

On the way upstairs, Jack checked that the front and back doors were locked. *How long will you have to live like this?* he wondered. *Weeks? Months? Years? The rest of your life?*

Naomi stuck her head out of her room. "I'm going for a lie down," he told her.

She looked at him with that old anxiety in her young eyes. "Aren't you feeling very well?"

Jack resisted the instinct to tell her he was fine. "I'm tired. It's been a long day." He ruffled her hair. "Don't worry, I won't miss bath time."

Laura's bedroom was furnished with modern, functional furniture. Pretty much the opposite of Rebecca's taste. She'd furnished their cottage with a mishmash of furniture from charity shops and vintage stores.

Rebecca. What happened? Where did it all go so wrong?

He looked out of the window. A woman was pottering about in a front yard across the street. There was no one else around. Nor were there any silver cars. He drew the curtains and flopped onto the bed. When he closed his eyes, faces rushed at him one after another – Rebecca's, Camilla's, Dale's, Abigail's, Zoe's, Erica's. And over them all loomed a yellow-green face that might have been conjured up in a childhood nightmare.

CHAPTER 22

It was pitch dark when Jack awoke with a gasp. Someone had covered him with a duvet. 3:43 a.m. read the bedside clock. He'd slept through bath time and a long way beyond. Laura must have bedded down on the sofa.

If that's how you want to play it...

The killer's parting words rose into his mind again. He groped for his phone, scrolled through the news feed and had a glance at Naomi's Facebook account. A bud of relief opened inside him. There was no news of a fresh attack and there had been no activity on the account.

He padded onto the landing and peeped into Naomi's bedroom. She was sound asleep. He went downstairs. The soft sound of snoring from the living-room told him Laura was also asleep. He headed into the kitchen to make a cup of tea. The wine bottle was on the work surface. Empty. It seemed he wasn't the only one who'd been hitting the bottle too hard. He sighed. There was no wonder really. For the past couple of months, Laura had been dealing with full-time work, Naomi and a brother on the verge of a nervous breakdown.

Jack smoked a cigarette out of the backdoor, then took his drink up to bed. There was no way he was getting back to sleep. He felt wide awake, hyper-alert. He sat sipping tea and scanning the list of people who'd bought, sold or rented property in Greater Manchester through Barlow & Coe. It was arranged chronologically from most recent to oldest, dating back a year from Abigail's death. He Googled any customers who lived within the triangle formed by Abigail, Zoe and Erica's murder scenes. Some had left little or no online trace of themselves. A few maintained websites or blogs. Several seemed almost to live through social media, posting the minutiae of their daily existences. There were people from all walks of life – teachers, shop workers, therapists, IT workers, receptionists, plumbers, labourers etc. But all of them had one thing in common – no discernible connection to the victims besides geography.

It was light outside by the time Jack was finished. He took a long shower, kneading the tension out of his neck. Laura was eating breakfast when he went downstairs. "Sleep well?" she asked.

Jack nodded. "You should have woken me. I only meant to close my eyes for a half-an-hour."

"I couldn't bring myself to." Laura eyed his shirt. "Take that off. I'll iron it. We can't have you going to work in a creased shirt on your first day."

Naomi came into the kitchen. Faint lines disturbed her forehead. "Are you OK now, Dad?"

Jack tousled her hair. "Yes, sweetheart." He moved the conversation on to lighter topics. "What lessons have you got today?"

Naomi rolled her eyes and shrugged – her standard response whenever she couldn't be bothered to talk about something. Jack smiled. That was fine with him. He wasn't much for chit-chat in the morning either.

Half-an-hour later Jack was bundling Naomi into his car for the school-run. "Good luck," said Laura.

"I don't know what time I'll be finished."

"That's OK, I'll pick up Naomi."

"Make sure you're there on time. And if anyone you don't know approaches you, call me straight away."

Laura frowned. "You're not still fretting about that Facebook nonsense, are you?"

"Just humour me will you, Laura?"

Jack puffed his cheeks as he ducked into the car. It wasn't easy to pull the wool over Laura's eyes. Nor did he want to. If Naomi really was in danger, then Laura was in danger too. In which case, she had a right to know what was going on. But what the hell was he supposed to tell her? *I'm being blackmailed by a psychopath,* obviously wasn't an option. He put the question to the back of his mind. He had another minefield to negotiate before it needed answering.

He went through the same procedure as on the previous day – watch Naomi all the way into school, check to make sure no one else was watching her, check her phone locator. As he returned to the car, he lit a cigarette. The cigarette was long finished by the time he'd fought his way through rush-hour to headquarters. He took a deep breath and headed into the building. The corridors were busy with officers coming on and going off duty. A claustrophobic feeling prodded at him as he caught a crowded lift to the SCD's floor. He knocked on Paul's door.

"Come in," called Paul.

Jack entered. "Morning, sir."

"Morning, Jack. Relax. Like I said, you only need to observe rank in front of the team." Paul eyed him intently. "Nervous?"

"Yes, but I'm raring to go."

"Glad to hear it." Paul rose from behind his mountain of paperwork. "I'll show you to your desk."

Jack's new colleagues already had their heads buried in phones, computers and files. He nodded at them and said, "Morning." The only names that had stuck in his mind were DI Emma Steele and DI Steve Platts – the former because he'd instantly liked her, the latter for the opposite reason. Steve looked unsmiling at Jack. The feeling appeared to be mutual. Paul led Jack to a desk neighbouring Emma. She was still trawling through CCTV footage from the RBS branch where Erica Cook had worked. She gave Jack a friendly, albeit jaded smile.

"Still hard at it," said Jack.

She pointed to her blonde hair. "This'll be grey by the time I'm done."

"Emma knows this division inside out. Any questions, just ask her," Paul said briskly. "You need a building pass-card. Oh and a mobile phone. I'll get them sorted out for you." He glanced at his wristwatch. "Morning briefing is in about twenty minutes, so I'll leave you to settle in."

Paul strode from the room like a man fighting a losing battle against time. "It tires me out just looking at him," said Emma. "Has he always been like this?"

Jack nodded. "Natasha, his wife, used to complain that she hardly ever saw him. I used to say to him, you want to be careful, nothing's worth putting your marriage at risk for."

"He should have listened to you."

Jack frowned curiously. "What does that mean?"

Emma hesitated to reply. "If the DCI's said nothing, then it's not my place to."

"They're getting divorced," Steve put in with a smirk.

Jack's eyes widened. "Since when?"

"Since a few weeks ago. The DCI hasn't breathed a word about it. Only reason we know is because I went to his house on business and he wasn't there. His wife told me he's living in a Premier Inn. Poor sod. Mind you, they do a bloody good Peri Peri burger at the Manchester Central Premier Inn."

"Prick," Emma muttered loud enough for Steve to hear. He blew her a kiss.

Jack wondered why Paul hadn't mentioned the breakup to him. Was he too embarrassed? For the most part, Paul kept his work and personal life separate. Still, they'd been friends for years. They'd gone to each other's wedding. Natasha and Rebecca hadn't been particularly close, but they'd got on well enough. *Rebecca. Maybe that's it,* thought Jack. *Maybe he doesn't want to burden me with his troubles because of Rebecca... Rebecca...*

He flipped open his wallet. A photo of Naomi smiled out from it.

"She's gorgeous," commented Emma. "What's her name?"

"Naomi."

"She looks like you."

No she doesn't, thought Jack. Rebecca's eyes stabbed at him from Naomi's face. He remembered the first time he'd looked into Rebecca's eyes. It was like he'd been struck by a bolt of lightning from a clear sky. He closed his wallet. He couldn't bring those memories here or he might as well hand in his badge right now.

A man in his late twenties or early thirties with a face as yet unmarked by the rigours of the job approached. "I'm Gary," he said. "We met briefly yesterday. I've been working on the Moss Lane Pharmacy and Barlow & Coe lists. Emma tells me you've been going through them. Come up with anything interesting?"

Jack gave Gary the shortlist of names he'd made, along with whatever information he'd dug up online. "I don't think it'll be of much use."

"No, this is great, thanks. It looks like most of these people live in Didsbury–"

"Pfft," interrupted Steve. "Give me a break. Our guy isn't some Guardian-reading ponce from Didsbury," he slid a glance at Jack, "or Chorlton."

Jack pretended not to notice. He'd come across plenty of blokes like Steve on The Force: alpha males who started pissing all over the place whenever a potential rival wandered into their territory. The best policy was to ignore them. Take away their oxygen.

"How do you know it's a guy?" asked Emma.

"Of course it bloody is." Steve pointed to the crime scene photos. "A woman wouldn't do something like that. Not unless she was some psycho dyke."

Rolling her eyes, Emma said sarcastically, "DI Steve Platts, the face of progressive policing."

Steve came back with a retort, but Jack had already zoned out of the conversation. He was looking at Paul who'd just marched into the room in a manner that suggested he had big news to tell.

Jack's heart was suddenly in his mouth. *Someone's either found Camilla and Dale or a new victim. Oh Christ, don't let it be a new victim.*

"OK everyone, listen up," began Paul. The room fell silent. "Two bodies have been found in Chorlton. A male and a female. Both approximately early thirties. The female fits the victims' profile and has injuries consistent with our perp's MO. The male also appears to have been fatally stabbed. A call came in from the female victim's mother, a Mrs Lilith Winter, an hour ago. She was worried because she hadn't been able to contact her daughter in two days. The daughter's name is Camilla Winter. Apparently she's quite a well-known opera singer. She was in a show at Manchester Opera House last Saturday night. So we know she was killed sometime after that. Two constables from West Didsbury Station got Camilla's landlord to let them into her flat. We haven't got a definitive ID yet, but the description fits Camilla. The man is believed to be her boyfriend, Dale Hopper of Broom Lane, Levenshulme. That's about all we know right now. This scene is potentially already several days old." Paul clapped his hands. "So come on, let's not let it get any older. Gary, Steve, I want you to canvas the neighbourhood. Emma, Jack, you're heading over to Didsbury to break the news to the mother."

Jack could have thrown his head back in relief – partly because he'd dodged the bullet of talking to neighbours who might have seen him lurking near Camilla's flat, but mainly because no one else had been killed. He wasn't surprised Emma had landed the unenviable task of breaking the news to Lilith Winter. She had a direct but gentle way about her that made her a natural candidate for such duties.

"What do we know about Lilith?" asked Jack.

"She's sixty-four. A widow. Camilla was her only child. No employment history. No criminal record."

Jack's heart gave a squeeze for Lilith. She'd outlived her husband and child. He couldn't imagine anything worse than that.

Paul resumed firing out orders and the team sprang into action.

CHAPTER 23

A convoy of marked and unmarked vehicles exited GMP HQ carpark. Jack's mouth was bone-dry. He'd used to live for the thrill of heading to a crime scene, his stomach queasy with anticipation. But the thrill was gone. Only the queasiness remained.

Sirens blaring, the convoy skirted the city centre and raced south along Princess Road. They passed Alexandra Park where Zoe Saunder's screams had echoed unheeded into the night. *This wouldn't be happening if you hadn't been too drunk on vodka and self-pity to go to her aid,* thought Jack. *Zoe might be alive, so might Erica, Camilla and– Stop! You can't change what's happened.*

When the other vehicles turned right towards Chorlton, Emma turned left towards Didsbury. She pulled over outside a handsome Victorian house on a tree-lined road. A gravel driveway led from stone gateposts to a pillar-flanked front door. To either side of the pillars were tall bay windows. High above them a Gothic spire stabbed at the sky. The large garden was in need of attention. The paths, driveway and flowerbeds were riddled with weeds. Trees and bushes competed for space, casting deep shadows. The house gave off a similar air of neglect. Its brickwork bore the green scars of leaky guttering. Its paintwork was cracked and curled.

They got out of the car and crunched along the driveway. The house loomed over them, blotting out the sun. "Mrs Winter must have money," commented Emma. "Places like this are worth an absolute fortune around here."

"Looks like she's fallen on hard times to me."

Jack noted that the curtains were closed in one of the upstairs windows. It made him think of Rebecca. For the last few weeks of her life, she'd refused to allow the bedroom curtains to be opened. She'd lain in semi-darkness, someone for whom the sun had become a tormenting reminder of a world that, seemingly for reasons unknown to anyone but herself, she wanted no more part of.

They climbed several stone steps and Emma knocked on the front door. Jack could see the tension in her face. Breaking the news of a loved one's death was one of the hardest parts of the job. You never knew how people would react. Some went silent. Others became hysterical. A few refused to believe their ears. One woman had even launched at Jack like a wildcat as if being the bearer of bad news somehow made him responsible for its cause.

The door was opened by a slim, somewhat sallow-faced woman with shoulder-length straight grey hair. Thick glasses perched on a prominent nose, magnifying dark brown eyes. She was wearing a functional blue blouse, black trousers and sturdy shoes. "Can I help you?" Her flat-vowelled Manchester accent was as deadpan as her expression.

"Are you Mrs Lilith Winter?" asked Emma.

"No. I'm her nurse."

Emma displayed her warrant card. "I'm Detective Inspector Emma Steele. This is Detective Inspector Jack Anderson. We're here to talk to Mrs Winter about her daughter."

"Oh I see. Have you found Camilla?"

"Can I ask your name please?"

"Stella Lloyd. Would you like me to pass on a message?"

Emma jotted down the name. "We need to speak to Mrs Winter in person."

"You know that she's seriously ill?"

"What's wrong with her?"

"Emphysema. She may only have months left to live."

"I'm sorry to hear that. May we come in? This is an urgent matter."

"Mrs Winter is very weak. If you're here with bad news, please break it to her as gently as possible."

How do you gently tell someone that their daughter's dead? wondered Jack as they followed Stella into a high-ceilinged entrance hall. A glass chandelier dangled above a chessboard-tiled floor. A gold clock ticked on a dark-wood sideboard set against the wall of a long hallway.

Jack's nostrils flared at a sulphurous odour. "What's that smell?"

"Acetylcysteine," said Stella. "It's administered by nebuliser to clear mucus. Very effective, but it smells like bad eggs."

She led them up a broad staircase carpeted in once plush but now threadbare scarlet. Dusty gold-leaf framed paintings of hills and moors decorated the walls, adding to the air of faded opulence.

"When did you last see Camilla?" asked Emma.

"About a week ago. She's not been round much lately. She's been busy rehearsing for her show."

Sunlight slanted through a stained-glass window, casting a hazy rainbow glow over the landing. Stella rapped on a panelled door. "Mrs Winter, there are police officers here to see you.

A brittle, breathless voice replied, "Come in."

They entered a large, gloomy bedroom where the sulphurous smell was so strong it made Jack's eyes water. The window was cloaked by thick curtains whose floral pattern matched the red velvet flock-wallpaper. The only light was a faint glow from a lamp beside a four-poster bed. A plastic medicine trolley and an oxygen cylinder flanked the bed. A dressing-table was crowded with framed photos of Camilla. Some had the polished look of publicity shots. Most were family scenes. Jack's gaze lingered on what looked to be a teenage Camilla between a dark-haired woman and a tall, dark-haired man. The woman was elegantly beautiful – plump lips, high cheekbones, cat-like eyes, a mane of gently curling hair. Reminiscent of

Elizabeth Taylor in her prime. The man was handsome too. But his chiselled features were offset by steel-rimmed glasses, a serious expression and a high-forehead that gave him a dry, scholarly air.

Propped up on a mound of pillows, Lilith was swathed in a lacy nightgown and silk duvet. Her hair was an unruly shock of white, her skin was jaundiced and slack, her lips were dry and bloodless. Only her eyes hinted at the beauty she'd once possessed. They glistened like blue gems from between heavy lids. A tube snaked from the cylinder to an oxygen mask clutched in Lilith's arthritic-knuckled right hand. Her chest rattled with each laboured breath.

"Hello, Mrs Winter, my name's Emma–"

Lilith waved away the introductions. "Just tell me," she said in a prep-school accent, grimacing as if each word was painful to form.

"It might be best if we spoke privately." Emma glanced at Stella.

The nurse stood her ground. "I think I should stay in case Mrs Winter needs me."

"Stella stays," said Lilith. She had the manner of someone used to being obeyed.

"I'm afraid it's not good news, Mrs Winter," said Emma. "At approximately eight o'clock this morning, officers gained entry to your daughter's flat. They found a deceased adult female fitting her description and deceased adult male who we believe to be one Dale Hopper."

Jack noted approvingly that Emma maintained eye contact with Lilith and didn't pussy-foot around the matter-at-hand. Directness was always the best policy in these situations. As for Lilith's reaction... There wasn't one – at least, not one he could see. Slowly, she lifted the oxygen mask to her face. She kept it pressed there for a full minute, her eyes bulging as she dragged air into her crippled lungs. Lowering the mask, she asked, "How did Camilla die?"

"We don't know yet. Like I said, we're not one hundred percent certain that the deceased is your daughter."

"It's her." A fatalistic light glimmered in Lilith's eyes as if there was something inevitable about what was happening.

"How can you be so sure?" put in Jack.

Lilith seemed to notice him for the first time. She reached up as if to smooth her hair, but her hand stopped then dropped back onto her stomach. She gave a hiss as if to say, *What's the point?* "Camilla always comes to see me after an important performance."

"When was the last time you saw or spoke to your daughter?" asked Emma.

"Saturday night. She rang me on the way home from the opera house. She was–" Lilith ran out of breath. She sucked at the oxygen mask again, before continuing, "She was in a taxi with *that* boyfriend of hers." Her tone suggested she had a less than high opinion of Dale.

"How long had the two of them been together?"

"Not long. Nine or ten months. Why? Do you think he killed her?"

"We have no evidence to suggest so. Can you tell me about the conversation you had with Camilla?"

"She was as happy as I've ever known her. Her performance in La Traviata had been a great success." Lilith made a flourish with her hand that reminded Jack of Camilla. "She was going away with Dale for a couple of days to celebrate. She promised to come and see me as soon as she got back."

"Where were they going?"

"Does it matter? She's dead." A scrape of emotion shook Lilith's voice. "My Camilla is dead."

Emma was silent while Lilith collected herself. Then she asked, "What was Camilla and Dale's relationship like?"

Lilith prepared herself to speak with a blast of oxygen. "Dale was..." she sought for the right words, "not marriage material. He had an ingratiating way about him. Like a used car salesman. I told Camilla, by all means enjoy him. Just don't allow yourself to fall in love with him. A man like that will ruin your life."

Jack wondered whether Lilith was speaking from experience. His eyes strayed back to the family photo. Gabriel Winter – assuming that's who the man at her side was – didn't look like that kind of man.

"Exquisite isn't she," said Lilith.

"Yes," agreed Jack. A slight thickening of his voice threatened to give away just how exquisite he thought Camilla was. He pointed to the bespectacled man. "Is that Camilla's dad?"

"Yes. Gabriel died ten... no, eleven years ago. Heart attack. He was a cardiologist. Quite famous in his field. Ironic don't you think?"

Jack looked at Lilith. Was that an upturn of bitter amusement at the corners of her mouth? Or was she simply struggling for breath? He moved in as if for a closer look at the photo, but instead cast his gaze over Lilith's medication. The prescription stickers were marked 'Peak Pharmacy. Wilmslow Road'.

Emma brought the conversation back on track. "Did Dale ever verbally or physically abuse Camilla?"

Lilith made a dismissive gesture. "Big mouth, no spine. That was Dale. They had their arguments, but there's nothing unusual in that. If you don't argue, there's no passion. Don't you agree?"

The question was directed at Jack. He thought about the arguments Rebecca and he used to have in the early years of their relationship. Fiery rows sparked by petty jealousies and followed by intense lovemaking. Sometimes it had seemed as if they argued just to make up. He slammed a mental trapdoor on the memories. "How long were you married?"

"Thirty one years. We married in 1975. I was twenty-two. Gabriel was two years older and studying medicine at Manchester University. We were children by today's standards. We met at the Twisted Wheel – a nightclub

that played Northern Soul. Gabriel loved that music. We bought this place in
'78." Lilith glanced around wistfully. "It was a different house back then. I
used to throw parties and all of Manchester's high-society would come. But
that stopped when–" A deep, racking cough broke off her words.

"When what?" pressed Jack.

Lilith tried to speak, but couldn't catch her breath. She put a handkerchief
to her mouth. When she took it away, there was blood on the material.

Stella stepped forwards to give Lilith a sip of water.

"Can you think of a reason anyone might have wanted to hurt Camilla
and Dale?" asked Emma.

"Mrs Winter's answered enough questions for now," the nurse said
firmly, strapping the oxygen mask over Lilith's face.

Lilith closed her eyes. "Camilla," she murmured. "Oh my little darling."

"We'll be in touch as soon as we have anything more to tell you, Mrs
Winter," Emma said as Stella ushered the detectives from the room.

Lilith opened her eyes and beckoned Jack to her side. He stooped over
her, intrigued as to what she might be about to say. She must have known
she didn't have long to live. Perhaps she was wanted to confess something.

"Cigarette," she whispered.

He looked at her in astonishment. Was she trying to cadge a cigarette?
She mouthed the word again, adding, "I can always tell a smoker." She ran a
finger over the deep lines around her lips.

Jack glanced at Stella, who was eyeing them suspiciously. "I don't think
your nurse would approve."

"Then don't tell her." Lilith nudged her hand against Jack's thigh below
the level of Stella's sight.

"It could kill you."

Lilith gave him a look that said as clearly as if she'd shouted it, *What have
I got left to live for?*

She had a point, reflected Jack. If he lost Naomi that would be the end of the line for him. He would have slipped Lilith all the cigarettes he had, let her smoke to her heart's content, except for one thing – with or without realising it, she might know something crucial to the case. "Sorry," he said, straightening.

Compressing her lips, Lilith turned her eyes away from him as if she'd decided he wasn't worth knowing.

As Stella showed them to the front door, she said, "Mrs Winter asked you for a cigarette, didn't she?"

"Yes," admitted Jack.

"Please tell me you didn't give her one."

"I didn't."

"Good, because just one could finish her off. That's not to mention the dangers of smoking around oxygen cylinders."

"What was Mrs Winter's relationship with her daughter like?" asked Emma.

"She thought the sun shone out of Camilla's backside," Stella stated bluntly. "She's nearly bankrupted herself supporting her. The life of a glamorous opera star doesn't come cheap." She opened the door. "Please don't come here again. Mrs Winter hasn't got long left. Let her live out her final days in peace."

Emma gave the nurse her card. "If anything important comes to mind or if Mrs Winter takes a turn for the worse, please call me."

As they returned to the car, Emma sighed, "Bloody hell that was rough. If that was me, I'd be glad I didn't have long left to live."

"So what now?" asked Jack.

"We'll head over to Chorlton. Let's grab something to eat on the way. I didn't have time for breakfast."

"Good to know you've got your priorities straight," Jack commented wryly.

"Can't do this job on an empty stomach. There's a cafe in Withington that does the best fry-up around."

The prospect of getting up-close-and-personal with a corpse clearly didn't bother Emma as much as her grumbling belly. Jack smiled despite himself. He'd missed being around that kind of mortuary rationality.

"Funny old bird, isn't she?" Emma said as they drove. "I get the feeling Mrs Winter was a real bitch back in the day."

"What makes you say that?"

"Woman's intuition. Did you see the look on her face when she was talking about her husband? There wasn't much love lost there. I bet she gave him hell."

Emma's phone rang. "It's the DCI," she said. Jack's heart kicked. Had there been another new development? Had someone seen him prowling around on the night Camilla and Dale were murdered? Was there a witness waiting to ID him? Emma put the call on loudspeaker. "Hello, sir."

"Where are you?"

"We're on our way to you," said Emma. "We finished talking to Mrs Winter a short while ago. Nothing much to report. Mrs Winter's bedridden. Emphysema. She hadn't seen or spoken to her daughter since Saturday."

"You can give me a full report later. Don't come here. I need you to head to Clarity Advertising Agency. Dale Hopper worked there."

"Where's that?"

"City centre. Quay Street. They're expecting you."

"Are they aware of the situation?"

"Not yet."

The implication behind Paul's words was clear – Emma and Jack had another unpleasant duty to perform.

"How are things going there?" Jack couldn't resist but ask.

"Well the bodies are at least forty eight hours old. The female's been cut open like the others. You can imagine the stink."

Jack didn't want to imagine what two days of decomposing in the summer heat had done to Camilla. "Any witnesses?"

"Not that we know of."

The news didn't do much to ease Jack's anxiety. Manchester Opera House and The Cuban cocktail bar were also on Quay Street. He'd hoped to avoid going anywhere near those places for the foreseeable future. There was also the question of whether any of Dale's colleagues had been in The Cuban on Friday night. If so, his career with SCD would be short-lived to say the least.

"Well that's breakfast out the window," Emma said ruefully as she changed direction.

CHAPTER 24

Clarity Advertising Agency was one of several businesses housed in a tall Georgian stone building on Quay Street. The opera house was a short distance to the west. A little further away in the other direction was the cocktail bar. A receptionist buzzed Jack and Emma in and directed them to the top floor. They were met out of the lift by a sharply dressed thirty-something man.

"I'm Thom," the man introduced himself, extending his hand. Jack didn't recognise him and there was no flicker of recognition in Thom's expression. Thom led them to a plush office with 'Thom Cooper. Creative Director' on the door. The walls were covered with framed adverts for various brands. He directed them to a sofa and perched himself on the edge of a desk. "So what's this about?"

Emma went into her, *I'm afraid I've got bad news,* spiel. Thom pressed his hands to his face. "Oh my god, Dale and Camilla are dead." As if struggling to make sense of the words, he repeated, "Dale and Camilla are dead. Are you sure it's them?" His reaction was a touch melodramatic, but appeared genuine enough.

"Ninety nine percent."

"How? Who? Why?"

"We're treating it as murder. As for the 'who' and 'why', that's what we're trying to find out."

"Whatever I can do to help, just tell me."

Emma exchanged a glance with Jack. He knew what she was thinking: *This man's got nothing to do with the murders.* The first thing a guilty person said was: *Well I didn't do it.* "Thank you, Mr Cooper," she said. "We need to talk to your staff."

"No problem. You can use my office." Thom shook his head. "This is insane. Fucking insane. How could anyone hurt Camilla? Such a beautiful, gentle woman."

Gentle. Camilla hadn't struck Jack as particularly gentle. Not like Rebecca. She was the gentlest person he'd ever known. She'd never hit or even shouted at Naomi. Not once. Rebecca and he had occasionally fallen out. But even during their fieriest rows, she'd always been careful not to say anything truly hurtful. When they had their first lover's tiff, she'd cautioned him, *Be careful what you say, Jack, because believe me, words can do just as much damage as fists.*

Jack pushed down the memories. "Did you know Camilla well?"

"Not very. Do you know The Cuban bar just along road from here?"

His stomach contracted. "Yes."

"I used to see her drinking in there sometimes. Well, I mean you could hardly miss her with that face and those big baby blues."

Big baby blues. Jack's thoughts strayed further. *Rebecca. What happened?*

"Is that where Camilla and Dale met?" asked Emma.

Thom nodded. "The first time Dale saw her, he said he was going to make her his wife. He was only half-joking. I told him she was out of his price range."

You were right, Jack silently agreed.

"Camilla wasn't interested in Dale," said Thom. "But he kept plugging away until she agreed to go on a date."

The memories pushed back so hard that Jack lost his grip on the present. Suddenly he was jogging on the coastal cliffs of East Sussex. He saw a woman fall to the ground. He rushed to her aid. She'd twisted her ankle. He'd always thought love at first sight only existed in novels and movies. But when she looked him in the eyes, he knew was wrong. He helped her to her car. He was so flustered by his feelings that he only remembered at the last moment to ask her name. "Rebecca," she said. He gave her his number and asked her to call and let him know how her ankle was doing...

"...stalker."

The word brought Jack back to the room with a jolt. He blinked, still seeming to hear from an impossible distance the whisper of waves breaking against cliffs – the cliffs where it had started and where it had ended. "Sorry I was miles away," he apologised. "What was that again?"

"Dale was convinced Camilla had a stalker," repeated Thom. "He came into the office last Saturday morning to go through slogans for an ad campaign. He was hungover. I asked if he'd had a good night. He said yes, except he'd had to warn off some nutter who was eyeing up Camilla. He reckoned he'd seen the guy hanging around outside Camilla's flat the day before."

"At what time?"

"He didn't say."

"Did Dale tell you what this man looked like?" asked Emma.

Jack's breath stopped as he waited for Thom's reply.

"Only that he was a scruffy looking dude."

"By 'scruffy', you mean what? He was unshaven? His clothes were a mess?"

"I don't know. Dale didn't say."

Jack still didn't breathe. It was obvious what Emma's next question would be.

"Where did Dale's confrontation with this 'scruffy' guy take place?"

"The same place I mentioned before, The Cuban."

There it was. Jack's chest deflated. A slew of conflicting thoughts raced through his mind, arguing back and forth. *You're fucked. You're totally fucked! You should have seen this coming. You've got to tell the truth.* He gave a sharp little shake of his head. *Yes, dozens of people saw Dale confront you, but many of those people will have been drunk by the end of the evening. And drunk people tend to forget things. No way will you be recognised. You hadn't shaved for days. On top of which, you're medium build, medium height, short brown hair – an everyman, unmemorable, ordinary. But what about CCTV? Stop jumping ahead. The bar might not have CCTV. Of course it fucking does! Oh Naomi. I'm so sorry, sweetheart. I'm so, so sorry. Get a grip. You're in this now. You've got to see it through.*

"Were Dale and Camilla out alone?" asked Emma.

"No. Some of Camilla's fellow cast members were with them. Don't ask me who though. Anyway, Dale and I went through the slogans, then he erm…" A catch came into Thom's voice. He cleared it and continued, "He left and that was the last time I saw him. The last time I'll ever see him. I can't… I can't get my head around it."

You will do, thought Jack.

For months after Rebecca's death, he'd harboured a tiny, agonising hope that one day she would walk back into the house. He'd concocted all sorts of fantasies: she hadn't drowned, she'd been washed up unconscious somewhere, suffering from temporary amnesia; or she'd done a Reggie Perrin; or aliens had abducted her. Anything would do, just so long as he didn't have to accept reality. But even for him there had come a time when he couldn't live in denial anymore. He'd been sorting through Rebecca's things and one thought had suddenly bludgeoned him over and over – *She's dead and you'll never see her again* – until he collapsed to his knees.

Thom fetched the agency's staff into his office one by one. Some were in floods of tears. Others seemed relatively unaffected. All sang the same tune – they hadn't seen or spoken to Dale since before the weekend, they didn't think Dale would have hurt Camilla, they didn't know of any reason anyone would want to hurt them, they couldn't believe – or more accurately, couldn't comprehend – what had happened.

It was early afternoon when Jack and Emma left the offices of Clarity.

"Fancy a bite to eat? My shout," offered Jack. Inevitably, Emma would want to check out The Cuban, but if he could delay doing so there was a chance something more urgent might come up or he could fabricate an excuse to duck out of accompanying her.

"Sounds good. We'll just have a quick chat with The Cuban's employees."

Jack's gaze travelled beyond her to the bar's crimson awnings and glass doors. "Shouldn't we call the DCI first?"

"What for?" Emma added jokingly, "I think we're big enough to make our own decisions."

In desperation, Jack said, "OK. Tell you what, you talk to the employees. I'll get on the phone. See if I can find out which of Camilla's fellow cast members were out with her and Dale on Friday."

Emma frowned. "You'd let me walk in that bar on my own?"

Jack had no answer for that. He knew what Emma was getting at. For all they knew, Camilla's 'stalker' might be acquainted with The Cuban's employees. He might even be friends with them. If Jack didn't have Emma's back, he was worse than useless – he was dangerous. No one would want to work with him. He'd become an outcast on his first day. Even worse, his colleagues might come to suspect he had an ulterior motive for not wanting to be seen in The Cuban.

"Sorry, Emma, I wasn't thinking."

She smiled. "Forget it.

Jack motioned for her to lead the way. He lit a nerve-calming cigarette. His footsteps faltered outside the bar. Emma glanced at him. He dropped his cigarette and ground it out with his heel. *Just get it over with. If they've got you on CCTV, you're done for no matter what. Walk confidently. Act with authority. You're not that sad-sack who Dale confronted. You're DI Jack Anderson.*

The front doors were locked. Emma knocked. A woman popped up from behind the bar counter and called to them, "We're closed."

Emma took out her warrant card. "Police. We need to speak to the manager."

The woman lifted the counter flap and opened the doors. "That's me."

Her face wasn't familiar to Jack, but he couldn't be sure she hadn't served him drinks. His brain had been like scrambled eggs on the night they were there to inquire about. They stepped inside. Sunlight was streaming through the floor-to-ceiling windows. Jack made sure he stood with his back to the glare. *Say nothing. Let Emma do the talking.*

"I'm DI Emma Steele and this is DI Jack Anderson. Can I ask your name?"

"Leah." No recognition showed in the manageress's eyes as she looked from Emma to Jack. "What can I do for you?"

"Who was working here last Friday night?"

"There were quite a few of us. Friday's our busiest night."

"Are any of them here now?"

"Yeah, Adam and Millie. Do you want me to fetch them?"

"Please. And we'll need the names and contact details of any others."

Leah disappeared through a doorway. A moment later she returned with the staff members. Once again, Jack didn't recognise them and they didn't appear to recognise him. "We're interested in an incident that occurred here on Friday night," Emma informed them.

"There were a few minor incidents that night," said Leah. "You know how it is, long hot days plus too much alcohol equals trouble." She shrugged as if to say, *What can you do?*

"The incident involved a man named Dale Hopper." Emma showed them a photo of Dale. "Do any of you know him?"

The question received a, "No," from Adam and Millie.

"He's seems familiar," said Leah.

"He works at Clarity Advertising Agency, a few doors along from here."

Leah shook her head to show the name meant nothing to her.

"He was in here with Camilla Winter," said Emma.

"The opera singer?" put in Adam.

"That's right."

Adam pointed to a booth. "She was sitting over there with her friends. I remember because... because she's one of those people you remember."

"I heard something kicking off on Friday," offered Millie. A ripple of tension passed through Jack as she said, "Some guy was shouting. Something about someone looking at his girlfriend. I didn't pay much attention. Maybe Dave saw what happened."

"Dave's our doorman," said Leah. "I've rung him. He's on his way here. If anyone can help you, it's him."

"What time did this incident occur at?" Emma asked Millie.

"I'm not sure. Maybe half-nine or ten o'clock."

"Do you have CCTV?"

"Yes," said Leah. "I can show you the footage from last Friday."

She led Jack and Emma to a room at the back of the building. She switched on a flat-screen TV. The screen was divided into nine segments, marked 'Cam 01-09'. Three of the segments displayed footage. Camera one was directed at the front entrance. Camera two overlooked the barroom. And camera three was in a corridor by the toilets. Jack's legs were trembling. He put a hand against a wall to steady himself as Leah opened the DVR system's main menu. His mind raced for an explanation as to what they were about to see.

"I'm sorry," said Leah. "The footage isn't there."

At those words, Jack felt like dropping to his knees and offering thanks to someone, anyone! For once, luck – or whatever – seemed to be on his side.

"What do you mean?" asked Emma.

"The hard drive's empty. It's been wiped."

"Is there any way to retrieve the footage?"

"Not that I know of."

"Who has access to this room?"

"Everyone who works here, but only me and Dave are trained to operate the CCTV. He must have formatted the hard drive."

"Would you be willing to let our techies look at the DVR?"

"Sure."

"Could you step out of the room? And if Dave turns up, bring him to us."

Leah nodded and left. "What do think?" Emma asked Jack.

He was still dazed with almost incredulous relief. "Seems too coincidental."

"Too bloody right it does. Do you remember what you said when you saw the footage of the guy who spoke to Zoe in The Alchemist?"

"I said he looked like a bouncer."

"What if you were right? He might be mates with this Dave."

Jack was silent as if considering the possibility. The voices in his head were arguing again. *Dave could get into a lot of trouble over this... Relax. He might get a grilling but it won't go any further than that... What if it does?*

Leah came back into the room with a burly man wearing sunglasses. Jack suppressed an urge to lower his head. *Stand up tall,* he told himself. *Act like DI Jack Anderson and that's all this guy will see.*

"This is Dave," Leah introduced the doorman.

Emma told him why they were there. Dave yawned. "Sorry, I was working a door until four in the morning." He lifted his sunglasses and squinted at the photo of Dale. "Yeah, I recognise him. He comes in here once or twice a week. He had words with some bloke last Friday. Told him to fuck off. I didn't get involved."

Emma swiped to a photo of the man from The Alchemist. "Was this the other bloke?"

"No. The other bloke needed a shave, but he didn't have a proper beard and he was nowhere near as ripped as that dude. He was average build..." Dave pointed to Jack. "Like him."

"What did he look like?"

"I dunno, just an average white guy."

"Hair colour?"

Dave shrugged, yawning again. "It was over in a second. I hardly looked at the bloke. I was looking at what-did-you-call-him?"

"Dale."

"Yeah him. He was the one giving it all that." Dave made a talk-talk-talk signal.

"Did you see anyone else acting suspiciously inside or outside the bar that night?" asked Jack. *Someone filming on their phone through the front window, for instance*, he would have liked to add.

"No."

"Have you deleted last Friday's CCTV footage?" asked Emma.

"No."

"Well someone has."

Dave glanced at Leah. She gave a shrug. He shifted on his tree-trunk legs as if cottoning on that he might be under some kind of suspicion. "What's this about anyway?"

"I'm not at liberty to say, but this is an extremely serious matter." Emma looked from Dave to Leah. "If either of you know anything about the missing footage or the man Dale confronted, you'd be well advised to tell us."

Dave spread his hands. "I've told you everything I know."

"Same here," said Leah.

"Then I'm afraid you'll both have to accompany me to Greater Manchester Police Headquarters for further questioning."

Dave scowled. "This is bullshit."

"Easy now, big man," warned Jack. His voice was calm, although his heart was still palpitating from when Dave said, *Like him.*

Dave glowered at him before dropping his gaze. Jack kept an eye on the doorman as Emma phoned Paul. The conversation was short and sweet. She got off the phone and said to Jack, "The SOCOs are on their way."

"Oh for fuck's sake," said Dave, who was clearly familiar with the acronym for Scenes of Crime Officer.

"You won't be able to open until the SOCOs are finished," Emma told Leah. "We also need fingerprints from you and your staff, so if you could please get us their contact details."

Leah nodded and hurried from the room again. Emma ushered Dave after her. She and Jack seated themselves in the bar to await the SOCOs. Dave made for a booth at the opposite side of the room.

"Paul said to tell you good work," said Emma.

"I didn't do much."

She glanced towards Dave. "You didn't blink when that meathead tried to stare you out. That's good enough for me."

Jack smiled, grateful for the praise although he didn't deserve it. He kept his hands below the table. They were trembling – whether from the DTs or dumped adrenaline, he couldn't tell. All he knew was that he'd been a hair's breadth away from being taken in for questioning along with Dave and Leah. He reflected that at least now he had the perfect excuse to look through city centre CCTV for the killer and the silver car. The only problem was that he was just as likely to find himself on the cameras. And he wouldn't be the only one examining the footage. Paul was doubtless already on the phone to the council's CCTV Control Room. There was every chance that his reprieve would only be temporary.

CHAPTER 25

Along with the SOCOs, two constables arrived to take Dave to Headquarters. Paul wanted to interview him personally. Leah remained behind, for the moment, to help with rounding up her staff. It took the rest of the afternoon to fingerprint and question them. One barman – a Columbian student – had seen a man hurrying from the bar at around ten o'clock on Friday, but hadn't seen his face. All he could add to what they already knew was that the man had short, medium brown hair. As for the cast of La Traviata, following the performance they'd dispersed across the entire country and beyond. Emma managed to contact two cast members who'd been in The Cuban. Neither had anything to add to the physical description.

"Medium build, short brown hair, scruffy stubble." Emma reeled off what she knew about Camilla's suspected stalker. "Could this guy be any more average?"

Something Thom had said came back at Jack like a boomerang: 'I told him she was out of his price range.' *Christ, if Camilla was out of Dale's price range, then Rebecca was out of my universe. I should have known it was too good to be true. I should have known...*

At half-past three, Jack dodged out of The Cuban to phone Laura. "I picked our little princess up as per your instructions," she told him. "She's safe and sound. We're on our way home."

"Hi Daddy," said Naomi. "Is work going OK?"

"Yes, sweetheart," replied Jack, feeling a sting of longing at the sound of her voice. "I've missed you today."

"I've missed you too, Dad. When will you be finished?"

"I don't know. It could be late." *Very late if things go bad,* thought Jack. "I'll try to get back before you go to bed. Be good for your aunt."

"I will be. Bye, Dad."

It was after five when they wrapped things up at The Cuban and returned to HQ. The atmosphere in the Incident Room was subdued. It was the nearing the end of a long day's graft. Team members were going over statements, tapping away at keyboards, following up on phone calls. Jack joined them. Out of the corner of his eye, he saw Emma writing on a stick-it-note. She slapped the note on the wall next to the photo of the man from The Alchemist. It read: 'Mr Average. Medium build. Short brown hair. Scruffy stubble.' Beside the vague description, she drew an arrow pointing to the photo and a question mark.

Paul strode into the room, purposeful as ever. He read the note, nodded approvingly, then clapped for everyone's attention. "Good work today. We've made real progress."

Two more people are dead. Can that be called progress? Jack felt like saying.

"I've just finished talking to Dave Goodall, the doorman from The Cuban," continued Paul. "He's sticking to his story that he didn't tamper with the security footage. He's got a conviction for ABH from 2015, for which he received a CSO. That's pretty much a job qualification for someone in his line of work. I see no reason to hold him. As for the footage, the computer techs tell me it's gone for good. The DVR system is working fine, so it wasn't down to a hardware or software error. The manageress, Leah Simmons, also claims she didn't delete the footage. So the questions are: who did and why? And do the answers have anything to do with these two people?" He tapped the photo and the stick-it-note. "If indeed they are two different people."

Steve Platts pointed out the obvious. "The bloke from The Alchemist isn't exactly Mr Average. He's built like a brick-shithouse."

Jack decided it was time for a bit of misdirection. Nothing that would knock the investigation off the rails. Just enough to nudge it away from him.

"You took the words from my mouth, Steve. It's also worth pointing out that Camilla was a beautiful woman and a well-known singer. She must have had admirers, fans and journalists pestering her all the time. Maybe that's all Mr Average was."

"What about Dale seeing the stalker–" began Emma.

"Suspected stalker," corrected Jack.

She gave him a frowning look as if reassessing her opinion of him. "What about Dale seeing the *suspected stalker* outside Camilla's flat the previous day?"

"Who says it was the same guy? There are a hell of a lot of Mr Average's out there."

"So you think Mr Average is a red-herring," said Paul.

"Not at all, sir. I'm just saying it's a long way from a given that Mr Average has anything to do what happened the following day."

"And I'm just saying I find it difficult to believe the incident in The Cuban has nothing to do with what happened the following day," countered Emma.

"Why?" asked Steve. "Dale was a hot-head. He saw someone eyeing up his woman and got jealous. Happens all the time."

Jack glanced gratefully at Steve for his unexpected support. Perhaps the guy wasn't a complete prick. *Or maybe my first impression was right,* he readjusted as Steve continued, "My first wife was a real bombshell. Legs up to her armpits. Tits like Sam Fox. She used to have blokes buzzing around her like flies on shit. I was always having to tell some horny bugger or other to fu–"

"Thank you for that pearl of insight, DI Platts," interrupted Paul. "You all have valid points. We're already prioritising identifying this guy." He indicated the CCTV-still. "Mr Average now has the distinction of joining him at the top of the pile. Steve, Gary, I want you talk Camilla's neighbours again. Find out if they saw anyone fitting Mr Average's description lurking outside her flat last Thursday. It'll probably come to nothing. Like Jack said, there are a lot of Mr Averages out there. But who knows, we might get lucky. Emma, Jack, I want you to go through the city centre CCTV footage. I'll contact a guy I know at the Evening News who owes me a favour. He should be able to get an appeal for witnesses up on their website today. Mr Average has been lucky so far, but someone in The Cuban must have got a good look at him."

As Paul handed out instructions to the rest of the team, Jack said to Emma, "So how do you want to do this? Shall I take the cameras to the west of The Cuban and you take those to the east?" He'd headed west along Quay Street after leaving the cocktail bar.

She replied with a curt nod. Jack's relief was tempered by the frosty atmosphere that now existed between them. He liked Emma, but a choice between putting her back up or putting Naomi's future at risk was no choice at all. As Jack got to work, Steve leant in and said, "That was a clever move."

Jack's heart skipped. What was a clever move? Had Steve somehow cottoned-on that his motives for casting doubt on Emma's Mr Average theory were less than honourable?

"Eighty percent of the city centre is east of The Cuban. You'll be off home in no time," Steve observed with a note of admiration. He glanced at Emma. "Mind you, I reckon it's landed you on her shit-list. Welcome to the club, mate."

Jack pushed out a crooked smile as if to say, *You got me.* He hated himself for it, but Steve was a potential ally and those were thin on the ground right now.

CHAPTER 26

Jack brought up a CCTV map. He mentally reran the route he'd taken out of the city centre after leaving The Cuban. He'd made his way westwards along Peter Street, then down Deansgate. He remembered running past the lofty glass tower of The Hilton and under the bridge that carried the Metrolink over great Bridgewater Street. After that it became hazy.

Over a hundred cameras controlled by the council were dotted across the city centre. There were no cameras in the direct vicinity of the opera house on Quay Street. There was one a short distance east of The Cuban on Peter Street. Another was located to the west at the junction of Deansgate and Great Bridgewater Street. He clicked on it and scrolled through the relevant footage. At 9:52 p.m. the camera zoomed in on some lads squaring up to each other. He recalled crossing the road to avoid them. In doing so, he'd also avoided the camera.

Once again he felt that exhilarating sense that perhaps, just perhaps, his luck was turning. It only lasted for seconds.

The next camera that could have picked him up was at the intersection of Medlock, Whitworth and Albion Street. At 9:54 p.m. a man ran into the camera's field of vision. He was only on camera for the space of a breath, but it was enough. Jack's eyes darted around the room. Emma was engrossed in her own task. Steve appeared to be dozing in his chair. No one else was nearby. He hit rewind and watched himself pass across the screen again. The image was a little blurry. His face wore several days' growth of stubble. It was difficult to make out his features in any real detail. But still, anyone who knew him would recognise the man on-screen.

Jack looked to see if the camera had picked up anyone who might have been following him. No one else came into the frame. At the sound of someone entering the room, he closed the footage. It would be held on file at the council's CCTV Control Room for thirty one days unless requested otherwise. He would simply have to hope Emma didn't check out the footage for herself. She had no reason to so long as she trusted him. That was something he would have to work hard on.

There were no more cameras between the City Road Inn, Albion Street camera and the Mancunian Way motorway that traversed the southern edge of the city centre. Jack turned his attention to the Peter Street camera – the camera closest to The Cuban. He was no longer looking for himself. He was looking for small silver cars and anything else that caught his eye.

He started the footage way back at half-past nine on Friday morning – approximately the time he'd arrived in the city centre. He'd spent the entire day watching the opera house, waiting for a glimpse of Camilla. Maybe the killer had too.

During the next few hours of footage, a lot of small silver cars passed through the camera's field of vision. Jack noted down all of their registrations. Hundreds of people going about their daily business came and went too – suited workers, delivery drivers, student types, mothers pushing prams, beggars, traffic wardens, street cleaners. Some, like the beggars, lingered for a while. Others moved quickly through the frame. No one caught his eye.

Time wound on both on and off the screen. At seven o'clock, Steve roused himself and said, "Right, I'm off for a pint. See you tomorrow."

At eight, Jack phoned Naomi. "Sorry, sweetheart, but I'm going to miss your bedtime again," he told her. "Don't worry, I'll be there when you wake up to take you to school."

"OK, Dad."

He detected a wobble in Naomi's voice. She was someone else whose trust he would have to earn. "I love you. Sleep well."

"Promise you won't work all night, Dad. You need to sleep too."

Jack hesitated to reply. The killer didn't operate on a nine-to-five basis; they were out there day and night, prowling around. How was he to have any chance of catching them if he wasn't willing to do the same?

"Promise," Naomi repeated. The wobble had become a tremor.

What's wrong with Mum?

She's just tired, sweetie. She'll be fine once she's had a good night's sleep.

Those words hung between them like a dark cloud. Jack sighed. "I promise."

Her voice more relaxed, Naomi asked if he wanted to speak to Aunt Laura. He said no, got off the phone and refocused on the screen. He needed to work fast if he was going to keep his promise.

The other detectives gradually followed Steve until there was only Jack and Emma left. Emma's face was hard with concentration. She showed no sign of giving up anytime soon. It was cracking on for ten o'clock by the time Jack finished going through the Peter Street footage. He'd compiled a list of over fifty registration numbers. Stars denoted how many times each car had made an appearance. He rubbed his eyes. Naomi was right – he needed sleep. His nerves felt as wrung out as an old dishcloth. *Just a couple more hours*, he told himself.

But before he started on the list, he needed something to keep himself going. He pushed back his chair. "Do you want a coffee?" he asked Emma. She either didn't hear or ignored him. He wouldn't have blamed her if the latter was the case. Being ignored was the least of what he deserved. She was scrutinising grainy footage of three men and two women at the Blackfriars Street and Deansgate crossroads – a quarter-of-a-mile north of The Cuban. She'd printed out several images of brown-haired men of medium height and build – none of which were Jack.

He gulped down his coffee and got back to it. As he logged onto the PNC, he found himself thinking about the last time he'd used it. That hadn't been on the up and up either. He'd been trying to trace Rebecca's final movements leading up to her death. The only thing of vague interest he'd discovered was that the Automatic Number Plate Recognition system had captured her Toyota outside the Hastings Premier Inn two hours before she died. What had she been doing there? It wasn't on her direct route to the cliffs. He'd shown her photo to the hotel staff. None of them had recognised her. Perhaps she'd been taking a last look around the town where she was born.

Was that what you were doing, Rebecca?

It doesn't matter what she was doing, he scolded himself. *This right here, right now, this is what matters.*

He ran the registrations through the DVLA database. The first was a Renault Clio registered to a Craig Hill, Union Street, Glossop. There were no vehicle reports attached to it. He checked to see if Craig had a criminal record – clean as a whistle. He Googled him and found a Facebook profile matching his driver's licence photo. Craig worked at a solicitor's in Central Manchester. He was 6'3" and rake thin. Jack put a cross beside the reg and moved on to the next one: a Skoda Fabia with an outstanding speeding fine. The owner was an eighteen-year-old girl with a Bristol address. Ruby Dunn. Google led him to a Facebook profile for a girl of that name who lived in Portishead. Skinny redhead. Looked like she couldn't punch her way out of a wet paper bag. He wrote her name down next to the corresponding reg followed by 'extremely unlikely'. The next was a Ford Fiesta ST. Its owner was a thirty-three-year-old man with a Keswick address – Jason Riley. Jason had several convictions for drunk and disorderly behaviour dating back to 2007. Punishments ranged from an official caution and a fixed penalty notice to an ASBO banning him from drinking in Keswick town centre. Interesting, but a chaotic drunkard was hardly the type to carry out a series of murders and leave no trace of himself behind. He wrote 'very unlikely'. Then came a

Peugeot 107 that belonged to a fifty-seven-year-old Rochdale woman. The car was clean. So was the woman. Another 'extremely unlikely'.

Ten o'clock turned into eleven, then twelve, then one... The list was littered with crosses. The only person Jack had found of any interest was a Stockport man with a history of sexual assaults on pre-teen girls. The only problem was the man was eighty-years-old and several inches shorter than Camilla. Could he have overpowered her? Jack very much doubted it.

There were still twenty-odd registrations left to check out. There was no way Jack could go through them all and get any sleep. *One more try, then call it a day.* He typed in the reg 'WT60 IMU'. He didn't expect it to lead anywhere. Sod's Law dictated that, if there was anything of real interest on the list, he wouldn't find it until the last registration. The car was a Fiat Punto that had been picked up heading west along Peter Street. A sunshade obscured its driver's face. The time stamp was 6:23 p.m., roughly an hour before Camilla had emerged from the opera house. That meant that unless the Punto had turned onto Deansgate, it had passed Jack. He checked through several nearby cameras to see if they'd captured the Punto. None had.

The Punto's owner was a Rhys Devonport, sixty-four-years-old, last known address: Victoria Road, Chester. Jack's eyes narrowed as they moved from the part of the database controlled by the DVLA to the section only the police had access to. Rhys Devonport had been reported missing on 1st December 2016. The case was still active. He checked out Rhys's personal details – 'POB: Wythenshawe, Manchester', 'DOB: 16-02-1953', 'Height: 5'10"', 'Weight: 191', 'Eye Colour: Blue', 'Hair Colour: 'Black', 'Race: White North European', 'Scars, Marks, Tattoos etc: Purple birth mark on left buttock', 'Circumcision: Yes', 'Build: Heavy/Stocky'.

Jack pushed his lips out thoughtfully. Rhys was big enough to overpower the female victims, but not too big to be the masked figure. And the South Manchester connection made things even more interesting. Rhys was from

Wythenshawe. So were Erica Cook and her parents, Roger and Stacy. Roger was fifty-eight. Stacy was fifty-six – close enough in age to Rhys to have encountered him as children hanging around the area's streets.

He scanned through the missing person report for other salient information. 'Occupation: Unemployed', 'Names Of Places Frequented: George & Dragon pub, Liverpool Road, Chester'. The date of last contact was '20-11-2016'. Twelve days before Rhys was reported missing. So either he lived alone or there was another reason for the delay. Perhaps he often disappeared for short periods. 'Previous Known Addresses: Jacksons Edge Road, Disley, Stockport'. 'Next of Kin: Brenda Devonport'. 'Relationship to missing person: Sister'. 'Marital Status: Single'.

He Googled 'Rhys Devonport, missing' and came up with several articles in Chester newspapers. He clicked the top one. 'Police Searching For Missing Chester Man' read the headline. Underneath was a picture of a smiling Rhys – florid drinker's face, good head of swept back hair, handsome in a raffish, shop-worn kind of way. 'Rhys Devonport was last seen in the George & Dragon pub on Liverpool Road. A spokesman for Cheshire Police said Rhys was a regular at the pub. Fellow regulars became concerned when Rhys stopped calling in for his evening drink. Rhys is described as white, average height, well-built, with mid-length wavy black hair. He may be wearing a dark green wax jacket, pink shirt, blue jeans and tan coloured shoes. He may also be driving a silver Fiat Punto with the registration beginning 'WT60'.

Jack entered the Punto's details into the Automatic Number Plate Recognition database. The plate had been caught on camera on the M602 near Salford on 10-12-2016. The driver was too lost in shadow to make out clearly. They appeared to be wearing a short-sleeved navy blue top. Their eyes were obscured by sunglasses. They were fair skinned, which fitted with Rhys's description. Their hair looked dark, but that could have been due to the shadows.

Jack's gaze flicked back and forth between the ANPR image and the photo of Rhys in the newspaper. The more he looked, the more he felt sure the driver wasn't Rhys. The shoulders weren't broad enough, the face was too long and narrow. But if it wasn't Rhys, who was it?

He looked on Google Earth at where Rhys lived in Chester – boxy three-storey block of flats in a built-up area. He looked at where Rhys used to live in Disley – big detached house behind a tall hedge and gate, overlooking a cricket field. Rhys Devonport, it seemed, had gone down in the world.

Perhaps it was Rhys in the car, mused Jack. Perhaps a woman had screwed him over – a petite, dark-haired woman with looks to literally kill for. He tried to visualise the masked figure in Camilla's window – bulky coat that obscured their body shape, a head shorter than Dale. Could it have been Rhys? One thing was beyond doubt. Rhys wasn't the man who'd spoken to Zoe in The Alchemist. If he was still alive, Rhys was sixty-four-years-old. The other man looked to be mid-thirties at most.

Rhys appeared to have fallen on hard times, he was a heavy drinker, he most likely lived alone. But was he in a relationship? Did he have an ex-wife? Did he have children? Why had he moved to Chester? The person to ask was Brenda Devonport. He looked her up on the vehicle database. She lived in Eccles, only a few miles from where the Punto had been picked up on camera. He would have to proceed with extreme caution in any dealings with her. If Rhys was in contact with his sister, word might get back to him. Which wouldn't be good if Rhys *was* the killer.

Jack resumed reading the missing person report. The landlord of the George & Dragon, a Terry Turner, had made the initial call to the police. He stated that Rhys had been a regular for over ten years and came in the pub most days. On his last visit Rhys had seemed his usual self. Rhys was known to live alone. The attending officer had checked out his flat and found that it was empty. There were no signs of a disturbance. Rhys's car wasn't in the residents' carpark.

There was also a brief description of a conversation between the officer and Brenda Devonport. 'I spoke by telephone to Rhys Devonport's sister, a Miss Brenda Devonport. Brenda lives in Eccles, Greater Manchester. She stated that she has had no contact with her brother in six years. She also said Rhys went missing for several weeks in August 1999 when his marriage broke down. She believes that Rhys will return to Chester.'

Brenda's statement raised several questions. Most obviously: who had Rhys been married to? And why had that marriage broken down?

Jack navigated to the 'Public Record Search' website and searched the Divorce Records. He found a listing for 'Devonport, Rhys, Born 1953, Manchester, Greater Manchester, England.' He downloaded the record's transcription. A divorce petition had been issued at Stockport County Court in October 1999. The petitioner was a 'Diane Devonport'. The respondent was 'Rhys Devonport. There was a co-respondent 'Stanley King'. The District Judge held that the 'respondent has behaved in such a way that the petitioner cannot reasonably be expected to live with the respondent. AND that the petitioner has behaved in such a way that the respondent cannot be reasonably expected to live with the petitioner.' The conclusion was clear: Diane had filed for divorce after becoming involved with another man, but Rhys was no angel either.

Jack chanced his arm on a Vehicle File search for a 'Diane King'. There was a woman by that name living at an address in Disley. Surely that had to be the ex-Mrs Devonport. No convictions. No outstanding charges. Google brought up a listing for 'Diane's Beauty Salon', also in Disley. The website offered 'A full range of beauty treatments'. Diane King was the salon's owner. There was a gallery with photos of a well-preserved, well-made blonde giving beauty treatments. She looked more than a match for Rhys. What she didn't look was anything like the killer's victims. Brown eyes and dark eyebrows marked her out as a bottle blonde. He looked on Google Earth at where she lived – neat suburban semi. Diane had gone down in the world too, although she appeared to be doing a lot better than her ex-husband.

Jack glanced at the time: 2:12 a.m. Despite Diane's dissimilarity to the victims, the lead was still worth looking into. Even if Rhys's disappearance wasn't related to the murders, it would distract attention from Mr Average. The next step was to speak to Diane and Brenda, but that would have to wait until a more sociable hour. Jack switched off his computer and rose to his feet, turning to say night to Emma.

His stomach lurched as his phone rang. Who the hell was calling him at this hour? Emma glanced at him as if wondering the same thing. There were only two people he could think of: Laura if there was something wrong with Naomi, and...

He took out his phone. 'No Caller ID'.

CHAPTER 27

Without a word to Emma, Jack left the incident room. The hallway was empty. He answered the call as he headed for the lift.

"Did I wake you?" The whispery voice was like fingernails clawing his raw nerves.

So you're not watching me right now, thought Jack. He didn't like revealing that Laura and Naomi were home alone, but he decided honesty was the best policy. Lying was just as likely to put them at risk as protect them. "No. I'm just leaving Headquarters."

"My, my, you have been a busy boy." There was no note of surprise in the reply.

Maybe you're watching me after all. Maybe you're testing me. The lift arrived and Jack got in. "What do you want?"

"You can start by thanking me."

"What for?"

"You help me, I help you. That's how this works, remember? Well I've done more than my bit to help you today."

Jack's forehead creased. He opened his mouth to ask, *What are you talking about?* But before the question could pass his lips, his eyes widened in realisation. "You deleted the security camera footage."

"Well I wouldn't say I deleted it entirely, if you catch my meaning. I just made sure your colleagues wouldn't see it for now."

Jack clenched his teeth. The killer was amassing enough evidence to bring him completely under their control. He wondered what else they had on him? Footage of him watching Camilla gasp her last breaths? Photos of him at La Traviata? Perhaps they'd been stalking him even before he started stalking Camilla. Maybe they had evidence that could place him at Alexandra Park on the night of Zoe's murder. If so, they could put him away not just for three or four months, but for the rest of his life.

Calm down, he told himself. *If they had that kind of evidence, they'd have used it from the beginning to make you cooperate.*

"It's your turn, Jack," said the killer. "Give me everything you've got."

The lift reached the ground floor. "First let me get to my car. It's too risky to talk here."

It only took a minute to get to the car, but it gave Jack a chance to put his thoughts into order. He had to play this just right, divulge enough to satisfy the killer without giving away anything of real importance. "We're releasing timelines of Abigail, Zoe and Erica's last known movements."

"I'm not interested in that, Jack. I want to know what information the SCD has that they're not making public."

Jack thought about the bearded man from The Alchemist. Did the voice on the phone belong to him? The killer had been clued up enough to get hold of the security footage from The Cuban. Why then would they be careless enough to be caught on CCTV in The Alchemist? It didn't add up. But then again, you never knew. So many criminals were an unfathomable mixture of cleverness and stupidity. If the killer *was* the bearded man, telling them about the CCTV might cause them to change their appearance and get rid of valuable evidence. Unless they were serious about wanting to be caught...

Jack couldn't bring himself to do it. There was plenty of other relatively inconsequential information he could try to placate the killer with. "The size of the victims' wounds suggests that the same knife may have been used in all–"

"No, Jack," the killer interrupted. "No, no, no. E minus. Must do better. Much better."

Jack ran his tongue nervously over his lips. The killer was beginning to sound angry. And an angry serial killer was no good for anyone. "Plain-clothes officers are on the streets watching out for women who look like the vic–"

"Stop! Fucking hell, Jack, all your bullshit's giving me a headache. I thought you'd be grateful enough to show me some appreciation, but oh no..." The killer trailed off, before continuing more calmly, "I can see we'll have to do this the hard way."

The line went dead.

"Shit, shit," hissed Jack, hoping he hadn't aggravated the killer into doing something terrible. His thoughts returned to Naomi and Laura. He stabbed the key into the ignition and screeched out of the carpark.

His phone pinged. He snatched it up. There were three picture messages. He pulled over and opened them. His skin prickled as if an icy wind had blown. All three photos were of dark-haired, blue-eyed women in their twenties or thirties. One of the women was walking along a pavement. She was dressed in a black trouser suit. There was a brick wall in the background. Another was sitting cross-legged on a patch of grass. She was wearing a vest-top and denim shorts. A pile of books at her side hinted that she was a student. The third woman's hair was more brown than black, but she had gorgeous eyes that reminded Jack of Rebecca when they first met – so bright and full of life...

His phone rang again – 'No Caller ID'. He answered it before the second ring. A mixture of relief and loathing swept through him as the killer asked, "Have you seen the photos?"

"Yes."

"I want you to choose one of them."

"Why?"

"Just choose one."

Jack swiped between the women. There was a brick of tension in his stomach. He stared into the third woman's beautiful eyes. No. He couldn't bring himself to choose her. The black-suited woman looked in a hurry to be somewhere. There were dark smudges beneath her eyes and two rings on her wedding finger. Those smudges might indicate sleepless nights of mothering a baby. There were no such marks on the cross-legged young woman's face. No rings on her fingers. She looked as if she didn't have a care in the world. It had to be her. *I'm sorry,* he silently told her. "The student in the park."

A little chuckle. "You're so clever, Jack. Only thing is it's the middle of summer. Not many students around Manchester at the moment. You're right about the park, though. I love walking in parks, people watching."

I bet you do. I bet you imagine what it would be like to be them, to live their lives instead of your own pathetic existence.

"So here's how it works, Jack. If I catch you in a lie or think you're holding something back, the girl you chose will be the next to die. Picture what she'll look like when I've finished with her. You don't want that on your conscience, do you?"

"No."

"So you'll play by the rules?"

"Yes."

"Then give me the good stuff."

Good stuff. What good stuff could he give out without jeopardising the investigation? The partial shoe print and synthetic hair fibre were unquestionably off limits. "No fingerprints have been recovered from the crime scenes. No sexual discharge either." Jack couldn't resist the impulse to add, "They think that means you might be impotent."

Another laugh. "What do you think it means?"

"They might be right. We're contacting local GPs and sexual dysfunction counsellors to find out if you've sought treatment."

"That's a good idea, Jack."

No trace of anxiety. That one's a non-starter unless the bastard is bluffing.

Jack stopped the train of thought in its tracks. Second-guessing was a bad habit, although that didn't mean it wasn't worth poking around, seeing if you hit any sore spots. "They also think you're most likely a white male over thirty, single, separated or divorced, that you may have a history of mental illness and or a criminal record, and that you're local to South Manchester."

"Sounds like you're talking about yourself."

"I pointed that out to my DCI."

"Be careful or you might end up a suspect."

"That wouldn't happen."

"Why not?"

"Because I'm not insane."

"And I am. Is that what you're saying?"

"For the perpetrator, killing is an obsessional, almost erotic compulsion that grows stronger with every act. Those are the police psychologist's words not mine. Does that sound like a sane person?"

"I'm not qualified to say, but the psychologist was right. The compulsion does grow stronger with every act." The killer's voice quickened. "It's getting stronger right now. I'm not sure I can resist it. Oh god, I need to see blood. I need to smell it. I need it. I need—"

The line fell silent. Jack's pulse was pounding in his face. He was picturing the cross-legged girl bloodied, slashed, torn. "Are you still there? Can you hear me? Don't hurt her. I'll help you. Tell me how to help you."

The voice came back on the line. "Last chance, Jack. Stop trying to wind me up and tell me what I need to know."

He scoured his mind and found a red rose. "A piece of flesh is missing from Erica Cook's left thigh where she had a tattoo of a red rose and cupid. SCD thinks the killer... Thinks you might have taken it as a trophy or to get the same tattoo done yourself. If I were you, I'd avoid tattooists for the foreseeable future."

"Better, Jack. But I think you've got even more." A silent moment passed. "I'm waiting, Jack. Think about that beautiful girl. Her life is in your hands. I'm going to count to five, Jack. After that you know what happens. One... Two... Three..."

Jack's mouth opened and closed. What else did he have? *The blood trails.* No, that wouldn't cut it. *Rhys Devonport.* No, that could put Brenda Devonport and Diane King in danger.

"Four..."

"We have CCTV footage of an as yet unidentified man talking to Zoe in The Alchemist cocktail bar," Jack blurted out.

The line was silent again for several nerve-wracking seconds, then the killer said, "You just saved that girl's life, Jack. You should feel good about yourself right now."

Then why do I feel like a total piece of shit? thought Jack.

"What does this man look like?"

"He's about your height, but built like a bodybuilder. Shaved head, blonde beard, dressed all in black."

"Ooh, he sounds scary. You might have found your man."

The flippant response suggested that the unidentified man and the killer were two different people. Once again, Jack wondered whether the killer was trying to bluff him out. And once again, he reminded himself that such second-guessing only played into the killer's hands.

"Have you got anything else?" asked the killer.

"No." The word was spoken like a full stop.

"OK, I'll buy that for now. I'll be in touch again soon. Happy hunting, DI Anderson," taunted the velvety voice.

The killer hung-up. Jack took a deep breath, resisting an urge to hit something. He needed to conserve his energy for finding this bastard.

He scrutinised the photos of the three potential victims again. The woman in the trouser-suit had a dark mole on her left cheek. Not much use for identifying her unless she turned up dead. He zoomed in on the cross-legged woman's books. Their titles were too blurry to read. The third woman was sitting at a piano, but looking sideways at the camera. She had on a smart blouse and jacket. The photo was different to the others in two ways: the woman knew she was being photographed and she was indoors. There was a professional glossiness to the image. Unless the killer was a professional photographer, they hadn't taken this photo. In which case, where had they got it from?

Jack uploaded the photos to Google Images and did a reverse image search. The outdoor photos turned up nothing of interest. A little thrill ran through him. The glossy image brought up an exact match. The woman was Fiona Jenkins, a private music teacher at Harmony Music Manchester. According to their website, she offered expert tuition in piano and vocal coaching. He searched the Electoral Roll and Phone Book and got two more hits. A 'Fiona Jenkins' lived on Alan Road, Withington – less than a mile from Camilla's flat. She was unmarried and fifty-years-old.

Jack's gaze returned to the website photo. It had clearly been taken a fair few years ago. Fiona looked to be in her mid-thirties at most in it. Did the killer only know Fiona from the photo? Or had they seen her in the flesh? If so, why were they deviating from their MO of targeting victims in their twenties and thirties? And how had they found her? Did they have a professional interest in music? Or perhaps Camilla had a connection to Harmony Music Manchester. He searched Harmony Music's website, but found nothing that answered his questions.

He brought up a Google Earth image of where Fiona lived – big Victorian house that had been converted into flats on a busy road where no one would pay attention to a stranger hanging around.

His troubled gaze lingered on Fiona's phone number. Should he warn her? He'd chosen one of the other women, so she didn't seem to be in immediate danger. It occurred to him that if the killer asked him to choose again, he could pick Fiona. And then all he would have to do to catch the killer was lie in wait for them to come after her. *All*. That made it seem simple. It wasn't simple by any means. He would be playing Russian roulette with Fiona's life. No, he couldn't do that without her knowledge and the backup of his colleagues. But that wasn't an option either. The best he could do was an anonymous warning.

He downloaded a 'Voice Changer' app that allowed him to record his voice and play it back. Like the killer, he chose an androgynous voice. He thought about what he should say – he needed to leave Fiona in no doubt of the danger she was in – before speaking into his iPhone. "Hello Fiona. You don't know me, but I know you. I've been watching you like I watched those other women. You might have heard of them. Abigail Hart, Zoe Saunders, Erica Cook, Camilla Winter. They're all dead now. I killed them. And I'll kill you too unless someone stops me. I don't want to kill you, Fiona. But I can't help myself. I need to kill and kill again. The need is getting stronger. I'm not sure I can resist it. Oh god, I need to see blood. I need to smell it. I need it. I need–"

Jack stopped the recording and played it back. It gave him a strange tingle in his head to hear his distorted voice saying the killer's words. He drove west across the city and pulled over at an isolated phone box. He dropped coins into the slot and, pulling his sleeves down over his hands, dialled Fiona. The call went through to an answering service. He was glad. His message was terrifying enough without it being received in the middle of the night. He put his phone to the receiver and pressed play.

The shit would hit the fan when Fiona got his message. She would go to the police and they would put her under protection. Then they would pick the message apart, stakeout her flat, maybe even try to set a trap for the killer using her as bait. What if the killer got wind of it all? How would they react? *There's no point worrying about that now,* Jack said to himself. *You'll deal with that if it comes to it.* The most important thing was that no harm came to Fiona. He'd done what he could for her. Now it was time to turn his attention to his own family.

He drove fast to Laura's house and let himself in with the key she'd given him. Alert to the slightest sound, he crept upstairs. He breathed with relief at the sight of Naomi and Laura sleeping soundly.

After securing the doors and windows, he lay down on the sofa. His body was exhausted, but his mind was too overwrought for sleep. He stared at Fiona's photo. She wasn't as beautiful as Camilla and she was a world away from Rebecca, but still... Those Mediterranean blue eyes. You could drown in them. He'd used to stare into Rebecca's eyes for hours. Sometimes it got to where she would she would say, "Enough, Jack. Stop looking at me."

He ground his knuckles into his forehead. How had life come to this? Not so long ago, he'd had a beautiful wife on one arm and a wonderful daughter on the other. Where had it all gone so wrong? He'd tried to be a good husband and father, but it had counted for nothing. One incomprehensible instant had shattered his world.

You're not going to do this to yourself. You're going to keep your promise to Naomi.

With a shuddering breath, Jack closed his eyes and faced the nightmares once again.

CHAPTER 28

"Morning Daddy."

Jack opened his eyes. He'd been wondering how he would make it through another day of work without falling off the wagon, but at the sight of Naomi all his doubts disappeared. She was smiling – not a carefree smile, but a smile nonetheless. She was already wearing her school uniform.

"I made you breakfast," she said, handing Jack a plate of toast and a mug of tea.

"Thanks, sweetheart." He sat up, rubbing his gritty eyes. "What time is it?"

"It's eight o'clock. Aunt Laura said to let you sleep for as long as possible."

Sleep. The fitful doze he'd eventually dropped into barely seemed to qualify for that term. Naomi watched Jack eat as if she was the parent and he was the child. "Is it OK?" she asked.

"It's delicious."

Naomi's smile broadened. With every kind word and kept promise, she was becoming happier and more secure. Jack's throat was suddenly so tight he couldn't swallow. *Please don't let me let her down again. Please, please...*

Laura came into the room in her nurse's uniform. "Morning, little brother. That was a hell of a long first day."

Jack pushed the toast down with a mouthful of tea. "I'll try to knock off at a more reasonable time today, but you might have to pick Naomi up again."

"That's fine. I'm only doing a half-shift. I saw on the news that they've found–" Laura broke off with a glance at Naomi as if realising what she'd been about to say wasn't suitable for little ears.

Jack nodded to show he knew what she was talking about. "That's why I was up half the night."

"Found what?" asked Naomi.

"Nothing you need worry yourself about," said Jack. He gave his mug back to Naomi. "Can I have another cup of tea please, sweetie?"

Naomi headed for the kitchen. "How close are you to catching whoever's doing it?" asked Laura.

"Not close enough."

"You'll get there."

Jack looked at her doubtfully. "If we catch this scumbag, it won't be down to me. I'm not the copper I used to be, Laura."

"You've only been back one day. Give it time. And don't push yourself too hard. Do you hear?"

Smiling wearily, Jack nodded.

"Good. Now go get yourself in the shower."

A shower and a second cup of tea later, Jack felt ready to face the world. He kept glancing at his phone during the drive to the school. Why hadn't Paul called with news of 'the killer's' message to Fiona? Perhaps Fiona was still asleep. Naomi was chattering on about her school friends. It was good to hear here talking about things girls her age were supposed to talk about. He went through the usual routine – goodbye kiss, watch her into school, look around for anyone suspicious – before heading to HQ.

The Incident Room was busy, but not busy enough to suggest any big new developments. Maybe Fiona had gone to work without listening to her messages. Jack wasn't overly concerned. No news also meant that no fresh bodies had been found.

Emma was still at her desk, scanning through CCTV footage of night-time streets. Her bloodshot eyes told a tale of long fruitless hours of searching. Her desk was littered with the evidence of a raid on the cafe vending machines – chocolate bar wrappers, crisp packets, cardboard cups, cans of energy drink.

"Have you been here all night?" asked Jack.

"Uh-huh."

"Any progress?"

"No."

"Why don't you take a break? Get some breakfast. I'll take over."

The offer wasn't made purely out of generosity. He needed to get back on Emma's good side.

"Thanks, but I'm OK."

Steve strutted into the office as if he was in charge. His moustache twitched. "Bloody hell, it smells like something died in here."

Emma flashed a glare at him. "Something *will* die in here if you don't keep your gob shut."

Steve held up his palms. "Whoa, wrong time of the month?"

"Fu–" Emma started to explode, but checked herself. She turned to Jack. "I've changed my mind. I'll take you up on your offer." She tapped a sheet of paper. "Those are the cameras I've been through."

Jack wafted her towards the door. "Go get some decent food inside you. And don't rush back. I'll let the DCI know the score."

With a tired nod of thanks, Emma left the room. Jack took her seat and perused her notes. She'd trawled through hours of footage from cameras to the west of The Cuban. She'd printed out dozens more images of Mr Averages. Jack flicked through them. His wild-eyed stalker alter-ego was nowhere to be seen.

Paul approached, sipping a super-sized coffee. The bags under his eyes suggested he hadn't got much sleep either. Living in a budget hotel was clearly taking a toll on him. Jack thought about his empty house. Rewind sixteen months and he would have offered Paul a place to stay. Of course, Paul would have had to open up to him about his marital problems first.

"Morning Jack. Where's DI Steele?"

"Getting breakfast. She's been working all night on her Mr Average theory."

"Do you still think Mr Average is a red-herring?"

"I never said he was. I just don't think it's as promising a lead as Emma thinks. I may have found something though." Jack was careful to keep his wording vague, as he continued, "It's a bit random, but I was running number plates caught on camera near The Cuban last Friday and I came up with this."

Jack pulled up Rhys Devonport's missing person file. Paul raised an intrigued eyebrow as he read it. "5'10", stocky, dark hair. I suppose Devonport could be Mr Average, except the doorman says Mr Average is thirty, forty tops. Devonport is too old. It could be that you've stumbled across a lead in a separate case. You'd better give Cheshire Police a call."

"What about Brenda Devonport?"

"By all means speak to her and anyone else of interest."

"I'd like to put eyes on Brenda. Gauge what she's about."

"Fine, but take Emma with you."

"I not sure she's in a fit state."

"The fresh air will do her good. Besides, Jack, you're not ready to be out there on your own."

"I'm fine."

"Are you?" Paul asked with a meaningful look that Jack decoded as: *Have you managed to stay off the sauce?*

"Yes."

"I'll send someone over to Chorlton in case Camilla's neighbours saw the Punto or anyone fitting Devonport's description."

Jack was relieved Paul hadn't asked him to undertake that particular task. There was as much chance that Camilla's neighbours had seen him hanging around as Devonport. Paul gave him a keep-up-the-good-work pat on the back. Then he continued on his way around the room, chatting with other team members. Jack watched him, reflecting that Paul was made for command. He had that essential ability of all good commanders – to be both aloof and caring at the same time.

Jack returned his attention to Rhys Devonport's file. The chief investigating officer was a DS Michelle Coyle. He gave her a call and explained the situation. "This is the first movement on the case in months," she told him. "I was starting to wonder whether Rhys is still with us."

"He may not be. It's not possible to ID him from the footage. Is there anything you can tell me about Rhys that isn't in the file?"

"He's not a well-liked bloke. He fell out with his sister Brenda years ago over something or other. There's no love lost between him and his ex-wife Diane either."

"Have you spoken to Diane?"

"Several times. She's a piece of work. Openly admits she couldn't care less if Rhys is alive or dead. Mind you, you can hardly blame her. According to her, he treated her like shit for twenty years. Mostly just womanising and boozing, but he apparently beat her up when she told him she wanted a divorce. She didn't report the assault."

"Does Rhys have any other exes?"

"Not that I'm aware of. No other living relatives either. No children. Apart from the blokes he drinks with in his local, he's all alone. It's sad really. I'm surprised it only took twelve days for someone to notice he was missing."

"Is it possible Rhys has been bumped off by an angry husband?"

"Anything's possible, but we haven't managed to track down any of the women he had affairs with. The way Diane tells it, they were mostly one night stands in Blackpool. Rhys used to spend a lot of time in Blackpool."

"*Mostly?*"

"She mentioned one woman Rhys may have had a long term-affair with in the eighties, but she didn't have a name for us."

"What about a physical description?"

"Yeah but nothing of any use. White, brunette, thirty-something."

Roughly the same age and hair colour as the victims. The lead had just got more interesting. "What about eye colour?"

"Sorry, I can't remember if Diane said."

"Did you ask Brenda about this woman?"

"Yes. She claims to have no knowledge of her."

Jack caught a note of scepticism in Michelle's voice. "But you don't believe her."

"I wouldn't say that. I just think she knows more than she let on."

"Why would she withhold information that might lead us to Rhys?"

"I got the feeling Brenda disapproves of her brother's lifestyle. I think she'd rather just forget all about him. Like I said, it's a sad case."

They all are, thought Jack.

"Do you really think Rhys could be involved in the murders?" asked Michelle. "He comes across as a real git, but I wouldn't have pegged him as a killer."

Would you peg me as a stalker and a corrupt copper? Jack felt like replying. "My DCI seems to think not, but you know how it is."

Michelle made a noise that indicated she did indeed know how it was – all leads had to be followed up as far as possible, especially in such a serious case. "Well good luck. And call me if you need anything."

Jack thanked her and got off the phone. The conversation had done nothing to sway him either way about Rhys. Plenty of people disappeared off the charts for one reason or another. It was particularly easy for loners like Rhys to do so. Often they resurfaced after weeks, months or even years. Sometimes they were never seen or heard of again. It stood to reason that a man like Rhys would have enemies: wronged women, cuckolded husbands. Perhaps one of them had killed him and left him to rot in a ditch. Or maybe he'd sold his car and taken himself off to live out his final years in Thailand. Jack hoped the latter was the case. Even a 'git' like Rhys didn't deserve to die a violent death.

CHAPTER 29

The morning briefing was a largely negative affair. No potential witnesses had come forward in response to the article in the Evening News about Dale's confrontation with Mr Average. Nothing of real interest had come in to the tip hotline. Nor had Forensics come up with anything significant from Camilla's flat. No connection had been found between Camilla, Dale and the other victims. No one had gone into any local tattooists to get a red rose and cupid tattoo since Erica's murder. No impotent psychopaths had sought help from therapists in the area. There had been no more sightings of the mystery man from The Alchemist. There was one glimmer of positivity. A Mr Harold Yates in the flat above Camilla's had been woken up by banging sometime around midnight on Saturday. He hadn't thought much of it because Camilla and Dale had had something of a stormy relationship. It wasn't uncommon to hear them arguing and throwing things around. Mr Yates's information backed up the coroner's estimated time of death for the victims.

The briefing was breaking up when Emma returned. Her eyes were clearer and the colour was back in her cheeks.

"You're looking more alive," said Jack.

"I feel it, thanks."

Stifling a yawn, she settled back into her seat. "How was the briefing?"

Jack gave her a quick rundown. She cocked an eyebrow when he told her what their day held in store. "I'm with the DCI on this one," she said. "If it wasn't for the mystery brunette, I'd hazard a guess that there's no connection between the Rhys Devonport case and ours."

"I'm not convinced there's a connection either, but it's worth looking into."

"Does Brenda Devonport know we're coming?"

"No and I don't want her to. It's been a few months since she had any contact with Cheshire Police. I want to catch her off guard."

Jack and Emma made their way down to the carpark. "I'll drive," said Emma. "There's something I want to do before we head over to Eccles."

Jack glanced at her curiously. Had she come up with a lead of her own? He doubted it. He'd read her notes. She had nothing. Emma drove south to the A57, then Princess Road. He guessed where they were going. His guess was proved right when they pulled over outside Camilla's flat.

Blue and white police tape was still stretched across the carpark's entrance. Two police vehicles and a bored-looking constable were in-situ. Emma stared at the scene, fingers pressed to her lips. She reminded Jack of himself – not himself now, but the person he'd been before Rebecca died. There was a determination about her that would have put a dog with a bone to shame. Usually he'd have counted himself lucky to work with her. Right then it made him as tense as a compressed spring.

Emma's gaze moved to the cemetery. She got out of the car. Jack smoked a cigarette as he followed her into the cemetery. It gave him an eerie feeling being there, like returning to somewhere familiar yet alien. He was careful not to look at the altar tomb where he'd spent several drunken days and nights. But he couldn't stop himself from looking at Camilla's bedroom window and picturing her sat there brushing her coal-black hair. Emma meandered back and forth, examining graves as if their occupants could tell her what she wanted to know.

"What are you hoping to find?" asked Jack. "This entire area's already been checked out."

Instead of replying, Emma approached the altar tomb and ran a hand across its spires and arches. She stooped to peer into the crack that Jack had peered out of at Camilla. Then she moved to sweep aside the ivy that veiled the collapsed wall. Jack's heart was palpitating. Had he left something – a vodka bottle, a cigarette nub – in the tomb? "Anything?"

"No. This would have been a good spot to watch Camilla from, don't you think?"

"Yes," Jack reluctantly agreed.

Emma got on her phone to Forensics and requested that the altar tomb be checked over inside and out.

Jack ground his teeth. The tomb was made of rough, friable stone. The chances of usable latents being recovered were slim. There was a good chance, though, that he might have left behind clothing fibres and hair fragments. The clothes weren't a problem. He could get rid of them. But if brown hair was recovered, it would lend further credence to Emma's Mr Average theory.

They waited for Forensics to arrive, then returned to the car. Emma put Brenda Devonport's address into the Satnav. The tinny voice led them to a rough and ready area of terraced houses, local shops, chippies, pizza takeaways, Indian restaurants and pubs.

Next stop was a kerb adjacent to a small park. Some kids were kicking a ball around. A pair of scruffy blokes were sharing a bottle of something on a bench. Jack grimaced, thinking about how many hours he'd spent pissing his life away.

They made their way through the park. Its far side was overlooked by a row of redbrick, bay-windowed terraced houses that matched the name of the street: 'Pleasant Road'. Trees stretched their branches over the park railings, dappling the street with shadows.

"No silver Punto," said Emma, scanning the cars parked outside the houses.

Jack peered around a tree at a paunchy man in his sixties or early seventies who was pottering about in a front yard, pulling up weeds and watering flowers – not Rhys Devonport unless he'd lost his hair and shrunk several inches. Net curtains veiled the house's front windows.

A woman of a similar age to the man soon emerged from the house – tanned face, glasses, black bob, frumpy shorts and t-shirt, and a distinct resemblance to Rhys. Brenda handed the man a mug. She looked harmless. Although that didn't mean she *was* harmless.

Taking a leaf out of the killer's book, Jack deactivated the caller ID on his iPhone. Then he messaged Brenda, 'Hello'. She took a phone out of her short's pocket, looked it and showed it to the man. He said something and she shrugged. She tapped at her phone. Jack's phone buzzed as a reply came through.

'Who is this?'

'It's me.' responded Jack.

Brenda spoke to the man again. Now it was his turn to shrug. She sent another message, 'Is this Rhys?'

She'd taken the bait. Jack didn't reply. Brenda stared expectantly at her phone. After a minute or two, she messaged him again, 'Where are you? Are you OK?'

So Brenda had been telling the truth – she wasn't in contact with her brother. This time Jack replied, 'Sorry. Think I sent this to the wrong number.' He didn't want to give Brenda false hope.

Brenda's companion gestured as if to say, *I told you.* Pocketing her phone, she squatted down to help weed the flagstones.

"That was a crafty little trick," Emma commented in a tone that suggested she wasn't sure whether she approved.

They headed back to the car and drove round to Brenda's house. Her companion had disappeared off somewhere. She was pruning a rose bush. She frowned when the detectives showed their warrant cards.

"We're here about your brother," said Jack.

"Well that's some coincidence." Brenda's accent was working-class Mancunian. "Just minutes ago I got some odd text messages that I thought were from Rhys, but it turned out they'd been sent to the wrong number. Do you want to see them?"

"I don't think that's necessary, Miss Devonport," said Jack. "It sounds innocent enough. Can we speak inside?"

Brenda led them along a narrow hallway into a living-room that looked as if it hadn't been updated since the seventies – brown three-piece suite, faded curtains, sworled carpet. A crucifix hung on the wall above a gas-fire.

"We have new information about Rhys," began Jack. "Last Friday his car was picked up by CCTV on Peter Street in Manchester city centre."

Brenda put a hand to her heart as if to calm it. "He's alive."

"I'm afraid we haven't been able to identify the driver. Do you have any idea why Rhys might have been there?"

"No."

"Does he know anyone who lives or works in that area? Or does he have a favourite pub or restaurant thereabouts?"

"I couldn't tell you. I've said this before and I'll say it again, I've had no contact with Rhys in years. The last I heard he was living on his own in Chester." Brenda sighed as if saddened by her words.

"Why don't you keep in contact?" asked Emma.

The sadness spread to Brenda's watery brown eyes. "We're very different Rhys and I."

"In what way?"

"Are you religious?"

"No."

Brenda looked at Jack. "What about you?"

He hesitated to reply. Religion wasn't a subject he'd been comfortable with since Rebecca's death. Part of him wanted to believe what the vicar had said at her funeral – that there was a light beyond life. But when he thought about death all he saw was darkness. "Not particularly."

"Neither is Rhys. He thought he could do as he pleased and there would be no punishment. But sinners are always punished. God makes sure of that, in this life or the next. Rhys never once visited our mum in hospital after she had her stroke? Said he couldn't handle it, but in truth he just couldn't be bothered. That was the last straw for Mum. She just gave up. I hardly spoke to Rhys for years after Mum died. Then, after what he did to Diane, well..." Brenda trailed off with a shake of her head.

"You mean the boozing and one night stands," Jack stated flatly. Brenda's words had needled him. *Sinners are always punished*. Bollocks! More times than he cared to remember, he'd watched helplessly as criminals – thieves, rapists, even murderers – walked free on technicalities. Where had God been then? Never mind the next life. What about this one? What about right fucking now? If sinners were always punished, why weren't good people always rewarded? Where had trying to do the right thing got him? What had he done to deserve this waking nightmare?

"Yes." Brenda's voice had a frosty edge that warned Jack to get his emotions under control.

"Did Rhys ever talk about the women he had affairs with?"

"Rhys knew better than to talk to me about that part of his life."

"I know this is difficult for you, Miss Devonport, but anything you could tell us would be a big help. We're particularly interested in a brunette he might have had an affair with in the eighties... White... Thirtyish."

Brenda pursed her lips and pushed at her glasses. Jack and Emma exchanged a glance that verified their thoughts were on the same page – *She knows something.* "The only woman I remember him with other than Diane was a blonde," said Brenda. "I bumped into them in a restaurant in the city centre. Don't ask me the name of the place because I don't remember. This would be in about '84 or '85. Do you know what Rhys did? He introduced me to her bold-as-brass. He was shameless. I gave him a piece of my mind. Told him Mum and Dad would be turning in their graves."

"What was her name?"

Brenda was silent another moment, then said, "Helen something or other." She looked at the floor as if ashamed. "When I saw Rhys in that restaurant, he was smiling and laughing like he was the happiest man in there. But I could tell it was an act. I knew he needed my help, but I told myself there was nothing I could do for him. Truth is, I wanted him to suffer for everything he'd done. So now Rhys is missing and I pray for forgiveness every night for forsaking him."

Smiling and laughing like he was the happiest man in there. But I could tell it was an act... Those words cut Jack even more deeply than Brenda's spiel about sinners always being punished. He found himself thinking about the way Rebecca had smiled when he got down on one knee and proposed to her – like he'd made her the happiest woman in the world. Had *that* been an act?

He felt no more irritation towards Brenda. Only sympathy. He'd been willing to sacrifice just about everything to help Rebecca, but since her death he'd spent many days and nights trapped in an iron grip of shame. He couldn't imagine how much worse it would have been if he'd turned his back on her.

"Can you remember anything else about this Helen?" asked Emma.

"Only that she looked about the same age as Rhys."

Jack did a quick mental calculation. Rhys would have been thirty-two or thirty-three-years-old at the time. "Helen could be our mystery brunette," he said to Emma. "Bottle of hair-dye. Hey presto."

"Do you think Rhys might be with this woman?" asked Brenda.

"They could have rekindled their relationship."

Brenda's forehead creased as if she was unsure what she thought of the possibility. "But why would he take himself off like that without telling anyone?"

"People do that kind of thing all the time. Even people with families of their own. They walk out the door one day and are never seen again." A lump formed in Jack's throat. He changed the subject. "As I understand it, you and Rhys grew up in Wythenshawe."

"That's right. Mum and Dad had a bungalow on Sale Road."

"I'm not very familiar with the area. Is that anywhere near Greenbrow Road?"

"Yes. We used to walk along Greenbrow Road to get to school."

Jack exchanged another glance with Emma. Once again, he could see his thoughts mirrored in her eyes. Either Roger or Stacy Cook could have lived on Greenbrow Road back then, possibly in the same house as now. People often inherited the house they'd grown up in.

"What school did Rhys go to?" asked Emma.

"Newell Green Highschool."

"Rhys is sixty-four, so he would have been there from... 1964 to '68. Give or take a year."

"That sounds about right."

"Assuming they went to the same school as him, Roger would have been there from approximately 1970 to '74 and Stacy from 1972 to '76," put in Jack.

"Who are Roger and Stacy?" asked Brenda.

Jack showed her a photo of Erica flanked by her parents. All three were smiling. Not deliriously happy smiles. Just ordinary, everyday smiles. What he wouldn't have given to be able to smile like that. "That's Roger and Stacy Cook of Greenbrow Road, Wythenshawe. Do you recognise them?"

"No."

Jack showed Brenda a photo of the man from The Alchemist. "What about him?"

She shook her head. "What have these people got to do with Rhys?"

"Possibly nothing."

"Did Rhys have an affair with this Stacy Cook?"

"I'm sorry, but we can't discuss those kinds of details. Well I think that's everything." Jack looked at Emma. She gave him a nod to indicate she had no more questions.

Brenda followed them to the front door. "Hopefully we'll have more to tell you soon," said Jack.

"My brother's not a bad man," she said. "He just lost his way. We all lose our way sometimes, don't we?"

With a quick nod, Jack turned and made for the car. That lump was back in his throat.

CHAPTER 30

"What do you think?" Emma asked as they drove away from Brenda's house.

"I think she's telling the truth," said Jack.

"Me too."

"Do you reckon this 'Helen' could be Stacy Cook?"

"Possibly, although an eight years age gap is a bit much for her to have looked the same age as Rhys."

"OK, so where to now?"

Jack gave Emma the address for Diane's Beauty Salon in Disley. The Satnav directed them south west along the M60. "Maybe Helen is an old friend of Rhys's," suggested Emma. "Could be someone he went to school with. Have a look online. All my old school class photos are on Facebook. I'll bet it's the same with Newell Green."

Jack Googled 'Newell Green High School 1964-68'. He followed a link to a list of notable alumni, but found nothing of interest. He tried 'Newell Green High School past pupils'. "You're right."

There was a Facebook page with a mixture of black-and-white and colour class photos. He found one listed as taken some time between '1965 and 1968'. It had been posted by a 'Simon Kemp'. The pupils looked about thirteen or fourteen-years-old. They were lined up in four ascending rows. Those at the front were sitting cross-legged on the floor. The next row was sitting on chairs. The third and fourth were standing. The boys were wearing smart blazers, shirts, ties and shorts. The girls were wearing buttoned-up cardigans and knee-length pleated skirts. Several of the pupils had been tagged with their names – Doreen Simmons, Alan Cooper, Janet Mills, Tommy Bishop, Helen Bancroft. Others had been identified in the comments. The boys in the front row were named from left to right as 'Neil Monk, Graham Thomas and Rhys Devonport'.

Rhys's wavy hair was swept back in the same style he'd worn it at the time of his disappearance. He was looking into the camera with a lazy-eyed, louche smile. Not the callow grin of an early teenage boy.

The boys in the other rows – including Simon Kemp – were also identified, but no more of the girls. Simon Kemp had commented that he'd tagged all the girls he remembered. Jack could think of someone who might know the names of the other girls, particularly those Rhys was friends with – Brenda.

Jack showed Emma the photo. He pointed out Rhys, then pointed to a pretty girl with big eyes that peered from under a straight blonde fringe in the row behind. "Her name's Helen Bancroft."

Emma chuckled as if she couldn't quite believe they'd got a hit.

Jack flipped open their Toughbook mobile data terminal and searched the PNC databases for Helen Bancroft. It didn't take long to find a likely candidate. "Helen Bancroft-Harding, born July 1953, deceased November 2005," he read out. "Helen lived in Wilmslow. Where's that?"

"It's a village a few miles south of Wythenshawe."

"Her widower, a Lawrence Bancroft-Harding, still lives at the same address."

"Give him a call. But tread lightly. Assuming Helen Bancroft-Harding is the same blonde Brenda saw Rhys with and assuming she was married, there's a good chance they were having an affair. Lawrence might not know about it. Imagine the effect finding out could have on him?"

Jack thought about Rebecca. If he found out she'd been having an affair, would it make her death harder or easier to bear? *It's pointless asking yourself such things. Paul was right, Rebecca would never have done that to you.*

He dialled Lawrence's home number. No answer. There was a mobile number. He tried it. A man picked up and said, "Hello?"

"Is this Mr Lawrence Bancroft-Harding?"

"Yes. Who's this?" Neutral middle-class accent. Lawrence's voice was slightly raised to make himself heard over traffic in the background.

"This is Detective Inspector Jack Anderson of Greater Manchester Police."

"Oh right... erm. What's this about?" The question was curious, not nervous. Lawrence didn't sound like a man with anything to hide.

"I'm searching for information about someone who may have been acquainted with your wife."

"Helen died in 2005." There was a little hitch in Lawrence's voice. "Cancer."

Jack felt a pang of empathy. He knew what it was like to nurse someone through a terminal illness. Many people didn't consider depression to be a real disease. They thought depressed people were merely sad. But feeling sad didn't make you roll around sobbing in agony. It didn't leave you too fatigued to lift a hand. "I'm aware of that. I'm hoping you can help me."

"Ask away. I'll do my best."

"Am I right in thinking your wife attended Newall Green High School in the mid-1960s?"

"You are."

"The man I'm trying to trace was in the same school year as Helen. His name is Rhys Devonport. Is that name–"

Click. The line went dead. "He hung up."

Emma arched an eyebrow. "I'd say that's a yes on both scores. Helen Bancroft-Harding was the woman Brenda saw Rhys with and Lawrence knows about the affair."

Jack tried phoning Lawrence back. No answer. He left a message, "I appreciate this is a difficult subject, Mr Bancroft-Harding. However, I do need to discuss this matter with you as part of an ongoing investigation. Please call me back on this number as soon as possible."

"Do you want to detour to Wilmslow?"

"No. I don't think Lawrence is at home. I'll give Brenda a call. See what she has to say." Jack dialled Brenda, remembering at the last second to reactivate caller ID. "Do you have internet access?" he asked her.

"Yes."

"Do me a favour, go on line. I'm going to direct you to a photo."

"Just a moment... OK, go ahead."

Jack told Brenda where to find the Newall Green High School photo. "The girl in the second row, third from the right is Helen Bancroft. Could she be the same person you saw Rhys with in the restaurant?"

"I couldn't say. I was a few years ahead of Rhys at school. Our paths rarely crossed and he didn't bring girls home at that age. Our parents wouldn't have allowed it."

"What about the other girls? Do you recognise any of them?"

"I'm not sure. It was over fifty years ago. Let me have a think about it and I'll call you if anything comes back to me."

Jack thanked Brenda and got off the phone. He shook his head in response to a glance from Emma. "Oh well, it was worth a go," she said.

CHAPTER 31

A few miles away from Disley, the urban landscape opened out into rolling fields speckled with pockets of woodland. Disley's outskirts consisted of detached houses set well back from the road. The centre of the village was a busy crossroads overlooked by stone terraced houses, a bank, several small shops and a pub.

Diane's Beauty Salon was just off the main road. The name was emblazoned in pink above images of slim women with too-perfect hair, teeth and skin. Diane was sitting behind the reception counter, doing her nails and looking bored. She smiled at Jack and Emma as they entered the salon. The smile disappeared when they flashed their warrant cards.

"Have you found him? Is he dead?" Diane asked. She was well-spoken but with a telltale hint of Moss Side. There was no concern in her voice. She almost seemed hopeful.

"Rhys is still missing," said Jack. "We're concerned for his welfare."

Diane gave a snort. "If anyone knows how to look after himself, it's *that* man."

"We'd like to ask you a few questions," said Emma.

Diane looked at her as if she was something she'd just scrapped off the soles of her high-heels. "What? Now?"

"If it's convenient."

"Well no it's not actually. I don't know what you expect me to tell you that I didn't tell that other copper. I can't remember her name?"

"DS Michelle Coyle," said Jack.

"Yeah, that's her."

"We're sorry for the disturbance, Mrs King, but it would be a great help if you could spare a few minutes."

Diane huffed resignedly. "I wasted twenty one years of my life on that man, so I don't suppose a few more minutes matters."

"We may ask questions you've been asked before, but please try to answer them as fully as possible."

"Yeah, yeah, just get on with it will you?"

"When were you last in contact with Rhys?"

"A long time ago. Not long enough though. I think it was when our Decree Absolute came through in 2000."

"Sounds like the divorce wasn't amicable," said Emma.

Another snort. "It was like World War bloody Three."

"Why did your marriage break down?" asked Jack.

"Because that man is a cheating piece of shit. He stuck his disgusting little thing in more holes than a porn star during our marriage. So you know what, I decided it was my turn to have a bite of the cake. And as luck would have it, I met the love of my life. When I told Rhys I was leaving him for Stan, he beat me black and blue then legged it to Blackpool. I've still got the scar where the bastard split my head open."

"Did he physically abuse you throughout your marriage?"

"No."

"Would you say he had an alcohol problem?"

"He was a heavy drinker, but not an alchy. He's too in love with his looks to ruin them with drink."

"Can you give us the names of the women he had affairs with?"

"There were several who used to come in his shop that I'm sure he was knocking off. One had a posh name." Diane paused as if trying to summon up the name, then continued, "I've got a terrible memory for names."

"Was it Helen Bancroft-Harding?" asked Emma.

Diane thought for a moment, then shook her head. "Although he probably shagged her 'n all, whoever she is. He used to travel all over on buying trips. He was often away all week. When he came home, I'd find things in his pockets – receipts for flowers and jewellery. His clothes would stink of other women. Sometimes there was even lipstick on them. He didn't care you see. He was brazen about it. He thought as long as he kept bringing good money in, I'd turn a blind eye. And he was right. But then I found out that business wasn't as good as he'd led me to believe. In fact, we were in debt up to our eyeballs."

"So you didn't leave Rhys because you met another man?"

"Did I say I did? I loved Stan to bits, but he wasn't exactly rolling in cash. I'd got used to a certain way of life. Big house, flash cars, five star hotels. I wasn't about to give all that up. I grew up in Cheetham Hill. Probably would have spent my whole life there if it wasn't for Rhys."

For the first time, Jack detected a trace of fondness for her ex in Diane's tone. Cheetham Hill – aka the 'Counterfeit Capital' of the UK – had a reputation as one of the roughest areas of Manchester. "How did you meet Rhys?"

"I used to work in a salon on Cheetham Hill Road. Rhys came in for a manicure one day. He was a vain prick. Thought he was god's gift. Had all the chat-up lines and liked to flash his cash. I knew he was a womaniser, but he promised me I'd never have to work again. That was good enough for me. But then the prick ploughed all his money into a load of bad investments. And now I'm back doing nails. I suppose that's what I get for being a gold-digger." There was no shame in Diane's voice, just matter-of-fact contempt – whether for herself, Rhys or both of them, Jack couldn't tell.

"What business was Rhys in?"

"Antiques. He owned a shop and auction house called 'Devonport's Antiques Shop and Auction House'." She laughed – not a soft chuckle, but what sounded like a smoker's laugh. "Rhys didn't have much of an imagination, but he had a good nose for business. He could sniff out a bargain from across a crowded room."

"What were these 'bad investments' you mentioned?"

"Oh I don't know. Dodgy stocks and shares and all that crap. We lost everything – the business, the house, the cars, the villa on the Costa Blanca."

"And that's when you told him about Stan?"

"Yup. Is this gonna take much longer?"

"We're almost done. Can you think of anywhere Rhys might be? A favourite place where he used to go."

"He always loved Blackpool." By way of explanation, Diane added, "Full of cheap tarts, isn't it."

"Did he used to stay anywhere in particular in Blackpool?"

"No. Any old slag's bed would do."

"Have you ever had black hair?"

A look of bemused irritation came over Diane. "What sort of question is that?"

"Please just answer the question."

"I've had black hair, brown hair, red hair, every single bloody hair colour there is going," snapped Diane. Her over-plucked eyebrows angled into a thoughtful V. "I'll tell you who had black hair. Her Ladyship."

"Who?"

"The posh bitch whose name I can't remember. That's what I used to call her. She used to come into Rhys's shop back in the early eighties."

"Early eighties as in what? Eighty one, eighty two?"

"More like eighty three or four. Not long after me and Rhys got married. She was very classy, nice clothes, good body. And she had money too. She bought some expensive pieces. Rhys was always nice to her, but he kept a professional distance. And that made me suspicious. You see, he's one of those blokes who can't help but turn on the charm with good looking women. You know the type, a schmoozer, always trying to cop a sly feel. But with her he was different. He almost seemed in awe of her. I remember winding him up about it. I'd say, 'Has Her Ladyship been in today? I hope you remembered to bow.' It used to get him proper angry and we'd have these blazing rows about her." Diane smiled crookedly at the memory.

"Do you remember anything else about her?"

"Yeah, she had these amazing blue eyes. I fucking hated those eyes."

Jack and Emma looked at each other. Was this it? Was 'Her Ladyship' the link they were searching for?

"I want you to have another go at remembering Her Ladyship's name," said Jack. "Take your time."

Diane closed her eyes. After a minute, she shook her head. "I can't remember it for the life of me. Thing is, it got the point where it was easier to block all that crap out. Funnily, I *can* remember the two priciest pieces she bought."

Jack fished out a pen and paper. "Go on."

"There was a mahogany display cabinet. It had three or four glass doors. Cost about £10,000. Serious money back then. The other thing was a sapphire ring, blue like Her Ladyship's eyes and surrounded by dozens of little diamonds. It took my breath away. It was absolutely gorgeous and had a price tag to match: £25,000. I was mad jealous at the thought of Her Ladyship swanning around with it on like she owned the world. Thinking back on it, I wouldn't be surprised if Rhys gave her the cabinet and ring as presents. The bitch might have cost him his business as well as his marriage."

"You had no proof that Rhys was having an affair with this woman?"

"No, but he was. Rhys always had to have the upper hand in our marriage. But with her I think it was the other way around. She was the one pulling the strings. Rhys would probably have left me for her if she hadn't already had a ring on her finger."

"She was married?"

"Of course she was. Where else would she have got money like that from?"

"Maybe she worked for it."

Diane let out a sharp laugh. "That woman never worked a day in her life. I deal with women like her all the time: spoilt wives with nothing better to do than get facials and go shopping with their husband's bank cards."

"Do you know where Her Ladyship lived?"

"No."

"What about invoices or receipts from the business? Did Rhys hold onto them?"

"All that stuff was binned years ago. Anyway, Rhys wasn't big on paying tax. A lot of business was done cash in hand, under the counter." Diane added, "I didn't know about any of that until things went tits up."

Jack's expression made it clear he couldn't care less about tax avoidance. "How old would you say Her Ladyship was back then?"

"Early thirties. Something like that."

"And her name definitely wasn't Helen Bancroft-Harding?"

"I didn't say definitely."

"What about Stacy Cook?"

"I said she had a posh name. Stacy Cook isn't a posh name."

Another name sprang into Jack's mind. "Lilith Winter."

Diane's eyebrows angled downwards again. "Lilith Winter," she repeated. "Now that name does seem familiar."

"Could that be the name? Could Lilith Winter be Her Ladyship?" pushed Jack.

"I..." Diane's eyes widened in realisation. "I know where I've heard it. She's the mum of that opera singer who was killed."

"But that's not the only place you remember it from, is it? You remember it from when Lilith used to come into Rhys's shop."

"Jack," Emma said in a cautionary tone. To Diane, she added, "Excuse us a moment, Mrs King."

Jack followed Emma outside. "You're leading her," she said to him.

"It's got to be Lilith," said Jack. "Think about it. Stacy Cook is a fifty-six-year-old cashier from Wythenshawe. Her husband Roger is a bus driver. They're not exactly the type to spend thousands on antique furniture and jewellery. On top of which, she would have only been twenty-two or three at the time. Ellen Saunders is fifty-six-year-old Preston housewife. Greg Saunders is a prison counsellor. Same deal as Stacy. And Suzanne Hart is a fifty-one-year-old PE teacher. She would have only been seventeen or eighteen in '82. Now think about Lilith. She's sixty-four."

"Which makes her the right age to be Her Ladyship," conceded Emma.

Jack nodded. "And think about her house. It's full of antiques. Did you notice if she was wearing any rings?"

"No."

"We've got to go there and find out."

Emma considered the suggestion, then nodded. "OK, let's do it."

As they went back into the salon, Diane asked, "Do you think Rhys might have something to do with those murders? Is that what this is about?"

Jack reeled out the same line he'd given Brenda. "I'm sorry, but we can't discuss the details of an ongoing investigation."

"Well if you do, you're barking up the wrong tree."

"Why do you say that?" asked Emma.

Diane's glistening pink lips curled contemptuously. "He hasn't got it in him to do something like that. His mum Joan used to call him soft lad. She was right. Apart from that one time when I told him about Stan, he was all this." She made a talk-talk-talk signal that brought Dale to Jack's mind. Was that where Camilla's attraction to Dale had stemmed from? "Joan and Ken – Rhys's dad – had a lovely bungalow on Sale Road," went on Diane. "It was on a corner with a magnolia tree outside. They were lovely people. Spoilt

Rhys rotten. He wouldn't have lasted five minutes in the shithole where I grew up." Her lips softened into a sigh. "Ken was killed in '82. Car crash. The shock was too much for Joan. She had a stroke. She only lasted a month or two after that. Now they had true love. Like me and my Stan. I often say to Stan, I hope I die before you."

Jack was instantly back with Rebecca. She'd said similar things to him. Only instead of 'hope' she'd used the word 'know'. *How can you possibly know something like that?* he would ask. To which she would reply, *I just do.* At those times her eyes would glaze over with a kind of frightened acceptance as if she was watching the future rushing towards her like an avalanche.

He wrenched himself into the present. "What happened to the bungalow? Did Rhys and Brenda sell it?"

"Rhys bought out Brenda's share. It stood empty for years. I think Rhys used it as somewhere to shack up with his tarts. He sold it at auction in '98. Got a lot less than he would have done if he'd put it up with an estate agent. He must have needed money fast."

"Do you know who bought it?"

"No."

"This is an awkward question, but why didn't you and Rhys start a family?"

"What's that got to do with anything?"

"I wondered if Rhys had fertility problems."

An old sadness clouded Diane's face. "No he didn't."

Jack understood the reason behind her expression – she was the one with fertility problems. He didn't press for further details. "Did Rhys have children from other relationships?"

"Not as far as I'm aware, but it wouldn't surprise me." Diane looked at her lap. The last two questions seemed to have knocked the wind out of her.

Jack gave her his number. "If you remember Her Ladyship's name, give me a call."

"I wouldn't hold your breath. Rhys used to say my brain was as useless as other parts of my body."

"Well name or no name, you've been a big help to us."

Diane gave Jack a faint smile that suggested her hard exterior concealed something softer.

"We'll call you if–" Emma started to say.

Diane's smile disappeared. "Don't bother."

Jack glanced back as they left the salon. Diane had resumed filing her nails. There was no trace of sadness on her heavily made-up face. *How does she do it?* he wondered with a kind of awe. *How does anyone do it?*

CHAPTER 32

"Rhys and Diane, a match made in hell," said Emma.

Jack opened his mouth to agree, but closed it without saying anything. His thoughts turned to his own marriage. *What room do you have to judge? Their marriage lasted longer than yours.*

"Next up Lilith Winter," continued Emma. "Apologies for doubting your lead, Jack. The way things are going you'll have this case cracked in time for lunch."

Her tone was jokey, but Jack caught a serious note. She was letting him know that he'd gone a long way to making amends for yesterday's missteps. "*We'll* have it cracked," he corrected. There was an unspoken meaning to his words too: *We're partners. I've got your back.*

Emma gave a little nod of understanding. "What if Lilith's not Her Ladyship?"

"Then we'll get hold of Lawrence Bancroft-Harding. And if he won't speak to us, we'll head over to Sale Road. Maybe Rhys took Her Ladyship there. It's a longshot, but one of his old neighbours might remember seeing them together."

"I hate to be a Doubting Deborah again, but I agree with Diane. From what we know about Rhys, I don't see him being our perp. He's a narcissist for sure. And he's shown some inclination towards violence. But it's a long way from there to killer. If Rhys is the killer, why now? It's seventeen years since his divorce. What set him off?"

"I'm not sure this has got anything to do with his divorce. Even with black hair, Diane would look nothing like the victims." Jack thought about

Diane's fleshy lips, generous curves and earthy brown eyes that were so different to the icy beauty of Camilla or, indeed, Lilith in her younger days. "Also, Diane's in her late fifties. She would have been about twenty when she married Rhys and about forty when they divorced. The killer's victims are all in their late twenties and early thirties."

"That still doesn't explain why Rhys would suddenly go on a murder spree."

"He's alone, getting old, losing his looks. Perhaps he blames Her Ladyship for the way things turned out for him."

"So why not just kill her? Why take it out on strangers? And if Rhys isn't the killer, what's happened to him? And who's driving round in his car?"

This time, Jack had no reply. So many questions. No answers.

They pulled over outside Lilith's house. As on their previous visit, the curtains were drawn in her bedroom window. Jack was struck even more strongly by the sense of faded beauty that hung over the place. It had only been a matter of days since they were last there, but the paintwork somehow looked more cracked and faded. The weeds were taller and thicker. Would Lilith have likewise grown frailer and closer to death?

"How do you want to play this?" asked Emma.

"Let's play it cautious until we've seen either the sapphire ring or the display cabinet. I'll mention Newell Green and see if it gets any–"

Emma's phone interrupted Jack. She put it on loudspeaker and Paul's voice came through. "Are you still in Eccles?" He sounded tense.

"No, sir," replied Emma. "We're in Didsbury."

"What are you doing there? Actually, never mind, I need you to head to Tasle Alley."

"Where's that?"

"City centre. Just off Albert Square." Paul paused almost as if for dramatic effect. "We might have another one on our hands."

An image jumped at Jack of a young woman sitting cross-legged on grass with books at her side. It couldn't be her, could it? *You just saved that girl's life, Jack.* That's what the killer had said. "What does she look like?"

"The call only came in a few minutes ago," said Paul. "A member of the public found a deceased female. That's all I know right now. DI Platts and DS Crawley are en route to the scene too. Call me as soon as you get there."

"Will do, sir," said Emma. She cut the call off and turned on the flashing blue bumper lights. "Looks like Her Ladyship will have to wait."

Traffic pulled over to let them by as they sped towards the city centre. Fifteen minutes later, they arrived at Albert Square – a large cobbled area dominated by the Gothic clock-tower of Manchester Town Hall. A crowd had gathered towards the far side of the square. People were balanced on the rim of a stone fountain, trying to get a better look at what was going on across the road. A constable was stationed at the entrance to Tasle Alley – a narrow backstreet hemmed in by tall buildings. A police car was blocking the north entrance to the square.

They pulled over just beyond a memorial statue of Prince Albert, got out and approached the constable. He stood aside as they displayed their IDs. "In the bushes to the left of the tree," he said, pointing to a brick wall with thick bushes behind it. "It's not a pretty sight," he warned.

"Who found the victim?" asked Emma.

"Some homeless guy. He's in the car."

"We'll have a look at the body, then we'll speak to him."

The wall grew from shoulder to head height as it progressed along the alleyway. On the far side of it and the bushes was a gated carpark at the rear of a seven-storey modern, brick building. There was a second constable at the opposite end of the otherwise deserted alleyway.

"Looks like we've beaten Steve and Gary to it," Emma said with more than a hint of *Ha! Screw you.*

The right-hand side of the alleyway was walled-in by a row of four, five and six-storey brick and stone buildings that appeared to have been haphazardly joined together. Steel bars were bolted over their basement and ground floor windows. There were several windowless, graffiti-scarred doors that could only be opened from the inside. Jack pointed to flattened sections of cardboard in one recessed doorway. "Looks like rough-sleepers use these doorways."

Across the alleyway a spindly tree angled rightwards, stretching for a patch of sunlight. Fresh green leaves were scattered across the pavement as if someone had clutched at the bushes to haul themselves over the wall. Emma pointed to several oily black-red smears on the flagstones. "Someone lost a lot of blood here."

She stepped around the blood and rose onto her tiptoes. Jack hung back. The image of the cross-legged girl – the girl he'd picked to be the next victim – filled his mind. *Please don't let it be her...*

Emma puffed her cheeks. "He was right. Not pretty."

Jack didn't want to look, but he forced one foot in front of the other. *Please, please don't let it be her...*

He peered over the wall. The woman was curled up foetally in a bush. Her orange legs were a patchwork of minor cuts and bruises. A white high-heel shoe hung off one foot. The other was bare. Her skin-tight pink miniskirt was torn and bloodstained. It had been pushed up over her hips, exposing faeces-stained buttocks. She wasn't wearing underwear. One large breast hung over a lacy bra. Her hands rested on it as if they'd been posed. There was blood on her long fingernails – her killer's blood? Her head was flung back. She looked as if she'd done twelve rounds with a heavyweight: eyelids swollen shut, lips pulped, nose crushed. There was a deep indent where her skull had been caved in by what must have been a horrifically powerful blow. Her hair – her light brown, blonde highlighted hair – was matted with gore.

Relief and anger surged up inside Jack. It wasn't the cross-legged girl. Not unless she'd got a fake tan, a boob job, put on twenty or thirty pounds and dyed her hair. But it was still a young woman whose life had been brutally cut short.

"Blunt trauma wounds to the head and face," observed Emma. "I can't see any knife wounds."

"Me neither. Doesn't look like she's been dead all that long. She may have been posed post-mortem. But if she was, it's different to the others and she wasn't left in plain sight." Jack pointed to the bloodstained pavement. "She probably died there sometime last night, then the killer made a half-hearted attempt to conceal her body. The Town Hall's only a few hundred metres away. There must be lots of CCTV cameras around here. Very high risk. Obviously this woman's hair is a different colour to the other victims."

"So you don't think she was killed by our perp."

"I didn't say that. Perhaps the killer decided to try their hand at something different. Spice things up. Or perhaps it was just circumstance, opportunity. This woman could have been drunk, already collapsed on the pavement and the killer thought, *What the hell, easy mark.*"

What Jack said was true enough. It was dangerous to discount a link based on changes in the MO alone. Perhaps this was the killer moving into a new phase of their evolution. Alternatively, perhaps someone had clumsily tried to pass off this woman's murder as the work of the serial killer.

They left the alleyway. More uniformed officers had arrived. The south end of the square was blocked off too now. There was still no sign of Steve and Gary. A camera crew was setting up near the Albert Memorial.

The 'homeless guy' was a scrawny, bearded man somewhere in his twenties or thirties – it was often difficult to guess the age of rough-sleepers. A few months on the streets could put years on a face. The man had the hollowed-out features of a junkie. Someone had bought him a coffee, which he cradled in hands that shook either from shock or withdrawal. Emma ducked into the backseat. Jack stooped at the door.

"What's your name?" asked Emma.

"Kieron."

"And where are you from, Kieron?"

"All over." Kieron thumbed towards the alleyway. "I've been kipping there for the last few weeks."

"Did you sleep there last night?"

"No. But I hid my stuff in those bushes. When I went to get it, that's when I saw her."

"What time was that?"

"I dunno. An hour ago or something like that."

"Did you touch the body?"

"No fucking way. She was dead. Nothing I could do to help her."

"Do you know the woman?"

"I don't know nothing about nothing. I just found her."

"Does anyone else sleep in the alleyway?"

"Sometimes. I dunno their names. I keep myself to myself." Kieron sniffed and shivered. "Can I go now please? I've been waiting here ages. I'm starving."

For a fix, thought Jack. This guy clearly wouldn't be much help. What if this woman was the killer's sixth victim? The killer was a watcher. They'd watched Erica Cook. They'd watched Camilla. And Jack was ninety-nine percent certain they'd been watching him. Maybe they were doing so right now. His gaze traversed the crowd. Several scallies were jostling for position at its front. A smartly dressed young couple were holding hands. His eyes passed over them, looking for someone alone. He hesitated on a man in a grey suit: mid-thirties, white, medium height and build, clean-shaven. He was chatting on a phone, laughing. A dickhead, quite possibly. But that didn't make him a murdering psychopath.

Jack scanned over a boisterous contingent of teenagers, a man who had the look of a rough-sleeper, a little old man in a flat-cap, a pair of well-to-do looking ladies. His gaze landed on a face near the back of the crowd. It belonged to a shaven-headed man with a blond beard and hulking shoulders.

Jack did a double-take as if he doubted what he was seeing. No, his eyes weren't deceiving him.

He dropped his gaze back to the car's interior. "Do you want a sandwich or something?" he asked Kieron.

"Yeah, cheese and pickle."

There was a Subway beyond the crossroads at the north side of the square. "Back in a minute."

"Get me one too," Emma said as Jack turned away.

He casually approached a pedestrian-crossing, watching the bearded man out of his peripheral vision. He waited for the green man and sauntered across. Instead of continuing straight on towards Subway, he turned right. He lost sight of his target behind a bronze statue of a man on a marble plinth. He darted back across the road between stationary traffic and peeked around the plinth. A knot formed between his eyebrows. The bearded man was gone. Darting glances all around, he spotted him walking towards the Town Hall. He could hardly have missed him. The man looked like a steroid poster-boy. A tight t-shirt showed off the overdeveloped musculature of his back and heavily tattooed arms. Jack started after him.

The man made his way along Princess Street to the left of the Town Hall. He glanced over his shoulder. His eyes met Jack's for a split-second. They showed no sign of alarm and he continued at the same pace, seemingly unconcerned. Jack didn't buy the act. He closed the distance between himself and the man, overtaking other pedestrians. At the far end of the Town Hall, the man crossed Princess Street and headed into a side-street. He darted another look behind him. This time Jack was close enough to see his eyes widen. As the man jerked his head to the front and broke into a sprint, Jack shouted, "Stop, police!"

The man paid no heed, pumping his arms like a hundred metre runner. Jack gave chase, passing a row of cafes and bars. The man turned a corner. When Jack reached it, he saw that the distance between them had increased. He didn't panic. The man's muscular frame was suited to short bursts of speed, but over longer distances Jack was confident he would have the edge. He'd used to go running several times a week down on the Sussex coast. He just hoped the subsequent months of abusing his body hadn't completely drained his petrol tank. The man dashed across a road, narrowly avoiding being mown down by a Metrolink tram. Jack lost sight of him again.

When the tram had passed, the man was gone. Jack's eyes scoured the streets. The road ahead was deserted except for a few parked cars. To his left, the pavements were speckled with office workers going about their business. To his right, across the tramlines, what looked like a coachload of tourist-types were gathered outside a grand stone building. Steps led up to a Greek-temple style porch fronted by tall Ionic columns. Vertical hanging flags identified the building as 'Manchester Art Gallery'. Was the man hiding amongst the tourists? Had he run into the gallery?

"Shit," Jack hissed. *Which way? Which way?*

He approached the tourists. Out of the corner of an eye, he spotted a figure rising from between the cars parked along the left-hand side of the gallery. It was the bearded man! His impatience had cost him. A few more seconds of hiding and he would have made good his escape.

Jack gave chase again. The man ran like a maniac across a busy crossroads. Jack's lungs were burning. Sweat was running down his face. The object of his pursuit also appeared to be feeling the exertion. The tables had turned. Centimetre by centimetre, Jack was reeling him in. The man darted into an alleyway of barred windows and rusty fire-escapes. Jack focused on regulating his breathing, inhaling into his stomach, feeding his muscles with oxygen.

The man shot him another glance and, seeing that the gap was closing, put on a burst of speed. *That's it you big bastard,* thought Jack, *burn yourself out.* Jack maintained his pace, dropping his shoulders, shaking out his arms.

A sunlight-streaked road. Another shadow-draped alleyway. The man stumbled into a woman, knocking her over. He righted himself and ran on, but his movements were markedly slower. Jack was gaining on him again, not centimetre by centimetre, but metre by metre.

They passed the entrance to a multi-storey carpark near the end of the alleyway. Jack could hear the man's rapid breaths. *Just a few more strides and you're mine.* He dived forwards, tackling his target around the waist. The man went down heavily, his face slapping into the tarmac. Jack attempted to put him in a chokehold. The man tucked his chin, bucked, twisted and thrust his feet into Jack's midriff. Jack reeled backwards into a wheelie bin. The man scrambled to his feet and hunched into a loose boxing stance. Blood was streaming from his nose. He was breathing like a winded bull. But he clearly wasn't about to surrender without a fight.

"You really want to do this?" asked Jack.

The man motioned him forwards. Jack clenched his fists in front of his face, forearms parallel, elbows tucked in to protect his midsection. The man was shorter than him, but a good few stone heavier. Jack had come up against bigger men before. The key was to stay light on your feet, slip their punches, make them chase you, wear them down whilst conserving your own energy. And when they had nothing left in the tank, strike fast and hard.

The man moved in and threw a haymaker. Jack bobbed to the outside of the strike, hooking a punch into his opponent's chin. The man staggered, but didn't go down. Jack danced away from a flurry of punches. Most missed their mark. A couple glanced off his forearms. He circled, waiting for another opening. He darted out a jab and continued to circle. *Stick and move. Stick and move...* He peppered the man with stiff jabs, opening several cuts.

The man's mouth hung open, gulping air. His fists were down by his stomach. Two sure signs that he was almost out on his feet. Now was the moment to move in for the kill. Jack slipped a telegraphed punch and fired off a powerful straight right. With surprising agility, the man evaded it and wrapped his arms around Jack. That was when Jack realised his opponent had been playing possum.

A foot hooked behind Jack's calves, tripping him backwards. The breath whistled out of his lungs as he slammed into the ground with the man on top of him. The alleyway swam in front of Jack's eyes. When it came back into focus, the man was straddling his waist like a schoolyard bully. An elbow that felt as if it had come from the clouds smashed into Jack's forehead. Warm blood flowed into his left eye. Another elbow crashed home, followed by several hammer-fists that Jack partially blocked. The man reached his thick fingers towards Jack's throat.

Move! Jack yelled at himself. *If he gets his hands on your throat you're done for.*

Jack bucked his hips, pitching the man forwards, forcing him to brace his hands against the tarmac. He grabbed the man's right arm with both hands, stepped his right foot over the man's left leg, bridged his hips again and rolled. It was a Brazilian Ju-Jitsu move he'd learnt in self-defence training. He'd done it plenty of times in practice, but never in a real situation. He felt almost as much surprise as relief when, in the blink of an eye, the positions were reversed.

Instead of throwing strikes, Jack went for the eyes with his thumbs. The man screamed and twisted. Jack allowed him to roll over. He cranked the man's head back with his left hand. Sliding his other hand under the man's beard, he grabbed the bicep of his own opposite arm and squeezed like an anaconda. He wasn't trying to constrict the windpipe. He wanted to close the carotid arteries, cut off the blood supply to the brain. That way unconsciousness was guaranteed in seconds.

The man reached back, clawing blindly. Before his fingers could find their target, he went limp. Jack didn't loosen the chokehold. The voices in his head were arguing again. *What if this is the serial killer? If you let him live, he'll destroy you... Not if you get his phone... You can't take that risk. He might have another phone. At the very least, he killed that woman in the alleyway. Why else would he have run? He deserves to die... Maybe, but that's not your choice to make...*

Uncertainty twisted Jack's features out of shape. The man had been unconscious for perhaps thirty seconds. Another thirty and his oxygen-starved brain would suffer irreversible damage. Jack began to count. *Five... Ten...* This would be murder, pure and simple. *Fifteen... Twenty...* He closed his eyes as if to shut out a sight too terrible to look at.

You've got to do it for Naomi... No, Naomi wouldn't want this. She wouldn't want a murderer for a dad... Like an echo of thunder, one word drowned out all the others: *Murderer!*

CHAPTER 33

A shudder wracking his body, Jack released the man. Had he done the right thing? All he knew was that he couldn't have lived with *that* word. He glanced around at the sound of an engine. A car was pulling up at the lower end of the alleyway. He wiped blood and sweat from his eyes. Gary Crawley was in the car's passenger seat!

Jack quickly went through the man's pockets. He found a cheap-looking phone, a set of keys and a wallet. As Gary and Steve got out of the car, Jack put the man into the recovery position whilst surreptitiously pocketing the phone.

Steve's expression was more amused than shocked by the sight of the bloodied, unconscious man. "Holy shit, looks like you've killed King Kong."

"Fuck you," Jack retorted breathlessly.

Steve laughed. "You know what, Jack, I'm starting to like you."

"Bloody hell," exclaimed Gary. "It's the bloke from the CCTV footage. The one who talked to Zoe Saunders in The Alchemist."

Steve took a closer look at the man. "Bugger me, so it is."

Blood dripped from Jack's forehead onto his torn jacket as he rose unsteadily to his feet. "He ran from me."

"We know. We saw you leaving Albert Square. We followed you, but lost you near the art gallery."

As Gary clicked on the handcuffs, the bearded man stirred and slurred out something unintelligible. Another shot of adrenaline flushed through Jack. A rear-naked-choke put people out fast, but they recovered fast too. In a minute or two the man would be conscious and Jack would, potentially, be a few words away from being put in handcuffs himself.

Jack opened the wallet. It contained a driving licence. "Shane Hardy. He lives in Rusholme."

"Only a mile or two from the murders," remarked Steve. "King Kong here could be our boy."

Gary tapped Shane's cheek. "Hey dickhead, what did you think you were doing running from a police officer?"

Shane's bloodshot eyes opened. Jack forgot to breathe as Shane glared at him. Several seconds passed. Shane said nothing.

"I think it's love," teased Steve. "Let's get him on his feet. These lover boys need a trip to the hospital."

"I'm fine," said Jack.

"You need stitches." Steve took a photo of Jack with his phone and showed it to him. There was a cut like an upside down smile over his eyebrow.

Steve and Gary lifted Shane upright. The big man's legs wobbled like jelly as they guided him to the car. Jack ducked into the backseat. Gary handed him a first-aid kit. He pressed a gauze pad to the cut. As they drove out of the city centre, Steve got on the phone and informed Paul of what was going on.

"I'll meet you at the hospital," Paul said over loudspeaker. "This could be the break we've been waiting for. Good work, Jack."

Steve hung up. "Yeah, good work. A bit of old-fashioned police brutality never did anyone any harm."

Jack couldn't tell whether Steve was joking.

Minutes later they were pulling up outside the glass facade of Manchester Royal Infirmary. Shane still hadn't spoken a word. Despite his situation, he appeared calm and inscrutable. *This isn't his first time in the back of a police car,* thought Jack. *This guy knows silence is his best defence.*

A nurse escorted them through the busy A&E waiting-room to the treatment area. A doctor set to work on Jack, injecting a local anaesthetic, stitching the cut and applying a dressing. "I'd like to send you for a skull X-ray," said the doctor.

"Thanks, doctor, but I'll pass."

Grimacing, Jack got off the trolley-bed. He ached all over. Tomorrow morning he really would feel as if he'd wrestled King Kong. The doctor wrote him a prescription for painkillers and gave him a date to return to have the stitches removed. As the doctor left the cubicle, Jack took out Shane's phone and switched it on. 'Enter Passcode' flashed up. He shoved the phone into his pocket as Laura entered in her nurse's uniform. Her mouth formed a tight O. "What happened?"

"I tripped," Jack said, mustering up a crooked smile.

Laura cocked an unamused eyebrow. "Have you ever considered another line of work?"

"You were the one who wanted me to return to work."

"I just want what's best for everyone."

"Yeah, well that makes two of us." Jack heaved a sigh. The next few hours could decide his and Naomi's future. He just had to hope Shane had no incriminating photos or videos stored on another device – that's if he even *was* the killer.

Laura turned as someone entered the cubicle. A faint frown crossed her face at the sight of Paul. They'd met once before. Jack's thoughts went back to that night two years ago. Paul and Natasha had wanted to get the lowdown on Manchester. Jack, Rebecca and Laura had gone to their house for a meal. It had turned out to be an awkward evening. Partly because Paul and Laura's political views were at the opposite ends of the spectrum – they'd butted heads over everything from drug laws to the 2011 riots. But mainly because Rebecca had drunk too much and ended up telling them both to, *Shut the fuck up!* The incident had stuck in Jack's mind because it was so out of character. Rebecca usually wouldn't have said boo to a goose. Later on when they were alone, he'd tried to find out what made her so angry, but he hadn't been able to get a word out of her.

"Hello Laura," said Paul.

Laura returned the greeting politely but coolly. She motioned to Jack. "Shouldn't he be on light duties?"

"This isn't Paul's fault," said Jack. "This is the way I wanted it."

"Well some might say you don't know what's best for yourself."

"I need to speak to Paul."

"You shouldn't be doing any more work today. You should be resting." Laura directed a meaningful glance at Paul.

He returned a strained smile. "Don't worry, I'll look after him."

Laura gave him a look as if to say, *You'd better.* She turned to Jack. "I'm going to call you later and make sure you're following doctor's orders."

Jack gave a mock salute.

Laura said a curt goodbye to Paul and left. He gave a small shake of his head. "Got to say, Jack, your sister puts the wind right up me."

"You're not the only one."

"How's your head?"

"Tip top. Next stupid question."

Paul's lips widened into a more natural smile. "I've just seen the other guy. You're a braver man than me. I wouldn't fancy tangling with him."

"So what do we know about Mr Hardy?"

Paul took out his notepad and read with obvious relish, "Shane Hardy. Thirty-two-years-old. Married to Paige Hardy. Thirty-one-years-old. They have a daughter, Maya, three-years-old. Address: Ashfield Road, Rusholme. Occupation: all round bad boy. Previous convictions: drugs, criminal damage, GBH, arson, burglary. In 2003 Shane spent six months in Forest Bank for arson. In 2006 he graduated to Strangeways for slashing a man's face with a broken bottle. He did two years. After his release, he stayed out of prison for one whole year. In 2009 he did eight months in HMP Risley for cultivating cannabis. In 2011 Shane got himself in trouble yet again. This time for dealing MDMA, Rohypnol and Ketamine in a Bolton nightclub. He did another two year stint. Guess where?"

Paul's question was almost gleeful. There was only one answer that could have got him so excited. "HMP Preston," said Jack.

"Correct. And who works at HMP Preston? None other than Greg Saunders. Zoe's dad. We don't yet know if Greg and Shane came into contact with each other, but even so..." Paul jabbed a finger at his notepad. "This is it Jack. This is the connection we've been looking for."

"Shane's just one of thousands that will have passed through HMP Preston in that period," cautioned Jack.

Paul shook his head. "Shane lives on the south side of Manchester and he was seen talking to Zoe in The Alchemist on the night of her murder. One coincidence I could buy. But three? No way."

Jack had to admit the evidence was damning. The hulking career criminal from Rusholme and the soft-spoken killer appeared to be one and the same person. Something occurred to him. "Have you checked Shane's shoes?"

"No."

"Well..." Jack tailed off meaningfully.

They headed over to a cubicle with two constables outside it. Shane was hunched on the bed, watched over by Steve and Gary. There were several stitches in his busted lip. He looked at Jack and Paul with unreadable eyes.

"Take your trainers off," said Paul.

"What for?" asked Shane.

It was the first time Jack had heard him speak. His was voice was a smoker's growl, his accent was Manchester scally.

"Just do it or we'll do it for you."

Shane kicked off his trainers. Paul retrieved them. Size nines, zigzagging tread pattern, no extra wear on the inner heels. He exchanged a glance with

Jack and the two men retreated out of Shane's hearing. Jack pointed out the obvious. "Those shoes didn't make the footprint in Alexandra Park."

"That doesn't mean Shane isn't our man. All it means is the footprint was probably made by someone out walking their dog."

I'm just calling to find out how my favourite accomplice is doing. Those words of the killer's echoed back to Jack. "Or the killer has an accomplice."

Paul made a doubtful, but not outright dismissive noise. The possibility wasn't inconceivable. Serial killer teams were extremely rare, but not unknown – Brady and Hindley, the Wests... He gave Jack an appraising look. "You should go home."

Home. Jack's stitches pulled tight as he frowned at the word. Where was home? "I have to do my paperwork."

"That can wait."

"What about Shane?"

"I'll deal with him. You've done more than enough to earn the rest of the day off. Besides, your sister will have my head on a platter if I let you work."

"Oh, did you send someone over to Chorlton to speak–"

"Yes," broke in Paul. "No one saw Devonport's Punto. Now that's your lot. Get going."

Jack saw that there was no arguing with Paul. "You'd better call me if there are any developments."

Paul nodded and beckoned Steve over. "Take Jack back to HQ." As Jack turned to leave, Paul added, "Sorry for ever doubting you, Jack."

Jack made no reply. That was the second undeserved apology he'd received that day.

"I had my doubts about you too," Steve said as he and Jack made their way to the car. "I thought you were just another do-gooder, but you're alright."

Jack accepted the damning praise. After all, it was well deserved. Back in the alleyway, he'd come within seconds of making himself a traitor to everything he once believed in.

As they drove away from the hospital, Jack's thoughts returned to Lilith Winter. What could a thug like Shane Hardy have to do with a woman like her? Nothing, that's what. They only lived three or four miles from each other, but they inhabited different worlds. Did that mean the Rhys Devonport case and the murders weren't connected? It came down to one question: was Lilith Her Ladyship? If so, the cases were almost certainly connected. If not, then it was just a matter of waiting and seeing what Shane had to say – or rather, didn't have to say – for himself. The thought of it was enough to make Jack reach for his cigarettes.

"Can I bum one of those?" asked Steve.

Jack gave him a cigarette and they smoked in silence. He gave thanks for small mercies.

His phone rang: 'Laura'. She'd probably discovered that he'd refused to be X-rayed. He didn't have the energy to argue with her. He let the call go through to voicemail.

"Who was that?" asked Steve.

"My sister. She's a nurse at the Royal Infirmary."

"She worries about you, eh?"

"Yeah. A lot."

"You're lucky to have a sister like that. Mine couldn't give a shit about me."

He may be a Neanderthal, but he's right again, thought Jack. What the hell would he do without Laura?

Steve dropped Jack off and said with a grin, "Don't worry about loverboy. I'll keep him nice and warm for you."

CHAPTER 34

Jack headed to his house. The thought of hanging around Laura's place waiting for Paul to call – or perhaps even show up at the door accompanied by a couple of constables – somehow didn't seem right. If the worst came to the worst, Jack wasn't sure how he would react. What if he lost his mind? Started smashing thing or even tried to hurt himself? He didn't want there to be any chance of Naomi or Laura seeing that. Besides, the blows to his head hadn't made him forget that there were things at the house he needed to get rid of.

The house was its usual silent self. Jack stared at the tower of clothes rising from the laundry bin. What had he worn in the tomb? That time was a blur of alcohol. *Just get rid of the whole bloody lot.* He reached for a blue shirt that had been a present from Rebecca. She'd loved to see him in blue. The fabric was soft with wear. He shook his head at the thought of getting rid of the shirt. Underneath it was a t-shirt with a tear in the hem. The sight sparked his memory. He'd snagged it on the iron spikes atop the cemetery gates. Another memory followed hot on that one's heels. He rifled through the pile until he found a pair of jeans. He felt in the pockets and withdrew a cigarette butt stained with lipstick. He put the filter to his nose. It gave off a faint sweet scent. Camilla's scent.

After stuffing the t-shirt, jeans, a jacket and trainers into a plastic bag, he drove towards the edge of the city, dumping each item in separate bins along the way. He couldn't resist but to light Camilla's cigarette and take a deep drag on it, before dropping it down a drain.

Back at the house, Jack had a go at unlocking Shane's phone. He tried Shane, Paige and Maya Hardy's year of birth. No dice. He chanced his arm on a selection of the most obvious four digit passcodes: '1234' '1111' '0000' '1212'. A message flashed up 'The phone is disabled. Try again in one minute.' He waited and tried again with no luck. He knew he should destroy the phone, but couldn't bring himself to do so. If the video and photos the killer had sent were on there, it would not only dispel any doubts about Shane's guilt, but also go a long way to putting his mind at rest about Shane's ability to hurt him.

Jack removed the SIM card in case his colleagues found a way to ping the phone's location. He stared out of a window like a lost child. What now? He could go to see Lilith. He could try to contact Lawrence Bancroft-Harding again. He could have a look at the Sale Road bungalow. Or... Or he could follow doctor's orders. His head was reeling like a boat in a storm. Yes, the best thing for him to do was rest up. But that wasn't the only reason he lay down on the sofa and closed his eyes. Part of him was afraid that if he looked any deeper into the possibility of a connection between Rhys and Lilith, he might actually find one. And unless he could then find a link between Rhys, Lilith and Shane, that meant the killer was still out there. It meant more women might die. It meant his colleagues would have another chance to get to the killer before him. But worst of all, it meant Naomi and Laura wouldn't be beyond the killer's reach.

The minutes ticked interminably by. Rebecca laid siege to Jack's thoughts. The vodka whispered to him, *I'll put a stop to her game.* He kept glancing at his phone, muttering, "Ring, you bastard thing," and then reassuring himself, *No news is good news.*

He snatched up the phone at the ping of an email.

His forehead contracted. 'Lucrezia Moretti. RE: Website Contact'. Finally the maker of the Ugly Mask had replied, but did he even want to know what she had to say? He was half-tempted to delete the email. But if he did so and Shane wasn't the killer and someone else died, it would be on him.

He opened the email. 'Dear Mr Anderson. My apologies for the delay in replying. I've been away on holiday. I was shocked to read your email. I hope the crime didn't involve anyone getting hurt. I assume you want a list of my UK customers. I'm reluctant to provide that information without verifying that you are who you say you are. Could you please send me some identification? Distinti Saluti, Lucrezia Moretti.'

After emailing Lucrezia a scanned copy of his warrant card, Jack fell into a fitful dream about Rebecca. He was trying to kiss her, but she kept turning her face away. On and on it went, for what seemed like hours...

The phone woke him up – 'Paul Gunn'. Was this the moment it all came crashing down? He almost hoped it was. In some ways, it would be a relief. Dry-mouthed, he put the receiver to his ear. "What news?"

"Oh, have I got news for you."

As soon as he heard Paul's upbeat tone, Jack thought, *He doesn't know!*

"Where to start?" continued Paul. "The Tasle Alley woman is Shane's wife, Paige. Well, ex-wife now. And get this, she turfed him out of their house a month ago. Apparently, Shane's a real womaniser. In the words of his mother-in-law, Carole, he'll, 'Shag anything with a pulse.' Carole says Shane was desperate to reconcile with Paige, but Paige wouldn't take him back. She also says Shane threatened to kill Paige, their daughter and himself if Paige didn't change her mind."

"Where's he been living?"

"We think he's been sleeping in his jeep."

Jeep, noted Jack. Not *Fiat Punto*.

"What we do know for sure," said Paul, "is that last night Paige went into the city centre with friends. She became separated from them in the K2 Karaoke Nightclub. That's just around the corner from The Alchemist.

Carole says Paige has been going to K2 once or twice a week since splitting up with Shane."

"Which explains why he was in the area on the night of Zoe's murder."

"Yeah, he couldn't find Paige so he took his anger out on Zoe instead."

"What about Greg Saunders?"

"That's the other bit of news. Shane *did* come into contact with Greg in HMP Preston. And there's something else too." Paul's voice rose for the finale. "At the time Shane was incarcerated there, a photo of Greg's wife and children went missing from his office. It was suspected that a prisoner stole it. Searches were made, but the photo was never recovered."

Surely that was it? The confirmation that Shane *was* the killer. Jack could almost hear the ring of the final nail being hammered into Shane's coffin. Shane had already done four stints inside. His fifth would be his last. There was a question Jack barely dared ask. "What's Shane had to say for himself? Or is he still playing mute?"

"No. He admits to knowing Greg. He even admits to having seen the photo. According to him, every bloke in his cellblock tossed off over Zoe and her mum. He claims he was looking for Paige when he recognised Zoe from the photo. He says he tried it on with her, but she wasn't interested."

"Sounds credible."

"I'd agree if it wasn't for the little matter of Shane murdering his wife four days later."

"Has he admitted it?"

"No, but he will do. He played it careful with Zoe, Abigail, Erica and Camilla. But I think emotion got the better of him with Paige. Mark my words, Jack, we're going to nail him to the wall."

"What about the fact that Paige doesn't look like the other victims?" Jack didn't want to argue against Shane having murdered all five women – he wanted Shane to be guilty and get put way for life – but Paul might sense something was off if he didn't voice doubt. Every angle had to be explored, every detail analysed. That was the essence of the job.

"Her face looks the same as the others to me."

Jack thought about Paige's pulverised face. There was no arguing with the image. "You know what I mean, Paul. She's bigger and she's got different coloured hair."

"According to her mum, Paige is always dying her hair different colours. One week she's a blonde, the next she's a brunette, the next a redhead. And she's got blue eyes. You want to know what I think? Shane killed those other women to throw us off the scent when all the time his real target was Paige."

"Maybe," agreed Jack. *I want you to catch me.* Those words of the killer's suggested another possibility. "Or maybe he couldn't care less about the police. After all, he threatened to kill himself along with his wife and daughter." Jack shuddered. A tiny part of him could relate to Shane's threat. After Rebecca's death there had been a fleeting instant when it flashed through his mind: *Our lives are over. I might as well throw Naomi and myself off the cliffs.*

"By the way, I've been singing your praises to the Super. You could be in line for a commendation."

Jack made an indifferent, "Hmph." There was a time when a commendation would have meant a lot to him. Not anymore.

"Try not to sound too overjoyed."

"Sorry, Paul, I've got a lot on my mind."

Paul sighed. "Tell me about it."

Jack wondered if Paul was referring to his impending divorce. Now hardly seemed like the time to mention it though. "I'll see you tomorrow."

"Don't come in if you don't feel up to it, Jack. And make sure Laura knows I did as I was told."

"You really are scared of her, aren't you?"

"Too bloody right I am."

Smiling thinly, Jack got off the phone. The smile disappeared as he ran back through the conversation. Everything seemed to have fallen into place. The killer was in custody. He hadn't mentioned Jack's involvement. *So why do I still have this gnawing doubt?* He thought about the soft voice on the phone and Shane's smoker's growl. He thought about the things the killer had said, the mind games they'd played. Did Shane Hardy, a low rent drug dealer, a man reduced to living in his jeep, have it in him to put on that performance? *Yes*, Jack said to himself. Shane had been educated in some of England's toughest universities of crime. He'd spent two years in Strangeways with the cream-of-the-crop – gangsters, armed robbers, rapists, murderers. He would know all the tricks of the trade. As for the androgynous voice, a Voice Changer app, such as he himself had used to leave a message for Fiona Jenkins, would do the trick.

"Shane's the killer," he said to himself. As if to emphasise the words, he snatched up Shane's phone and smashed it against the hearth.

His mind turned to Fiona. Paul hadn't mentioned her. She seemingly still hadn't heard the message. Either that or...

The lines around Jack's eyes lengthened. Had Shane killed twice in one night? Perhaps Fiona had been the appetiser before the main course. Shane was a rage killer. He wanted revenge on Paige for kicking him out, but he was also desperate to reconcile with her. He'd sidestepped that contradiction by taking his anger out on strangers. For a while that had sated his violent urges. But maybe last night his rage had taken complete control and he'd succumbed to his ultimate fantasy – killing his wife.

CHAPTER 35

Jack glanced at his watch. It was time to pick Naomi up from school. He could decide what to do – or not do, as the case may well be – about Fiona Jenkins afterwards. Naomi had to take priority. As he got into his car, his phone rang. He snatched it out. *Please god, don't be No Caller ID!* He let out a breath. It was Laura. This time, he answered her call. "Sorry I didn't answer when you rang earlier. I was with a colleague."

"How are you feeling? Any dizziness, nausea, blurred vision?"

"I'm fine., I'm on my way to pick up Naomi."

Laura tutted. "You should be resting. I would have picked her up."

"I told you I'm fine. I'll see you soon."

As Jack had told her to do, Naomi was waiting in the playground with her teacher. Her lips curving into a broad smile, she ran to Jack. The smile vanished at the sight of the gauze pad taped to his forehead. "What happened to your head?" she asked, her eyes even bigger than usual with worry.

Jack was ready for the question. He'd already decided to make light of it. "I got it chasing a suspect. I haven't had to do anything like that since I was walking the beat. I need to get back in the gym big-time."

"Did you catch the suspect?"

"Yeah. You should have seen the size of him. Muscles like the Incredible Hulk." Jack made a chopping motion. "But he was no match for my superior Kung-Fu." He detected a trace of a smile at the corners of Naomi's lips. It was like the sun reappearing from behind a cloud.

"You don't know Kung-Fu."

"Oh yeah? So what do you call this?" Jack playfully jabbed at Naomi's ribs.

She giggled and squirmed away, "Stop! Get off!" Jack straightened and she looked up at him with serious eyes again. "I don't like it when you get hurt, Dad."

"Neither do I," Jack's voice softened reassuringly. "Fortunately I spend most of my time behind a desk. My job's actually pretty boring."

Naomi gave him a doubtful look. He moved the conversation on. "What do you fancy for tea? We could pick up pizzas on the way back to your aunt's."

"Pizza, yay!"

As they made their way to the car, Jack's gaze moved over the parked and passing cars. No silver Punto. *Relax,* he told himself, *Shane can't harm Naomi now... But what if he's not the killer?* He pushed the doubt away. *Stick to the facts. And the facts say Shane's the killer.*

They pulled up outside Laura's house at the same time as her. Fussing around Jack like a worried hen, she ushered him to the sofa. "Stay," she ordered.

As they ate, Naomi excitedly told her aunt about Jack's fight with the 'Incredible Hulk'. After the meal, Naomi went upstairs to change out of her school uniform and Laura asked Jack, "So do you think The Incredible Hulk killed those women?"

Jack wanted to say yes. He wanted to tell Laura there was no more need to worry about Naomi's Facebook prowler or anything else for that matter. But the doubting voice cautioned him, *Give it another day or two. See what happens.* "I'm certain he's guilty of at least one murder."

His thoughts returned to Fiona Jenkins. It was just after five o'clock. About now she would likely be heading home from Harmony Music Manchester. With a decisive movement, he rose to his feet. There was only one way to make sure Fiona was OK: he had to put eyes on her.

"Where are you going?" Laura asked in surprise as he headed for the front door.

"I have to do some work."

Laura shook her head. "Oh no, no way. You're not fit–"

"Please, Laura," broke in Jack. "This is something I've got to do. It shouldn't take too long." He summoned up a smile for his sister. "Don't look so worried. Things are looking up. Naomi and I should be out of your hair very soon."

"I don't want you out of my hair. I don't care how long you both stay here, so long as you're happy."

"I know. Now stop fretting. I'll be back soon."

Jack closed the door and checked it was locked. Twenty-odd minutes later he was pulling up outside Fiona Jenkins's flat. The journey to Withington was only five miles, but the roads were congested. Alan Road was a broad through-road lined by handsome Victorian villas. Fiona lived on the ground floor of a three-storey redbrick house. Her curtains were closed. There were no vehicles in the driveway. It looked as if no one was in. He glanced at the dashboard clock: 5:28. *She's a private music teacher,* he said to himself. *She probably doesn't work a nine-to-five.* He lit a cigarette and settled back to wait.

Quarter-of-an-hour later, a blue Nissan pulled into the driveway. A thirty-something man got out of it. He checked one of three mailboxes attached to the wall by the door before heading inside. Another fifteen minutes passed by. Half-an-hour. No one else showed up. Glancing around to makes sure he was alone, Jack got out of the car and approached the front door. Letters were poking out of the mailbox for 'Flat 1'. It appeared Fiona hadn't been home in at least a day. *It doesn't have to be anything sinister. She might just be away on holiday,* he tried to reassure himself.

He drove to a phone box and called Harmony Music Manchester. "Is Fiona there?" he asked when someone picked up. "I'd like to book a lesson with her for this week."

"I'm afraid she's away until the second of September."

Surely that confirmed Fiona was on holiday. "OK, thank you."

Jack returned to Laura's feeling better about Fiona. But he still couldn't shake off the doubts. Every minute or two, his eyes flicked towards his phone. *Just switch it off,* he said to himself. But he knew he wouldn't. *What if the killer's still out there?* Everything hung on that question.

At nine o'clock he took Naomi upstairs for her bath. Laura offered to do it, but he needed the distraction. As he kissed Naomi goodnight, she asked, "When are we going home, Dad?"

Home. There was *that* word again. Jack stroked her hair. "Soon, sweetheart."

"Good. I like it here, but I want to be in our house. I want it to be just you and me."

Jack turned away so that Naomi didn't see his eyebrows pull together. Would it ever truly be just the two of them? Would Rebecca ever stop haunting him?

Back downstairs, Laura had made his bed up for him. "You need an early night," she told him.

No, what I need is something to knock me out for the night, Jack felt like replying. The killer had rung him every day since Camilla and Dale's deaths. Twice those calls had come in the small hours of the night. There was no way Jack was getting any sleep without the help of something. A bottle of vodka would do the job, but those days were behind him. He turned the telly on.

"And don't stay up too late watching that thing," Laura said as she left the room.

Jack held in a sigh. Laura was only trying to help, but sometimes her helpfulness veered into controlling. When they were kids, she'd seemed to spend more time than their parents nagging him. *Jack, do this. Jack, don't do that.* It had made for a fractious relationship. Things had got better between them when she moved to Manchester. He didn't want their relationship to regress to what it had been. He made a mental note to move back into the Chorlton house as soon as possible. If Shane continued to be the prime suspect, that might only be a day or two. *If, if...*

His eyes returned to his phone. Silence. Drawing in a long breath, he put the evening news on. The screen showed a constable at the Albert Square end of Tasle Alley. It was reported that a young woman's body had been found and a suspect had been taken in for questioning. No names were mentioned. Nor was it officially confirmed that the woman's death was connected to the other murders. Although the report's references to 'The Manchester Ripper', as the press had dubbed the killer, made it clear the police considered it to be so.

Turning the telly down low, Jack got into his sleeping bag and closed his eyes. He was immediately bombarded by images from the day: Brenda Devonport and Diane King's sad faces; Paige Hardy's dead one... *Just let them come and let them go*, he told himself. *Let them come and let them go.*

It didn't work. A long time seemed to pass. He opened his eyes to look at the time: 10:05. *Shit!*

All night it went on like that. The faces, the doubts, the phone, the question. By the small hours, he almost wanted the phone to ring and No Caller ID to flash up. At least that would free him from this torturous uncertainty. Four o'clock crawled by. Five. Six... The phone remained silent. He repeated his mantra, "Shane's the killer." But yet another troubling possibility followed on the heels of his words. What if the real killer hadn't got in contact because of Shane's arrest? Maybe they were hoping the unnamed suspect would cop for all the murders.

At half-past six, hollow-eyed, Jack got up. His head was pounding. His body ached as if it had been stretched on a rack. He took painkillers and a long shower. He examined the stitches on his forehead. There was no sign of infection. Laura frowned when she came downstairs to find him in his suit. "Don't tell me you're going into work."

"Well it's either that or lie around here all day thinking about you know who." *Rebecca.* The name hung unspoken in the air.

The lines on Laura's forehead became more pronounced. "You've got a point there. But if you feel dizzy or faint, you must stop working at once and–"

"Yes, matron," Jack cut in. Lack of sleep had eroded his patience. He'd used to teasingly call Laura 'matron' when she bossed him around as a child.

She exchanged her frown for a sarcastically amused expression. "OK, Jack, if that's the way it is I'll leave you to it."

"Oh come on, Laura, I was only kidding," Jack said as she turned to leave.

She headed out the front door without replying. Jack sighed. That was another thing Laura had always been good at – making him feel guilty. It seemed all the females in his life – Rebecca, Naomi, even Camilla – made him feel that way sooner or later. Was it their fault or his? Perhaps there was something lacking in him, some spark of empathy that would allow him to better understand their needs. Or maybe that was simply the way of things. Maybe it was impossible for love to exist without guilt.

The depressing thought was pushed aside by Naomi calling to him. He helped her get ready for school, grateful for the mindlessness of the morning rituals. A short time later, he was dropping her off at the gates and going through his other less mindless morning ritual before heading to HQ.

CHAPTER 36

The sight of the self-consciously modern building inspired only a mild feeling of dread. There was a confidence to Jack's stride that wasn't entirely bravado as he made his way to the Incident Room. Anyone looking at him would have seen a man at ease with his surroundings. Anyone, that is, except Rebecca. She would have seen through him in an instant. Her eyes would have laid bare his doubts and fears. He'd never been able to hide anything from her. The same wasn't true in the opposite direction. Jack considered himself a good reader of people. But if she wanted to, Rebecca could lock her thoughts away from him as securely as money in a vault.

Emma was already at her desk. So were Steve, Gary and half-a-dozen other detectives. Emma glanced stonily at Jack. Steve broke into applause. "Here he is! Gorilla-Killa."

The other team members, except Emma, joined in clapping. Jack acknowledged them with a nod as he sat down at his desk. "I'm sorry," he said to Emma. "I should have given you the heads up about Shane."

"So why didn't you? Instead of giving me some bullshit about fetching sandwiches?"

"If he'd seen us both leaving the scene, he might have suspected something was up."

Emma expelled a sharp breath that told Jack what she thought of his reasoning. "I thought we were a team. Obviously I was wrong."

Steve mimicked a rear-naked-choke. "You should've seen the chokehold this one put on Shane. It was like something from a cage fight. Come on, Jack, show us how it's done."

Emma smiled thinly. "Go on, Jack, go play with your new pal."

"He's a dickhead," Jack replied out of the side of his mouth.

"So you should get on with him then."

Jack's silence acknowledged that he deserved the retort. If he'd been the one left sitting in the car, he would have been equally pissed off.

More detectives strolled in with their morning coffees and laptop bags. Each took a moment to congratulate Jack with a thumbs up or a few words.

Paul appeared, wearing his usual all-work-and-no-play face. "Morning, DI Anderson. How's the head today?"

"Not too bad, thanks, sir."

"Good because we've got a busy day ahead of us. Right is everyone here?"

"Yes sir," came the communal reply.

"Before I start the briefing, we owe our newest team member a round of applause. A very nasty piece of work is off the streets because of Jack."

More clapping greeted Paul's words. Steve beat his chest and made gorilla sounds. Jack felt a genuine flush of pleasure at the show of camaraderie. For the first time, he could almost imagine himself working there for many years to come.

The room quietened as Paul began, "First up on today's agenda – Shane Hardy. After I'm done here, I'm formally charging him with resisting arrest, assaulting a police officer and the murders of Paige and Zoe."

There was a general murmur of approval, but Emma said, "I think you're jumping the gun on the murder charges, sir. I've spoken to the staff at The Cuban and Clarity Advertising, and to Camilla's fellow cast members. None of them recognise Shane. He's not Mr Average."

"You can't know that for certain, DI Steele. No one we've spoken to got a good look at Mr Average. And even if a reliable witness comes forward and confirms that Shane isn't Mr Average, that doesn't mean he's not our perp. As Jack and Steve suggested the other day, Mr Average may well have nothing to do with any of this."

"We've got enough to detain Shane without charges for a couple more days," persisted Emma. "Jack and I came up with some promising leads yesterday. Why not hold off on charging Shane until we find out where they go?"

"I take it you're referring to the possibility of Lilith Winter being involved with Rhys Devonport."

"It stands to reason that if Lilith was involved with Rhys, and if there's no connection between Shane, Rhys and Lilith, then we might be charging an innocent man." Emma looked to Jack as if seeking his support.

Resisting an urge to avoid her gaze and stay silent, he agreed, "Emma's right."

Paul's eyebrows lifted. "I didn't expect anyone – especially not anyone here – to accuse Shane of being innocent."

"As far as I'm aware, sir, Shane hasn't changed his story that he had nothing to do with the murder of his wife, Zoe Saunders or the other victims," Emma countered.

Paul indicated she was right with a nod. He flipped through a notepad. "Estimated time of death for Paige is between two and four a.m. on Thursday morning. Shane claims he was asleep in his Jeep Cherokee on Elton Street at that time. DC Clarke's been over there this morning."

"There was nothing much to see," put in Olivia Clarke – a fresh-faced twenty-something. "Just a patch of woodland, fly-tipped rubbish, a scrap yard and old factory buildings. I spoke to the scrap yard's owner and the occupants of nearby houses. No one saw Shane or his jeep on Thursday night."

"So Shane has no alibi. We found his jeep on King Street, a hundred metres from Tasle Alley. According to him, he was driving through the city centre when he saw a crowd gathering in Albert Square and decided to find out what was going on." Paul consulted his notes again. "There were two bin liners of clothes, a sleeping bag, a pillow, toiletries, a small amount of cannabis, a lot of empty cider bottles and a hammer in the jeep. Shane claims he kept the hammer for self-defence. The hammer is clean. However, traces of blood have been found on the passenger seat. Shane says Paige suffered a nosebleed in the jeep around the time of their breakup."

"I'll bet she did," smirked Steve

"As you all know, we're also trying to establish whether Shane has alibis for the murders of Abigail, Zoe, Erica and Camilla." A pleased-as-pie note found its way through Paul's professional demeanour. "So far the answer is a big fat no. On the night of Zoe's murder, Shane claims he went straight to his jeep after leaving The Alchemist cocktail bar. He says he was too drunk to drive and fell asleep on the backseat until he was woken the next morning by a traffic warden and told to move on. We haven't yet managed to track down the traffic warden. As for Abigail, Erica and Camilla's murders, Shane says he can't remember where he was. He's blaming his lack of memory on heavy drinking."

Jack shifted in his seat. Shane's explanation had uncomfortable echoes of his own alcohol–induced memory blanks.

"That's convenient," Gary commented dryly.

"Isn't it?" agreed Paul. "Shane has scratch marks on his right cheek. At first he claimed they were inflicted by Jack. But when he was told that blood and skin has been found under Paige's nails, he said he went to see her at their house last Saturday and she hit him. Paige's mother, Carole Logan, has confirmed that Shane did indeed come to the house that day. But she says Paige refused to open the door to him. This has been backed up by a neighbour who saw Shane banging on said door. If the blood and skin turn out to be Shane's, I'd say that seals his fate as far as Paige's murder goes."

"I'd say so too," agreed Jack.

"What about you, DI Steele? Still think Shane's innocent?"

"I never said that's what I thought, sir," said Emma. "I agree, it looks to be almost a certainty that Shane killed his wife."

"But you're not convinced about Zoe and the others."

"No I'm not. At the very least, I'd like to find out if it was Lilith who bought the sapphire ring and display cabinet from Rhys."

Paul mulled over Emma's request. "I need someone to ask Mrs Winter whether she knows Shane. I don't suppose it would do any harm if that someone had a nose around the house. But I don't want Lilith questioned about Rhys. And that's non-negotiable. She's just lost her only child. I will not have her put through any more distress. Is that understood?"

"Yes, sir."

"One more thing. I need you to see both the ring and the display cabinet, otherwise we drop the Rhys Devonport and Mr Average lines of inquiry and hit Shane with everything we've got. Agreed?"

"Yes, sir," Emma repeated less eagerly.

"Jack?"

"I have no issue with that, sir," said Jack.

"Good. Then the two of you can head over to Didsbury after the briefing."

Jack touched a hand to his forehead. The *what ifs* were suddenly ringing out in his mind like church bells.

Paul continued the briefing in what was, by his standards, an almost jaunty tone. Considering Shane's lengthy criminal record, there was no chance of him being granted bail. It could take a year or two for the case to go to trial. Unless the case collapsed before then, a violent offender was out of circulation for the foreseeable future. Now it was all about building the case. Shane's life had to be picked apart in minute detail. If he'd spanked his daughter, kicked a neighbour's cat, pulled the legs off a crane fly, Paul wanted to know about it.

Afterwards, Paul motioned Jack aside and said, "About the commendation. Looks like it's going to happen. Congrats, Jack. At this rate, you'll be running the division in a few months."

Jack's lips curled wryly. "No thanks. I can do without that headache on top of the one I've already got."

CHAPTER 37

They'd driven halfway to Didsbury in stony silence before Emma said, "Thanks for backing me up."

"No problem," replied Jack, just barely disguising the fact that Lilith Winter was the last person he wanted to see. He didn't believe for a second that Lilith knew Shane. As for whether Lilith knew Rhys...

He popped a couple of painkillers out of a blister strip and swallowed them dry. Emma said nothing else during the journey. Jack got the message loud-and-clear: he was out of jail, but still on probation.

When they arrived at the house, Jack said, "Remember, no questions about Rhys."

Emma made a mouth-zipped motion. "So how are we going to get a look around without arousing suspicion?"

"How about if I ask to use the toilet while we're talking to Lilith?"

"You're just full of sneaky tricks, aren't you?" Emma's tone wasn't complimentary.

Jack knocked on the front door. He seemed to smell the rotten egg stench of Acetylcysteine even before Stella opened it. Spots of what looked like blood speckled the nurse's smock. She frowned at the detectives as if they were unwanted door-to-door salesmen. "I asked you not to come back here unless you absolutely had to."

"Don't you watch the news?" said Emma. "We've arrested a man on suspicion of the murders. We need to ask Mrs Winter a few questions about him."

"What could Mrs Winter possibly know about a man like that?"

"That's what we're here to find out."

"Do you have to do this right now? Mrs Winter's having a bad day."

"We won't take long," said Jack. "We just need to show her a photo of the suspect."

Exhaling an annoyed breath, Stella motioned for them to follow her. Jack swallowed hard as they ascended the stairs. It smelt as if Lilith had already died and begun decomposing. Two doors were open on the landing – the bathroom door and a door to a cupboard full of bedding and towels. There was a mound of bedding marbled with red, brown and yellow stains outside Lilith's room. Stella turned to them and put a finger to her lips before entering the room.

The bedroom was as silent as a funeral parlour, except for the thin rasp of Lilith's breathing. Only her head was poking out from beneath a clean white sheet. Her eyes were closed. An oxygen mask was strapped over her mouth and nose. Snakes of white hair wound their way across the pillows. She looked as if she'd been drained of all colour. But as Stella approached the bed, Lilith's eyelids parted revealing eyes that shone like wet diamonds.

"The police are here again," said Stella.

"What do they want?" Lilith's voice was like dry leaves rustling in a breeze.

"They've arrested Camilla's killer."

"We don't know for certain that our suspect is the killer," corrected Emma. "We need you to have a look at a photo and tell us if you recognise the man in it." She proffered a photo of Shane.

Lilith's bony, liver-spotted left hand emerged from under the sheet to take it. Jack felt a jolt in his gut as if he was a passenger in a speeding vehicle that had slammed on the brakes. There were two rings on the third finger of Lilith's hand – a gold wedding band and a silver ring set with a glittering sapphire crowned by diamonds. That had to be it! The ring Her Ladyship bought from or was given by Rhys. His brain started to whirr. *Shane's not our perp. Fuck! Shit! Calm down, don't jump to conclusions. Lilith might recognise Shane. Oh god, please recognise him, please recognise him...*

Lilith stared at the photo for a few seconds. With what seemed to Jack a crushing sense of inevitability, she shook her head.

"Are you sure you don't recognise him?" he asked, desperation edging into his voice. "Maybe he knocked on your door once trying to sell you something. Or maybe you spoke to him in a shop."

Lilith sucked as much oxygen as possible into her toiling lungs, then removed the plastic mask. "I wouldn't give a man like him the time of day if he asked for it," she replied witheringly, flicking Shane's photo away as if offended by the very suggestion that she would recognise him.

Jack fought to hide a grimace. Even with the painkillers, his head felt ready to crack open. The doubts were running amok. *Shane's just some copycat who used the other murders to try to get away with killing his wife. And the prick even botched that. Paul's right about the killer trying to misdirect us, only not in the way he thinks. Paige wasn't the real target, Camilla was... Or perhaps she wasn't. Maybe all this is just coincidence and bullshit. Shane could still be our perp. But why would Shane be driving Rhys's car? Maybe he wasn't. But then who was? Does it even matter? Oh god, what a mess...*

"That's a beautiful ring," Emma said casually as she retrieved the photo. "Is that a blue diamond?"

"No, it's a sapphire," said Lilith.

"Did your husband give it to you?"

Lilith stared icily at Emma for a few grating breaths, then said, "Yes."

The lie was as clear as the sapphire. But Lilith displayed no hint of awkwardness or embarrassment. If anything there was a challenge in her tone as if she was daring them to disbelieve her.

Jack chewed his tongue as he was hit by an almost overpowering urge to demand, *Tell us about Rhys Devonport. You had an affair with him, didn't you?*

Come on, your Ladyship, give us all the gory details. Did he take you to his parents' bungalow? Did Gabriel find out? Is that what gave him a heart attack?

Emma nudged his shoe. He took the prompt. "Can I use your toilet?"

"It's next to the bathroom," said Stella.

Jack left the room, pulling the door to behind him. He went downstairs quickly and quietly. The dining-room and living-room seemed to him the most likely places to find the mahogany display cabinet. The first door on the right led to a room furnished with a stiff-backed sofa and a pair of matching armchairs arranged around an elegant coffee table. Thick rugs covered a parquet floor. To either side of a marble and cast-iron fireplace were shelves filled with books. At the centre of a mantelpiece book-ended by porcelain dogs stood a pewter cremation urn. A grandfather clock ticked in one corner. There was no display cabinet. Jack couldn't resist but take a closer look at the urn. 'Gabriel Winter 1954-2006' was engraved on it.

Fifty-two-years-old. Gabriel hadn't lived to see his daughter reach her twenty-first birthday. If Camilla even *was* his daughter. Poor bastard.

Jack moved on to the next door. It led to a study with a green-leather topped desk and walls of books with titles such as 'Braunwald's Heart Disease', 'Interventional Cardiology', 'Hurst's The Heart', 'Current Medical Diagnosis and Treatment' and 'A Clinician's Guide to Medical and Surgical Abortion'. The room had a musty unused smell.

The third door led to a store cupboard crammed with cleaning products, air-fresheners, a clothes horse, rusty paint tins, a box of jumbled tools and the like. The fourth door opened onto a sun-splashed dining-room. A sturdy oak dining table and eight chairs with barley-twist legs occupied the centre of the room. Expensive-looking porcelain dining sets were piled on an antique sideboard. French doors overlooked a patio, beyond which was an overgrown lawn shadowed by trees.

No mahogany display cabinet. Several minutes had passed since Jack left the bedroom. Stella and Lilith might be starting to wonder what he was up to. He hurried to open the final hallway door. He just had time to glimpse a large, dated kitchen – dark wood cupboards, white marble work surfaces, scarred brown linoleum – before a voice behind him asked sarcastically, "Did you get lost, Detective Anderson?"

He turned towards Stella, smiling as if he hadn't been caught out. "I was just having a nosey around. I love big old houses like this."

"Well it'll likely be coming up for sale soon. Although I think it'll be beyond your price range."

Jack didn't allow his smile to slip at the caustic comment. He followed Stella up to Lilith's bedroom. Emma was thanking Lilith for her time. The old lady didn't appear to be listening. She was staring at the sapphire ring as if the detectives' questions had roused memories that had lain dormant for years.

Stella put out a hand to stop Jack from re-entering the room. He was glad. He wasn't sure he would have been able to resist asking Lilith about Rhys. Stella repositioned the oxygen mask over Lilith's face before ushering the detectives to the front door.

"How much longer do you think she's got?" asked Emma. Jack knew she was thinking the same as him – if Lilith died she might take the killer's identity to the grave with her.

"It's difficult to say," answered Stella. "Maybe weeks. Maybe only days." She looked at them as if to ask, *Is there anything else?* When no more questions were immediately forthcoming, she closed the door without a goodbye.

"She caught me downstairs," explained Jack as they returned to the car.

"Did you see anything that might be the cabinet?"

"No. I looked in the living-room, dining-room and study. I didn't get a proper look at the kitchen. But then again, a ten-thousand quid display cabinet isn't the sort of thing you put in a kitchen."

"Gabriel Winter might have done if he knew where it came from."

"He might also have chopped it into expensive firewood. I would have if I was him."

"So you think Lilith was lying about her ring?"

"I think Lilith's Her Ladyship."

Emma was thoughtfully silent for a moment. Then she said, "Assuming you're right – which I don't doubt you are – Lilith and Rhys were seeing each other in the early eighties. Camilla was born in '86, so..." She left the possibilities that could follow dangling tantalisingly.

"So..." echoed Jack. "What now?"

"I say we do as you suggested yesterday. Head over to Wilmslow and talk to Lawrence Bancroft-Harding. Then check out the Sale Road bungalow."

It was Jack's turn to lapse into silence. The killer hadn't called him in over twenty-four hours. The evidence against Shane was still damning. If Lilith had lied about the ring, she might also have lied about Shane. Or there might be a link between them that she wasn't aware of. Jack sucked his lips uncertainly. Did he really want to go any further down the Rhys and Lilith rabbit-hole before exhausting all other lines of inquiry? No, he did not. "OK, but let's find out what the DCI has to say first."

"You know what he'll say. His condition was that we had to see both the ring and the cabinet. He's fixated on Shane."

"And I suppose you're not fixated on Mr Average."

"Fair enough, maybe I am. But Shane wasn't the man Dale confronted. Nor was Rhys. So who was it? Who was stalking Camilla? And who's driving around in a car belonging to a missing man who had an affair with Camilla's mum?"

"I don't know. What I do know is everything you just said is speculation."

"Speculation," Emma parroted as if she couldn't believe her ears. "You said yourself you think Lilith lied to us."

"Exactly, I *think* she lied. You haven't got one hard fact that points to Mr Average as the killer. Shane was caught at the scene of his wife's murder. Shane spoke to Zoe on the night of her death. Shane knows Zoe's dad from prison. *Those* are the facts. I'm not willing to go against orders based merely on what you or I think."

Emma wrinkled her forehead. "You know what, Jack. I can't work you out. One minute you're going all lone wolf, the next you're a stickler for the rules."

He smiled ruefully. "Well if you ever do work me out, let me know because I've been trying to do the same thing for years."

Emma didn't return his smile. As they drove to Headquarters in yet more stony silence, Jack tried to convince himself that his self-righteous little speech about 'facts' hadn't simply been another attempt to put an end to Emma's obsession with Mr Average. He failed miserably.

CHAPTER 38

"No," said Paul. "Nothing you've told me has changed my mind."

Emma stabbed her finger at a sketch she'd made of Lilith's sapphire and diamond encrusted ring. "I described that to Diane King. She's positive it's the ring Her Ladyship got from Rhys."

"What does that prove? Diane's not even certain Rhys had an affair with Her Ladyship. This is all just..." Paul sought the right word, "gossip. Even if they had an affair, there's no law against it."

Jack caught an uncharacteristically personal tone in Paul's voice. He wondered whether Paul was worried people were gossiping about his and Natasha's impending divorce. If so, Jack could sympathise. He'd spent months feeling as if everyone – even strangers in the street – were whispering about him. A red flush was creeping up Paul's neck. A sure sign he was getting angry. Jack darted Emma a cautioning glance, but she pressed on regardless, "You're missing the point, sir."

"Am I? Then why don't you enlighten me, Detective Inspector Steele?"

"The point is, either Shane was driving Rhys's car last Friday or–"

"Why couldn't it have been Rhys driving his own car?" cut in Paul. "Seeing as we're throwing wild theories out there, have you considered this? Let's say you're right about Rhys and Lilith. Let's even say Rhys not Gabriel is Camilla's dad. In that case why would it be so strange that Rhys was in the vicinity of the opera house?"

"I don't suppose it would be," conceded Emma. "But why was Rhys there on that particular night?"

"Who knows? But it comes down to this, would Rhys have killed his own daughter? And if he did, would Lilith lie to protect him? I just can't see that being the case?"

"Me neither. Which leaves us with Mr Average?"

Paul rolled his eyes and slapped his palm against his desk. "Dear god, please somebody save me from Mr-bloody-Average."

"Have you looked at the file I've put together on Lawrence Bancroft-Harding? He's 5'9", medium build, brown hair–"

"Yes and he's also seventy-one-years-old. We've been down this road before with Rhys. Both are too old to be your mystery man."

"Fair enough, sir, but that doesn't rule Lawrence out of the picture."

"So let me get this straight, Detective Steele. You're suggesting that Lawrence Bancroft-Harding, a retired dentist without so much as a speeding fine to his name, might have taken up serial murder in later life as... as what? A hobby?"

"Lawrence has good reason to hate Rhys," said Emma, maintaining her composure in the face of Paul's sarcasm. "Maybe he killed Camilla to get at Rhys. And like you speculated about Shane, the other women were killed to throw us off the scent."

Paul heaved an ever-so-patient breath as if he was dealing with a stubborn child. "Jack, you spoke to Lawrence. What did you make of him?"

"He sounded on the level," said Jack. "But I only spoke to him for a minute before he hung up."

"Exactly. If Lawrence had said, *I've no idea who Rhys Devonport is*, that might have rung alarm bells. But instead he hung up on you. A guilty person doesn't hang up on the police."

"He could have panicked," suggested Emma.

"Our killer doesn't panic. Our killer knows how to deal with the police. Our killer isn't some geriatric widower who suddenly turned into Jack the Ripper thirty-odd years after his dead wife had an affair. Our killer is a musclebound sociopath with a long-term history of crime and violence." Between each sentence Paul stabbed a finger into the desktop for emphasis. "Do you see where I'm going with this?"

"Yes, sir."

"Now here's what's going to happen. You're going let Lilith Winter die in peace. You're not going to disturb Lawrence Bancroft-Harding either. I'm not sure what you expect to find out from him anyway. Men don't tell women they're having an affair with about other women they're also having an affair with. That kind of thing tends to spoil the mood. What you are going to do is pass on all the information you've got regarding the Devonport case to Cheshire Police. Then you're going to focus solely on linking Shane to Abigail, Erica, Camilla and Dale's murders. Is that understood?"

"Yes sir," Emma said again, this time with Jack in chorus.

"Good." Paul wafted them from his office.

"He could be right about Rhys wanting to see his daughter," Jack said as they headed to their desks. He'd felt a rush of gratitude when Paul pointed out that possibility. It hadn't silenced his doubts, but it had turned the volume way down on them. He was annoyed but not surprised that he hadn't thought of it himself. His mind was being pulled in so many directions – Rebecca, Naomi, the past, the future...

"So it's all just one big coincidence, is it?" shot back Emma.

"I'm starting to think it could be, yes."

"Keep telling yourself that, Jack, and you might actually believe it."

All afternoon Jack immersed himself in Shane Hardy's life. Shane was born in Rusholme in 1985 and had spent his entire life there. His parents, Denise and Carl, had likewise grown up in the area. Carl had done several stints inside for burglary, handling stolen goods and other petty crimes. Denise was a barmaid in a local pub. In 1998 she'd been fined for possession of Class B and C drugs. The apple, it seemed, had not fallen far from the tree. Shane had three sisters. All of whom were married with kids and lived in or around Rusholme. Shane had attended The Manchester Academy High School on Moss Lane, a stone's throw from the pharmacy where Zoe Saunders had worked. That might have been of interest if Shane hadn't left school sixteen years before Zoe started work at the pharmacy.

Shane had never had a job – at least, not one for which he'd paid tax. Paige had been a hairdresser at a salon in Longsight. Not the type of place Lilith or Camilla would go to have their hair done. She'd been in the year below Shane at The Manchester Academy. Her parents, Carole and Neil Logan, lived just round the corner from Shane's parents. Jack wondered what they would happen if they bumped into each other on the street. He couldn't imagine it would be pleasant. Carole and Neil seemed like decent people. Carole worked in an off-licence. Neil was a lorry driver. Neither had a criminal record. Maya, Shane's three-year-old daughter, was now living with them. She was the one Jack felt sorriest for. Although in a strange way, maybe she'd been lucky. Shane would have messed her up for sure if he'd stayed in her life. This way she would have an upbringing that would give her a chance to avoid the mistakes her dad had made.

By the end of his shift, Jack had found nothing that connected Shane to Lilith and Rhys or to any of the victims besides Paige and Zoe. But neither did he have the energy left to listen to the doubting voices in his head. He wanted to get home to Naomi. He wanted to give her *that* same chance.

Emma was engrossed in whatever it was she was doing. Perhaps she was following orders. Or maybe she was back on the trail of Mr Average. Jack wasn't all that interested. Let her waste her time on a wild goose chase. He said bye. She flicked him a terse wave. It seemed he was back in jail. Fuck it. He refused to feel guilty. He'd done everything he could to get to the truth... Well, almost everything. To hell with the rest of it. It wasn't his responsibility. Orders were orders.

On the way out of the building, he poked his head into Paul's office. Paul wasn't there, but the hum of his computer suggested his absence was only temporary. Jack's gaze landed on the photo of Paul, Natasha and their two kids. He reflected that Paul was probably glad of the murder case workload. It gave him a reason not to spend his evenings knocking around a Premier Inn with only his worries for company. Something Paul had said came back to him: *Men don't tell women they're having an affair with about other women they're also having an affair with.* Had he been speaking from experience? Had Natasha caught him playing around?

Jack didn't dwell on the questions. The reason behind Paul living in a Premier Inn would come out in time. Or it wouldn't. Either way, it was none of his business.

CHAPTER 39

On the way to Laura's, Jack stopped off at a toy shop. What did eight – nearly nine – year old girl's want? he wondered, browsing shelves of princess outfits and plastic jewellery. He chose a teddy bear with a broken heart held together by a plaster.

When Laura saw the bear, she said, "Very subtle. I suppose you're the plaster."

"I'd like to be."

Naomi was lying on the sofa, twiddling with the silver bracelet on her wrist – a sure sign that she was thinking about her mum. Her fingers flinching away from the bracelet, she looked at Jack with eyes like a cloudless sky.

Rebecca... What happened?

He smiled. Not at Naomi, but at how quickly the question came and went. "Hi, sweetheart." He held out the teddy bear. "I know you've got more stuffed toys than you know what to do with, but I saw it and I just couldn't resist."

She took the bear and cuddled it. "He's gorgeous!"

"OK, so who wants to go out for something to eat?"

"Me," exclaimed Naomi. "Pizza."

"We had pizza last night."

"So?"

Laura laughed. "Didn't you know, Jack? You can never have enough pizza."

He drove them to a local Italian restaurant. Laura glanced approvingly at Jack when he ordered a soft drink with his meal.

"Is Elsa still coming to see you?" he asked.

Naomi nodded. "Every day."

"If she's really a stray maybe she can come to live with us."

"You mean at Aunt Laura's house?"

"No. I mean at our house."

"We're moving back home. When?"

The question scared Jack – not because he didn't want Naomi to live with him, but because he didn't want to take any more chances with her happiness. "How about at the weekend?"

Naomi nodded eagerly, then looked apologetically at Laura. "If that's OK with you, Aunt Laura?"

She smiled. "Of course it is, darling. I'm happy if you're happy."

Jack smiled too, resisting the urge to throw his arms around Naomi. He didn't want any big displays of emotion. He wanted things to be steady, level... normal.

The pizzas arrived. They tucked in and the conversation returned to lighter topics. Jack didn't think about the murders. More than that, it was the first time he'd been out for a family meal since Rebecca's death and not had to fight back tears.

"Can Elsa sleep in my bedroom?" Naomi asked. "Please say she can, Dad."

"She can."

"Yay!"

Jack raised a cautionary hand. "Once she's been checked over by a vet. We'll also have to do a bit of investigating. Make sure she doesn't have an owner."

"I'll ask at all the houses on the street tomorrow."

"Not on your own you won't. I'll come with you."

Laura raised her glass. "This calls for a toast. Here's to Elsa finding a new home and me getting my spare room back." As Naomi pushed her bottom lip out in pretend-hurt, Laura added with genuine sadness, "I'll miss you loads, Naomi. I've loved having you to stay and if you ever need me, you know where I am."

"While we're at it, I have something else to celebrate," said Jack. "Paul's put me up for a commendation for catching the thug who gave me this." He pointed to his injured forehead.

"Who's Paul?" asked Naomi.

"He's my new boss. You remember Paul. We worked together in Sussex. He sometimes used to come to our house. Although the last time you saw him, you were only been about six. So maybe you wouldn't remember him."

"Has he got black hair?"

"That's him, although it's more grey than black these days."

"Oh yeah, I remember him. He's nice." Naomi paused thoughtfully, before adding, "I don't think Mum liked him very much though."

Jack frowned. "Why do you say that?"

"Mum and me were out shopping one day and we saw him. He said hello but Mum didn't say anything back."

"She probably didn't hear him."

"She did because she looked straight at him."

Jack's frown hardened. "When was this?"

"It was about a year before Mum... You know, before she–" Naomi's voice seemed to snag on something.

Jack nodded to indicate that he knew. He didn't want to say the word either. His knife and fork suddenly seemed impossibly heavy. They clattered to his plate. He touched a hand to his forehead, his expression trapped somewhere between pain and bewilderment. The stitches were throbbing as if something was trying to rip them apart.

"Jack," said Laura, sounding cautious and concerned.

"What's wrong, Dad?" asked Naomi.

"I..." His voice was weak. "I have to go."

"Go where?"

Jack saw something close to panic in Naomi's eyes. *All I care about is my daughter.* He'd tried so hard to convince himself that that was true, but his reaction exposed the lie. He rose to his feet. Laura caught hold of his hand. "Don't go, Jack."

I'm sorry, he mouthed, pulling his hand from hers and turning away.

"Why is he leaving? Is it my fault?" Jack heard Naomi asking as he made for the exit. Her words hit him so hard that he almost doubled over. *No it's not your fault. It's your mum's fault, it's my fault, it's the world's fault, but not yours,* he wanted to tell her, but the current carrying him along was too strong to resist.

"Think, Jack!" Laura called after him. "Think about what you've got before you do anything you'll regret."

Think. The word seemed to echo in Jack's ears as he ducked into his car. Laura knew him better than anyone alive. She knew exactly what was going through his mind. He brought up Paul's address on his phone and punched it into the Satnav. He started to turn the ignition. Stopped. Shook his head. It was absurd. Just fucking absurd to even entertain such thoughts. Rebecca would have been off in her own world as usual. That's all there was to it. Perfectly innocent.

He reached to open the door, but his hand fell short. The encounter between Rebecca and Paul had taken place a year or so before her death. That must have only been weeks before Paul moved up to Manchester. Why hadn't Paul mentioned that Rebecca blanked him? For that matter why had Paul relocated to the North West? London had been practically on his doorstep. He could have found all the action he wanted there without uprooting his family. Before taking the GMP job, Paul had shown no inclination to venture north of the Watford Gap. He was a Sussex man, born and bred. So why leave? And above all why had Natasha kicked him out? Jack had to know. Just had to. He wouldn't be able to rest until he did.

He started the engine and stabbed at the accelerator. Paul lived in Cheadle, just south of Didsbury. He wouldn't be home, of course, but it wasn't him Jack wanted to speak to.

CHAPTER 40

Jack bullied his way through evening traffic to Paul and Natasha's house – a bland new-build on a cul-de-sac. A casually dressed woman was unloading shopping from a Volvo in the driveway. Natasha had changed little since Jack last saw her. She still had a blonde bob and a trim figure. The only differences were that she looked noticeably older and she wasn't smiling. Natasha always used to be smiling. She was the opposite of Paul – easy-going, down to earth, no hidden agendas. That was why their marriage had worked so well – or at least that was the way it had appeared to Jack.

He got out of the car. "Hello Natasha."

She pivoted on her heels at his voice. "Jack." She sounded more surprised than pleased to see him.

"How are you?"

"I'm good." Natasha's reply was less than convincing. "How about you?"

"I'm confused."

"About what?" Natasha's eyes darted towards the house as if she was looking for a reason to get away from Jack.

"Where are Imogen and Dylan?" Paul had a teenage daughter and a son two years older than Naomi.

"Imo's at her boyfriend's. I hardly ever see her these days. Dylan's in the house on his iPad. You know how kids are."

"Actually I don't. I've not spent much time with Naomi recently."

"I'm sorry to hear that. Are you OK, Jack? You seem... tense. Do you want to come in?"

Jack detected a note of reluctance in the offer. "You seem tense too, Natasha."

"Do I?" Natasha tried to smile Jack's words away, but all she could manage was something closer to a grimace. "I'm just tired."

"It's exhausting being a single parent, isn't it?"

Natasha dropped her pretence of a smile. She sighed. "Yes, it is."

"I was gobsmacked when I heard about you and Paul. I always thought you two were perfect for each other."

"So did I. Turns out I was wrong." Natasha's voice was tightly controlled, letting slip only a hint of bitterness. "I'd rather not talk about this in the street."

"Let's go inside then."

Natasha seemed thrown by the suggestion as if she'd forgotten her offer of a moment earlier. "Oh... OK."

"Let me help you with those." Jack took the shopping bags from her. She closed the Volvo's boot and led him into the house. The interior was every bit as soulless as the exterior – laminate floors, neutral colours. It was exactly the kind of house Paul would go for. And exactly the kind of house Rebecca would have despised. Could she really have been attracted to him?

The idea seemed almost laughable. But then again, had he ever really known what Rebecca was attracted to? Perhaps she herself hadn't known.

Natasha pointed him into the kitchen. "Just dump the bags there, thanks."

The kitchen was clean and tidy. Natasha transferred cheese, butter and milk from the bags to an already well-stocked fridge. Despite the breakdown of her marriage, on the surface at least, she appeared to be holding things together well enough. She filled a kettle. "Tea? Coffee?"

Jack shook his head and stared at Natasha as if waiting for an answer to an unasked question.

She didn't flinch from his gaze. "Don't look at me like that, Jack. Paul used to give me that look when he was about to interrogate me about something or other. It always made me feel like I'd done something to feel guilty about, and before I knew it I'd be apologising for no reason." The bitterness reared its head more visibly, giving her lips an unattractive twist. "Well I'm done with apologies. They don't get you anywhere. All they do is make people think they can shit all over you."

Natasha broke off as if she'd said more than she intended. As she turned to take a mug from a cupboard, Jack noticed a tremor in her hand. He maintained his silence. He knew when to force his way to answers and when to hold back and let them come to him. Natasha banged down the mug. "Don't play games with me, Jack. Just tell me what you want to know."

"I want to know why my wife ignored your husband when they saw each other in the street a year before she died."

Everything inside Jack wound itself into a breathless knot as he waited for Natasha to reply. She looked at him uncertainly, her shoulders hunched. Then she dropped another nuclear bomb on the scorched remains of his world. "I've thought about telling you so many times. I've even picked up the phone and started to dial your number. But no matter how much I wanted to hurt Paul, I couldn't bring myself to do it to you. Not after what you've been through."

Jack's breath was suddenly coming in panic-gasps. *You were right! Oh Christ, you were right! Rebecca and Paul had been... They'd been having an...* He lurched over to the sink. "I'm going to be sick." He retched but nothing came up. *They'd been having an affair. Rebecca couldn't cope with the guilt so she killed herself.* Was that it? Was that the answer he'd been searching for? Tears streamed down his face. It was too much. Too much... His eyes strayed to a knife on the drainer. He saw himself spilling his guts with it, like a disgraced Samurai committing hari-kari. As if reading his thoughts, Natasha gently took hold of his shoulders and guided him to a chair.

He crumpled into it like a broken doll, burying his head in his hands. He felt himself sinking into a bottomless ocean of grief. As if from a long way off, he heard Natasha saying, "Here, drink this?"

Cracking his eyelids, Jack saw that she was proffering a glass of water. He nudged it away. "Got any vodka?"

"Are you sure? Paul told me about your drinking problem."

"*Paul.*" Jack spat out the name as if it was poison. "You still talk to him?"

"No, but I'll have start doing so for the sake of the kids."

As if on cue, a sandy-haired, freckly boy appeared at the door. Dylan glanced apprehensively from Jack to Natasha. There were smudges under his eyes. He didn't look like the happy-go-lucky boy Jack remembered. "What's going on, Mum?"

"Nothing for you to worry about, Dylan. This is Jack, a friend of mine and your dad's from Sussex."

"Naomi's dad," said Dylan.

"That's right. He's not feeling well. Go back up to your room." Natasha ushered Dylan upstairs. She returned with a bottle of vodka and poured two measures.

Jack tossed his back, poured himself another and downed that too, grimacing as if he was swallowing bitter medicine. Natasha sipped her drink, eyeing him uneasily as a third measure went the same way. Jack wiped his mouth with the back of his hand. That familiar numbness was creeping over him, but he had a long way to go before he got to where he wanted to be. A fourth drink gave him the courage to ask, "When did you find out about them?"

"I don't think we should talk about that now."

Jack repeated the question in a voice that wouldn't be denied.

Natasha heaved a sigh. "A fortnight ago."

"How?"

"Just by chance. Paul left his phone on the side." Natasha glanced towards the work-surface. "He got a text message. Something to do with work. I read it, then started going through his phone. I don't know why. Maybe on some level I suspected he'd been up to no good. Anyway, I found..." Her forehead creased into deep furrows. "I found some messages Paul and Rebecca had exchanged."

The tide of nausea rose again. "What did they say?"

"You don't want to know. Believe me, Jack, you don't want those images in your head."

Fuck me harder, Jack. Harder. Harder! Strangle me, Jack! Rebecca's words pulled at his brain like fishhooks. "Did they mention anything about hurting each other? Physically I mean."

Natasha's expression answered his question even before she said, "How did you..."

"Something Rebecca once said. How long did it go on for?"

"Paul says about six months. From March to August in 2015. But Paul's a liar."

"Six months," Jack said, his voice cracking. *Six months. Seventeen Weeks. 119 days.* How many times had they met up in that period? How many times had they fucked? Where had they fucked? In a hotel? In the back of a car? In their respective marital beds? All of those places? Had Rebecca dressed up for him? Worn lingerie or even fetish gear? Had they done it over and over, like wild animals in heat? Had they taken care not to leave marks on each other? Had they used protection? Had it just been a physical thing? Or had there been more to it? Had they whispered sweet nothings to each other? Had they held each other all night long? Had they discussed breaking up with their spouses? Why did they stop seeing each other? Who broke off the affair?

So many questions. Jack felt choked by them. He grabbed the vodka bottle and upended it to his lips.

"Don't do it to yourself," said Natasha. "It's not worth it?"

"So what is worth it?" spluttered Jack.

"Nothing's worth killing yourself over."

"That's not what Rebecca thought."

"It still might have been an accident."

"Bollocks." Jack slammed the bottle down like an exclamation point.

"Please. You'll scare Dylan. He's been really struggling since Paul moved out. He hero-worships his dad."

Natasha's plea cut through Jack's anger. She was right. He shouldn't be here in this state. Vodka bottle in hand, he stood up. "Thank you, Natasha."

"What for?"

"For telling me the truth."

A sad smile touched her lips. "There have been enough lies."

Jack started to nod agreement, but he realised doing so would in itself be a lie. Rebecca and Paul's deceit had led him here, but now he was caught in his own circle of deception. He headed for the front door.

Natasha followed him. "You shouldn't be driving, Jack. Stay a while and have something to eat."

He shook his head. "You don't need my madness in your house on top of everything else."

"You're not going to do anything to Paul, are you?" There was a queer note in Natasha's voice as if she wasn't sure what she wanted the answer to be.

"Right now, I'm going to find somewhere to drink myself unconscious." It was a lie – at least the 'right now' part was – but Jack didn't want Natasha to warn Paul what was coming his way.

She stepped forwards and put her arms around him, repeating softly, "It's not worth it."

Jack pulled away as if a snake had hissed in his ear. *A fortnight ago.* Natasha's words flickered like sparks in his brain. Today was the 28th of July.

Abigail Hart was killed on the 16th. "The murders started just under a fortnight ago."

Natasha wrinkled her forehead. "What murders?"

"The ones that have been all over the news."

"Oh you mean the murder of that opera singer, Camilla something or other, and those other women."

"Camilla Winter, Abigail Hart, Zoe Saunders, Erica Cook." Jack spoke each name like an accusation. "Hasn't it occurred to you that all those women bear a striking resemblance to someone we knew?"

"No because I don't have a clue what they look like. I haven't had much time for watching the news."

"Rebecca. They look like Rebecca." Jack brought up a newspaper photo of Camilla on his phone.

Natasha's eyebrows lifted. "I see what you mean. It's uncanny. But what's that got to do with..." She trailed off, realisation dawning in her eyes. She stared at Jack in astonishment, then said with a hollow laugh, "I didn't think there was anything left that could surprise me. How wrong I was. So let me get this straight, you think I killed those women because they look like the bitch that destroyed my marriage."

Jack's jaw muscles pulsed. Even after everything, it stung to hear Rebecca called a bitch. "Where were you on the night of the 16th?"

Natasha laughed again. "The same place I've been every night since I kicked Paul out. Right here, looking after Dylan and Imogen. Unlike you, I've got no family around here that I can offload my children onto. I've got no friends either." There were tears in her eyes. "I'm all alone in this city. You know what I'd like to do? Put the kids in the car, drive back to Eastbourne and never set eyes on this shithole again."

A flash of lucidity cut through Jack's miasma of grief and alcohol. It was true. How the hell would Natasha have found the time to stalk the victims and him? Moreover, she was about 5'2''. Too short to be the figure he'd seen in Camilla's flat, unless she'd been wearing stilettos – hardly the best choice of footwear for stalking and killing. "I'm sorry, Natasha. I'm not thinking straight."

"Yeah, you've got that right at least. No wonder Rebecca cheated on you if this is how you treat people who show you kindness."

Jack nodded as if to say, *I asked for that*. He turned to continue to his car. As he opened the door, he felt a hand on his arm. "I'm sorry," apologised Natasha. "I shouldn't have said that. I know how it feels to be lied to by someone you love. It destroys your trust in everyone and everything."

Jack smiled gratefully at Natasha for her understanding. "You should go back to Eastbourne."

"I will do as soon as I can pluck up the courage."

Jack gave her hand a squeeze. "Bye, Natasha."

She waved half-heartedly as he drove away. He took another mouthful of vodka and tossed the bottle onto the passenger seat. Oblivion would have to wait. He needed to keep what remained of his wits about him for a while longer. *Fuck me harder, Jack. Harder. Harder! Strangle me, Jack!* Those words tore chunks out of him. Tears ran like silent rivers down his face. "How could you, Rebecca? How could you do this to us? I loved you so much!"

Tower blocks played peek-a-boo with the setting sun as he sped into the city centre. "I did everything I could to make you happy. Why wasn't that enough? What did you want from me?" The questions only led to more questions. Why had Rebecca wanted to be strangled? Had she derived some warped pleasure from having the air throttled out of her? Or had she believed she deserved to be punished for something? *Strangle me, Jack!* She'd said that to him about seven years ago. Well before her affair with Paul. So what had she deserved to be punished for back then? Had there been other affairs? Or did it go deeper than that? Had she wanted to be punished just for being herself? Just for being born? Just for daring to try to lead a normal life with a husband and child?

Jack realised with a jolt that he'd reached his destination. He pulled over outside the high-rise Premier Inn. He thought about how Rebecca's Toyota had been captured on camera outside the Hastings Premier Inn shortly before she died. Was that where she and Paul used to meet up? Had she gone there that day to reflect on what she'd done? Perhaps Paul was staying at the Manchester Central Premier Inn because it reminded him of her. Jack's fists flexed at the thought.

Laura's words echoed back to him again as he got out of the car: *Think about what you've got before you do anything you'll regret?* "Rebecca didn't think about it before she fucked Paul," he retorted out loud. "She didn't care about anything but herself, so why should I?"

He prowled into the hotel lobby and showed his warrant card to the receptionist. "What room is Paul Gunn in?"

The receptionist looked at her computer. "314. Is Mr Gunn in some sort of trouble?"

"He's my boss."

"I can call his room if you like."

Jack shook his head. He caught a lift to the third floor. 'Ssshhh... This is a quiet zone.' said a sign on the wall. A bitter smile ghosted over Jack's lips. Things were about to get noisy.

He pounded his fist on the door of room 314.

CHAPTER 41

Paul answered the door in his dressing-gown. His forehead lifted in surprise. "Ja–"

Before he could get the word out, Jack's fist slammed into his chin. He staggered backwards, rocking like a skittle. Jack advanced and threw a left hook that sent Paul reeling onto the bed. Paul flung up his hands to deflect any more punches as Jack loomed over him.

"Please, Jack," slurred Paul, his eyes swimming with concussion.

"I thought you were my friend."

"I am."

"Friends don't fuck their friends' wives!" exploded Jack.

"I'm sorry."

"Sorry's not enough. Not even close. Tell me why I shouldn't beat you shitless?"

"I didn't mean it to happen. Neither of us did. We were drunk."

Jack scowled dismissively. *Drunk. The eternal excuse.* "When?"

"Does it matter?"

"Yes."

"It was March, two years back. You were away on a–"

"Counter terrorism course," cut in Jack. He'd spent two days in London watching the MET perform anti-terror training exercises. He'd enjoyed the spectacle, but he'd been worried about Rebecca. She'd recently started a new job and was stressed out by the demands of juggling full-time work and motherhood. He'd offered not to go, but she'd insisted she was fine.

"I'd lost my phone," said Paul. "Do you remember I'd been at your house the day before? I thought it might be there, so I stopped off on the way home from work. Rebecca invited me in. She was drinking wine. She offered me a glass. She was in an odd mood. Down one minute. Way up the next. I'd never seen her like that before. I was concerned. I didn't want to leave her alone."

Jack made a scornful sound. "How caring of you."

Paul eyed him nervously. "Are you sure you want to hear this? What good can it do now?"

Jack replied with the kind of glare he usually reserved for criminals trying to worm their way off a hook.

"One glass of wine turned into two," said Paul, his Adam's apple bobbing. "Before we knew it we halfway through a second bottle."

"Did you talk about me?"

"I don't remember what we talked about. I remember Rebecca went upstairs to check on Naomi. When she came back down there were tears in her eyes. I asked what was wrong. She said she wasn't a good mum. I tried to tell her she was, but she kept shaking her head. I put my arms around her and... and we kissed. I don't know which of us instigated it. It just happened."

"Then what?" pressed Jack, his voice squeezed to a hoarse whisper by the tension in his chest.

"No." Paul's reply was shaky but determined. "That's not for you to know."

Spittle flecked Jack's lips as he snarled, "She was my wife!"

With a flinch, Paul said, "It should never have happened. It was wrong. We both knew that."

"So why did you do it?"

"I don't know. Honestly I don't. All I can tell you is it went on for a few months and then it ended."

"Who ended it?"

"Neither of us. We just knew there was no future in it. And..." Paul hesitated as if unsure he should say what was in his mind.

"And what?"

"Sometimes Rebecca would look at me with this... this pain in her eyes. It frightened the hell out of me."

Jack rocked on his heels as if absorbing a punch. "You knew she was on the verge of a breakdown and you took advantage of it."

Paul suddenly rolled away from him and scrambled to his feet. He assumed a defensive stance, hands raised, palms out – ready to fight but offering peace. "I didn't know and I didn't take advantage. It wasn't something I gave any thought to. Like I said, it was just something that happened."

"Just something that happened," Jack parroted in a voice laced with violence.

"Jack, calm down. It won't do anyone any good if one of us ends up in hospital or worse."

"Just something that happened," Jack repeated as if it was a toxic mantra that justified whatever he might do.

"Yes, exactly that. It wasn't about love. The sex wasn't even that great. It..." Paul groped for the right description. "It was selfish and meaningless and... and that's all it was. Rebecca never had a bad word to say about you, Jack. She loved you."

Jack had spent half his life trying to understand why people did things that destroyed the lives of others and themselves. But this was as far beyond his comprehension as quantum physics. "How can you love someone and do this to them?"

"I wish I could answer that," Paul said with a hopeless look. "Maybe then Natasha would take me back."

"You don't deserve her."

"You're right, but I love her."

Jack wrinkled his nose as if he smelled shit on Paul's breath. "You don't know what love is."

"Yes I do. I love my family and I want to make up for what I've done."

"Rebecca's dead," Jack said with ominous finality. "How are you going to make up for that?"

"That's not my fault. Rebecca hated herself for some reason that went way beyond me and her."

As much as he wanted to, Jack couldn't dispute that. *'I hate myself more than I can tell you.', 'I shouldn't be a mother.', 'I'm a horrible person.', 'I don't love Naomi. How can I bring up a child I don't love?'* Those were only a few of the things Rebecca had said in the months following Naomi's birth. He'd reassured her over and over that she would grow to love Naomi. And as the fog of depression lifted, Rebecca had appeared to fall in love with her baby.

But had that really been the case? wondered Jack. Or had Rebecca been faking it? If so, she'd been very convincing. Perhaps she'd been trying to convince herself as much as anyone else, but had lost the will to fight her true feelings – or lack of them. Maybe she hadn't ever loved anyone, him included. *What does it matter now?* he asked himself. But the question was hollow. It mattered.

"Why was she like that?" Jack's voice was more plaintive than angry.

"I've no idea. We didn't talk much."

Again, Paul's words had the ring of truth. When Jack married Rebecca, she'd been outgoing, even extroverted. But at the lowest point of her post-natal depression he'd struggled to get more than a few words out of her. Even after recovering, she'd talked and laughed a lot less than she used to. He'd sometimes wondered what happened to the woman he fell in love with. Not that he'd ever stopped loving her. If anything, the more he'd sensed her slipping away, the tighter he'd held on to her. He'd told himself their disconnection was a natural part of being together for so long. Like those silent old couples you saw in restaurants. He'd tried everything he could think of to reconnect with her – date nights, romantic weekends away, family holidays. In the end, it hadn't been enough. She'd become a virtual stranger. He felt that more acutely now than ever. Had he ever truly known Rebecca? Or had she worn a mask that concealed her true nature in the way that the killer's Ugly Mask perhaps revealed theirs?

"I've no right to ask this," said Paul, "but Natasha won't speak to me. Could you tell her how sorry I am and that I love her?"

"You've got some fucking nerve. Why should I?"

Paul's face quivered with regret. "Because I've lost everything over something that meant nothing. A few moments of insanity."

"Don't give me that bollocks, Paul. You knew what you were doing. Why should you get away with it? Why should anyone get away with the shit they do?"

"I don't want to get away with it. I told you, I want to make amends."

Jack took out his warrant card. "I suppose that's why you gave me this, to make amends."

"No... Well, maybe that was part of it," admitted Paul, "but that's not all it was. You're the best copper I know, Jack."

Jack thought about himself covering up his presence at Camilla's flat. He thought about himself refusing to follow up the Helen Bancroft-Harding lead. "No I'm not." He made to hand his ID to Paul.

Paul shook his head. "Keep it."

"Do you really think we can work together after this?"

"Put in for a transfer. Do whatever you need to do. Just don't throw away your career because of this. Please, Jack."

"Actually, Paul, you know what? You're right. But why should I be the one to move jobs? I'll stay at GMP and you can fuck off elsewhere. That is unless you want to see my face every day and be reminded of the misery you've caused."

"I don't need to see your face to be reminded of that." Paul sounded crushed.

Jack unclenched his fist. The urge to pound it into Paul was gone. All that was left was smouldering contempt. "You might want to start looking for a new job soon anyway. Natasha's talking about moving back to Eastbourne with Imogen and Dylan. I told her she should do it."

Anger flashed in Paul's eyes. The two men eyeballed each other. Paul blinked and lowered his gaze. Jack's lips curved into something that only resembled a smile. "And I thought I was pathetic."

"We're all human, Jack," pleaded Paul. "We all make mistakes."

"Yeah, and we all have to live with our mistakes." As Jack turned to leave, he added sardonically, "See you tomorrow, sir."

CHAPTER 42

Jack knocked back a slug of vodka. The bitter liquid took the edge off his post-adrenaline tremors. He felt a twinge of guilt for his cheap shot about Natasha moving back down south. That kind of petty vindictiveness wasn't him. Rebecca's voice rang out in his head: *Fuck me harder, Paul. Harder. Harder! Strangle me, Paul!* The words were the same as always, except for one tormenting difference. A fresh surge of anger swept away the guilt. He pounded a fist into his thigh, muttering in a half-sob, "Bastards. Fucking bastards."

He stopped on the way to his house to buy more vodka. He slammed open the front door and staggered upstairs. He emptied a drawerful of photos of Rebecca onto the bed and tore them up whilst shouting, "You've ruined me. I hate you. I wish to god I'd never met you!"

Finally, there was only one photo left – the wedding photo of Rebecca and him in the church porch. Their eyes! So full of happiness and love. How could something so beautiful turn into something so ugly? With an agonised groan, he clutched the photo to his chest and collapsed atop a mattress of torn dreams.

His gaze fell to his wedding ring. Since Rebecca's death, he'd occasionally caught himself rubbing it when thinking about her. Sometimes he looked at it and was transported back to the moment she'd slid it onto his finger. It had never crossed his mind to take it off. Even now, the thought of doing so made him feel sick. He forced down another mouthful vodka, but retched it back up.

Fuck me, Paul. Strangle me...

Just keep drinking. Keep drinking.

Jack returned the bottle to his lips. It wouldn't be long now before he couldn't think or feel anything at all.

His phone rang. He took it out and wasn't surprised to see 'Laura'. He let the call go through to voicemail, then listened to her message: "Don't do anything stupid, Jack. Naomi and I both love you to bits. Please call or text. We're worried sick–"

That was as much as he could bear to listen to. He cut off the message, slurring, "I'm sorry. I'm so sorry..."

I'm so sorry. Those words reminded him of something else. He scrolled down to Rebecca's final message: 'I love you and Naomi more than I can bear. I'm so sorry.'

So sorry for what? For Paul? For killing yourself? For marrying me and having our baby? For all of it?

Jack deleted the message and closed his eyes, hoping for darkness. But all he saw was an expanse of blue as endless as an ocean horizon. Bit by bit, he blotted it out with more vodka...

It was pitch dark when the phone roused him from his alcoholic blackout. For an instant, he didn't know where he was or even what year it was. He reached out, seeking Rebecca and found nothing. Then it all came rushing back, wrenching a guttural, animal-like moan from deep inside his chest.

He looked at his phone. The moan stopped. For a breathless moment, there was silence. Then he burst into a shrill laugh that bordered on hysteria.

'No Caller ID'.

"Fuck you!" Jack shouted at the phone. He turned his gaze to the ceiling... or something beyond. "Fuck you! Fuck you!"

The ringing stopped. Another few seconds of silence. It started again. 'No Caller ID'.

Jack put the phone to his ear. What else could he do? The voice stroked him like a flame. "Surprised to hear from me, Jack?"

"Surprised?" laughed Jack. "Why should I be surprised? Shit, I wouldn't be surprised if you walked into this room right now and stuck a knife in my stomach. I might even thank you for it."

"You sound drunk, Jack."

"So what if I am?"

"Something's happened, hasn't it? Something to do with Rebecca."

Jack ground his teeth. This bastard could see through him like an X-ray. He had a sudden urge to spew it all out, the whole sordid tale. Empty it into the killer like vomit into a toilet.

"Talk to me." The voice was soft, but in a different way. Gone was the demanding, taunting tone. Its place had been taken by... By what? Not sympathy. No, this was something else. Something closer to pleading.

Jack wanted to get it out so badly that he could taste the bitter words. But even as drunk as he was, he knew it would do more harm than good. Information was power. The job, not Rebecca, had taught him that. It was a simple equation: the more information you had on someone, the more power you had over them. "What do you want me to say? You were right, I'm like you. I'm a worthless piece of shit."

"We're not the worthless ones, Jack. They are."

They. Who were *they*? The victims? Someone else? He parroted Emma's words from the day before. "Keep telling yourself that and you might believe it."

"You don't know me, Jack. You don't know what I've been through. But I know what you're about. It's all poor me. Why did life do this to me? Me. Me. Me."

"Oh fuck you," Jack spat into the phone. "At least I don't go around murdering people."

"No, you just ruin kids' lives, don't you?" The killer shot back. "You make them promises you can't keep."

"This isn't my fault."

"Isn't it? Did someone else put that bottle in your hand and force you to drink from it?"

There were tears in Jack's eyes. "She did this. Not me. It was her. It was Rebecca."

"Tell me about Rebecca."

"Please leave me alone. Leave me alone..." Jack slurred off, then added, "I... I'll tell myself this was a bad dream. You never rang. Shane will go down for the murders and we'll both be free to go on with our lives."

"And you'd be OK with a man going to prison for crimes he didn't commit, would you?"

"Did you kill that woman in Tasle Alley?"

"No."

"Then Shane did. And he deserves to go to prison for the rest of his life anyway. So what's the difference?"

Laughter came down the line. Again, it wasn't taunting. It was more disbelieving. "I've never known anyone as good at lying to themselves as you, Jack. You wouldn't be able to live with yourself. It would destroy you knowing I was still on the streets."

He shot back a disbelieving laugh of his own. "What do you care if it destroys me?"

"Tell me about Rebecca," the killer said again.

Jack threw his head back and yelled, "Argh!" at the ceiling. "You want to know about Rebecca. Alright, I'll tell you about her. I thought she was better than everyone else – more beautiful, more understanding. To me, she was perfect. She had this way about her. When she walked into a room, people would stop and stare. Sometimes I felt embarrassed to be beside her. Like I wasn't good enough to have her on my arm. She seemed to feel things – pain and pleasure – more deeply than other people. Once, not long after we got together, we were walking home from a night out and it started raining – one of those summer storms when the heavens open up. Rebecca spun round and round. She wanted me to dance with her, but I... I just stood watching..." Jack faded into the memory.

There was a brief silence. "I'm going to hang up now." There was another new note in the killer's voice. Weariness? Sadness? It was difficult to tell.

"Wait," exclaimed Jack. "What happens next?"

"You have to catch me. It has to be you, Jack. You alone."

"Why me? Why does it have to be..." He trailed off. The line was dead.

Jack lay motionless, struggling to make sense of his vodka-drenched thoughts. *I've never known anyone as good at lying to themselves as you.* Those words swirled in his mind. The bastard was right. He'd lied to himself that Rebecca loved him. He'd lied to himself that she didn't commit suicide. He'd lied to Laura. But worst of all, he'd lied to Naomi. He'd told her he would never be apart from her again. Yet here he was, wallowing in self-pity while she worried herself sick about him. Perhaps, like Shane's daughter, Naomi would be better off if he went to prison. He shook his head hard. He wasn't a murderer like Shane. *We all lose our way sometimes,* Brenda Devonport had said. And she was right. He'd lost his way. The question was had he wandered too far to find the way back?

He shook his head again. "All you've got to do is catch this fucker."

Oh, is that all? Ha, ha!

"Shut the fuck up," he shouted at the doubting voice.

Lawrence Bancroft-Harding. The name rose through the murk of his mind. He needed to speak to Lawrence. But in his current condition, he would struggle to make it to the front door, never mind Wilmslow. *Probably a good thing,* he reflected. Paul had pleaded with him not to throw his career away. But Paul was a fucking snake. *If you disobey orders, he might use it as an excuse to kick you out of SCD. Best to speak to him before making a move.*

Jack scowled. The thought of Paul made his head pound with violent urges. *No,* he said to himself. This wasn't about Paul and him. This was about Naomi. For her, he would swallow his pride. For her, he would treat Paul with all the respect due to a superior officer.

He snatched up the vodka bottle and flung it into the darkness. It clattered against something. His eyes rolled. The alcohol was pulling him back under. Before giving in to it, he texted Laura: 'Please don't worry. I'm OK. Tell Naomi we're still on for the weekend. I love you both too.'

CHAPTER 43

Jack spent a long time showering, shaving and styling his hair. He put on a clean suit and adjusted his tie. He adjusted his face into a professional expression. Mask in place, he left the house.

He could still feel the lingering effects of the vodka. His head was hammering and the ground seemed to shift beneath his feet. Coffee and painkillers would soon sort that out.

His phone rang. 'Laura'. He answered it. "Hello, sis."

"Hi Jack. How are you this morning?"

"I won't lie, I've got a nasty hangover."

Laura sighed. "What are we going to do with you, Jack?"

"Is Naomi OK?"

"She keeps asking me to take her out to look for you. I said no. I'm taking her to school, just like any other day."

"That's good."

"Did you see him last night?"

"Who?"

"Don't play games with me, Jack. You know who?"

"Yes I saw him. And yes we exchanged more than harsh words."

An apprehensive rise came into Laura's voice. "You didn't..." She trailed off as if afraid to ask the obvious question.

"No I didn't kill him. I wanted to, but I didn't."

A breath of relief came through the earpiece. "He's not worth it. He's not worth even one second of your time."

"Someone else said pretty much the same thing. I'm starting to think you're both right. Listen, I'll see you later. It might be late. I don't know what time I'll get off work."

"You're going into work?" Laura asked in surprise.

"Uh-huh. Just like any other day."

"Well be careful. And if you feel like punching that prick again, just remember what really matters."

"I will."

Jack got off the phone. He drove to Naomi's school and parked a little way along from it. After a while, he spotted Laura and her. His chest gave a squeeze. Naomi wasn't smiling. That worried look was back. The one he'd first seen when Rebecca fell ill. He didn't get out of the car. Yes, he'd done his best to make himself presentable. But nothing could disguise his bloodshot, pained eyes. Seeing him now would only add to Naomi's worry. He would see her when it was all over.

Because it would be all over today. One way or another.

He watched Naomi into school before continuing on his way. Upon arriving at HQ, he unhesitatingly headed up to the Incident Room. His mask almost slipped at the sight of Paul chatting to Emma. Paul was sporting a big phoney smile that vanished as Jack approached. There was a nasty bruise by Paul's right eye. He blinked as if anticipating a punch being thrown at him. Jack's composure returned. *You're the one with the upper hand,* he told himself. *This piece of shit can't touch you.*

"Morning DI Anderson," Paul said stiffly.

"Morning sir," Jack replied in an unreadable tone.

Emma glance from one man to the other as if she suspected something was off. Jack wondered if Paul had spun her some bullshit about where the bruise came from. He cast off the thought. *Remember what really matters. You're going to catch that bastard out there. And then you're going to go see Naomi.*

"Can I have a word in private?" asked Jack.

Paul hesitated to reply – only briefly, but enough to suggest he wasn't sure he wanted to be alone with Jack. "About what?"

"Shane Hardy."

Relief flickered in Paul's eyes. "You can say what you need to say here."

"OK, sir. Shane killed his wife, but he didn't kill the others."

"You sound very certain of that."

"I am."

Paul spread his hands as if to say, *Go on.*

Instead of explaining himself, Jack said, "I want to speak to Lawrence Bancroft-Harding."

"Why should I agree to that? What's changed since yesterday?"

Jack stared at Paul with eyes like stones. "Everything."

Paul blinked again. "OK, Jack, you win," he said quickly. "Let's discuss this in my office."

Jack could feel Emma's eyes following him and Paul from the room. He could almost hear her wondering about the sudden freezing over of relations between the two friends. That was good. It would give him a little more leverage.

As soon as they were in his office, Paul turned to Jack and said in a tone that mixed anger and anxiety, "So is this how it's going to be? Are you going to be constantly trying to make me look small in front of the others?"

"You don't need me to make you look small, sir," Jack said in a calm voice that didn't match his words.

"Do you remember what I said before you returned to work, Jack? I said that if you fell off the wagon, you were out. All I have to do is get on the phone to the Super and request a urine test and you're finished."

Jack thumbed towards the Incident Room. "And all I have to do is tell that lot how you got that bruise and you're finished. Oh you'll still have a job, but you won't have their respect. And you'll never rise any higher than

DCI. I mean, who's going to promote an officer that might screw around with their wife?"

A flush of impotent anger climbed Paul's throat. He darted his tongue back and forth across his lips as if considering what his next move should be. "What do you want from me?"

"I've already told you, I want permission to speak to Lawrence Bancroft-Harding."

"Why? What's so important to you about him?"

"Do I have your permission, sir?"

Paul's face was a minor symphony of tics at Jack's continued refusal to explain himself. Jack drew a bitter pleasure from watching him squirm. *Is this how the killer feels when they speak to me?* he wondered. Paul's features slumped in resignation. "Yes, you have my permission." As if trying to claw back a small measure of control, he added, "But you and DI Steele have only got today to look into your lead."

"I'm better off working alone. If Emma's with me, I might let slip something I'll regret."

The bunched muscles of Paul's jaw told Jack that he was holding back an explosion of wounded pride. Paul gave a sharp nod.

"Thank you, sir."

With this parting show of disingenuous deference, Jack left the office. Emma was waiting in the corridor. "Did he give you permission?"

"Yes."

"How did you get him to change his mind? Have you dug up something new?"

"No."

"I don't understand. Then what–" Emma broke off as Jack headed for the lifts. "Wait up. I need to get my jacket."

"I'm working alone today."

Emma frowned. "But this is our lead. Why would you work it alone?"

Jack jerked his chin towards Paul's door. "Ask him."

Emma dodged in front of Jack and fixed him with one of her direct stares. "What's going on, Jack?"

He held her gaze expressionlessly. She gave a little nod as if to say, *OK, if that's how it is,* and stepped aside. He felt like shit for giving her the cold shoulder, but that was the way it had to be. There were things he might have to do that she couldn't be around.

CHAPTER 44

Lawrence Bancroft-Harding lived in a detached house on an affluent street. The curtains were open. An Audi was parked in the driveway. It looked like Lawrence was in. Jack put a set of handcuffs and his steel baton in his jacket pockets. As much as he would have taken satisfaction in proving Paul wrong, he was ninety-nine percent sure Lawrence wasn't the killer. Jack was getting to know the owner of the soft voice. Paul's reasoning was sound: they weren't the type to panic and hang up. But more than that, there was something in their past, some trauma that went back to childhood. *No, you just ruin kids' lives, don't you? You make them promises you can't keep.* He'd caught a scrape in the killer's voice when they said that. They hadn't simply been talking about Jack and Naomi. They'd been talking about themselves. Had someone made them a false promise?

Jack could find no such trauma in Lawrence's childhood. Lawrence had grown up in a comfortable middle-class household. His dad had also been a dentist. His mum had been a housewife. They were married for over fifty years. When his dad retired, Lawrence had inherited his practice and ran it until his own retirement two years ago. After his dad's death in '95, Lawrence had taken his mum in. She'd lived with her son and daughter-in-law until her death in '02 – just three years before cancer had claimed Diane. Those weren't the actions of a sociopath. They were the actions of someone whose upbringing had taught them to lead a decent life.

Of course it could all be a mask, a disguise – hence the handcuffs and baton.

Jack knocked on the front door. It was opened by a bespectacled man with mild grey eyes and a broken-veined complexion. His hair might once have been brown like Mr Average's, but now it was snow white. He was slightly stooped with narrow shoulders. Hardly the type to be running around murdering young women. But then again, you never knew. Jack kept one hand on the baton's grip. The man looked as if he hadn't been up long – blue dressing-gown, slippers. A faint frown disturbed his forehead as Jack asked, "Are you Lawrence Bancroft-Harding?"

"Yes. Who are you?"

Jack displayed his warrant card. "We spoke on the phone. I'm investigating the disappearance of Rhys Devonport."

Lawrence's frown hardened. "Sorry, I can't help you."

He made to close the door, but Jack jammed his foot against it. Lawrence wasn't going to get out of talking to him this time. "I assure you this won't take long."

"Please move your foot."

"A man is missing. He could be dead."

Lawrence compressed his lips as if holding back from saying something he might regret.

Jack called his bluff. "We can do this at the station if you like."

Lawrence stared at him undecidedly for a moment, then sighed. "I suppose you'd better come in."

They went into a living-room furnished with a chintzy three-piece suit – not the type of thing a man would choose. The fireplace was a shrine to Lawrence's wife. Photos of Helen crowded the hearth and mantelpiece. In some she was alone, in others she was with Lawrence. She had thick blonde hair, blue eyes and a broad smile.

"She was a beautiful woman, don't you think?" said Lawrence.

Jack nodded. Helen had certainly been beautiful, but she hadn't been in the same league as Camilla or, for that matter, 1980s Lilith.

Lawrence seated himself in an armchair. There was a glass of white wine next to it. Noticing Jack looking at the glass, Lawrence said, "Leftover from last night."

You're not a very good liar, thought Jack. There was still condensation on the glass. It hadn't been poured long ago. He swallowed dryly. God, how he longed to down the contents of the glass and whatever remained in the bottle it had come from.

"White wine was Helen's favourite. I never used to much like it. Now it's all I drink."

Lawrence settled back in his chair, stretching out his legs and crossing his feet. Jack glanced at his slippers. He estimated them to be about a size eight or nine. There was no sign of excess wear on the inner heel. "You're not currently in a relationship?"

"Not since Helen died twelve years ago. Twelve years," Lawrence repeated. "That's a long time to be drinking alone. No partner. No kids. Just me. What about yourself? I see you're married." He indicated the gold band on Jack's ring finger.

Jack's brow wrinkled as he glanced at his wedding ring. He saw that Lawrence still wore his ring too. *Twelve years... a long time to be drinking alone.* Was that what the future held? If he had a future. "I have a daughter. She's eight."

"You're lucky. Helen and I decided not to have children for the sake of her health." Lawrence's eyes drifted off to some other place for a second. "She would have made a wonderful mum."

"I understand that Helen and Rhys were good friends."

Lawrence gave him a sardonic look. "You can say it, Inspector. They were lovers."

"When was this?"

"From '84 to '85." Lawrence's tone was matter-of-fact, but a ghost of old pain haunted his eyes.

"And were you and Helen married at the time?"

"Yes."

"How did you find out about the affair?"

"How does anyone find out about these things? Helen broke down and confessed one day. She ended the affair and we did whatever was necessary to save our marriage."

Jack looked at his wedding ring again, wondering how he would have reacted if he'd found out about Rebecca's affair when she was alive. Would they have tried to make a go of it? Or would they have split up?

"I'm not the least bit surprised Devonport's gone missing," said Lawrence. "I always knew that one day he would pick the wrong bloke's wife to mess around with." A spark flickered in his eyes. "When I found out what he'd been up to with Helen, I wanted to kill him myself. I might have done so too if she hadn't begged me not to. Even years later, I sometimes thought about tracking him down and beating the living daylights out of him." With an almost ashamed downward look, he added, "Truth is, I would never have actually done it. I can admit that now. But when I was your age... Well, you know how it is."

Jack's pulse quickened. Did Lawrence somehow know about Rebecca and Paul? No, that wasn't possible. The older man was merely referring to the pride and ego of youth.

"I used to think I was a coward for letting Devonport get away with what he did," continued Lawrence. "I wasted years of my life on hating him. I almost destroyed what was left of my marriage because of it."

"What kept you together?" Jack had to ask.

"Cancer." Lawrence smiled sadly at the look of bemusement that came over Jack. "In '88 Helen was diagnosed with breast cancer and suddenly Devonport didn't matter anymore. Nothing quite puts things in perspective like being told the love of your life might die. As it happened, the treatment was successful. Helen went into remission and got the all clear. After that we had seventeen wonderful years together before the cancer came back. It could have been more if I hadn't held onto my hate for so long." His features contracted. "I sometimes wonder whether Helen would have got cancer at all if I hadn't put her through so much guilt."

"What about everything she put you through?"

Lawrence's eyes narrowed as if he sensed Jack's interest was more than simply professional. "Oh I suffered too. There were times when I felt like I wanted to die rather than endure the pain of knowing what Helen had done. But my pain was clean. Hers was dirty. And that kind of pain rots you from the inside. Makes you feel hollow and worthless. Does that make sense?"

Jack nodded, thinking about the way Rebecca sometimes used to writhe around as if something was eating away at her insides. With difficulty, he maintained a tone of professional detachment. "Do any of your friends or relatives know about the affair?"

Lawrence looked mortified at the idea. "No. As far as I'm aware, only two people besides myself, Helen and Devonport know about it. And one of those passed away years ago."

"What are their names?"

"Gabriel and Lilith Winter."

A glimmer of surprise found its way through Jack's mask. Here was another link. Another piece of the puzzle. What other pieces did Lawrence possess? "As in Camilla Winter's parents?"

"Yes." Lawrence shook his head. "Terrible, terrible thing what happened to Camilla."

"Did you know her?" Jack's fingers curled more tightly around the baton as he waited for Lawrence's reply.

"No. I never met her."

"Then how did you come to know Lilith and Gabriel?"

Jack stepped sideways as Lawrence rose and approached the fireplace. Lawrence picked up a black-and-white photo and showed it to him. Jack's eyes widened with surprise for a second time that morning. It was the Newell Green High School photo. "This was taken in '67." Lawrence pointed. "That's Helen. That's Devonport." His finger moved to a girl behind Rhys whose centrally parted dark wavy hair was just long enough to cover her ears. She was slim but not skinny, with a swan-neck and a long, unblemished face. Her rosebud lips wore a slightly upturned Mona Lisa smile. She was looking down at the back of Rhys's head. "And that's Lilith."

So Lilith didn't come from money. Were her cut-glass accent and haughty mannerisms just another one of the masks that people wore? wondered Jack.

"Lilith and Helen were best friends until Devonport came between them," continued Lawrence. "I'd assumed it was Lilith who sent you my way."

"No. It was Rhys's sister, Brenda."

Lawrence opened his mouth as if to say, *Ah.* "How did she know about Helen and Devonport?"

"She didn't. She only knew that Rhys was seeing someone named Helen in the mid-eighties." Jack indicated the photo. "Then I saw that online and put two and two together."

Lawrence frowned as if something had occurred to him. "You don't think Devonport's disappearance has anything to do with Camilla's murder, do you?"

"We've no reason to suspect it," Jack lied.

"But you do know that Devonport had an affair with Lilith too?"

"Yes, although we're a bit hazy on the details."

Lawrence smiled thinly. "I can just imagine what Lilith said when you mentioned Devonport to her."

"Lilith's not in much of a fit state to say anything. She has emphysema. She doesn't have long left to live."

"Oh, I'm sorry to hear that," Lawrence said with what seemed genuine sympathy. "I never much liked Lilith. She always thought she was so much better than Helen. Her parents were wealthy, but they fell on hard times. That's how she ended up at Newell Green. She despised the place. I remember once at one of Lilith's dinner parties Helen made some passing remark about their schooldays. The look Lilith gave her. It could have frozen the soup. Their friendship was toxic. To me, it seemed like the only reason Lilith was friends with Helen was because she could treat her however she wanted and Helen would put up with it. Lilith was good at manipulating people. And she had a ruthlessly ambitious streak. Like Thatcher. Nothing was ever going to stand in her way. But she had one weakness."

"Rhys Devonport."

Lawrence nodded. "Devonport had been hopelessly in love with Lilith since their schooldays. And she was in love with him too. But he couldn't give her what she wanted – social status. So she married a man who could, but who she didn't love. Tragic, isn't it? That would have been the end of the story, but Devonport had other ideas. He pursued her until she gave in. That was sometime in '82. Lilith used to get Helen lie for her. One time Gabriel phoned our house looking for Lilith. Helen pleaded with me to tell him Lilith and her were out shopping. I wasn't happy about it, but what else could I do? Lilith ended the affair in '84."

"'84," parroted Jack. Camilla was born in '86. That meant Rhys wasn't her dad. It also meant Lawrence had no reason to hurt her.

Lawrence nodded. "And a few months later Helen and Devonport..." He closed his eyes and shook his head. "In some ways I blame myself for what happened. I should never have let Lilith treat Helen the way she did. I should have told her what I thought of her – that she was a controlling, nasty piece–" He broke off with a flick of his wrist as if wafting away a bad smell. "What's happened has happened."

"Do you think Rhys was trying to make Lilith jealous?"

"I think that's exactly what he was trying to do. Of course, he didn't say that to Helen."

"What did he say?"

"I don't know. Devonport's what you might call a charming bastard. I met him once by chance at an antiques fair. This was well before his affair with Lilith. He could have sold coal to a miner. A real life Del boy. He was all over Helen. Hands like an octopus. Alarm bells should have been ringing even then, but I trusted her. Well you do, don't you? When you love someone, you think only the best of them. You don't believe for a moment that they could..." Lawrence's voice faltered. He pushed out a smile. "But anyway, that's life, as they say."

Yes, thought Jack. *That's fucking life.* "Why did Lilith break off the affair?"

"Because she fell pregnant."

Jack frowned in confusion. "But Camilla was born two years after Lilith ended the affair."

"That's right. Obviously Lilith wasn't pregnant with Camilla in '84."

"You're saying Lilith had another child before Camilla?"

"All I can tell you is what Helen told me. Lilith had done the maths and knew it had to be Rhys's baby. She was in a real state. She refused to have an abortion. She's Catholic. It never made much sense to me. She could cheat on her husband, but when it came to having an abortion, uh-uh, no way."

"So what did she do?"

"What could she do? She had to tell Gabriel about the affair."

"And how did he take it?"

"I've no idea. He can't have taken it very well, though, because after that Lilith broke off all contact with Helen."

"Why?"

"I assume because Helen had covered up for Lilith and Devonport. Helen was devastated. I've never seen her so upset. Not even when she was diagnosed with cancer. I'm sure that's why she did what she did with Devonport – just to try to provoke a response from Lilith. Both she and

Devonport were willing to ruin their lives over that woman. Makes you think, doesn't it?"

"Yes," agreed Jack, although it made him want to do the opposite. He would have given almost anything to shut his mind down to all the cheating, lying and deception done in the name of love. "And did Lilith respond?"

Lawrence shook his head. "She and Helen never spoke again. We only heard about Camilla's birth and Gabriel's death through mutual friends."

"Did Rhys know about the '84 pregnancy?"

"Not as far as I'm aware."

"So what happened to the baby?"

Lawrence spread his hands in a 'who knows' gesture. "I've often wondered that myself. Perhaps Lilith had a miscarriage."

But what if she didn't? Jack asked himself. Lawrence seemingly had no reason to hurt Camilla, but Rhys might have. Jack suddenly found himself thinking about a book he'd seen in Gabriel's study: 'A Clinician's Guide to Medical and Surgical Abortion'. It had caught his eye because it seemed out of place. Had Gabriel performed a forced abortion on Lilith? And had Rhys somehow found out about it after all these years? Maybe Lilith had confessed to him because she was dying. And maybe Rhys had killed Camilla in revenge for Gabriel killing his child. It made a twisted kind of sense. A sort of balancing of the books.

Jack thought about Lilith's reaction – or rather lack of one – upon first hearing the news of Camilla's death. It was almost as if she'd known what was coming. But why wouldn't she have pointed them to Rhys? *No, you just ruin kids' lives, don't you? You make them promises you can't keep.* Perhaps Lilith had promised herself to Rhys when they were children. And now she was paying the price for breaking that promise.

"Thank you Mr Bancroft-Harding."

"I hope I've been of help. Despite everything, I wouldn't want Devonport to come to a bad end."

There was no trace of sarcasm in Lawrence's voice. Jack squinted at him as if he was trying to decipher a complex equation. "Did you truly forgive your wife?"

"Yes," Lawrence replied without hesitation.

"What about Rhys?"

"You mean have I forgiven him too? I've never thought about it, but I suppose have. Perhaps I should even be grateful to him."

Jack's eyebrows drew together. "Why?"

"Helen and I wouldn't have been as close as we were if it wasn't for him. The cancer played a big part, but it was the affair that first made me realise just how much Helen meant to me. Actually I feel sorry for Devonport. I found true happiness with a woman I love. The woman he loves wants nothing to do with him."

"If you feel that way, why were you so reluctant to talk about Rhys?"

Lawrence smiled coyly. "Just because I don't hate the bastard anymore, doesn't mean I can stand the sound of his name. You've asked me a lot of questions, Inspector. Now can I ask something of you?"

"Go ahead."

"Please don't contact me again. It's not that I don't want to help. It's just..." Lawrence's smile became almost bashful. "I only want to remember the good things about Helen."

Jack returned to his car with mixed emotions. Part of him was in awe of Lawrence's ability to put love before ego. But another part sneered that Lawrence's magnanimity wasn't wisdom it was weakness.

He couldn't see any reason to think Lawrence hadn't been truthful. If Lawrence was going to seek revenge on Rhys and Lilith, surely he would have done it back when he first found out about the affair. Or soon after Helen's death in 2005. Why would he wait another twelve years? It wouldn't make sense. Especially not when you considered that he'd led a happy life with Helen.

Jack closed his tired eyes, but instantly snapped them open. The back of his eyelids were like screens projecting stomach-churning images of Rebecca and Paul. Could he have forgiven her? It was pointless torturing himself with the question. Unlike Lawrence, he hadn't had the chance to find out. But what about Paul? Could he forgive Paul? The idea seemed as far-fetched as time travel.

"Rhys," he murmured. That was who he needed to focus on now. Not himself. Not Rebecca. And definitely not Paul.

But where the hell was Rhys? He wasn't in Chester. He wasn't at his sister's. He certainly wasn't at Diane's. And Cheshire Police had checked out his old Blackpool haunts. That left only one place Jack could think of.

He punched 'Sale Road' into the Satnav.

CHAPTER 45

Sale Road passed through a residential area of modest semis and terraces with the occasional low-rise block of flats and small shopping parade thrown into the mix. It wasn't difficult to locate the bungalow where Rhys and Brenda grew up. The magnolia tree in its front garden was in full pink bloom. The little detached bungalow's roof peeped over a scraggly privet hedge. A short driveway led to a garage with windowless double-doors. The driveway was empty. The front window curtains were closed. No one appeared to be home.

Jack drove on for a short distance and did a U-turn before parking up. He watched the bungalow for ten minutes.

An old man came out of a neighbouring house and began trimming his side of the hedge. A woman walking two dogs stopped to talk to him. The old man gestured animatedly with his secateurs at the overgrown hedge.

He doesn't look happy, thought Jack. *Might be worth having a chat with him.*

Jack waited for the dog-walker to continue on her way, then got out and approached the old man. "Excuse me, sir. Have you got a moment?"

The man squinted at him. "Are you a salesman?"

"Quite the opposite. I'm interested in buying a property in this area." Jack didn't want to announce that he was a policeman without knowing what the old man's relationship was to Rhys. Besides, sometimes the best way to get the information you wanted from someone was to engage them in casual conversation. "Is this your house?"

"Yes. I've lived here over forty years and I'm not interested in selling."

"What about your neighbours? Do you think any of them might be interested?"

The man prodded at the hedge. "I wish this one bloody-well was."

"Sounds like you've had trouble with them."

"It's rented. We've had more people living there than I can count. Most have been nice enough. Some have been a pain in the arse. There was this one family a few years back. Four bloody kids–"

"Who lives there now?" Jack interrupted before the old man could go off on a rant. He didn't want to stand around outside the bungalow for any longer than necessary.

"Dunno. Never seen them. The curtains are always shut. Sometimes there's a light on. I think the place is empty most of the time. Definitely has been for the past couple of weeks. I've heard a car coming and going in the middle of the night. I reckon whoever it is must work nights. Either that or they're a vampire."

Perhaps you're closer to the truth than you realise, thought Jack, simulating a smile at the dry remark. "Do you know who the letting agent is?"

"Yes, because I keep having to get on to them about this bloody hedge. People with pushchairs have to walk in the road. It's dangerous. I'd cut it myself, but you know what it's like these days. I'd probably end up in court or–"

"Who did you say the letting agent is?"

"Barlow and Coe." The old man pointed in the direction Jack had driven from. "Their office is two minutes that way."

"Barlow and Coe," Jack echoed. Abigail Hart had worked in their city centre branch. The pieces of the puzzle were coming together fast. He'd gone through the list of Barlow & Coe's customers, Googling any that lived within the triangle formed by Abigail, Zoe and Erica's murder scenes. Wythenshawe fell just outside that area. "Thanks for that."

Jack returned to his car, noting the bungalow's street number and the cylinder lock on its upvc front door. Burglars had a field day with those locks. They could be snapped with a few simple tools. He'd learnt how to do it as a constable regularly called out to incidents where people were locked in and unable to reach their door. It was quick, but destroyed the lock. Not good for OAPs who couldn't afford a replacement. A better way was to use a bump key. He'd had a set specially made. It had come in very handy over the years – and would prove so once again if Barlow & Coe didn't have, or refused to hand over, a spare key for the bungalow.

He drove to a parade of shops. Barlow and Coe was housed in a small office with photos of properties in its window. A smartly dressed thirty-something woman was sitting behind a desk. A name plaque identified her as 'Scarlett Brooks'. Smiling, she asked, "Can I help you?"

Jack showed Scarlett his warrant card. "I'm trying to find out about a tenant who rents a property through you." He told her the bungalow's address.

Scarlett consulted her computer. "The tenant's name is Jordan Murphy."

"Jordan Murphy?" murmured Jack. Who the hell was Jordan Murphy? Was Rhys using an alias? "When did he rent out the bungalow?"

"Thirteenth of November 2016."

A week prior to Rhys's last date of contact. Surely that wasn't a coincidence. "Have you met Mr Murphy?"

"No, but I've spoken to him on the phone."

"So there's just one man living there?"

Scarlett nodded. "Although to be honest, when I first spoke to him I thought he was a she."

"Oh, why's that?"

"Well he's softly spoken and he's got one of those names that could belong to a boy or a girl."

The killer's sexless voice seemed to tingle in Jack's ears. "Does Mr Murphy have an accent?"

"Not that I can remember."

Softly spoken. No accent. It had to be the killer! "I was chatting to one of the neighbours. He says the bungalow's empty most of the time."

"This neighbour didn't happen to be a Victor Meldrew lookalike, did he?"

"That's him."

Scarlett's lips thinned into an unsurprised smile. "That would be Mr Tullett. He runs the local neighbourhood watch. And boy does he like to keep an eye on his neighbourhood. If you get my meaning."

Jack returned a smile to show that he did. He was itching to have a look inside the bungalow. For that to happen without going through official channels, he would need Scarlett's cooperation.

"He's been giving me earache about the bungalow's overgrown garden," continued Scarlett. "I keep telling him, it's the tenant's responsibility to look after–" She broke off, frowning as if something had occurred to her. "There were some policemen in here the other day. They were asking about Abigail. The girl who was–"

"Yes, I know," interrupted Jack. Time was ticking on.

"Has this got something to do with her?"

"Yes."

Scarlett put a hand to her mouth. "Oh my god, you don't think Mr Murphy is the Ripper, do you?"

"I'm sorry, I can't–"

"Oh of course, you can't discuss an ongoing investigation." Scarlett smiled. "I watch way too much police stuff on TV."

"Did you know Abigail?"

"Not very well. She worked in our city centre office. I only met her twice. She was a lovely girl."

"Listen, Scarlett, what I really need is to have a look inside that bungalow."

Scarlett looked at Jack uncertainly. "One minute." She rose and went through a door at the back of the office. She returned with a key. "I shouldn't be doing this but..." She handed him the key. "That's for the backdoor. You catch the wanker who killed Abigail."

I'm going to, Jack wanted to reply. But there were no guarantees in life. That was another lesson Rebecca had taught him. "Thanks for this. I'll bring it back when I'm done."

Jack returned to the bungalow and parked up in the same spot. The driveway was still empty. The curtains were still closed. Mr Tullett was still cutting the hedge. Jack didn't want to get caught up in conversation with the old man. He glanced at the time: 12:34. Best to give it a while longer anyway in case Rhys or Jordan or whoever rented the place was indulging in a long lie-in.

He booted up the Toughbook. A search revealed several Jordan Murphys in the North West – none of which were registered as residing at the bungalow. One caught his eye. This Jordan had a record. In 1996 he'd been convicted of drunk driving, fined £1000 and banned from driving for a year. That held little interest, unlike what happened in 2009. In March of that year, Jordan had been questioned in relation to accusations of sexual abuse at Rainbow's End Children's Home in Blackpool. He'd run the home from 1997 to 2009, when a fourteen-year-old girl named Hannah Meadows accused him of molesting her. After an investigation by Lancashire Police, the Crown Prosecution Service had decided there was insufficient evidence to bring charges against Jordan. But some mud had obviously stuck because he'd relocated from Blackpool to Blackburn – where, according to the DVLA database, he still lived. He was described as no longer working with children.

Rainbow's End Children's Home – in '84 Lilith had suffered an unwanted pregnancy. The offspring of such pregnancies sometimes ended up in children's homes. *Blackpool* – Rhys's favourite seaside haunt. Those were the type of coincidences that would set any detective's brain tingling.

Jack thought back to the killer's rant about putting kiddy fiddlers' heads on spikes. If Jordan was the killer, those words didn't add up. Assuming Jordan was guilty of molesting Hannah, he'd had years to reflect on his crime. Why would he suddenly be filled with self-loathing? And how did such self-loathing translate into serial murder? Perhaps it was all part of the killer's game. An act, a bluff. Sexual predators – especially child molesters – were, by nature, arch-manipulators.

Jack looked at Jordan's particulars: 'POB: Burnley General Hospital, Burnley', 'DOB: 09-04-1958', 'Height: 5'8"', 'Weight: 176', 'Eye Colour: Brown', 'Hair Colour: Brown', 'Race: White North European', 'Scars, Marks, Tattoos etc: tattoo of blue rose on left shoulder', 'Circumcision: No', 'Build: Medium', 'Occupation: Recruitment Consultant and joint owner of M&J Recruitment Agency', 'Names Of Places Frequented: not known', 'Next of Kin: Stuart Murphy and Anthony Murphy', 'Relationship to Jordan Murphy: Sons', 'Marital Status: Married to Maria Murphy'.

Tattoo of a blue rose – a red rose tattoo had been cut from Erica Cook's thigh. The 'coincidences' were adding up. Another thing bothered Jack though. If Jordan was the killer, why would he rent the bungalow under his own name? Jack seemed to hear a whisper of the soft voice, *I want you to catch me...*

He scrutinised Jordan's mugshot – bald as an egg; salt-n-pepper goatee; washed-out complexion; broad, large-featured face; deep-set, grey eyes. Jordan's face was tired but inscrutable. He didn't look like the sort who would easily crack under pressure.

You'll find out if you're right about that soon enough, Jack thought grimly.

He navigated to M&J Recruitment Agency's website. On the homepage there was a photo of the agency's premises – stone building, steel and glass entrance, swanky sign. The agency dealt with a wide range of jobs, from legal, administration and sales to dental and medical. He clicked 'Meet the Team' and was taken to glossy photos of M&J's employees. Top of the page was 'Maria Murphy, Managing Director' – a good looking middle-aged woman with auburn hair and blue eyes. Next to her, looking very different from his mugshot – smart suit, friendly smile – was 'Jordan Murphy, Sales Director.'

He looked up Hannah Meadows. She had a record: petty theft, shoplifting, being drunk and disorderly in public, possession of Class A drugs. For the first three offences, she'd been given fixed penalty notices. For the final offence, she'd received a conditional court discharge. So far so typical. At eighteen Hannah would have found herself ejected from the care system into a council flat. No money, no job, no prospects. Confused, alone and traumatised. Was it any wonder she'd turned to crime and drugs? His heart grew heavier as he read on. In April 2014, aged just nineteen, Hannah had died from a heroin overdose. He sighed. Fucking life. Fucking shitty world. He followed a link to a custody photo – hair tied into a scruffy topknot; pale, makeup-less face; tired, empty eyes – too tired and empty for a girl her age. But despite – or perhaps because of – it all, she was still heartbreakingly beautiful.

Rebecca...

There had been a similar emptiness in Rebecca's eyes, except she'd suffered no childhood trauma that Jack knew of. Her parents had doted on her, given her all the love a child needs. They weren't wealthy people, but they were comfortably enough off to make sure she hadn't wanted for anything. She'd been popular at school and academically gifted. She'd sailed through university and straight into a job at a prestigious consulting firm. To all appearances, she was a happy, successful young woman. But something had been gnawing at her, hollowing her out until she was nothing but a shell of herself.

What was it, Rebecca? What happened to you?

He forced his mind back to Hannah. Her hair was platinum blonde with dark roots and her eyes were blueish-green. Not an exact match to the victims, but close. Here then was motive: Hannah had besmirched Jordan's reputation. Perhaps he'd been planning his revenge on her before she selfishly OD'd, and so had to vent his anger on substitute victims. Jack wrinkled his forehead. There were several problems with that hypothesis. First, the victims were all significantly older than Hannah. Second, Jordan's life hadn't fallen to pieces after Hannah's accusation. He was running a seemingly successful business with his wife. Jack took a peek at Jordan's Blackburn house on Google Earth: modern detached, double-garage. From the looks of it, Jordan had moved on with his life and was doing very well thank you very much. Why risk everything now, three years after Hannah's death?

Jack stopped the questions. There were so many 'whys', but he wouldn't find the answers sitting here. He lifted his head in time to see Mr Tullett disappearing behind his house. It was a quarter-past-one. The street basked quietly in the midday sun. Jack's gaze slid across to the bungalow. *No one's in*, he said to himself. And if they were... well, they were about to have a rude-awakening.

CHAPTER 46

Jack crossed Sale Road and entered the bungalow's garden. The overgrown hedges made it difficult for him to be seen from the street. That was good. He didn't want anyone calling the police on him. He tried the garage door. Locked. In the garage's right-hand wall there was a cracked window blacked out with newspaper. He manoeuvred his car key through the crack and lifted the newspaper. Empty. The garden was a tangle of grass and weeds. Brambles snagged his trousers as he approached the backdoor. The back curtains were closed too.

He listened at the door. Silence.

He quietly slid the key into the lock and turned it. Steel baton in hand, he eased open the door and edged inside. His nose wrinkled at a faint, familiar smell. He was in a kitchen – orange cupboards, floral wall tiles, yellow Formica table, yellow and white striped linoleum, looked like a relic of the 70s. Dust frosted the work-surfaces. He opened the fridge and a sour stink jumped out. There was a bottle of curdled milk in the door compartment. The fridge was otherwise empty. He checked several cupboards – plastic cups, a wine glass. *No one's living here,* he thought. But that didn't mean the bungalow wasn't being used for something. He moved into the hallway and sniffed the air. The smell was getting stronger. It wasn't sour milk.

He padded across a dark carpet to a door a few centimetres ajar. The room beyond was furnished with a dark-wood dining table and six chairs. Cobwebs clung to a glass globe light-fitting. Garish floral curtains hung over the window. Nothing else but more dust and yellowed Anaglypta wallpaper.

The living-room was next – same carpet, same light shade, wallpaper and curtains. A threadbare three-piece-suite was arranged around a stone hearth. No television, ornaments or other signs of inhabitation.

He was drawn to the front door by a pile of mail below the letter-box – charity begging letters, home insurance offers, takeaway menus, political party crap, free newspapers. Junk mail the lot of it. Nothing addressed to anyone in particular.

There were three more doors. The first led to an empty box-room; the second to a dated avocado-green bathroom with mould-splotched tiles. A frayed towel hung on the radiator. A lump of soap with dark hairs on it was stuck to the sink. There was a whiff of old urine. Nasty but not as unpleasant as the other smell, the one that made Jack tighten his grip on the baton as he neared the final door. The edges of the door were sealed with masking tape. What had the bungalow's tenant been trying to seal in?

As he peeled the tape off, a fat fly emerged from between the door and frame. He opened the door and almost reeled backwards as the smell hit him full in the face. It was like a mixture of rotten eggs, cabbage and shit, with a tinge of nauseatingly fruity sweetness. Hundreds more flies speckled the walls and ceiling. He closed the door behind himself before they could escape.

There was a blow-up mattress on the carpet. Stained blankets were scrunched at the foot of it. A man, naked except for filthy white y-fronts, lay on the mattress, his arms stretched out to either side, his head resting on a pillow. His face, abdomen and stomach were grotesquely bloated. His skin was green and mottled with red and purple patches. Blood had leaked from his nose, mouth and eye sockets. A halo of black-brown slime surrounded him. Bloat – the breakdown of organs causing gases to accumulate – had long since set in. Fluids were being forced out of every orifice as the body liquefied from the inside out. Taking into account the warm summer conditions, Jack estimated that the man had been dead for at least a week, possibly even a fortnight.

Jack squatted down beside the corpse. He didn't gag. He'd seen bodies in a worse state. The face was unidentifiably swollen. Jack mentally scrolled through Rhys's personal details: 'Hair Colour: Black', 'Scars, Marks, Tattoos: Purple birthmark on left buttock', 'Circumcision: Yes'. The dead man's swept back hair was grey-black. Jack pulled down the y-fronts, exposing genitals as inflated as a bullfrog. The man was circumcised. He rolled the corpse onto its side. A circular birth mark was just visible through a sheen of putrefaction.

There could be little doubt that this was Rhys Devonport – which blew Jack's theory about Rhys taking revenge on Gabriel out of the water.

The only signs of injury were ligature welts on the wrists and ankles. Next to the mattress was an empty water bottle. Plastic cups were scattered across the carpet. Jack took a closer look at one. It was crusted with a sugary brownish residue – over-sweetened tea or coffee or possibly some kind of protein drink. The window was boarded up. In one corner was a plastic bucket with a toilet roll beside it. In another corner was a bundle of clothes – blue jeans, pink shirt, size ten suede loafers – and a stack of newspapers. He checked the pockets of the jeans and shirt. Empty. He leafed through the newspapers. The most recent was dated 'Thursday 13th July 2017' – twelve days ago and three days before the murders started.

His gaze landed on three more objects – a black ball gag, a tube of Savlon and a tangle of blood-stained twine – before returning to the corpse. Someone had been providing Rhys with food and drink, a bucket to piss and shit in, reading material. They appeared to have been keeping him alive, but he'd died anyway. Rhys had been in his sixties, a heavy drinker. He'd been missing since November 2016. He might have been kept prisoner here for seven or eight months. There was every chance that the strain of captivity had been too much for him. Perhaps the ligature welts had become infected, hence the antiseptic cream. Or maybe his heart had given out. Whatever the case, surely it was significant that he'd died around the time that the murders started.

But why had the killer kept Rhys alive? Why had they fed him, rubbed antiseptic into his sores, given him painkillers, perhaps even bathed him? Had they wanted something that they couldn't get from simply sticking a knife in his stomach? Perhaps they'd wanted him to suffer as long as possible for some real or imagined wrongdoing, and when he died the focus of their rage had transferred elsewhere. The only way to find out for sure was to keep pushing deeper into the nightmare.

He frowned uncertainly. If he called this in, half of GMP would descend on Jordan Murphy. But if he didn't call it in, there would be some difficult explaining to be done later on. If there even was a 'later on'. Tackling psychopathic killers wasn't exactly without risk. There was also Jordan's wife, Maria, to consider. She'd stuck by her husband after the Hannah Meadows episode. Perhaps she believed he'd been falsely accused. Or maybe she shared her husband's – alleged – sexual proclivities. She might even be involved in the murders.

It has to be you, Jack. You alone.

The frown faded. He'd done a deal with the devil. There was no turning back now. Rhys had lain undiscovered for weeks. A few more hours wouldn't change anything. *And what if something happens to you?* Jack asked himself. *Well then Emma will follow the same trail to Jordan.*

He rolled Rhys onto his back and resealed the door as best he could. If the killer – or killers – returned to the bungalow, he didn't want them to realise anyone else had been there.

He headed to his car and put Jordan's Blackburn address into the Satnav.

Why should anyone get away with the shit they do? He'd hurled those words at Paul as if it was a mystery. But there was no mystery to it. Some people got away with it because they were clever. Some because they were lucky. And some simply because no one cared about what they'd done. That last reason was what bastards like Jordan counted on when they targeted the likes of Hannah Meadows. Hannah had been the archetypal victim – alone, vulnerable, messed up, easily influenced. If Jordan had stuck to girls like her, he would have continued to get away with the shit he did. But for some reason he'd branched out into murdering respectable young women with families to fight for them. Or at least that was how it appeared. Maybe Jordan was just another piece of the puzzle. Either way Jack intended to find out.

"No one gets away with it," he promised himself. "Not today."

CHAPTER 47

Jack detoured to his house. He rifled through boxes and bags until he found what he was looking for – the bump keys. He put them in his pocket along with a screwdriver. If the Murphys were out and the opportunity presented itself, he might just take a sneaky look around their house. If he could get his hands on the incriminating video and photos, the deal was off.

He had to keep a close watch on his thoughts all the way to Blackburn. Whenever he caught himself slipping into tortured visions of Rebecca and Paul, he recited the questions he intended to ask Jordan. There were lots of them. Most were distinctly unpleasant.

The M66 was mercifully quiet. He made the journey in good time. The Murphys' modest detached was on the north side of Blackburn. The front garden was paved over to provide parking for a Range Rover. The curtains were open. Jack parked against the opposite kerb, wondering how to play his next move.

He took another look at the DVLA database. The Range Rover was registered to Jordan. Maria drove a Mercedes.

So Jordan was home alone. That is, unless Maria and he shared a car to work. Or unless the Merc was at the garage for repairs. Or unless one or both of their sons – Stuart and Anthony – was in the house. Or... Or...

Jack's best option was clear – stakeout the house until he was certain Jordan was alone. But he had no intention of doing so. This murderous farce had gone on long enough. His gaze travelled up and down the street. Satisfied no one was around, he got out of the car and slunk down the side of the house

A venetian blind was closed in a small downstairs window. The sight piqued Jack's interest. Why was the blind closed in the middle of the day? He could think of one seedy reason.

He edged an eye around the window-frame. There was a thin gap between the frame and blind. He could see a bookshelf, the corner of a desk, a printer, a hairy arm. Did the arm belong to Jordan? He glimpsed a shoulder adorned with a faded tattoo of a blue rose. The sight of the rose seemed like a sign. Here was an opportunity. It was risky, but he had to take it.

Jack crept to a backdoor. He didn't want to announce his presence and give Jordan a chance to dispose of evidence or possibly even arm himself. The door was locked. He tried the bump keys until he found one that fitted the lock. He pulled the key out one notch and hit it with the handle of the screwdriver whilst applying a light rightwards pressure. The lock didn't open. He tried again, feeling for the sweet spot where the bump key would shear all the lock tumblers simultaneously. The key turned.

His phone pinged. Tensing at the seemingly amplified noise, he ducked down and looked at the phone. It was a reply from Lucrezia Moretti! 'Dear Detective Inspector Anderson, I have attached a list of all UK customers who have purchased the Ugly Mask. I hope this is of help. Distinti Saluti, Lucrezia Moretti.'

Jack scanned through the list. There were fifty two names and addresses. Jordan Murphy wasn't amongst them. Of course, Jordan could have used a false identity. None of the names meant anything to Jack. He glanced uncertainly at the backdoor. The policeman in him knew he should take a step back and find out if any of the customers were connected to Jordan. But another other part of him – the part that couldn't bear the thought of a murderer and molester continuing his comfortable married existence for even one more day – said darkly, *Why waste time when you can get the answer straight from the horse's mouth?*

Jack opened the backdoor. It led to a utility room with a washing machine that was currently in use. There was a shoe rack next to the door. He dropped to his haunches and examined two pairs of trainers. One pair was a size six, the other a nine. Neither pair showed signs of wear resembling the footprint in Alexandra Park. He checked out two pairs of hiking boots and a pair of men's brogues. Same story.

The noise of the machine covered Jack's footsteps as he advanced into a kitchen – cooker, microwave, spice rack, shelf of cookery books. Nothing out of the ordinary. He cracked open the kitchen door. A hallway led to the front door. There were two other doors. He turned handle of the nearest one and entered a small study. Jordan was sitting at a desk in boxer shorts and a vest. Bifocals were perched on the ridge of his craggy nose. He flipped shut a laptop and swivelled his chair towards Jack. He flinched so hard his glasses fell off. His moustache and goatee split into a shocked O.

Jack brandished his warrant card.

Jordan's eyes bulged at him. "What... How did you get in here?"

"The backdoor was open."

"That's a lie. G-get out of my h-house," stammered Jordan. He had a gruff northern accent. Nothing like the killer's phone voice.

"Answer my questions and I'll leave. Who else is in the house?"

Jordan's mouth opened and closed dumbly. His eyes darted around as if seeking an escape route. He moved one of his hands.

"Keep your hands where they are." Jack's tone left no doubt that the consequences of disobedience would be dire.

Jordan swallowed hard. "I-I can b-barely see you without my glasses."

"OK, but no sudden movements."

Jordan put on his glasses and peered at Jack's ID. His expression moved from fear to indignation. He'd seemingly seen enough warrant cards to know a genuine one from a fake. "You've no right to be in here."

"I'll ask you one more time. Is there anyone else in the house?"

"My wife's at work."

"What about your sons?"

"Stuart's at college. Anthony doesn't live here. Look, I know my rights. You need a search warrant before you can enter private premises."

"That's correct, I do."

"Then where is it?" demanded Jordan.

Jack sighed. Suspects were like unruly children, constantly testing the boundaries. You had to crack down on them hard. Make sure they knew where they stood. "Let me make this very clear to you, Jordan. I don't have a search warrant. What I do have is evidence that places you at a murder scene in Wythenshawe."

He watched for the slightest sign that Jordan knew what he was referring to. Jordan scrunched his face in what appeared to be genuine bewilderment. "What the hell are you talking about?"

"Does the name Rhys Devonport mean anything to you?"

"No."

"Are you sure? Take a moment to think about it."

"I don't need to. I've never heard that name before."

"Then how did your name come to be on the lease for the bungalow where I found Rhys's body?"

Jordan threw up his hands. "This is crazy!"

"Move your hands again and I'll break them off," Jack stated matter-of-factly.

Jordan clamped his hands to the arms of his chair. "I've no idea what's going on here, but I'm telling you the truth. If my name's on that lease, it's either a different Jordan Murphy or..." His forehead pinched in thought.

"Or what?"

"Or someone's trying to frame me."

"Why would someone want to do that?"

"You must know my history. There are people out there who would love to see me in prison."

"What people?"

"People like you."

Jack stared hard at Jordan. "Are you insinuating that I'm lying?"

Jordan's stammer returned. "If w-what you're telling me is true, w-why are you here alone?"

"Because my colleagues don't know about any of this."

Jordan ran his tongue over his goatee as if trying to work out whether Jack's reply was a good or bad thing. "What do you want from me?"

"I want to know who killed Abigail Hart, Zoe Saunders–"

The look of alarm on Jordan's face made it clear he recognised the names. "What? Wait a minute."

"Erica Cook, Camilla Winter–"

"Just bloody wait!"

"You've heard those names before," said Jack.

"Of course I have. They're on the news all day long. Maria's obsessed with it all. You can't seriously be suggesting I've got anything to do with their deaths?"

"Why not? You're a child molester."

"I've never been convicted of a crime in my life, except drunk driving."

"Just because you weren't convicted of molesting Hannah, doesn't mean you're innocent." Jack pointed to the laptop. "If I was to take that to the GMP techies, I wonder what they'd find?"

"Nothing. It's my work laptop. And you've no more right to take it than you have to be in my house." Jordan puffed himself up with righteous indignation. "I've had enough of this. Either you leave right away or I'm phoning the police."

Jack knew a bluff when he heard one. "Go for it."

Jordan reached for a phone on the desk. His hand hovered over it before retreating to the armrest.

"I thought not," said Jack. "You don't want my colleagues prying into your affairs."

"And you don't want them prying into yours either," retorted Jordan. "Why is that? Just what's your game?"

"I've told you, I want to know who killed those women."

Jordan threw his head back exasperatedly. He composed himself with a long breath. "Hypothetically speaking, let's say you're right about my sexual preferences." He qualified his words, "You're not right, but we'll assume for a moment that you are."

"OK, hypothetically speaking you raped Hannah, drove her to heroin addiction and a premature death."

If Jack's response bothered Jordan, he showed no sign of it. "So if I've got a thing for young girls, why would I murder two men and four women?"

"You worked in Blackpool from 1997 to 2009. Rhys Devonport made frequent trips to Blackpool during that time. Perhaps you used to meet up with him and do whatever it is perverts like you do. Rhys was down on his luck in recent years. Maybe he was blackmailing you. As for the women. Their murders aren't about sex – at least not directly. They're about revenge."

"For what?"

Jack shrugged. "Losing your job at Rainbow's End. Women for being women. You tell me."

"I do not know Rhys Devonport." Jordan emphasised each word as if that somehow made them true. "I chose to leave Rainbow's End. And I'm glad I did. That job was nothing but stress. Look around you. I've been doing well since then. I run a successful business that provides care for hundreds of old and infirm people. And as for me hating women, I have a wife who I love very much. She's stood by my side through thick and thin."

Jack's lips crooked into a cynical smile. "Has this story got a title? How about, Jordan Murphy: Pillar of the Community and Paedophile? It's not very snappy, but it does the job."

"You can't talk to me like that!"

"You still don't get it, do you, Jordan?" Jack spoke slowly as if trying to make himself understood to a simpleton. "I don't give a shit about your rights. I came here for answers and I'm going to get them. One way or another." The conviction in Jack's words caught even him by surprise. He found himself wondering just how far he would go to get the answers he wanted. Would he hurt Jordan? Could he cross that line?

Jordan's face turned several shades paler. "I d-don't have the answers you w-want."

"I'm going to show you something and I want you to take a long hard look at it before you say anything. Do you understand?"

Jordan nodded. Jack opened the list of Ugly Mask customers and placed his phone on the desk. "Do you recognise any of those names?"

Jack watched closely as Jordan read the list. Was that a hesitation? A flicker of recognition? He couldn't be sure. Jordan shook his head. "No I don't."

"You're lying."

"Why would I lie?"

"I don't know, but you are. I've been in this game long enough to spot a lie. Now it's your turn. I want to see what's on your phone. And if I hear one more word about your rights, you'll force me to do something I don't want to do." Jack slid a hand into his jacket and started to take out the steel baton. He wasn't seriously thinking of using it, but if he'd read Jordan correctly the gesture would be enough.

Blinking, Jordan retrieved an iPhone from a shelf. He unlocked it and handed it over, saying in a forced tone of couldn't-care-less, "You won't find anything on it."

Keeping one eye on Jordan, Jack scrolled through the photos, videos, messages and call history. Most of the content involved Jordan's wife and sons. There were also WhatsApp exchanges between Jordan and his employees. The phone was clean. "OK. Now the laptop."

Jordan obligingly flipped it open and clicked through its contents – photos, videos, downloads, documents, emails, browsing history. Clean. Not even a Facebook account. *Shit.* This wasn't looking good.

"I told you," said Jordan.

"Where are your other phones?"

"What other phones?"

"You know what I'm talking about. Don't make me search the house, because I'll tear it apart brick-by-brick if I have to."

Jordan wasn't blinking anymore. He was staring steadily at Jack. "Go ahead."

Is this fucker playing with me? Jack felt his control of the situation slipping. It reminded him of the way the killer tied him up in knots. "Stand up and turn around."

"What for?"

Jack took out his baton and extended it. "Do it."

Jordan stood up. He was slightly shorter than Jack, but stockier. His gaze darted from the baton to Jack's eyes.

"You're wondering whether to have a pop at me," said Jack, his voice steely. "Try it. See what happens."

Jordan's tongue flicked across his goatee again. He held Jack's gaze for several charged seconds, then turned around. Jack pulled Jordan's hands behind his back and handcuffed him. "Jordan Murphy, I'm arresting you for the murder of Rhys Devonport. You don't have to say anything–"

"You're bluffing," interrupted Jordan.

Jack jerked him towards the door. "But it may harm your defence if you do not mention when questioned something which you later rely on in court." He tucked Jordan's laptop under his arm.

"Anything you find on that will be inadmissible."

"Maybe. Maybe not. But either way I'll make sure your wife and sons, your employees, your customers and anyone else you might give two shits about knows what floats your boat."

Jordan's face crumpled like a burst balloon. "OK. OK. That list you showed me. I recognised a name – Crystal Cuthbert."

Jack found the name: 'Crystal Cuthbert. School Hill, Bolton'. He'd never been to Bolton, but before applying for the GMP job he'd read up on Greater Manchester's crime rates and social problems. School Hill was up there with the most crime-ridden, deprived parts of the region. "Who is she?"

"I don't really know. She came to Rainbow's End in '98. She'd been in the care system her entire life. She'd been placed with several foster families but it never lasted long. She was a compulsive liar."

"Like Hannah," Jack remarked dryly.

"I–" Jordan started to protest.

"Yeah, I know, you never laid a finger on Hannah. What did Crystal look like?"

Glowering at Jack, Jordan answered, "Skinny white trash, black hair, blue eyes."

White trash? How the fuck did this piece of human waste dare to call someone white trash? Jack just barely resisted a compulsion to shove Jordan's face into the door. "You said you don't really know who Crystal Cuthbert is. What did you mean by that?"

"She's a foundling. She was left outside Saint Cuthbert's Church on Crystal Road in Blackpool. That's where her name comes from."

"What year was that?"

"Well she was fourteen in '98, so that would have been–"

"'84," murmured Jack. The year Lilith fell pregnant. Could it be? Could Crystal Cuthbert be Lilith and Rhys's daughter? "Saint Cuthbert's. That sounds Catholic."

"It is."

Right hair and eyes. Right year. Right religion. It has to be her! Was Crystal the soft voice on the phone?

"It's Crystal, isn't it?" Jordan exclaimed as if reading Jack's mind. "She's behind this."

"Have you had any contact with her since she left Rainbow's End?"

"No." Jordan's eyes grew huge at the sound of a vehicle pulling up outside. "Oh my god, it's Maria. You have to leave. Or take me out the backdoor. I don't care. Just don't let her see me like this."

Jordan's tone didn't seem to suggest there was any substance to Jack's suspicions about Maria. Nor did it suggest he was in any way happy or relieved to be caught. "Why? What have you got to be afraid of if you're innocent?"

"Please! I've told you everything."

"I very much doubt that. For starters, you haven't told me what you did to Crystal that would make her want to frame you for murder."

"I did nothing. Like I said, she was a vindictive, lying little–"

"This is getting me nowhere. I think it's time I spoke to Maria."

"No. P-please don't," Jordan pleaded.

Jordan tried to twist away as Jack opened the door. Jack applied pressure to Jordan's forearms, forcing them up between his shoulder blades. A whimper escaped Jordan's lips. His resistance gave out and he staggered into the hallway.

CHAPTER 48

Jordan hung his head like a man on his way to the execution chamber as Jack pushed him towards the front door. Jack felt Jordan trembling beneath his grip. Jordan seemed to be more afraid of his wife than he was of Jack.

A key turned in the lock. The door opened and an auburn-haired woman in a stylish trouser-suit and high-heels stepped into the hallway. She sucked in a sharp breath at the sight of Jack and her husband.

"D-Don't listen to him, Maria," spluttered Jordan. "He's not who he says he is."

"Unfortunately for you, Jordan, that's exactly who I am," countered Jack.

He held out his ID. The shock in Maria's hazel-brown eyes was replaced by something else – something almost expectant. Jack saw it and decided to test the water. "You know why I'm here, don't you, Maria?"

"No." Her voice was composed – unnaturally so considering the situation, it seemed to Jack.

"Then why do I get the impression you've been expecting something like this to happen?"

"Perhaps because this isn't the first time I've had to deal with the police. My husband–"

"Is a child molester," offered Jack.

"I've never been convicted of a crime in my life, except drunk driving." Jordan reeled out his habitual defence again.

"I was going to say my husband has been persecuted for years because of malicious lies spread by those he was trying to help."

"Except they weren't lies," said Jack. "Jordan molested Hannah. And where there's one victim like her, there are always others."

"That's why you're here. Someone else has made an accusation, haven't they?"

"If you say so."

Maria gave Jack a puzzled look. Or maybe it was a simulation of puzzlement. "What's that supposed to mean?"

"I'm going to say some names. Stop me if you recognise any of them. Rhys Devonport, Crystal Cuthbert, Lilith Winter, Camilla Winter. Any of them ring a bell?"

"No."

Jack cocked his head. It was his turn to act puzzled. "Strange. Jordan tells me you're obsessed with the Manchester Ripper murders." He prodded Jordan. "Isn't that right?"

Jordan nodded. He was staring at his wife in a way that suggested painful cogs were grinding into motion in his mind.

"OK, I recognise the name Camilla Winter," admitted Maria, unfazed that she'd been caught in a lie. "Am I to take it you're here because Jordan's a suspect?"

"Yes."

Arching an eyebrow, Maria glanced at her cowering husband. "You're having me on, aren't you? This must be some kind of joke."

"Is that the best you can do?"

She aimed a frown at Jack. "I'm getting sick and tired of your cryptic remarks."

"My apologies. It's just that when I tell someone their spouse is suspected of being a paedophile and a murderer, I expect them to shout, cry, become hysterical. What I don't expect them to do is calmly ask questions and make flippant remarks."

"Well like I said, this isn't the first time I've been here."

"Back in 2009 when Hannah accused Jordan, what made you stand by him?"

Something that might have been pain lined Maria's face. "I believed he was innocent."

"I *am* innocent," declared Jordan.

The lines faded as quickly as they'd appeared. "He's telling the truth," said Maria. "He was here with me on the night of Abigail Hart's murder."

"You seem very certain of that," said Jack. "Abigail was killed on the 16th of July. I can barely remember where I was two days ago, never mind that far back."

"I remember because we both drank too much wine and had to take the next day off work."

"That's right," put in Jordan. "We drank four bottles between us. I pretty much passed out on the sofa."

"I'd be willing to testify to that in court," said Maria.

Jack looked thoughtfully from Jordan to her. Nodding as if he'd made his mind up about something, he took out his keys and reached for the handcuffs.

"What are you doing?" Maria asked in surprise.

"What does it look like I'm doing? I'm letting him go. I don't think Jordan murdered Abigail or Camilla or Erica–"

"Based on what? My word? Surely you need more than that?"

Jack hesitated to unlock the cuffs. "Are you saying the alibi is false?"

"No. What I'm saying is, how can you be certain I'm not lying to you? I did it before. I could be doing it again."

Jack frowned. "I'm a little confused. I'm telling you your husband's innocent. I thought you'd be happy."

"I am."

"You could have fooled me. You know what really strikes me as strange? You haven't asked who Rhys Devonport and Crystal Cuthbert are. Why is that?"

"I... thought maybe you made up those names. That you were trying to trick me." Maria stumbled over her words. Only for a second, but it was enough for Jack. She *was* lying again, but not about the alibi. *I'm just calling to find out how my favourite accomplice is doing.* Recalling the killer's words, Jack's hand returned to the steel baton. Perhaps Maria was involved in the murders, just not in the way he'd thought.

It was enough for Jordan too. Anger emboldened his voice. "You bitch! You're trying to set me up. You and that little slag."

Maria gave him wide innocent eyes. "What little slag?"

"Crystal-fucking-Cuthbert. What did she tell you? Whatever it was, it's a lie. That slut doesn't know how to do anything but lie and–" Jordan stopped short as if he'd thought better of saying what was on the tip of his tongue.

"And what?" Maria asked in a voice that sounded like something between a warning and a threat.

Jordan blinked and dropped his gaze. "Bitches," he muttered, his shoulders quaking as tears of self-pity took hold. "You give them everything – love, a home, children – and what do you get in return? A knife in the fucking back."

"You've never given me anything!" retorted Maria, her eyes ablaze. "Except for Anthony and Stuart. And I as good as raised them by myself. All you cared about was Rainbow's End. Sometimes I didn't see you for weeks on end."

"That was the job."

Maria made a motion as if chopping up Jordan's words. "And what about when you lost that job?"

"I didn't lose it. I voluntarily left."

"You couldn't have stayed on at Rainbow's End if you'd wanted to. Your reputation was ruined. People didn't trust you anymore. They didn't want to know you. Or me. And what did you do about it? You hid in the house feeling sorry for yourself." Maria jabbed a long-nailed finger at her chest. "I started M&J Recruitment Agency. I made a success of it. I paid the mortgage. Me not you! If it had been left to you, we'd have ended up homeless as well as ostracised."

Jordan shook his head as if to say, *That's not how it happened.*

Maria lunged forwards as if to take a swing at him. Jack made no move to intervene. He wanted to see what other simmering resentments this spat brought to the fore. Her index finger stopped just short of her husband's face. "*I'm* the one who gave *you* everything. I gave you a family, a career, this house. But most of all I gave you my trust. And in return all you gave me was lies, lies and more lies!"

Jordan shook his head again, but Maria hissed, "Don't you dare. Twenty nine years we've been married. Twenty nine years! You've ruined my life. I won't let you ruin Stuart and Anthony's too."

"I've always been a good dad to them."

Maria scowled. "Do you remember how I tried to throw a party for Stuart's thirteenth birthday, but had to cancel it because not a single parent replied to the invites? Stuart was devastated. He kept asking why no one wanted to come. And you told him it was because there were a lot of small-minded people out there who believe all the lies and gossip they hear." Self-disgust shook Maria's voice. "You made them part of your lies. I'll never forgive myself for letting you do that. But it ends now. You're not going to corrupt the boys. Remember what I said in 2009? I said I'd kill you if I ever found out you'd done what Hannah Meadows said you did."

A hopeful light came into Jordan's eyes. "But I'm still alive. That means you don't fully believe whatever lies Crystal's told you."

The light faded as Maria replied icily, "No, darling. It means I want Stuart and Anthony to know the truth. And it means death's too good for a murdering paedophile like you. You deserve to spend the rest of your life in prison."

"I'm not a murderer!"

"Oh yes you are. You abused Hannah when she was fourteen. Five years later she was dead."

"I didn't stick the needle in her arm."

"No, but you might as well have."

Finding his confidence, Jordan sneered, "I hardly think that will cut the mustard in a court of law, *darling*. Nor will renting out a property in my name that has a dead man I've never met in it."

That sneer was too much for Maria. Jack saw her mask of composure fall off and smash on the floor. From the look on her face, he knew something painful was coming Jordan's way. She snatched up a terracotta plant pot and brought it crashing down on her husband's head. Jordan collapsed on to his face, screaming, "Help! Help me!"

Maria raised the plant pot to hit him again. Jack caught her arm. Her eyes swollen with rage, she made to prise herself free. He warned her not to with a slow shake of his head. She reluctantly allowed him to take the pot away. He gestured for her to sit on the bottom step of the stairs and bent to lift Jordan onto his knees. Blood was streaming from a gash on Jordan's bald scalp. "Y-You're a..." he stuttered at his wife, trailing off as if he had no words to describe what she was. His eyes reeled towards Jack. "You could have stopped her. I'll have your job. Oh god, I'm bleeding. I need to go to hospital. I demand–"

"You're in no position to demand anything," interrupted Jack. "If I were you, Jordan, I'd keep your trap shut or I might let her finish the job."

Jordan opened his mouth as if to say something else, but snapped it shut again. Jack turned to Maria. She was trembling like a restrained wild animal.

"Your husband's right." Jack's voice was calm, but he was coiled and ready for anything. "The lease alone won't be enough to get a conviction."

Maria stared at him silently.

"Play dumb if you like, but as things stand Jordan will get away with abusing another girl. That's what Crystal told you, isn't it? That Jordan abused her when she was at Rainbow's End."

Jack paused to see what effect his words had. Still no response.

"Listen carefully, Maria, because believe it or not I'm trying to help you. Do you know what the sentence is for accessory to murder? It's the same as if you'd committed the crime yourself. You said you want to protect your sons. You won't be able to do that from a prison cell."

This time Jack's words got through. Maria closed her eyes, pressing her lips into a pale line as if damming back her voice.

"Forget getting Jordan put away for murder," Jack persisted. "That's not going to happen. But you can still expose him for what he is. Crystal's word might not be enough to convict him, but it will be enough to ruin him. It might even inspire other victims to come forwards. Things have moved on since 2009. People know the police will take those kinds of allegations seriously now."

Maria's lips trembled. The words were getting through to her. Now it was time to offer the illusion of a way out. Jack had been through the process hundreds of times. Act as if you were the suspect's only friend, then sit back and let them hang themselves. It was a shtick as old as the police force itself.

"I'm giving you a chance, Maria. Tell me the truth or I'll be forced to take these cuffs off Jordan and put them on you. Once we get to the station, you won't be dealing with a sympathetic audience. My colleagues will pull your life apart piece by piece. And when they're done, they'll be nothing left of you. You'll be just another number on a prisoner admission form."

Maria's eyes opened. Exhausted acceptance had replaced her anger. She heaved a breath, then began...

CHAPTER 49

"I was eating lunch in a cafe near the office. A woman sat down at my table. I remember being surprised because there were plenty of empty tables. She said nothing. She just looked at me. This was back in October of last year." Maria fell silent as if considering whether she wanted to say more.

"You can't leave me like this," whined Jordan. "It's not right."

"*You're* not right," spat Maria. She stabbed a finger at her temple. "You're sick in there."

Jordan looked abjectly up at Jack. "I need a doctor."

"Keep it shut and you might see one before you bleed to death," said Jack. He motioned for Maria to continue.

She chewed the underside of her upper lip. Her eyes flicked past Jack. Glancing around, he saw framed photos on the wall of two young men with the same colour hair as her. A line like a vertical cut appeared between her eyebrows. Jack could guess what she was thinking. Does it run in the genes? Are they infected with the same sickness as their dad? Those questions would have tormented him if Stuart and Anthony were his kids. "They're good looking lads," he said. "I bet they've got girls dropping at their feet."

Maria's eyes flinched back to his. "What's that supposed to mean?"

"Was that how it was for you, Jordan?" asked Jack. "Did they drop at your feet?" The question was as unsubtle as it was cruel.

"You bastard," murmured Maria, tears glistening in her eyes. She swiped them away. "The woman in the cafe, the way she looked at me made me uncomfortable. It was impossible to tell what she was thinking. I asked her, 'Do I know you?' I'll never forget her reply. She–" Maria's voice caught in her throat. She cleared it and tried again. "She said, 'It's an ugly one don't you think? The way it bends to the right when it gets hard. And there's that birthmark on the foreskin. You know, the one that looks like a squeezed zit.'"

"Oh Christ, please stop." The voice was a dry croak. It came from Jordan.

Maria ignored him. "I didn't know what to say. I felt sick. I tried to leave, but she grabbed me and said, 'I'm going to tell you a story about a girl who was sent to Rainbow's End in 1998. Her name was Crystal Cuthbert. She was fourteen and had spent her life in care. Her parents abandoned her as a baby. She had no friends. There was a man at Rainbow's End. He was kind to her. He made her feel like she was worth something for the first time in her life. She became attached to him. Dependent on him. She believed he loved her. But he didn't know how to love anyone but himself. She didn't realise that for a long time though. Not even after he raped her. She thought she was special. She thought they were going to run away together. That little girl was me. The man was your husband.'" Maria's eyes came back to the room. "I knew she was telling the truth. How could I doubt it? Her story confirmed my worst fear: the man I loved was a monster."

"No," snivelled Jordan.

"Yes!" Maria hurled the word at him. "That's exactly what you are. A monster. Not fit to be around human beings. Shall I tell you what I did when Crystal described the vile ways in which you abused her? I picked up a knife and said, 'I'll kill him.' But Crystal said, 'I have a better way.' I asked what way, but she just carried on with her story. 'I was heartbroken when Jordan dumped me after three years,' she said. 'I couldn't understand why he did it. But I understand now. There were other girls he was more interested in. Girls the same age as I'd been when I first came to Rainbow's End. I hated him. I thought about telling someone what he'd done but I didn't think they'd believe me. Who was I? Some little skank. Jordan was an important person. So I said nothing. Next thing I knew I was eighteen and living in a council flat in Bolton. I still had no friends and I didn't want any. I trusted no one. I was in and out of work. Just shitty menial stuff. I was too angry to hold down a job for long. I'd go off on people at the slightest thing. I thought about my parents a lot. Who were they? Why had they abandoned me? Had they been too young or poor to look after me?'"

"Is there much more of this crap to go?" grumbled Jordan, blinking away the blood in his eyes. There was a defeated note in the question. He'd accepted that his marriage was beyond saving. All he wanted now was to get his head seen to.

"*This crap*," scowled Maria, glancing at the plant pot as if a bell had rung for round two of bashing in Jordan's skull.

Jack warned her not to with another shake of his head.

"She's making it up. Can't you see that?" Jordan appealed to Jack. "How could she remember word-for-word what Crystal said almost a year ago?"

"Because every one of those words has been eating away at my brain ever since," countered Maria. "I wish I could forget them. But I can't."

Jack guessed that both Jordan and Maria were right to some extent. Maria almost certainly didn't remember the conversation verbatim. She might even be embellishing it. But he didn't doubt that at the core of her story there was a nugget of truth.

"Where was I?" said Maria, her eyebrows scrunching together. "I can't think with this bastard interrupting me all the time."

"Too young and poor to look after me," prompted Jack.

"Oh yes. So Crystal told me how she drifted for several years. She said she would have gone on like that forever if it hadn't been for Hannah Meadows. The first she knew about the case was when she read a newspaper article about the CPS's decision not to press charges. She said, 'All I could think was, if I'd told someone what Jordan did to me maybe Hannah wouldn't have had to go through the same thing.' I told her she couldn't blame herself and she said, 'I know now it wasn't my fault, but back then I thought differently. I didn't go out of the flat for days. Didn't talk to anyone.

Didn't eat. Didn't pay my bills. I basically had a complete breakdown. The guilt was too much for me. I constantly thought about killing myself.'"

Jack's stomach gave a twist. *Rebecca. Was the guilt too much for you? Or was there more to it? Where did your pain come from?*

"'Revenge.'"

The word sliced through Jack's thoughts.

"'The thought of getting revenge on Jordan was the only thing that kept me from slashing my wrists. And he wasn't the only one I wanted revenge on. I used to daydream about tracking down my parents and making them pay for what they did. The problem was, I didn't know where to start on either score. There was no point going to the police about Jordan. I'd only have got the same treatment as Hannah. I sometimes used to follow him around with a knife in my pocket, trying to work up the courage to stick it in him. But I couldn't get past the feeling that death was too easy a way out. I wanted him to suffer the way I'd suffered. And besides, if I went to prison for killing him how would I fulfil my ambition of looking into my mum and dad's eyes as I told them about how Jordan raped me?'"

Jordan managed a whimper of protest at the damning words. Jack silenced him with a sharp nudge in the back.

Maria didn't appear to notice. Her eyes were lost in Crystal's story. "'I put up posters all over Blackpool asking if anyone remembered a pregnant woman who might have given up their baby in '84. No one came forward. I was at a dead end. And that's where I stayed for years. I got back into my old routine, drifting in and out of shitty jobs. I even made a friend. Her name was Angela. She was older than me and loved karaoke. She dragged me onto the microphone with her one night when I was drunk and I discovered that I had a talent. I could sing. Angela reckoned I had the voice and looks to make a go of it professionally. She even set me up with a gig at a workingmen's club, but when it came to it I couldn't get up on the stage. I just couldn't bear the thought of all those men looking at me...'"

Maria's forehead furrowed as if she'd reached a part of the story that she found particularly painful. Jack was thinking about Fiona Jenkins, the piano and vocal coach at Harmony Music Manchester whose photo Crystal had sent him. He resisted an urge to hurry on Maria. He didn't want to break the reverie she'd fallen into. Not when he was so close to solving the puzzle.

After a long few seconds, Maria said quietly, "'Then it happened. Hannah OD'd. I had another breakdown. This time it was much worse. I lay in bed staring at the walls for weeks. I would have stayed like that until I died if Angela hadn't called a doctor. I was sectioned. I took all the drugs they gave me. I told a therapist the story of my shitty life, everything except Jordan. I kept that part for myself. When they let me out, I looked up Angela, but she'd moved away from the area. So I was alone again. One day I decided to leave too. I packed a bag and headed down to London. I spent the next two years living in squats and on the streets. I learnt how to pickpocket, shoplift, break into places. I had a talent for those things too. I don't remember much about that time. I felt like a ghost. People seemed to look straight through me. One night a man tried to rape me. I carried a knife for protection. I stabbed him to death.'"

The policeman in Jack compelled him to ask, "Did Crystal tell you the man's name?"

Looking at him as if she'd forgotten he was there, Maria shook her head. "For days afterwards she was terrified the police would pick her up. But they never did. And she came to realise something: killing is easy. That's when she decided to return to Blackburn to kill Jordan. She'd only been back here a few days when something happened that felt like a miracle to her. She said to me, 'I was watching TV and I saw–'"

"Camilla," put in Jack, shuddering as he recalled how he'd felt the first time he saw her.

Maria nodded. "Camilla was doing an interview. Crystal showed me it on her phone. Camilla was tearfully talking about her mum's emphysema. She asked people to pray for Lilith. She mentioned her dad too. Gabriel Winter. A wonderful man who saved countless lives during his career as a cardiologist before he passed away. Camilla had Crystal's eyes, her hair, her nose and mouth. But she didn't have her..." Maria sought the right word, "blankness. I said to Crystal, 'She looks like she could be your sister,' And Crystal said, 'Yes, she does, doesn't she?' And then I understood. I asked if she was certain Lilith and Gabriel were her parents. 'No,' she said, 'but I'm going to find out with your help.' She'd been watching Lilith's house. The old woman was being cared for at home by private nurses. She asked me if I could get her a job there."

The final piece fell into place. "Stella," exclaimed Jack. He summoned up an image of the nurse. The grey hair, brown eyes and wrinkles. It was all another one of Crystal's disguises. Another mask.

Maria nodded again. "I asked how that would help deal with Jordan. And Crystal said, 'Believe me, I'll make sure he suffers for the rest of his life in a place where he can't hurt anyone.' I asked why I should trust her and she said, 'If I didn't mean what I'm saying your husband would already be dead.' How can you argue with that? So I pulled some strings and got Crystal a job as Lilith's nurse. I forged her an ID. Gave her some basic training. I've been around nurses long enough to know the job inside out. And late last October she started her new job. On her first day, she rang and told me Lilith had a long scar just below her bellybutton. She said, 'Lilith says it's not a caesarean scar, but I know it's where Gabriel pulled me out of her stomach.' Crystal's voice was shaking. I hadn't heard her like that before. She said, 'I could have forgiven them if they were young and poor. But they were neither of those things. They just didn't want me. Who knows why? What I do know is they gave Camilla all the love they never gave me. They made her into everything I could have been.' I asked Crystal what she was going to do and she said, 'I'm going to find out more.'"

"Was that the last time you heard from her?" asked Jack.

"No. She called again a fortnight later. She was very calm. She said, 'I know why they threw me away, I know who my dad is and I know what to do.' I asked why, who and what, but all she said was, 'Thank you for everything, Maria.' Then she hung up. Weeks went by. I felt sick every time he," Maria glowered at Jordan, "put his filthy hands on me. Weeks turned into months. Crystal didn't pick up the phone when I called. I was starting to think I'd made a mistake trusting her. Then on the sixteenth Crystal called and said, 'It's happening.' I asked what was happening and she said something strange. She said, 'I'm becoming somebody.'"

"At what time was this?"

"It must have been close to midnight."

I'm becoming somebody. Those words didn't seem strange to Jack. Not when you considered that Crystal had killed Abigail shortly before phoning Maria. She must have felt as if her life's purpose was taking shape.

"Crystal told me she needed something with Jordan's fingerprints on it," said Maria. "Jordan was passed out on the sofa so I took his wine glass. 'Leave it on the doorstep,' said Crystal. 'The police will be coming for Jordan soon.' I sat up listening out for her, but I heard nothing and in the morning the glass was gone."

Jack thought about the wine glass in the bungalow's kitchen cupboard. That would make the case against Jordan more convincing. But would it have been enough to secure a conviction? He doubted it.

"The next thing I knew it was all over the news that a woman had been murdered in Manchester," continued Maria. "When I saw Abigail's photo and heard how she'd been stabbed and cut open, I thought to myself, *Could it be Crystal? But why would she kill someone who's got nothing to do with any of this?* I hoped and prayed it wasn't Crystal, but when Zoe and Erica were killed in the same way and they both looked like Crystal, I knew it had to be her. Then Camilla was killed and I... I was..." Maria's expression finished the sentence: *I was horrified.*

CHAPTER 50

There was a brief silence, then Jordan sneered, "Bravo, darling. If my hands were free, I'd give you a round of applause. That performance deserves an Oscar."

"I didn't know Crystal would kill them," insisted Maria.

"Bollocks. You must have realised there was only one way that psycho bitch could set me up with a life sentence."

"I don't think Crystal intended to frame you for their murders," said Jack. "Connecting Rhys Devonport's murder to theirs would have been dangerous for her. Sooner or later, someone would have uncovered the connection between Rhys and Lilith."

"Rhys Devonport is Crystal's dad," Maria gasped in realisation. "He had an affair with Lilith."

"That's right."

"And Crystal killed him too?"

"She abducted him. Kept him prisoner. I don't know whether she killed him. It could be the strain was too much for his heart. Either way, the end result is the same."

"Did he know about Crystal? What I mean is, did Lilith tell him she was pregnant?" There was a pained hope in Maria's voice.

"Would it make it easier for you if I said yes?"

After a motionless moment, Maria shook her head.

"Those people are dead because of you," scoffed Jordan. "And you call me a monster!"

"No. They're dead because scum like you exists," corrected Jack.

Jordan hissed dismissively. "Are we done here? Can I go to hospital now?"

"It wasn't supposed to be like this," murmured Maria.

Jordan smirked, drawing strength from her weakness. "Don't worry, darling, I'll take good care of M&J Recruitment while you're in prison. I'll have to change the company name. We can't have it associated with a murderer, can we now? What do you think of J & Sons? It's time to bring the boys into the family business. Keep them close. They going to need their dad when they find out what you are."

"What I am!" The fire flared back into Maria's eyes. "What about what you are?"

Jordan put on a butter-wouldn't-melt face. "I'm an innocent man. That's what I am."

"I'll tell them—"

"You'll tell them what? That you're brainless bitch who was taken in and manipulated by a psychopath?"

Lines and twitches mapped out Maria's features. Reading the signs, Jack stepped between her and Jordan. "Do you believe me?" she appealed to Jack.

"I believe Jordan abused Hannah and Crystal."

"Then how can you let him go?"

"What other choice do I have?"

"He'll do the same to others, and he'll keep on doing it until someone stops him."

Jack knew that. He hadn't seen the slightest trace of remorse in Jordan.

"Please don't let him ruin anyone else's life," pleaded Maria. "I've been such a fool. I don't care if I go to prison just so long as he doesn't get away with what he's done."

No one gets away with it. Not today. Jack's promise rolled through his mind like thunder.

"You're right about the fool bit," mocked Jordan. "That's probably why you hit it off with Crystal. She's not the sharpest tool in the box either."

Jack looked at Jordan's smug face. *No one gets away with it. Not today.* The words reverberated too loudly to be ignored. Turning to Maria, he said, "Someone broke into your house. You're not sure how many of them there were. They grabbed you from behind, tied you up, blindfolded and gagged you."

"W-What are you doing?" The arrogance had drained from Jordan.

Maria's eyes widened to their fullest extent as Jack continued, "They didn't speak. Not a single word. They just beat Jordan to death."

"You're bluffing," gasped Jordan.

"Am I?" The question wasn't simply aimed at Jordan. Jack's brain was whirling with that and other questions. *What are you doing? This is insane! You can't seriously be considering this, can you?*

As if echoing the thoughts, Jordan said, "You c-c-can't do this. You're a policeman."

The questions kept coming with irresistible force. *Why should Jordan get away with it? Why should Lilith? Why should Crystal?* Jack glanced at a cordless phone on a windowsill. "I'll leave that within your reach," he told Maria. "Half an hour after I leave, dial 999. You don't have to say anything. They'll trace your call and send someone out."

"Why bother with the police?" asked Maria, her eyes goggling as if she wasn't sure this was really happening. "Why can't we hide the body?"

Jack pointed to the blood that was dripping from Jordon onto the carpet. "There's too much blood. No matter how hard you clean, they'll find a speck. Trust me, this is the best way. When the police realise nothing's been stolen, they'll figure it's a case of Jordan's crimes catching up with him."

"Help!" Jordan cried out at the top of his lungs. "Hel–" The breath whooshed from him as Jack thrust a foot into his back, pitching him onto his face. Jack pinned him there with a knee.

"Get a towel and a knife," he said to Maria.

She quickly fetched the required items. Jack cut the towel into strips and made to stuff a balled-up piece into Jordan's mouth.

"I admit it," blurted out Jordan. "I molested Hannah and Crystal. There were others too. I'll give you their names."

"How can I be sure the names would be real?" asked Jack.

"I secretly filmed them and took photos."

Jack thought about the way Crystal had filmed and photographed him. Had she cottoned-on to what Jordan was doing and taken twisted inspiration from it almost two decades later? "Where are they?"

"They're in the house. I'll show you."

Jack removed his knee from Jordan's back.

"He's playing for time," said Maria. *That* look was back on her face. Her fingers twitched as if impatient to get at Jordan's throat.

"No I'm not!" Jordan darted Jack a glance that said, *Keep her away from me.*

Jack lifted him upright and motioned for him to show the way. On wobbly legs, Jordan led them to the study. He jerked his chin towards a corner of the carpet. "Under there."

"Try anything and I'll break your arms," warned Jack, manoeuvring Jordan to a radiator and cuffing him to it. He peeled back the carpet, exposing floorboards that appeared to be firmly nailed down.

"Third, fourth and fifth floorboards from the wall," said Jordan.

Jack prised at the floorboards and found that the nails were loose. Beneath the floorboards was a cavity with a strongbox in it. He lifted the box out. It was padlocked. "Where's the key?"

"Plant pot."

There was a spider plant on the windowsill. Jack felt around in the soil until he discovered a key. He unlocked the box. DVDs were neatly packed into it. Each was marked with a name. They were arranged in alphabetical order: 'Alicia', 'Billie', 'Carrie', 'Hannah', 'Joanna', 'Kelly', 'Tara', 'Tonya'...

There were seventeen DVDs with twelve different names. Alongside them were six photo albums. Jack opened the top one. Sheets of transparent plastic held the obscene photos in place. Jack flipped through the pages to one marked 'Crystal'. The photos had been taken in what appeared to be a seedy hotel room. There was a bottle of gin on a bedside table. Crystal looked painfully young. Jack tried to see her face and nothing else. The resemblance to Stella was there, just barely. A photo on the following page revealed a small mole above Crystal's right eyebrow. That would be enough to explain how he'd found his way from Jordan to Stella.

He snapped the album shut. There was no need now to find out if he'd been bluffing, but he still burned to beat Jordan to a pulp.

Maria clearly felt the same way. With an enraged shriek, she sprang at Jordan. She landed a glancing blow before Jack hauled her off and pinned her against a wall. She subsided into trembling stillness as he said, "There's enough in that box to put him away for a long time. Not the rest of his life, but he'll be an old man when he gets out. And even after he's released, he'll be monitored until the day he dies. He'll barely be able to step outside his door without having to report his whereabouts. He'll never work again. Your sons will want nothing to do with him. No one will, except others like him, and he'll end up back inside if he's found to be in contact with them. His life will be a living hell. That's what you wanted isn't it?"

Maria nodded and Jack stepped away from her.

"I'm not the only one going to prison," taunted Jordan.

Jack fixed him with a violently calm stare. "You're thinking you're going to tell my colleagues about your wife and Crystal's deal."

"Why shouldn't I?"

It occurred to Jack that perhaps he should take a leaf from Crystal's book of mind games. "I'll give you two reasons: Stuart and Anthony. You said you've been a good dad to them."

"I have." Jordan shot a glare at Maria as if daring her to contradict him.

"Then don't ruin their lives. You're facing a ten or twelve year stretch. Maria will do a lot longer than that if you open your mouth. The business will collapse. You'll lose this house. Your sons will be cut adrift with no one to help them. They might end up like Hannah Meadows."

Jordan scowled. "I know what you're trying to do and it won't work. My boys will never end up like that brainless little bitch." With a gleam of parental pride in his eyes, he added, "They're survivors. Like me."

"OK, Jordan, then consider it from this angle. If you get Maria put away, I don't see how either of your boys ever talks to you again. But if you keep your mouth shut, I'll make sure they know you've done one good thing in your life. And maybe, just maybe – if prison changes you – there's a chance they'll want to know you when you get out."

"No, I don't want–" began Maria, but Jack flashed her a silencing look.

Jordan's eyes shifted uncertainly between Jack and Maria. They landed on Jack. "I have one condition. That *she,*" he hissed the word at Maria out of the side of his mouth, "doesn't poison Stuart and Anthony against me."

Jack looked askance at Maria. "I don't see any problem with that. It's not as though they won't know what he's about. And by the time he's released, they'll be more than old enough to make up their own minds about him. Besides, it's either this way or..." He left the alternative hanging.

Maria heaved a sigh and nodded.

"I want to hear you say I promise," said Jordan.

Maria's eyes flashed, but she reeled her anger in with a deep breath. A smile flickered over her lips as if something in Jordan's demand had reassured her. "Alright, Jordan, I promise I won't say a word to the boys about you. Not one word. Good or bad. But it won't make any difference because you'll never change."

She and Jordan stared at each other. Jack could feel the weight of all the years between them, all the heartache and broken promises. Jordan's lips quivered as if struggling to form a retort. He gave up, hanging his head like he was already a prisoner.

"OK," said Jack. "So here's the story. I came here to speak to Jordan and caught him looking at this lot." He pointed at the DVDs and photo albums. "He resisted arrest. That's how he got the cut on his head. Maria, you returned home to find Jordan in handcuffs. I identified Stella Lloyd from the photos. When I asked if you recognised the name, you realised she'd come to you for a job. And that's all there is to it. Stick to that story and things should work out as planned." *Unless Crystal or Stella or whatever other name she might go by blows the lid off the whole thing,* he added to himself. In which case, all of them were going down.

Jack's gaze moved between Maria and Jordan. Maria gave him a nod. Jordan looked like someone staring into his own grave. Satisfied, Jack asked Maria, "Have you got a first-aid kit?" She nodded again and he told her to fetch it.

When she returned, Jack opened an antiseptic wipe and made to clean Jordan's wound. "Let me," said Maria. As Jack glanced at her uncertainly, she added, "Don't worry, I won't go for him again."

With a tenderness Jordan didn't deserve, Maria cleaned and dressed his wound. He looked up at her hopefully. The hope vanished as she said, "This is the last time I will ever touch you, Jordan." His head dropped as she continued, "From now on you get to deal with your own cuts and bruises, cook your own meals, wash your own clothes, pay your own bills, along with the rest of the shit I've done for you over the years. Do you hear me? Hmm?" Her tone wasn't angry. Nor was it taunting or contemptuous or... or anything. It was just flat. As if she'd already severed all emotional ties with Jordan.

Jack uncuffed Jordan from the radiator, lifted him to his feet and re-cuffed him. With the strongbox under one arm, he steered Jordan to the front door. His gaze returned to Maria. "Remember, stick to the story no matter what.

My colleagues will most likely think Crystal was playing some sort of game with you because of Jordan. Which in a sense is true."

"You're going after Crystal, aren't you?"

"Yes. Are you going to warn her?"

"No. She has to be stopped."

Jack had to trust Maria. There was no other choice. She looked at him with a mixture of gratitude and curiosity. "Why are you helping me?"

He echoed Natasha's words. "Because I know how it feels to be lied to by someone you love."

"Thank–" Maria started to say.

Jack cut her off. "Don't." He didn't want her thanks. He'd freed her from Jordan's lies, but entangled her in his own. So many lies, one feeding into another, into another. From where did this endless stream spring? Where was it going?

Jordan's gaze remained fixed on the ground as Jack led him to the car. Jack put the strongbox in the boot and cuffed Jordan to an overhead handle.

"I just want to know one thing," said Jordan as they drove away. "Would you really have killed me?"

Jack remained silent. It wasn't simply that Jordan didn't deserve an answer. Jack didn't have one to give him.

CHAPTER 51

Truth, lies... All the way back to Manchester, Jack's mind was like a coin flipping over and over. Which side up would it land? All he could do was watch and wait. Truth, lies... He told himself he would take Crystal in unharmed. But what if he couldn't get hold of the video and photos? Truth, lies... Doubt crept into his expression. Did he even know what the truth was anymore? What if Crystal resisted arrest? What if she fought him tooth-and-nail? At what point would he be justified in hurting or even killing her? Where was the line? He looked in the rearview mirror as if seeking something he recognised.

Who were you, Rebecca?

He drove as if some relentless force was hurling him towards his destination. He pulled over across the street from Lilith's house and cut the engine. His eyes sketched the outline of the house. Was Crystal waiting for him? *Even if Maria wanted to warn Crystal, she hasn't been able to contact her in months,* Jack reminded himself. Or had Maria been lying about that too? He pressed his fingertips to his forehead. The coin was turning so fast he couldn't tell which side was which.

There was a knock on the driver side window. Jack's heart almost punched a hole through his ribcage when he saw who it was. He lowered the window. "Emma, what are you doing here?"

Emma's stare was hard and searching. "I spoke to Maria Murphy."

"How–" Jack started, but broke off. The answer to the question he'd been about to ask was obvious: Emma had found her way to Maria the same way

343

he had. His eyes ran up and down the street. There was no sign of any of his other colleagues. "Are you here alone?"

"Yes." Emma glanced at Jordan as if he was something nasty a cat had brought in. She motioned for Jack to get out of the car. He did so and she continued, "I wanted to give you a chance to explain yourself before I show this to the DCI." She unfolded a printout of a CCTV image tagged 'City Road Inn, Albion Street'. A man was frozen in the act of running. Emma had zoomed in on his unshaven features. "And don't tell me that's not you."

Jack was silent. The coin had reached its zenith.

"I'm waiting," pressed Emma.

"What can I say? I was drinking in the area."

"That's your story is it? You just happened to be out drinking in the same area as Camilla and Dale. And you just happened to be caught on camera running away from that area at around the time Dale and Mr Average had their altercation."

Jack nodded feebly. The coin plummeted groundwards.

"Two questions, Jack. Why did you try to conceal this from me? And why were you running?"

"I didn't tell you because..." his mind raced for a plausible reason and found one that could easily have been true, "I didn't want Paul to know I was out boozing a few days before returning to work. And I was running to get a taxi. It was just a coincidence."

"What about this? Is this coincidence too?" Emma handed Jack another printout. This one was of an email. The first sentence read 'Regarding samples taken from the altar tomb, chemical analysis of the ash has determined that the brand of cigarette is Marlboro.'

"You smoke Marlboros, don't you Jack?"

"Yes." In fact he could do with one right now. "Me and several million other people."

"Just another coincidence, eh?" Emma's tone wasn't simply sceptical, it was outright disbelieving. Like a magician pulling rabbits from a hat, she produced yet another printout – a CCTV-still of Manchester Opera House's lobby. The lobby was crowded with smartly dressed people. Amongst them, partially obscured but there for eyes that knew what they were looking for to see, was a man in a blue suit.

Jack closed his eyes at the sight of himself. The coin hit the ground – truth. *No one gets away with it today. Not even you.* "I'm Mr Average." The words came out in a rush. It burned his heart to think what it would do to Naomi if he went to prison. But the pain was outweighed by relief. Christ, the relief! It was like he'd heaved a concrete slab off his back. He didn't need to know where the line was. It was no longer up to him alone whether Crystal lived or died. "I was watching Camilla on the night she was murdered. I'd been watching her for days. I'm not sure how many. I was drinking a lot at the time."

"You were stalking her."

Jack didn't even try to argue otherwise. "I saw her by chance one night and–" A choking lump rose into his throat. "It was like I was seeing Rebecca..." His mind drifted off course. He caught hold of it. "I wanted to stop, but I couldn't. I had to keep going back there. I saw a masked figure in the flat. The figure killed Dale. I tried to save Camilla, but I was too late. The killer was gone and she was dying."

"If you tried to save her, why cover up your presence?"

"Because I've already lost so much. I couldn't face losing anything else."

"You let the killer get away. If you'd rung it in, we could have thrown a net over the area." Emma's tone was rebuking, but she looked at Jack with a trace of sympathy.

"That's why I'm here. To put things right."

Emma's eyes narrowed. She glanced at Lilith's house. "Are you saying the killer's in there?"

"What did Maria tell you?"

"Only that you'd arrested her husband and were on your way here."

Jack gave the house an uneasy look of his own. This wasn't the time to give Emma the whole sad story of Crystal's life. The longer they stood there, the greater the chance of Crystal getting wind of their presence. He opened the boot and took the relevant photo album out of the strongbox. He showed Emma the images of Crystal. "Does she look familiar to you?"

"No."

"What about if you gave her grey hair and glasses and changed the colour of her eyes to brown?"

Emma's furrowed brow smoothed out in sudden realisation. "Stella Lloyd."

"Camilla wasn't Lilith's only daughter. Lilith had an affair, got pregnant and abandoned the baby. That baby grew up to be an extremely troubled woman. Her name's Crystal Cuthbert, but she's using the alias Stella Lloyd."

"So Crystal killed her sister in revenge. But why kill those other women?"

"Maybe it was for practice. Maybe it was to confuse us." Jack thought about the scar on Lilith's stomach and the way the victims had been slashed open. "Or maybe it was a howl of rage for what Lilith did."

Emma nodded. "That makes sense. Crystal's killing her mother over and over."

I'm becoming somebody. Crystal's words offered another possibility. "Or maybe she just likes the way killing makes her feel."

Emma shot another look at Lilith's house as if to make sure no one was sneaking up on her. As much to herself as Jack, she said, "I need to call this in." She eyed him awkwardly. "Sorry, Jack, but I have to cuff you."

He wasn't surprised. He'd have done the same in her position. "You're a better copper than I ever was, Emma. I'm sure we'd have been good friends if it wasn't for all this. And I appreciate you coming to me before Paul." His lips thinned at the sour taste of the name. "You can put the cuffs on me after I've arrested Crystal."

Emma frowned. "That's not going to happen. We're going to wait here for backup to–" She stepped backwards, whipping out a can of pepper-spray as Jack started towards the house. "Stay where you are, Jack."

"It'll make a lot of noise if you try to stop me, Emma. Enough for Crystal to hear."

"I'm warning you," said Emma, but she didn't block his way. "Shit," she hissed, lowering the pepper-spray and hurrying after him. As they passed between the gateposts, she muttered, "I must be out of my fucking mind."

"Welcome to the club," Jack replied dryly.

CHAPTER 52

Staying low, Jack and Emma crossed the lawn. The house loomed over them, a brooding, watchful presence. They padded up the steps to the front door. Jack tried the handle. Locked. The door had a big old lock. Not the kind he could pick with his bump-keys. He signalled to head around back. They slunk along the side of the house. Honeysuckle and wisteria perfumed the warm air. It was the type of day when people flung their windows wide open. But all the windows were closed. The back garden was bathed in shadows cast by tall trees. The French Doors also had an old-fashioned lock. The windows were leaded. It wouldn't be difficult punch out a square with a baton and undo a latch.

"It's not locked," Emma whispered. She was at the backdoor.

Jack's eyes narrowed at her. Why wasn't it locked? It was almost like an invitation. "Extreme caution," he whispered back.

Baton at the ready, Jack eased the door open. It led into the kitchen. He saw what he hadn't been able to see from the hallway – a display cabinet. Surely it had to be *the* mahogany display cabinet. It was a beautifully crafted piece that would have graced any living-room. But it was tucked away in a gloomy corner, crammed full of pots and pans. Perhaps Gabriel had put it there. If so, it had got off lightly.

There was a pair of black lace-up shoes on the lino. Jack picked one up and checked the size – 7. He checked the soles. The tread was evenly worn. He frowned, perplexed. Then he pulled a corrective innersole out of the shoe. He showed it to Emma. She gave a nod of understanding.

Jack gently opened the door to the high-ceilinged hallway. The sideboard clock ticked – quiet, but loud inside Jack's ears. They didn't check to see what – if anything – was lurking behind the other doors. Their priority had to be making sure Lilith was safe, regardless of whether she had one day or a hundred left to live.

Emma tapped Jack's shoulder and pointed to the front door. The key was in the lock. Jack unlocked the door – in case they needed to make a quick exit – and pocketed the key. They started up the stairs. The threadbare red carpet barely deadened their footfalls. The floorboards were a minefield of creaks. Sweat seeped from Jack's armpits as he tested each step. It seemed to take a long time to reach the top. The bathroom door was open. An empty hoist dangled above the claw-footed bath.

Hardly breathing, Jack approached Lilith's door. As he opened it, the hinges gave out a wince-inducing squeak. Signalling for Emma to stay where she was, he entered the bedroom. The sulphurous smell was oppressively thick. He wouldn't have been surprised to find Lilith drenched in blood, her vital organs trailing out of her belly. But she appeared to be asleep. Even with an oxygen nose-tube strapped across her face, her breathing was a paper-thin wheeze. Her hair looked like a mat of spider webs. The sapphire ring sparkled on her bony finger as if illuminated from within.

Lilith stirred, but didn't wake up. She was probably on enough medication to knockout an elephant. Jack looked under the bed, behind the curtains and in the wardrobe. All clear. His gaze lingered on the photos of Camilla crowding the dressing-table. So beautiful...

Rebecca. How could you do it? I loved you so–

A noise shredded the silence. It sounded like the howl of a wounded animal. As Jack whirled around, Emma took several stuttering steps backwards into the room. The can of pepper-spray fell from her hand. She turned towards Jack, looking down and clutching her hands to her chest. Blood seeped between her fingers. She shook her head as if in incomprehension. Then her legs gave way. Jack tried to catch her, but he wasn't fast enough. Her breath whistled between her teeth as she thudded into the floorboards.

Jack flashed a look at the landing – no one was there – and dropped to his knees. Tears ran down Emma's cheeks as he unbuttoned her blood-soaked blouse. There were two wounds – one in the centre of her abdomen, the other a centimetre to the right of her sternum. They looked to have been made by a large blade. The volume of bleeding from the upper wound suggested the blade hadn't punched through the ribs. The abdominal wound was deep though. Very deep. He wiped the blood away with his sleeve to get a better look. More blood welled up to conceal the slot shaped opening.

Snatching at her breath, Emma gasped, "Is it bad?"

"You're losing a lot of blood." If he'd been the one wounded, Jack would have wanted the truth, the chance to make peace with his conscience or whatever in case the worst came to the worst. He needed to work fast. The first thing was to staunch the bleeding. His eyes darted to the medicine trolley. There were bandages, gauze pads, bedsore creams. Jack grabbed what he needed. He went to work on the abdominal wound, peeling open several gauze pads and pressing them against it.

"This is going to hurt," he said, rocking Emma from side to side to pass the bandage beneath her.

She groaned, her fingers curling into trembling claws. "I can't breathe." Her voice was as faint as a breeze.

Not good. Jack fumblingly tried to tie the bandage. *Shit. Shit. Calm down.*

"I'm scared, Jack."

"I know, sweetheart. I know."

He secured the knot tightly. Satisfied that he'd stemmed the bleeding, he moved on to the chest wound. There was a creak from the landing. His head snapped up. His breath stopped.

He saw the dress first – a blue shoulderless dress that followed the slender hourglass contours of its wearer. The same dress Rebecca was wearing in the photo that appeared in the newspapers after her death. His gaze moved up over the gentle swell of breasts to a pale swan neck curtained by straight black hair. The hair was styled in a centre parting. The way Rebecca had worn hers. The face between the curtains was soft yet angular with a small jaw that accentuated rosebud lips, a delicately tapering nose and... and... Those eyes. So blue and empty. The way Rebecca's had been empty in the last weeks of her life.

"Rebecca," Jack murmured like someone in a dream.

The woman glided into the room on bare feet. One hand was concealed behind her back. The other was stretched out as if appealing for Jack to come to her. "There's no such thing as perfection, Jack," she said in a voice of profound sadness. "You expected too much. I couldn't be who you wanted me to be."

The words drew Jack's breath out of him in a shudder. Was that the answer? Had he put Rebecca up on too high a pedestal? Was that why she'd fallen?

"It's not Rebecca," Emma found enough air to murmur.

But all Jack heard was that sad voice. All he saw were those unfathomable eyes. "I'm sorry, Rebecca. Please forgive–"

There was a squeak of bedsprings. Lilith was sitting up, her hair a wild white cascade. "What... Who are you?" she croaked.

In an instant the sadness dropped away and Jack was no longer looking at Rebecca, he was looking at Crystal. Crystal's face was harder than Rebecca's, more pinched. But above all, it was angrier. There was a rage in Crystal's eyes that could have burned a hole through Lilith.

"Who am I?" Crystal's voice was like a knife sliding from its sheath. "I'm your daughter."

"My daughter?" Lilith blinked as if trying to work out whether this was a medication-induced hallucination. Crystal watched with obvious satisfaction as horrified comprehension dawned over Lilith's ravaged face. "You... killed... Camilla." Rattling breaths punctuated the words.

"Yes, I killed your precious Camilla. I cut her open the same way Gabriel cut you open on the day you threw me away."

"How... How..."

Crystal anticipated the question. "How did I find you?" She mimicked Camilla's voice with eerie accuracy. "I couldn't have achieved any of this without my mother's love and support." A bitterly ironic smile formed on her lips. "If you hadn't given my sister everything she needed to be such a success, I'd never have found you. Nor would I have had read the love letters you keep hidden in your jewellery box. The ones where my dad tells you how much he loves you." She stabbed a finger into her chest. "Well what about me? Who's ever loved me?"

"Jack..." breathed Emma, trailing off into ominous silence.

Glancing down, Jack saw her eyes roll white. His mind flashed back to Camilla dying despite his efforts to save her. No matter what, he wasn't going to let that happen again. He pressed a gauze pad to Emma's chest wound and appealed to Crystal, "She'll die if she doesn't get medical attention."

"No one. That's who," Crystal continued to rant at Lilith. "Well now it's your turn to find out what it's like to have nothing and nobody. And when you die, dear mother, the last face you see will be mine."

"You're evil," said Lilith.

"I'm evil? I'm not the one who drove their husband to an early grave. I'm not the one who abandoned their child to a life of abuse. Shall I tell you how old I was when I was first raped?" Crystal laughed – a soft chuckle that was chillingly familiar to Jack. "A child rapist is the only person who's ever said 'I love you' to me. How fucked up is that?"

Jack furtively slid out his mobile phone and started to dial. Crystal whipped a bloodstained carving knife from behind her back. "Don't," she warned.

"She'll die," said Jack.

"Let her. What do I care?"

"Do something or she'll kill us all," Lilith rasped at Jack.

"Oh no, dear mother," said Crystal. "I'm not going to kill you. I'm going to care for you. I want you to live as long as possible. I'd have you live forever if I could. Exactly as you are now. Each breath so painful it makes you want to claw your own throat out. *That* would be perfection."

"You're insane."

Crystal laughed again. "Make up your mind, Mother. Which is it? Am I evil or insane? Whatever I am, it's your fault."

Lilith looked away from Crystal as if she couldn't bear the sight of her.

"Look at me!" demanded Crystal. "Look at what you've created. Abigail, Zoe, Erica, Camilla, Dale, Rhys, they're all dead because of you."

Lilith's gaze returned to Crystal. "Rhys is dead." For the first time there was fear in her voice.

Crystal's eyebrows lifted as if she'd just realised something. "You still love him, don't you? Oh this is..." she paused for the right word, "wonderful." Her face twisted in anguished fury. "I went to see my dad. I thought he might be happy to know he had a daughter. I thought wrong. No wonder you were attracted to each other. He was a selfish piece of shit just like you. I tried to make him love me. But he had no love left to give. You drained him dry."

A barrage of coughs hit Lilith. She doubled over, speckling the sheet with blood.

Emma's chest was heaving brokenly too. Her eyes drifted shut.

"Don't close your eyes, Emma," urged Jack. Her eyelids fluttered back apart. "That's it. Fight."

"No, don't fight it," Crystal said to Emma. "You'll only be wasting your last few moments of life. Because Jack's leaving here without you." Her blue gaze shifted to him. "Aren't you?"

"I've already told her everything."

A shade of uncertainty creased the skin around Crystal's eyes. "You're lying."

Gripping his baton, Jack rose to his feet. "Even if I am, it won't stop me from taking you in."

"Stay back, Jack. Remember what we talked about. Naomi. Some old man's cock. You can still stop that from happening. You can give her everything I didn't have. That's what you've wanted all along, isn't it?"

"'You'd never be able to live with yourself. It would destroy you.' That's what you said when I suggested letting Sean cop for all the murders. And you were right. It would." Jack glanced at Emma's frightened eyes. "So would letting her die. What good would I be to Naomi then? It's over, Crystal. You wanted me to catch you. Well here I am."

"Yes, but not while my poor dear mother is alive. Who'll care for her if I'm in prison? She can't go into hospital. She's too good to die in hospital." Crystal's voice was a schizophrenic mixture of sarcasm and sincerity.

"She won't have to. I'll pay for a private nurse if need be."

An expression of terrible weariness aged Crystal. She heaved a sigh. "You might be the only good man I've ever known, Jack."

"Put down the knife."

Crystal started to lower the knife. But then she was lunging at Jack, letting out that same howl he'd heard when Emma was attacked. He was ready for her. He brought the baton down on her wrist with bone-breaking force. She grimaced, but didn't drop the knife.

Jack dodged backwards as Crystal stabbed at his stomach. He stumbled over Emma. Crystal lunged at him again, catching him off-balance. He flung up the baton to deflect the blade. Steel clattered against steel. The blade scraped along the baton and sliced into the flesh between his forefinger and thumb. He felt no pain, only the warmth of blood. He dropped the baton, but caught hold of the blade. It cut into his fingers as Crystal tried to wrench it free. His hand was slippery with blood, but somehow he held on.

With another strange, keening howl, Crystal threw her weight against Jack. He toppled backwards and hit the floor with her on top. She reared up, pushing down on the knife with both hands. Its tip grated against his ribcage. He pushed back. Her eyes appearing ready to pop out of their sockets, Crystal strove to drive the blade deeper. But even with gravity on her side, she wasn't strong enough to prevent him from lifting her hands. The blade trembled in the air above Jack.

"Don't resist me, darling." The sadness was back in Crystal's voice. "I'm waiting for you."

Rebecca...

The name whispered in Jack's mind, sapping his will, draining his strength. The knife inched back downwards.

"That's it," soothed Crystal. "We'll be together soon. I promise you."

Oh Rebecca. My Rebecca. Why? Why?

A ghostly apparition materialised behind Crystal. Lilith's face was as white as her hair, except for a vivid streak of red on her chin. Her mouth was contorted into a gurning grimace as if she was battling extreme pain. Her thin, slack-skinned arms were trembling over her head. To Jack's amazement he saw that somehow, from Christ knows what depths of willpower, she'd summoned up the strength to lift her oxygen cylinder. She brought it down on Crystal's head with a dull thunk. Crystal collapsed forwards, unconscious. Lilith crumpled to the floor too, gasping as if she'd run up a mountain.

Breathing hard himself, Jack wriggled out from underneath Crystal and disarmed her. Blood blotted his shirt and dripped from his hand. Blood was running from Crystal's head, from Lilith's mouth and nose, from Emma's chest. So much blood it was difficult to see anything else.

Jack reached for his handcuffs before remembering they were on Jordan's wrists. He checked Emma's pockets. No cuffs. Emma's eyes were closed. He felt for a pulse in her throat and found one – barely. *You need to call for an ambulance. Now!* He spotted his phone under the dressing-table, scrambled for it and dialled dispatch. "I have an officer down. I need an ambulance and assistance." He gave the operator the address, moving to retrieve his baton. Crystal was as still as a corpse. Maybe she *was* a corpse.

"Cigarette."

For a second, Jack thought he was hearing things. In a voice like sand falling through an hourglass, Lilith repeated, "Cigarette."

Her face was turning from white to blue. She looked as if she only had minutes before she shuffled off to join Gabriel, Camilla and Rhys. There was no fear in her eyes. If anything there was a glimmer of impatience.

Who am I to turn down her final request? thought Jack.

He placed a cigarette between Lilith's lips and sparked his Zippo. A faint moan drew his attention. Crystal was alive! Her eyelids were flickering. She was regaining consciousness. As Jack's eyes darted around for something to restrain Crystal with, Lilith took the Zippo from him and lit her cigarette. She wheezed out smoke, her face contorting with pain and pleasure. His gaze landed on the bandages. They would do the job. He tore open a fresh box. A low but intense hissing started up behind him. Turning, he saw that Lilith had removed the tube from the oxygen cylinder and was twisting the flow regulator knob. The silk bedsheets were already on fire. As the oxygen hit them, they went up with a thirsty whoosh.

Jack lunged for the cylinder. Lilith threw herself on top of it, clinging to the regulator knob with the same deathly strength she'd demonstrated earlier. Feeding insatiably on pure oxygen, the flames raced across the bed and sprang onto the curtains. The dressing-table was going up in flames too, bubbling and blackening the photos in their frames.

It was too late, Jack realised. The fire was already raging beyond his control. At any moment, the pressurised cylinder could split open like a sausage in a frying pan. Then the massive release of accelerant would incinerate everything in the immediate vicinity. It was time to get the hell out. But he wasn't going alone. He turned to shake Crystal, trying to bring her around. She groaned but remained limp. He couldn't carry her and Emma at the same time. And Emma had to come first. Hooking his arms under Emma's legs and back, he lifted her. She sagged like a sack of compost.

Jack half-ran, half-staggered from the room and down the stairs. He awkwardly opened the front door. When he was ten or so metres from the house, he lowered Emma to the lawn. He turned to sprint back to the house. *Crystal has to live!* The thought drove his legs like pistons. *She has to!* It wasn't simply that he wanted her to face justice. It was the thought of never again looking into her eyes and seeing that unknowable sadness.

Lilith's bedroom window blew out with an echoing boom, belching flames into the sky. Jack threw himself to the grass, shielding his head from a hail of glass. He scrambled to his feet and continued running. No way could Crystal have survived the explosion, but he had to be sure.

Heat and smoke buffeted him as he entered the house. Covering his mouth and nose with his forearm and keeping low, he climbed the stairs. His eyes smarted. He could barely breathe. Vines of flame were spreading across the ceiling and walls. The landing was an impenetrable barrier of orange-glowing smoke. The heat was blistering. He took one more step towards Lilith's bedroom. Then he could go no further.

"Crystal," he shouted.

The only reply was the roar and pop of flames. He reluctantly retreated from them. There was a cracking, snapping sound. He sprang down the stairs as a section of the ceiling collapsed. His momentum carried him through the front door. He fell to his knees on the lawn, coughing and spluttering. Flames reached out as if beckoning him back inside as he crawled to Emma. Their glow lent the illusion of colour to her cheeks. But when he put his ear to her mouth there was nothing. Not even the faintest whisper of breath.

He hoarsely called her name, slapping her cheeks. Nothing.

He began CPR. Each thrust of his hand brought fresh wells of blood to the surface of Emma's chest. He breathed into her mouth. She exhaled his breath back at him. Then... Nothing...

From the near-distance came the wail of sirens. The noise rapidly grew louder, but not rapidly enough. Emma was dead. He'd failed again.

Tears tracked down Jack's sooty face as he lowered his head and awaited his colleagues.

CHAPTER 53

The curved needle slid into Jack's skin. The suture pulled tight, closing the gash between his thumb and forefinger. His chest wound had already been stitched and dressed. Somewhere nearby Emma's husband was sobbing. The sound hurt Jack more than any needle ever could do. After tying off the thread and applying a dressing, the doctor left him alone with the wails of grief.

The plastic curtain swished open. Jack's pupils contracted to pinpricks of hate. Paul returned his gaze warily, hesitating to enter the cubicle. "The doctor tells me you were lucky," he said. "The knife struck a rib over your heart."

"Lucky," Jack murmured as if the word was foreign to him, his voice raw from smoke and fatigue.

"What happened, Jack?"

What happened? The coin was in the air again. *Truth, lies, truth, lies... Lies.* Even if he couldn't be the dad he wanted to be, he could be there for Naomi. He could protect her from the Jordans of the world and make sure she didn't become one of the Crystals. "Emma and I tracked down the real killer."

"So you were right. Shane Hardy's not our man?"

"The killer wasn't a man – at least not the killer of Abigail, Zoe, Erica, Camilla, Dale, Emma and Rhys."

"Rhys Devonport's dead?"

"His body's in a bungalow on Sale Road."

Paul jotted down the address. "You said the killer *wasn't* a man. I assume that means you think they died in the fire."

Jack nodded. "Crystal Cuthbert."

"Who's Crystal Cuthbert?"

Jack took a moment organise his thoughts – he needed to get his story straight, but it was difficult with the sounds of grief assaulting him. Then he laid out the whole sordid, tragic tale – Lilith and Rhys's doomed love affair, Helen Bancroft-Harding's sad side story, Crystal's heart-breaking upbringing, her quest for revenge. He was careful to paint Maria as an innocent bystander.

"So you don't think Maria knew her husband was guilty?" said Paul.

"Perhaps somewhere in her mind." Jack's eyes gleamed like knife-points. "But you know how it is, sometimes we tell ourselves so many lies that they begin to feel like the truth."

Paul blinked away from him. "Christ, mate, what a mess."

Jack couldn't tell if he was referring to the fallout of Lilith's affair or his own. "I'm not your fucking mate."

Paul held up a placatory hand. "Emma's dead. Can we put aside our personal issues and concentrate on catching her killer?"

"Crystal is dead."

"Did you see her body?"

"No."

"Then we don't know for sure that she's dead."

"She's dead," Jack reiterated. "No one could have survived that explosion."

"I suppose we'll find out if you're right soon enough. Anything else to tell me?"

Something about the way Paul said it put Jack on his guard. "Not that I can think of right now."

"OK. Go home. Get a few hours rest. The IIO will want an initial account from you when you're up to it." Paul glanced towards a fresh outbreak of sobbing. More of Emma's loved ones had turned up. He released a heavy sigh. "I should go talk to them."

"Do you want me to come with you?" The thought of facing up to Emma's relatives was enough to make Jack break into a cold sweat, but he felt compelled to offer.

"I don't think that would be advisable, do you?"

Now it was Jack's turn to blink away from Paul. "No."

Paul ran a hand through his hair and buttoned his jacket as if making himself presentable for an important business meeting. He paused and said quietly, "I'll never stop regretting what I did. I'd give anything to go back and undo it, but I can't."

He left Jack with those words. Jack rose from the trolley-bed and exited the cubicle. At first his movements were slow, but they quickened with every step away from the relentless sobbing. By the time he reached the A&E waiting-room, he was almost running. He didn't stop until got to his car. Steve had taken Jordan into custody. The last Jack had seen of him, Jordan was being guided none too gently into the backseat of Steve's car. Would he keep his side of the deal? Only time would tell.

Jack had other concerns too. The footage of his altercation with Dale and photos of him stalking Camilla were still out there somewhere. Had Crystal's phones been destroyed in the fire? If not, he might yet be outed as Mr Average. Again, there was nothing he could do but wait and see what happened.

When Jack arrived at his house, he half-expected to find someone waiting to put him in handcuffs. But the only thing awaiting him was silence.

He stripped off his blood and soot stained clothes and got under the shower. Then he flopped onto the bed. He checked his phone. Laura had left a voicemail: "I saw on the news that there's a house on fire in Didsbury. They're saying it's got something to do with the Ripper murders. Is it true?"

Jack was too exhausted to talk to Laura. He texted her: 'We got the killer. I'll tell you all about it later.'

Not all, he corrected himself. There were certain things Laura could never know.

Jack eyelids were too heavy to keep open any longer. But instead of sleep, he found a new question lurking behind them: had he expected too much? Was that what had driven Rebecca into Paul's arms and, ultimately, to her death?

He shook his head. He was finished with trying to be a rational man in an irrational world, futilely seeking answers where none existed. Who knew the real reasons Rebecca, or for that matter Crystal, had done what they did? All he knew for certain was that he was alive and they were dead.

CHAPTER 54

As GMP HQ came into view, Jack puffed his cheeks at what the next few hours held in store. In the week since the fire, he'd been stuck in the purgatory of Post Incident Procedures. Officially he was on medical suspension, but he'd gone into headquarters almost every day for meetings with the Initial Investigating Officer, the Post Incident Manager and the Senior Investigating Officer – a trio whose duties ranged from officer welfare to determining whether there were grounds for officers to face misconduct or criminal charges.

"So far so good," Jack reminded himself, mentally reeling off the reasons to believe those words.

Top of the list was Jordan Murphy. Jordan was detained on remand awaiting trial. Since his arrest, four other of his victims had been tracked down and agreed to testify against him. His predicament was looking bleak, but he'd kept his mouth shut so far.

Next came a pair of CCTV films that made Jack wonder whether Crystal had been insane or merely stupid. The first was entitled 'Crystal Cuthbert aka Stella Lloyd making a deposit for Lilith Winter at RBS Chorlton' and included a brief cameo from Erica Cook. The sequel saw Crystal taking to the screen with Zoe Saunders in 'Crystal Cuthbert aka Stella Lloyd purchasing medical supplies at Moss Lane Pharmacy'. Through luck or choice, Stella hadn't used the pharmacy for Lilith's prescriptions, otherwise he would have found his way to her much sooner.

The films were closely followed by the incriminating photos and video of Jack – or rather, the absence of them. Whatever devices they were stored on had seemingly been reduced to ashes, along with pretty much everything else in Lilith's house.

Below that were some loose ends Jack had been working on tying up. He'd searched the streets around the scorched shell of Lilith's house for Rhys's Punto. He'd also checked out the block of flats in School Hill, Bolton that Crystal had used as the delivery address for the Ugly Mask. No Punto. No mask either. The flat itself was empty and, judging from the dust, had been so for a considerable time. The Punto and mask couldn't hurt him though. Just so long as someone didn't find them together and then find their way to Lucrezia Moretti. In which case, he would have a difficult time explaining how he'd come to contact Lucrezia only hours after Camilla and Dale's murders.

Jack parked up and made his way to the SCD's offices. Steve was waiting for him. He ushered Jack into an empty room. Steve had been his main line for information over the past week. Gone was the Neanderthal so desperate to assert his alpha status. Underneath Steve's arsehole demeanour there seemed to exist a decent enough, if somewhat insecure, bloke.

"I thought you might be interested in this." Steve handed Jack a folder containing the forensic report into the two female bodies recovered from Lilith's house.

The fire had raged out of control for hours, the oxygen accelerant generating sufficient heat to burn the bodies beyond visual recognition. The charring was not severe enough to prevent forensic identification. Lilith had been positively identified from dental records and recent chest X-rays. The second body was more problematic. The force of the blast had destroyed the lower part of the woman's face, so dental analysis was out of the question. The morphology of her pubic symphysis, hip bone and medial rib ends suggested she was between forty-eight and fifty-four-years-old.

Tension crept into Jack's face. Factors such as disease and lifestyle could skew estimations based on bone morphology. Crystal had been thirty-three, but those were thirty three hard years. The abuse, the breakdowns, the rough-sleeping, doubtless those factors had added years to her body. But eighteen years?

He continued reading. Skeletal analysis had found that the second body had size seven feet with fallen arches and was five feet six inches tall. That matched Crystal's particulars. DNA had been successfully extracted from bone marrow, but there were no matches on the DNA database. That meant a hairbrush, toothbrush or other object that might yield a sample for comparison was needed. But all such items had perished in the fire.

"Between forty-eight and fifty-four," Jack murmured thoughtfully. Crystal's alter-identity, Stella, had fallen within that age bracket. Either the conclusion of the morphological analysis was an anomaly or... or... "Shit," he swore softly. This was not good at all. He frowned at a voice in the corridor.

"Have you seen DI Anderson?" Paul asked someone.

"No, sir," came the reply.

Footsteps moved away from the door. Jack gave the folder back to Steve. "I'd better find out what he wants."

"Good luck with that," said Steve. He, along with the rest of the team, had doubtless clocked that Jack and Paul had, to put it mildly, fallen out. Unless they had something important to say to one another, the former friends now only communicated with curt nods, grunts and stony looks.

Jack peeked into the corridor. Paul was in the doorway of the Incident Room. Clamping down on a familiar rise of anger, Jack approached him. "I heard you were looking for me, sir." He was careful to observe rank. He didn't want to give Paul any excuse to censure him.

Paul threw him a deadpan glance, then his gaze slid across to Emma's empty desk. With a heavy heart, Jack looked at it too. The coroner hadn't yet released Emma's body. But when they did, there would be the agony of the funeral to look forward to. She would be buried with all the ceremony afforded an officer killed in the line of duty.

"Funny thing," said Paul, "Every time I come in here, part of me still expects to see Emma at her desk. Do you know what I mean?"

Jack knew exactly what he meant. For months after Rebecca's death, he'd felt something akin to surprise every time he stepped into the house and she wasn't there. He'd rather have eaten glass than talk about such things with Paul though.

"I need to speak to you in private," said Paul. Without waiting for a reply, he strode towards his office.

Jack followed a few paces behind, his eyes stabbing at Paul's back. Paul sat down and gestured for Jack to do likewise. "I have an appointment with Dennis Shaw," said Jack. Dennis was the Senior Investigating Officer and an old-school copper, the kind for whom loyalty to fellow officers was the first and last rule of policing. He wasn't about to serve a Notice of Investigation for misconduct or worse on an officer who'd nearly been killed trying to protect a colleague. Not unless he had no other choice.

"This won't take long," said Paul. From the way Paul's eyes searched his face, Jack guessed what was coming. "I know we've been over all this, but there are things I'm still struggling to understand. Why didn't you call it in when you discovered Rhys's body?"

Jack reeled out the same response he'd given several times before. "I wasn't sure whether you'd insist on sending in the SOCOs. I didn't want to risk the killer finding out that we knew about Rhys."

Paul gave a little nod as if he could just about swallow that answer. "What I really can't wrap my head around is why neither Emma nor you reported your suspicions to me before entering Lilith's house?"

"I can't speak for Emma. As for myself, do you really need to ask?"

Usually such an allusion to Paul and Rebecca's affair would send Paul's eyes blinking to the floor. But not today. The two men stared at each other. Paul picked up a handheld recorder and pressed play. Jack kept his face expressionless as an androgynous voice crackled into the room, "Hello

Fiona. You don't know me, but I know you. I've been watching you like I watched those other women. You might have heard of them. Abigail Hart, Zoe Saunders, Erica Cook, Camilla Winter. They're all dead now. I killed them. And I'll kill you too unless someone stops me. I don't want to kill you, Fiona. But I can't help myself. I need to kill and kill again. The need is getting stronger. I'm not sure I can resist it. Oh god, I need to see blood. I need to smell it. I need it. I need–"

"We found that message on the answering service of one Fiona Jenkins of Alan Road, Withington," said Paul. He handed Jack a photo of a brown-haired women with big blue eyes. "Fiona was reported missing three days ago. She's five feet six, flat-footed, fifty-years-old. Sound familiar?"

"When was the last contact?"

"Three days before Crystal supposedly burned to death."

Jack's mind raced. Was it possible? Could the lump of human charcoal on ice in the mortuary be Fiona Jenkins? "Have you done a DNA comparison?"

"That's another funny thing. I had Forensics go over Fiona's flat, but they came up with nothing. No hairs. No toothbrush. It's almost like someone made sure there was no way to get a comparative sample."

"What about Fiona's parents?"

"Both dead. Fiona has no living relatives. She's all alone in the world."

All alone. You would never have known from her smiling face. Another mask? "How come it took a week for her to be reported missing?"

"Her friends and colleagues – she teaches at a private music school – thought she was at a yoga retreat in Goa. Only thing is she didn't get on her outbound plane."

Jack was suddenly thinking about Naomi. She'd been living with him for the past four days. Laura was babysitting her at his house today. He wouldn't have let her out of his sight if he'd known about Fiona Jenkins. "Why have you kept this from me until now?" There was an edge of anger in his voice.

"I didn't want to worry you. Like I said, I was hoping to find a comparative sample to confirm whether the second body is Fiona."

"Bullshit," retorted Jack, half-standing. "You're just sticking it to me for not telling you about Rhys and Crystal."

"Careful, Jack. I'm your senior officer and you'll show me the proper respect."

Jack scowled. "Respect? What respect have you ever shown me?"

He stalked out of the office. Paul pursued him, saying, "You're not the only one who smells bullshit. There's something off about your version of events and I intend to find out what it is. Unless that is you've changed your mind about applying for a transfer."

Jack gave a sharp laugh. "It's going take a hell of a lot more than empty threats to change my mind."

"Well this situation can't go on."

"You're right. It can't." Jack's reply was full of unspoken meaning.

As if his batteries had finally run out, Paul's shoulders dropped and he heaved a sigh. "Natasha and the kids have gone to live with her parents in Eastbourne."

Jack looked at him with, if not sympathy, then at least a lack of hostility. "I'm sorry to hear that."

"Are you? It may well mean you get what you want."

"I didn't want any of this, but I'm trying to make the best of what I've got left. You should too."

"What does that mean?"

Jack spread his hands as if to say, *That's up to you to decide.*

They faced each other a moment longer, then Paul said, "Go see Naomi." He added hopefully, "Oh, and forget about my threat. Perhaps we can just call it even?"

Jack's lips pulled into a humourless smile. "You know what, Paul? You really are a cunt."

Without waiting to see what effect his parting shot had, Jack hurried on his way. As he exited the carpark, he dialled Laura. Her number was engaged. He tried the landline. No one picked up.

Relax, he told himself, *she'll be on the phone to one of her friends. Crystal's dead. Burned to a crisp. And even if she's alive, she planted Fiona's body because she wants us to believe otherwise. She'd have to be crazy to come out of hiding. Crazy...*

Crystal's eyes loomed large in his mind. He saw no rationality in them, only wild blue abandon. He tried phoning Laura again. Still engaged. "Fuck," he muttered, putting his foot down.

The journey to Chorlton took half the time to usual but felt twice as long. Jack scanned the cars parked along the kerb outside his house. No silver Punto. The front door was open. Naomi's little pink bike lay on the path, but she was nowhere to be seen. He pulled in behind Laura's car and ran into the house, calling out, "Naomi! Laura!"

Laura appeared at the top of the stairs. "What's going on?"

"I was about to ask you the same thing. Where were you?"

"I was on the toilet."

"Your phone was engaged."

"I got a call from work."

"Where's Naomi?"

"In the garden."

"Well she's not there now."

"She's probably around back." Laura started down the stairs. "She knows not to leave the garden."

Jack dashed through to the kitchen and peered out the window. The back lawn was empty. He craned his neck to make sure Naomi wasn't behind the garage. Nothing.

"Isn't she there?" Laura asked.

The taut lines on Jack's face answered her question. He sprinted upstairs to Naomi's bedroom. Elsa, the scrawny black-and-white cat they'd taken in, was curled up on the bed. No Naomi. *Shit! Shit!*

"Naomi, Naomi, Naomi," Laura called out in the street, her voice rising with each repetition.

The phone locator! Jack snatched out his phone and checked the location of Naomi's phone. A hand seemed to close around his throat. The phone was on the A56, south of Chorlton. He barely had time to wonder what that meant before there came a sound that turned his skin cold.

Brring... Brring...

Please don't be No Caller ID.

'Naomi' flashed up. Pressing the phone to his ear, Jack asked, "Where are you, sweetheart? Are you OK?"

"Yes, I'm OK, Dad," Naomi replied. There was a wobble in her soft little voice that sounded an alarm in Jack's brain. "I'm in a car and you won't believe who I'm with, Dad..." She faltered as if she herself couldn't believe it.

Jack's anxiety was threatening to spill over into full blown panic. He just about kept it in check. Now more than ever he needed to wear his policeman's mask: stay calm, say the right things, ask the right questions. "Why wouldn't I believe you?"

"Because it's..." Naomi wavered again, before blurting out, "It's Mum!"

There was a stunned silence. Jack knew Naomi wasn't with her mum. And yet... And yet there was such certainty in her words. Could Rebecca be alive? His heart throbbed painfully at the possibility. No! He couldn't afford to indulge such fantasies. He peeled his tongue from the roof of his mouth. "Put your mum on the phone, sweetheart."

"OK, Dad. Bye."

Another voice came on the line. "Hello Jack. Surprised to hear from me?" The voice had a gentle Sussex accent. It might conceivably have belonged to Rebecca. But Jack knew it *didn't* belong to her. Rebecca's voice had used to ripple in his ears like waves on a pond. This voice was flat. There was no music in it.

Jack's voice dropped to a razor-edged whisper. "If you hurt Naomi, I'll kill you." It wasn't a threat, it was a statement of fact.

"Hurt her? How could you think I'd do such a thing? She's our daughter."

She's not your daughter, you psycho bitch. Jack ground the words between his teeth. *Stay calm, say the right things.* "Listen to me, Crystal–"

"Who's Crystal?"

Jack bit down again. *Don't let her get under your skin. Just play along.* "Listen to me..." His throat constricted around the word. He pushed it out. "*Rebecca.* It's me you want. I'm the one who ruined your plan."

"What plan?" Crystal sounded baffled. "You were the one always making plans, Jack. Not me. I go where the wind takes me."

That was true. Rebecca had hated to make plans. She'd felt hemmed in by them. Stifled. *But this isn't Rebecca,* Jack reminded himself. *She's reading you like a fortune teller, probing for ways in. That's what she does.* "And where's that?"

"You know where."

I'm becoming somebody.

Jack's face pulled tauter as those cryptic words replayed in his mind. Perhaps Crystal had meant them literally. Maybe she was like an empty bottle. Something that became whatever it was filled with. Lilith had given birth to a baby without a name. That baby had become Crystal Cuthbert. And Crystal Cuthbert had become Stella Lloyd. Had Stella Lloyd now become Rebecca Anderson? If so, the right question wasn't: where would Crystal take Naomi? It was: where would Rebecca take Naomi?

Jack felt as if his legs might buckle. His voice scraped out. "The cliffs."

"You know me so well, Jack."

Do I? he wondered. *Did I ever really know you, Rebecca?*

"Better even than I know myself," Crystal continued as if replying to his thoughts. "I thought I wanted to be alone. I was wrong. I want to be with my family. But I'm not stupid, Jack. I know there's no way back for us."

"You're wrong about that, Rebecca." Jack tried to sound as sincere as he was desperate. It wasn't difficult. All he had to do was give voice to the fantasies that had tormented him since Rebecca's death. "We can still be together. We can be a real family again. Just you, me and Naomi."

"Just you, me and Naomi," Crystal echoed in a tone suspended between doubt and hope. "How do I know you're not just telling me what I want to hear?"

"I'll prove it. Just give me the chance."

The line was momentarily silent. Then, emphasising each word, Crystal repeated, "Just you, me and Naomi."

The warning behind the words was clear: *Involve anyone else and it will end badly.*

"Yes."

More agonising silence, interrupted by footsteps running up the stairs. Laura came into the room, flushed and breathless. She opened her mouth to speak, but Jack darted a finger to his lips.

"Alright, Jack," said Crystal. "We'll see you at the cliffs."

No, not there, Jack's mind yelled. *Anywhere but there.* "There must be somewhere closer to–" He broke off. The line was dead. He squeezed his eyes shut. Images and sounds rushed at him – the crowd, the cliffs the sea, the whoosh of waves, the whump-whump of rotor-blades...

"I can't find her," said Laura. "Who were you talking to?"

Jack's eyes snapped open. "I've got to go."

"Where?" Laura asked as he darted past her.

Without replying, Jack ran downstairs. Laura caught up with him at his car and grabbed his arm. "What the hell's going on, Jack?"

He tried to shake her off, but she tightened her grip. "I won't let you shut me out," she said. "Not where Naomi's concerned. Either you speak to me or I'm calling the police."

"No, you can't do that, Laura," exclaimed Jack. "She'll hurt Naomi. Maybe even..." He couldn't bring himself to say it. Just the thought of it made him feel as if he was about to plunge off a cliff.

"Who's she?" Laura's eyes contracted behind her glasses, then expanded like saucers. "You mean that insane woman. The one who's supposed to be dead. She's got Naomi, hasn't she? Where are they? Tell me."

"I can't. I have to do as she says. I know Crystal. I know what she's capable of. I've got to go now and I've got to go alone." As Laura shook her head, Jack snapped, "Yes. This is how it's going to be or I'll cuff you and lock you in the house."

Jack and Laura glared at each other for a few seconds, their eyes unyielding. Jack's expression softened into something more pleading than commanding. "You've got to trust me, Laura. This is the only chance we've got to get Naomi back alive."

Laura gnawed her lips uncertainly. Jack placed his hand over hers. *Please,* he mouthed. "I can do this."

She stopped chewing and pulled her hand away. "Then what are you standing here for?" There were tears in her eyes, but her voice had taken on an icily practical tone. "Go and fucking get her."

With a sharp nod, Jack ducked into the car. The engine flared as he sped away. He attempted to check the location of Naomi's phone again, thinking that maybe he could catch them up long before Hastings. 'Location Unavailable' came up. Crystal must have taken out the SIM card. He slammed a fist into the dashboard. "Oh god, if you hurt her... If you hurt her..."

He raced south out of the city. He didn't need the Satnav. He knew the route: M6, M1, M25, A21. Nearly three hundred miles. Just over five hours on a good day. He glanced at the clock: 10:22. The sky was faultlessly blue. It was the type of day when, standing on the cliffs east of Hastings, it seemed as if you could see forever.

CHAPTER 55

The journey passed in a white-heat of frantic activity. Change gear, accelerate, overtake, don't brake, don't stop. Don't stop! Vehicles, bridges, trees, fields, towns, cities... All of them swept by in a blur. Jack saw only what he needed to see: the road ahead, the signposts and the clock.

Then he was on a two-lane road, hemmed in by trees. He fought his way past every vehicle in front of him, flooring the accelerator, hammering the horn at oncoming traffic. His shirt was dark with sweat, his lower back and legs begged to be stretched. He didn't notice. Change gear, accelerate, overtake, overtake, overtake. *Beep! Beep!* "Move out of my way. Move you bastards!"

The road widened into a dual carriageway. The trees gave way to rolling fields. His petrol light blinked on. "Fuck!"

He screeched into a service station, filled the tank, threw the money at the attendant and ran raced onwards. Another two-lane road. Redbrick cottages. Tudor-framed pubs. Thick hedgerows. Sun-bleached wheat. Grazing cows. All of it so familiar. All of it unseen – that is until he hit the outskirts of Hastings.

The town began on the far side of an ugly grey overpass. His stomach twisted at what awaited him a short distance further along the road. Not the cliffs. They were still several miles away. But something almost as bad. Queasiness threatened to overwhelm him when he saw the Premier Inn. It was a nothing place. A bland brick building sandwiched between a pub and a car dealership. But he would rather have been struck blind than set eyes on it again.

Fuck me harder, Paul. Harder. Harder! Strangle me, Paul!

Every word was a razor blade slicing into Jack. For a second, he thought he was going to throw up and pass out all at the same time. Then he was beyond the building and Rebecca's voice was fading. There was a salty metallic taste in his mouth. Blood. He'd bitten a chunk out of the underside of his lip.

He hauled in a breath and refocused. Not much further now.

He took a left turn to avoid getting caught up in the traffic that crawled along the beachfront promenade. He climbed through streets of faded white and pastel-coloured houses towards newer, drabber suburban estates. The gradient steepened as he neared the edge of town. Then he was on a road that ran parallel to the coastline. Gaps in windswept hedges revealed glimpses of the sea. About a mile out of town, he turned onto a single-lane road that wound between banks of yellow gorse. It ended at a gravel carpark with a dozen cars and an ice cream van in it.

Jack's heart gave a thump. At the far end of the carpark, only a few metres from where Rebecca had parked on her final day, was the silver Punto. There was no one in it. He pulled alongside it, sprang out of the car and raced along a path that branched leftwards from the carpark. The path descended through fields of short, rough grass towards the cliffs. Crickets chirped. Gulls soared. About fifty metres away to his right was the grey box of the coastguard station. Its windows stared out to sea past a tall radar mast. Gorse blossom and salt perfumed the air. He'd loved this place and that smell all his life up until the day Rebecca died. He hadn't expected to visit here again, except in his dreams.

He left the path, sprinting down a steep grassy bank, stumbling, almost falling. The gorse ended. Twenty or so metres further on the grass ended even more abruptly. That was where they were standing. Close enough to the edge to make cold sweat pop out on his palms. They were facing out to sea, holding hands. Crystal was wearing the blue dress. Her hair lay over her shoulders as black as the cormorants that sunned themselves at the foot of the cliffs. Her feet were bare. In her other hand she was holding the Ugly Mask.

Jack could hear waves sloshing against the rocks a hundred-odd metres below. The tide was in. That wouldn't save Naomi though. The cliffs were sheer at the top, but flared outwards where successive slips of friable sandstone and clay had been deposited at their base. Anyone falling – or jumping – would be smashed into a boneless bag long before they hit the water.

Naomi looked tense – her head was down, her shoulders were hunched. She was standing the full length of her arm away from Crystal. *She's realised that Crystal isn't who she claims to be,* thought Jack. That wasn't necessarily a good thing. He needed to keep the situation as calm as possible.

He passed a 'DANGER. RISK OF IMMINENT CLIFF FALLS!!' sign. Crystal and Naomi were only fifteen metres away now. Neither showed any indication of being aware of his presence. Could he sneak up and grab Naomi? It would be a huge risk. A miscalculation could send them plummeting to their deaths. The question became moot as Jack's phone pinged. Naomi turned towards the sound, her hand pulling free of Crystal's.

"Dad!" she cried out as Crystal caught hold of her. Her eyes were swollen with tears. She strained towards Jack, but Crystal pulled her back like a dog on a lead. "She's a liar," sobbed Naomi. "She's not my Mum!"

"Don't worry, everything will be OK," he replied in a voice that only revealed a tremor of the fear surging through him.

"Will it?" put in Crystal. Her eyes were as empty as the horizon. More reminiscent than ever of Rebecca during those last weeks. She held up the hideously wrinkled mask. "That depends on which face you want me to wear."

Jack raised his hands, palms outwards. He tried to edge forwards so slowly as for it to be imperceptible. "It's not too late to stop this, Crystal..."

At the spasm of irritation that flashed across her face, he corrected himself, "Rebecca."

"It was too late the moment I was born," she said matter-of-factly.

"Come away from the edge. You want us all to be together. Well that can happen, but you've got to do as I say."

"There's only one way we can be together, Jack." A hollow light lit up Crystal's eyes. "Pain. That's all life is." She motioned towards the blue expanse at her back. "Out there, there's no more pain."

Staring into those bottomless eyes, Jack felt a tug of something. It reminded him of a thought that had flashed through his mind soon after Rebecca's death: *Our lives are over. I might as well throw Naomi and myself off the cliffs.*

No! he furiously told himself. *Never!*

Jack frantically sought for something to say that might give him control of the situation. There was only one thing he could think of. "I love you, Rebecca." As he said the words, he knew in his heart they were true. And he knew too that if Rebecca were alive, he would have forgiven her, just as Lawrence had forgiven Helen. It wouldn't have been easy, but he would have found a way. The realisation threatened to choke him as he repeated, "I love you."

With each word, he closed the gap a fraction more. Crystal's eyebrows were twitching. He could see the doubt in her eyes, but also the desperate need to believe him. "Tell me who I am," she said.

"You're my wife. To have and to hold. For better, for worse." Jack extended a hand towards Crystal. He was getting close. Almost close enough to lunge for Naomi.

There was a kind of mistiness in Crystal's eyes as if she was drifting off to some other place – perhaps a place where she, Jack and Naomi were all living happily together. She took up the vows. "For richer, for poorer..."

Jack's other hand crept towards Naomi.

"In sickness and health..."

Her fingertips were only centimetres away.

"To love and–"

Crystal broke off as Naomi interrupted in a frightened voice, "I want to go home, Dad."

Blinking as if she'd been snapped out of a trance, Crystal looked at Jack and Naomi's almost touching fingers. Her eyes came alive with a savage light of betrayal and she took a step backwards.

In what seemed like slow motion to Jack, Crystal toppled off the cliff. Naomi screamed as she too was dragged over the edge. Jack sprang forwards. His fingers closed around Naomi's skinny wrist. Her arms pulled taut between him and Crystal. He fought not to overbalance, leaning back with all his weight. Naomi's right foot flailed at thin air. She screamed again, her eyes goggling with pain and fear.

Jack's heels slid through the grass. He didn't let go. If Naomi was going to die, then so was he.

His feet found purchase against something solid. A stone? A root? Whatever it was, it prevented him from losing his footing. He found himself staring down past Naomi. Crystal's bare feet were braced against the rock face. That look of blank determination was back. One hand was clamped onto Naomi. The other flapped with a strange grace towards the sparkling sea. The Ugly Mask's thin black hair fluttered in the breeze.

Jack and she strained against each other, competing in a deadly tug-o-war. He could feel the gash between his thumb and index finger tearing open. He could feel every particle of sweat beneath his fingers. His grip was slipping. Slowly, slowly, slipping... His hand came up against the anniversary bracelet. The fine silver links provided just enough friction for him to hold on.

For endless seconds, the three of them teetered as if in suspended animation. Then it happened. Jack couldn't tell whether Crystal lost her grip or let go. But suddenly, in eerie silence, she was falling. He reeled backwards, dropping to the grass. Naomi lay sobbing against his legs. He enfolded her in his arms. "Daddy's got you. Daddy's got you," he breathlessly soothed her.

"My arms hurt," she said.

Jack examined her shoulders. The joints must have almost been torn out of their sockets, but there was no sign of dislocation. He manoeuvred her further away from the cliff's edge before moving to peer over it. Waves lapped at the pale cliffs. Crystal was nowhere to be seen. Just as Rebecca had been nowhere to be seen. He didn't feel glad that Crystal was dead. He didn't feel sad. He didn't feel much of anything at all. Naomi was safe. Nothing else mattered.

"Till death do us part," he murmured.

"Are you OK?" called a voice from behind him.

A woman was by the warning sign. Jack knew what would happen next. More people would stop to find out what was going on. The coastguard would scramble a search helicopter. Chances were, Crystal wouldn't be found. The tide would soon be on the turn and strong currents would carry her out to the same deep, dark grave as Rebecca.

He replied with a nod. His gaze fell to the gold band on his ring finger. He ran his thumb over its smooth surface. Something Lawrence had said returned to him: *Only remember the good things.*

He thought about Rebecca – that time she'd danced in the rain, the way she'd kissed him when he proposed to her, the tears of exhausted joy she'd cried the first time she held Naomi, her infectious laugh, her open-mindedness, her generosity, her gentleness. But most of all he thought about her eyes. Not her eyes at the end, but her eyes at the beginning...

Jack worked the ring over his knuckle and put it in his pocket. Recalling the ping that had given him away, he took out his phone. There was a text message from 'No Caller ID'. That meant the incriminating video and photos had, presumably, gone over the cliff with Crystal. He deleted the message without reading it. Then he gently scooped up Naomi.

"Why did that woman say she was Mum?" she asked.

"She was very ill, sweetheart."

"Ill like Mum was?"

"No, not like your mum."

Naomi was thoughtfully silent for a moment. There was a little knot between her eyebrows. "Are we going home, Dad?"

"You mean home as in Manchester?"

Naomi nodded.

Jack smiled down at her. "Yes, we're going home." As he carried her to the car, he said, "You know I loved your mum very much. I still do."

The knot disappeared as Naomi replied, "I know, Dad. I love her too."

ABOUT THE AUTHOR

Ben is an award winning writer and Pushcart Prize nominee with a passion for gritty crime fiction. His short stories have been widely published in the UK, US and Australia. In 2011 he self-published *Blood Guilt*. The novel went on to reach no.2 in the national e-book download chart, selling well over 150000 copies. In 2012 it was picked up for publication by Head of Zeus. Since then, Head of Zeus has published three more of Ben's novels – *Angel of Death, Justice for the Damned and Spider's Web*. In 2016 his novel *The Lost Ones* was published by Thomas & Mercer.

Ben lives in Sheffield, England, where – when he's not chasing around after his son, Alex – he spends most of his time shut away in his study racking his brain for the next paragraph, the next sentence, the next word...

If you'd like to learn more about Ben or get in touch, you can do so at www.bencheetham.com

OTHER BOOKS BY THE AUTHOR

The Lost Ones

The truth can be more dangerous than lies...

July 1972

The Ingham household. Upstairs, sisters Rachel and Mary are sleeping peacefully. Downstairs, blood is pooling around the shattered skull of their mother, Joanna, and a figure is creeping up behind their father, Elijah. A hammer comes crashing down again and again...

July 2016

The Jackson household. This is going to be the day when Tom Jackson's hard work finally pays off. He kisses his wife Amanda and their children, Jake and Erin, goodbye and heads out dreaming of a better life for them all. But just hours later he finds himself plunged into a nightmare...

Erin is missing. She was hiking with her mum in Harwood Forest. Amanda turned her back for a moment. That was all it took for Erin to vanish. Has she simply wandered off? Or does the blood-stained rock found where she was last seen point to something sinister? The police and volunteers who set out to search the sprawling forest are determined to find out. Meanwhile, Jake launches an investigation of his own – one that will expose past secrets and present betrayals.

Is Erin's disappearance somehow connected to the unsolved murders of Elijah and Joanna Ingham? Does it have something to do with the ragtag army of eco-warriors besieging Tom's controversial quarry development? Or is it related to the fraught phone call that distracted Amanda at the time of Erin's disappearance?

So many questions. No one seems to have the answers and time is running out. Tom, Amanda and Jake must get to the truth to save Erin, though in doing so they may well end up destroying themselves.

* * *

Blood Guilt

Is it ever truly possible to atone for killing someone?

After the death of his son in a freak accident, DI Harlan Miller's life is spiralling out of control. He's drinking too much. His marriage and career are on the rocks. But things are about to get even worse. A booze-soaked night out and a single wild punch leave a man dead and Harlan facing a manslaughter charge.

Fast-forward four years. Harlan's prison term is up, but life on the outside holds little promise. Divorced, alone, consumed by guilt, he thinks of nothing beyond atoning for the death he caused. But how do you make up for depriving a wife of her husband and two young boys of their father?

Then something happens, something terrible, yet something that holds out a twisted kind of hope for Harlan – the dead man's youngest son is abducted.

From that moment Harlan's life has only one purpose – finding the boy. So begins a frantic race against time that leads him to a place darker than anything he experienced as a policeman and a stark moral choice that compels him to question the law he once enforced.

* * *

Angel Of Death

Murderer? Or heroine? You decide...

Fifteen-year-old Grace Kirby kisses her mum and heads off to school. It's a day like any other day, except that Grace will never return home.

Fifteen years have passed since Grace went missing. In that time, Stephen Baxley has made millions. And now he's lost millions. Suicide seems like the only option. But Stephen has no intention of leaving behind his wife, son and daughter. He wants them all to be together forever, in this world or the next.

Angel is on the brink of suicide too. Then she hears a name on the news that transports her back to a windowless basement. Something terrible happened in that basement. Something Angel has been running from most of her life. But the time for running is over. Now is the time to start fighting back.

At the scene of a fatal shooting, DI Jim Monahan finds evidence of a sickening crime linked to a missing girl. Then more people start turning up dead. Who is the killer? Are the victims also linked to the girl? Who will be next to die? The answers will test to breaking-point Jim's faith in the law he's spent his life upholding.

✻ ✻ ✻

Justice For The Damned

There were no dead young women.
There was no serial killer.
Or at least that's what they said.

Melinda has been missing for weeks. The police would normally be all over it, but Melinda is a prostitute. Women in that line of work change addresses like they change lipstick. She probably just moved on.

Staci is determined not to let Melinda become just another statistic added to the long list of girls who've gone missing over the years. Staci is also a prostitute – although not for much longer if DI Reece Geary has anything to do with it. Reece will do anything to win Staci's love. If that means putting his job on the line by launching an unofficial investigation, then so be it.

DI Jim Monahan is driven by his own dangerous obsession. He's on the trail of a psychopath hiding behind a facade of respectability. Jim's investigation has already taken him down a rabbit hole of corruption and depravity. He's about to discover that the hole goes deeper still. Much, much deeper...

* * *

Spider's Web

'So he wove a subtle web, in a little corner sly...
And merrily did sing, "Come hither, hither, pretty fly..."'

A trip to the cinema turns into a nightmare for Anna and her little sister Jessica, when two men throw thirteen-year-old Jessica into the back of a van and speed away.

The years tick by... Tick, tick... The police fail to find Jessica and her name fades from the public consciousness... Tick, tick... But every time Anna closes her eyes she's back in that terrible moment, lurching towards Jessica, grabbing for her. So close. So agonisingly close... Tick, tick... Now in her thirties, Anna has no career, no relationship, no children. She's consumed by one purpose – finding Jessica, dead or alive.

DI Jim Monahan has a little black book with forty-two names in it. Jim's determined to put every one of those names behind bars, but his investigation is going nowhere fast. Then a twenty-year-old clue brings Jim and Anna together in search of a shadowy figure known as Spider. Who is Spider? Where is Spider? Does Spider have the answers they want? The only thing Jim and Anna know is that the victims Spider entices into his web have a habit of ending up missing or dead.

Printed in Great Britain
by Amazon